Ship

Alan Evans was an enthralling British writer of First and Second World War adventure thrillers, mainly based on naval battles. Carefully researched, and with his own experience of active service, the novels skilfully evoke the tension and terror of war. Many of the figures and events are based on real-life models.

THE COMMANDER COCHRANE SMITH NAVAL THRILLERS

SHIP OF FORCE

ALAN EVANS

CANELO

First published in the the United Kingdom in 1979 by Hodder and
Stoughton Limited

This edition published in the United Kingdom in 2020 by Canelo

Canelo Digital Publishing Limited
31 Helen Road
Oxford OX2 0DF
United Kingdom

A CIP catalogue record for this book is available from the British Library.

Print ISBN 978 1 80032 020 8
Ebook ISBN 978 1 78863 242 3

Look for more great books at www.canelo.co

Printed and bound in Great Britain by Clays Ltd, Elcograf S.p.A.

Author's Note

If I listed the names of all the people who helped me with this book, in Belgium, Dunkirk and Britain, it would fill a page or two. But my thanks to all of them.

This is a work of fiction, though set in the framework of events at the time. Any resemblance of any character to a real person, living or dead, is coincidental. In particular there was never a Dunkerque Squadron as portrayed here, nor such a Commodore.

Prologue

He was not tall, and was slight of build, thin-faced. His name was David Cochrane Smith, he wore the uniform of a Commander, Royal Navy and in that summer of 1917 he was just thirty years old. He walked across Horse Guards Parade towards the Admiralty to be told his fate. He had seen action too often and knew he was not a brave man, but while he could not deny his fear he could hide it as he did now. He knew a lot of his faults. He was self-critical but he could usually smile at himself, if wryly. He could not smile now. He wanted one thing in all the world and that was a command and he would fight for it because he was a fighter. But he was afraid.

Rear-Admiral Braddock stood at the window of his office that looked out over the Horse Guards and watched Smith until he disappeared into the building. Braddock waited at the window as the minutes ticked away. He was square and solid with a pointed black beard and thick, black hair but after three years of war both hair and beard were flecked with grey. He had entered the Navy in 1862 as a boy of twelve and built a career on courage, common sense and dedication to his profession, virtues like the man himself, solid, practical. He was a good officer, a good example of a type, not a man who got himself talked about in terms heroic or scandalous, sturdily respectable, not brilliant. He knew that. And thought the officer about to arrive was very different.

He turned and scowled as the knock came at the door and Smith entered, cap under arm. Braddock nodded. "Sit down."

"Thank you, sir." Smith sat stiffly on the straight-backed chair as Braddock stared at him frankly. Smith's fair hair showed the mark of the cap, an indented circle around his head. Not a handsome face. Not impressive. But three months before, in command of H.M.S. *Thunder*, an elderly armoured cruiser, Smith had fought two marauding German cruisers off the coast of Chile. And sunk them. The action had been bloody; *Thunder* had lost a third of her complement in killed or wounded. Smith had also previously sunk two German colliers, tenders to the cruisers but masquerading as neutrals. One of them he had blown up in a neutral port and the shock-waves of that explosion still shuddered through the diplomatic world – and shook the already shaky foundations of Smith's career.

Braddock stared into the pale blue eyes that met his, seemingly without emotion, and thought, 'You'd never think it to look at the feller.'

His wide desk held but one file and that was closed. Braddock knew its contents by heart and would not refer to it again. The spectacles he hated were hidden in a drawer; he could see his man well enough and could recite the details of Smith's career – and his background. Brought up in a Norfolk village by a retired Chief Petty Officer and his wife who ran the village shop. There were many who wondered how a boy from that background got into *Britannia* as a cadet. Braddock himself had wondered. But now he knew more about Smith than Smith did himself. And could not tell him.

Braddock said abruptly, "I sent you to the Pacific to get you out of trouble." There had been a woman, not the first by any means but that affaire had bordered on the scandalous and could have wrecked Smith's career. Braddock said nothing of that, but: "You did very well out there."

"Thank you, sir."

"That is the opinion of the public at large. A number of your superiors are not so enthusiastic and think you took enormous risks that were only justified by later events. They think you're eccentric, hare-brained and plain lucky. A wild man." He eyed Smith. "So you'll see why there *were* difficulties about your next appointment."

There was the slightest emphasis on the past tense and Smith said quickly, hopefully, "Yes, sir?"

"Yes. But — there was a suggestion that an anti-submarine flotilla be formed." Braddock said grimly, "Are you aware that the U-boats are winning the war at sea? That if they continue to sink ships at their present rate this country will be starved into submission?"

Smith hesitated. "I — didn't know it was that bad, sir."

"Well, it is. But keep your mouth shut. What do you think of an anti-submarine flotilla?"

"It might help, sir."

Braddock's thick eyebrows lifted. Didn't Smith want the bloody job? "You don't sound too confident."

"I think it can only supply part of the answer. I think—" Smith stopped.

Braddock prompted him impatiently, "*What* do you think?"

"That convoys are the answer. They worked in other wars, and in some waters in this one."

"The argument goes that a modern war and the U-boat impose new conditions."

"The 'beef' convoy is working, sir." Smith said it flatly, stating a fact. The 'beef' convoy ran between neutral Holland and England.

Braddock nodded slowly. "I agree. But — for now: an anti-submarine flotilla it's going to be. The suggestion comes from Commodore Trist who commands the Dunkerque Squadron, and it has been approved. He proposes 'a flotilla of destroyers and a ship of force as flagship'. I quote him verbatim. The ships to be allocated from his command as available and the flotilla still to be under his overall command." He finally opened the file that lay on the desk but only to take an envelope from it and hand it to Smith. "Your appointment."

Smith took it. "Thank you, sir. I'm grateful."

"Rubbish!" Braddock rumbled. He stared down at his hands spread big on the desk, then squinted up at Smith and said quietly, "Wait and see what it's like. But I pushed for you to get it because I think you will be able to do something with it." And then he hurried on, not giving Smith a chance to speak: "Another thing. Garrick and a Leading Seaman Buckley asked to serve with you again."

Smith blinked. They had served in *Thunder* in the Pacific, Garrick as First Lieutenant. Their asking to serve with Smith again was a compliment and he did not know what he had done to deserve it.

Braddock said, "Their request has been granted. Garrick gets his half-stripe and he's to have a command under you."

Garrick a Lieutenant–Commander now! Smith said, "That's grand, sir." He was pleased and it showed.

Braddock shrugged. "You should have had promotion yourself, but as I said, you're not everybody's favourite officer, not *anybody's* favourite officer. You stepped on too many toes in the Pacific." He asked, "Any questions?"

"No, sir."

Braddock could see Smith was eager to be away, excited at a new command – even possibly relieved? Had he been in doubt that he would get a command? Braddock believed in this young man and that he should be employed. He said, "Trist is over here for a conference and wants to see you. There's a messenger outside to take you along." He stood up and turned to the window again. He had a lot to think about and he thought best on his feet, but as Smith reached the door Braddock called in a near bellow, "Smith!"

"Sir?"

Braddock did not turn from the window. He said, "If you ever need help you know where to find me."

"Thank you, sir."

The door closed. Braddock went on, but muttering to himself with bitter resignation, "Because they won't let me out of this bloody office now."

He was too old, and too valuable where he was.

Smith followed the stooped and grizzled messenger as that pensioner creaked along the corridors of the Admiralty, but his mind was elsewhere. He *had* doubted he would get another appointment, thought they would try to bury him alive in some far, forgotten corner. He knew he had professional critics, a wild reputation and few friends. But he had hidden his doubt and now it seemed he was a lucky man and that he had a friend in the Rear-Admiral. And he had a flotilla. A flotilla! He wondered about the ships and the men, elated now. Destroyers! And a 'ship of force'! Did Trist have a cruiser in the Dunkerque Squadron? Or was one to be borrowed from the Harwich Force? A flotilla!

Then the messenger stopped at a door and tapped with arthritic knuckles. Now for Trist. Smith took a breath and entered the room.

Trist, like Rear-Admiral Braddock, also stood by a window, but this office was no more than a cubby-hole borrowed to interview Smith. The Commodore was tall, immaculate in his uniform with the thick, gold ring of his rank. He stared out of the window as if at distant horizons, jaw out-thrust and arms crossed, frowning as if in deep thought. Smith thought uneasily that it was a pose but then dismissed the idea as ridiculous. He did not know Trist and it would not do to start with any preconceived opinions.

Trist did not share that view. "Commander." He indicated a chair but before Smith was seated went on: "Let me be clear. I have no use for lady-killers nor glory-hunters. Understood?"

Smith let himself slowly down on to the chair, the elation draining away and anger taking its place. "Perfectly clear, sir. Neither have I."

"Um." Trist seemed unconvinced. He sat down behind the desk. An open briefcase lay on it and he tugged out a paper, sat reading it.

Smith waited in the silence, that unease on him again. Trist sat very straight in the chair, face set in that studied frown. A pose? The Commodore commanded the Dunkerque Squadron which in turn formed part of the Dover patrol under Vice Admiral Bacon. The Patrol

6

consisted of four hundred–odd craft, drifters, destroyers, minesweepers, minelayers, tugs and many others but all with one main task: to hold the Straits of Dover, deny them to the enemy and keep safe the traffic between Britain and France. Troopships and supply transports, hospital ships and leave ships, merchant traffic to and from all over the world entertaining or leaving the port of London, all passed through that narrow neck of water. Why should a man with a command like that need to pose?

Smith thrust the thought aside as Trist looked up at him and asked, "You can take up your command tomorrow?"

"Yes, sir." He had only to pack his bags. There were no farewells to be said, no partings.

Trist grumbled, "The Press and Parliament were all shouting for offensive action against U-boats so the Admiralty demanded it. My orders are to allocate the ships as available and this I have done." He consulted his notes again. "It seems Lieutenant Commander Garrick and a Leading Seaman Buckley asked to serve with you." He pursed his lips. "I don't approve of an officer trailing an entourage but in this case the powers that be decided. Garrick and Buckley joined the Squadron two days ago."

"I'm glad, sir." Smith said with stiff politeness. "Thank you."

Trist sniffed. "Nothing to do with me. I simply obeyed the orders of my superiors as every officer must." He peered significantly at Smith, who said nothing to that. Trist went on, eyes on his notes again. "Frankly I found Garrick a bit of an oaf; hardly a word to say for himself. But I assume he's competent and that will be something."

Smith stiffened in the chair but Trist did not notice. Smith stared at him coldly, thinking, Garrick an oaf?

Unimaginative and stolid, maybe. But he was a fine seaman, conscientious, loyal and there was none braver. He snapped, "Garrick is a good officer, sir. You don't need to worry about him."

Trist looked up sharply at the tone. "I can do without your reassurances, Commander. And Garrick will be your worry, not mine. *You* will answer for the flotilla to *me*. The orders are that it is to take offensive action against U-boats. That is a wide brief but the methods discussed were patrolling, and blockading or blocking the ports where the U-boats have their bases. The last two were considered impracticable so it comes down to patrolling. Any independent action you intend must first be authorised by *me* and *I* have work for you and these ships. Is *that* understood?"

Smith sat stiff-faced but raging at Trist and himself. He had started badly. He had received his appointment only minutes ago but already he was at odds with Trist. He said only, "Understood, sir."

Trist watched him suspiciously for a moment, then said, "Now. The ships available to you. I intended three destroyers. Two are in the dockyard and will be for some weeks, but *Sparrow* is fit for sea. And of course there is the monitor, *Marshall Marmont*, which Garrick commands..."

Smith stared at Trist as he talked on but thought only of the two ships.

Sparrow.

Marshall Marmont.

He knew nothing about them as individuals but he knew the classes of ship they belonged to and that was enough. Neither of them could be described as 'a ship of force'. He had known this would be bloody.

Part One

From a Find…

Chapter 1

She lay at anchor in Dunkerque Roads, the approach to the port that had sweltered throughout the day in windless, brilliant sunshine but now with the evening there was a wind from the sea that brought with it the rain. Smith stood in the well of the forty-foot steam pinnace that butted out from between the breakwaters and headed for the ship. She was H.M.S. *Marshall Marmont* and she was a monitor. That is to say she was built to bombard shore installations and so she was shallow-draughted and carried two fifteen-inch guns. She was not so much a ship as a floating gun-platform for those two big guns in their turret which towered ridiculously high on its mounting above her foredeck. Certainly she had no place in an antisubmarine flotilla.

Beyond the sheltering breakwaters of the French port there was a sea running that set the pinnace lifting and plunging. This was *Marshall Marmont's* pinnace and it was smart enough. The brass on the stubby funnel glittered, and polishing that was a labour of love; the smoke it poured out would leave it foul again within hours. Smith set his feet against the pitching, held on against it and stared at the monitor as he came up on her. She was only one of half-a-dozen monitors anchored in the Roads. Some of the others were twelve-inch gun monitors but there was also *Erebus* that mounted fifteen-inch guns.

They lay there along with a scattering of destroyers and drifters, the little fishing craft called into service by the Navy for various duties, but these patrolled the mine-net barrage laid across the Straits. The long line of nets with its electrical mines was supposed to stop U-boats making a passage through the Channel. It had caught very few U-boats and there was no knowing how many had slipped past it or crossed the submerged nets at night, running on the surface.

She was close now. *Marshall Marmont* was short and wide and the bulges built along her sides to give her extra protection against torpedoes made her wider. So she sat wide-hipped in the water. Like an upturned soup-plate, he thought, or with that high turret and the higher bridge and control-top behind it, and her square stern – like a flat-iron. She would sail like one, too. What the hell was Commodore Trist thinking of?

The pinnace slipped in alongside the monitor and hooked on. As Smith topped the ladder the pipes of the bosun's mates in the sick party shrilled and that was a sign of his achievement, his right to command but it did not cheer him. Then he stepped on to the quarter-deck with his right hand at the salute and saw Garrick returning that salute and fighting down the urge to grin. Then Smith smiled. Garrick was pleased to see Smith; for the moment that was all Garrick cared about and it showed.

Smith's well-worn bags and valise were brought aboard by the sideboys as Garrick presented *Marshall Marmont*'s officers, drawn up on the quarter-deck. Smith found a word for each of them, studied each face and committed it to memory in those short seconds of talk. Then the officers were dismissed and he stood alone with Garrick and glanced down at Garrick's sleeve. "Congratulations."

"Thank you, sir." Garrick's part in the Pacific action and Smith's report on that part had brought Garrick's promotion and command of *Marshall Marmont*. He said indignantly, "It beats me why you got nothing, sir. It's a disgrace!"

Smith knew why. The Admiral had told him. "Never mind that." He got down to business. "What about this ship?"

"She's a command and I'm grateful, sir." Garrick meant it.

Smith said dryly, "Don't be too sure. It's submarines we're going after, remember. Besides, I've heard some things. I crossed from Dover in a trooper and her master invited me on to bridge. He was good enough to air his knowledge of every ship in the Roads and the harbour. So?"

Garrick hesitated, glum now. "I don't know what you've heard but I've learned a lot these last two days. She's nearly new, not commissioned till 1915 but her engines aren't up to the job. She's slow and under-powered so she can barely make headway against some of the strong tides in these waters. Her best speed is six, or maybe seven knots. That's when her engines are working but they're—" He paused, choosing his words, then finished "—not very reliable."

Smith said brutally, "I've heard she's supposed to have spent more time in the dockyard than she has at sea." He stared out over the darkening sea at the dark port: Dunkerque was blacked out from eight p.m. because of the danger from air-raids. "I'm told they call her H.M.S. *Wildfire*."

Garrick admitted unhappily, "Yes, sir."

There was already an H.M.S. *Wildfire*: a 'stone frigate', a shore station that was a barracks and gunnery school.

Garrick said, "People from other ships make suggestions like: maybe we should take a tug along whenever we go to sea." Garrick added bitterly: "Often we do." He went on: "Or they say the Admiralty have a new artist and he's coming to paint us; he specialises in still-life."

Smith grinned lopsidedly. "I suppose it is pretty funny, to them."

"Maybe. But I blame that for the bad reputation the crew have ashore. The men get fed up and some drunk says a word too much and the fighting starts."

Smith was silent. *Marshall Marmont* was the 'flagship' of the flotilla with which he was to take 'offensive action' against U-boats. Her designers may have thought it just conceivable that she would be called upon to fight another ship, but hunt U-boats? No. She was supposed with her big guns to be a central strong point for the rest of his little flotilla. This was his 'ship of force'!

Garrick asked, "Have you been aboard *Sparrow*?"

Smith was sorry for Garrick. He had got him into this. Left alone, Garrick might have got a destroyer command. Destroyer? Smith's other ship was *called* a destroyer but – The fact was that back in the 1890s the navies of the world had been building torpedo-boats, fast little craft designed to attack and sink capital ships. Fisher at the Admiralty saw them as a potential threat to the British Fleets of big ships, demanded a vessel to counter them, and the result was the torpedo-boat destroyer, the TBD. *Sparrow* was one of these, one of the earliest 'destroyers', launched in 1899. At any high speed and in any bad weather these boats shipped water over the bows but their designers had foreseen this and so they had a curved hump of a foredeck – like a turtle's back — to shed the water. So they called them turtle-backs. These ships were also sometimes known as 'thirty-knotters' because they were designed for a speed of thirty knots. In her trials *Sparrow* just achieved that speed but had rarely done so later. For many years her best had been a bone-shaking twenty-six knots.

Smith said, "I reported to the Commodore and then paid a flying visit to *Sparrow*. I know that she's called *Bloody Mary*, and why." Because her crew had an even worse reputation than the monitor's for brawling ashore and because they were almost entirely Scots.

"'Bloody Mary, Queen o' Scots,'" Trist had quoted when Smith reported to him. "Lieutenant Dunbar who commands her has collected a sort of Foreign Legion aboard her, Scots like himself with one or two Irish. You'd be hard put to it to find an Englishman aboard. Dunbar himself guards his tongue but to my mind he borders on dumb insolence. You'll need to keep a tight hold on him and his crew."

Afterwards Smith had seen them and found Dunbar close-mouthed, obviously weighing up this new Commander.

Garrick said, "I'm afraid most of the brawling is between the crews of this ship and *Sparrow*, sir."

Smith knew that, too — bad news always got around. He shifted restlessly. "We've received sailing orders?"

"Yes, sir. The Commodore has called for all commanding officers at nine."

"All right. Let's make a start." They went down into the pinnace and it headed for the port.

Smith stood with Garrick in the well as the pinnace wound through the anchored shipping. He watched the low silhouette of *Marshall Marmont* recede astern as the pinnace headed for the port. Offensive action? With this – flotilla? It sounded more like a floating zoo with its men at each other's throats, his destroyer the black sheep of the Dunkerque Squadron and his monitor a lame duck. Garrick said, "One of the 'M' monitors left this morning." He pointed to a line of the 'M' class monitors, squat ships, low in the water like *Marshall Marmont* but smaller and mounting twin twelve-inch guns in a turret forward. "She was detached for 'Special Operations'. That's all anybody knows."

Smith nodded absently. He hunched his shoulders against the rain. Special Operations could mean anything... The pinnace ran into the port of Dunkerque, between the breakwaters and up the channel to pass between the bastion and the lighthouse. The French had an underground headquarters in the bastion. Close by was a French seventy-five-millimetre field gun, its wheels on a circular platform on top of a cone-shaped mounting so the trail hung down and the barrel pointed at the sky. The extemporised anti-aircraft gun was there because of air raids; this port needed all the guns it could get. It was bombed by Zeppelins and bombers, shelled by raiding destroyers and bombarded by fifteen-inch guns from behind the German lines in Belgium. It bore the scars. Twenty miles north at Nieuwpoort, the lines of trenches that faced each other across Europe ran down to the sea. In Dunkerque you could hear the mutter of gunfire that never stopped. At night the glow of the firing lit the distant sky.

The Trystram lock lay to starboard and its gates were open to admit a Coastal Motor Boat to the basin beyond. The CMBs were berthed in there and the Commander surely couldn't be happy about it; he would want them outside where they would not have to pass through a lock to get to sea. The CMB entering was one of the newer fifty-five-foot boats. Her ensign drooped at the yard because she was hardly moving as she slipped into the lock. But Smith knew these boats were capable of speeds up to forty knots and were the fastest vessels afloat. He could see the two torpedo chutes, not tubes, in the stern from which she fired her torpedoes. With her rounded hull curving inboard to form her deck and make her nearly a cylinder in shape she looked a bit like a torpedo herself, slim, fast, deadly. As she entered the lock someone flashed a light briefly from the quay above, showing the boat's commander where he stood in the cockpit at the wheel. He was a very young man of course, probably a Sub-Lieutenant. Coastal Motor Boats were a very young man's game. His oilskin glistened black with rain and spray and his face turned up to the yellow light was drawn. The light snapped out then and the CMB was lost in the gloom of the lock.

Marshall Marmont's pinnace thrust on up the length of the basin of the Port d'Echouage, past a tug and then the destroyers tied up at the quay to starboard, of which *Sparrow* was one. To port was the shipyard. At the head of the Port d'Echouage the way came off the pinnace as the engine slowed and she turned to slip in alongside the steps. Close by was the lock de la Citadelle that led to the basin where the French destroyers were berthed but right above was the quay where the fish market was held and its smell lingered.

Smith, by virtue of rank, was first out of the pinnace but then Garrick came up and they started to walk along the edge of the quay.

They headed for the Parc de la Marine and Trist's headquarters, walking quickly. On their left was the old seamen's quarter and as the doors of bars and cafés opened and closed they let out a murmur of sound and shafts of light, but for most of the time they were closed and the quayside lay dark and silent. There were gaps in the houses that made up the streets running back from the quay, marking where bombs had fallen. High above the town stood the Belfroi tower where the French had an observation post to watch for enemy aircraft or ships. But while they could warn of raiders, a lot still got through the guns and the fighters.

Smith walked in brooding silence. Garrick would be wondering about Smith's plans for the flotilla and the bitter truth was that he had none. Not for a creeping monitor and an ancient torpedo-boat destroyer. He knew Trist had plans for them.

But Garrick asked, "This business of offensive action against U-boats, sir. What do you think about it?"

Smith told him.

–

Behind them in the Port d'Echouage the tug *Lively Lady* was snugged-in against the quay across from the shipyard and only fifty yards from *Sparrow*. Victoria Sevastopol Baines woke in her tiny cabin aboard the tug and lay for some minutes staring up at the deckhead. She thought it needed a lick of paint and she'd tell George, the tug's master, about it. She believed in keeping the crew of the *Lively Lady* on their toes. The devil found work for idle hands. She lay still but not idle, planning work for those hands. Besides, she was long past the age for leaping out of bed.

Victoria's middle name gave the clue to her years; she had been born as the news of the fall of Sevastopol reached England. At the age of sixty-one she preferred to let waking take its time. At the same time, normally she disapproved of sleeping during the day as being a foreign habit. This day, however, she felt justified because the *Lively Lady* had orders to sail that night so she thought this little sleep was like the wise virgins tending their lamps. Well, the virgin part wasn't to be taken literally. There had, after all, been Captain Baines and the Captain had been a full-blooded man: she had borne him four sons. He had also been master and owner of the tug *Lively Lady* so his widow owned her now – and commanded her. Strictly the tug came under the orders of the Royal Navy and strictly she was commanded by her master, George, because he was Royal Naval Reserve and had a master's ticket. But Victoria who had no ticket at all, refused to accept such red tape. She commanded the tug and George and the Navy accepted it. Early in the war she had been outspoken about an officer's seamanship and he threatened to have her sent ashore. She had bawled at him from leather lungs: "*Ashore?* Put *me* ashore? *I'll* write to *The Times* about *you*, my lad! Tear a widow woman from her only means of livelihood and throw her on the streets? A woman that's trying to serve King and country and has four boys at sea this minute!" That was how she started. He heard a lot more but not the end because he wisely hauled clear before then.

Now she threw back the covers, knelt on the bunk and peeped out of the scuttle. The quay was a foot from her face and in the half-dark the pave of it gleamed wetly but the rain was not heavy. She thought a walk to stretch her legs and to get some fresh air would do her good.

The *Lively Lady* was not due to sail for three hours. She drew the curtains over the scuttles because she knew Frenchmen got on to the quay and everyone knew about *them*. She crawled stiffly out of the bunk, a stocky lady set solidly on thick legs, and lit the lamp. In its light she peered into the mirror with sharp blue eyes and scowled at the bird's nest of grey hair. She brushed it severely, setting it ship-shape in a tight bun. That done she washed and groaned red-faced into her stays, made all fast with two half-hitches then squeezed her feet into the high-heeled shoes. The young flibbertigibbet of a girl in the shop at Dover had tried to sell her a size six when she had worn a size five for close on fifty years. She'd even had the sauce to mumble some rubbish about her feet spreading. Fool.

She pulled her dress on over her head. Her hat went on the grey bun with a pin rammed in either side to secure it. She picked up coat, fur tippet, handbag and umbrella and went on deck. "*George!*"

Her bellow brought a tall, thin, sad man popping up from the hatch leading to the saloon.

"Yes, missus?"

"Do up me dress, George, there's a good lad."

George stepped around her and fastened the buttons between her shoulders, helped her on with her coat. "There y'are, missus."

"Thank ye, George. I'm going for a breath of fresh air. Mind you see we've got steam for sailing."

"Aye, missus."

"Don't let that Purvis feller get ashore to get drunk."

"No, missus."

"See you later then." Victoria put up her umbrella and walked across the plank to the quay.

George watched her go and said sadly, "Yes, missus."

She walked very straight in the back. As a young girl she had carried baskets of washing on her head for miles but that was far behind her. Her cronies in the Kent branch of the Temperance League knew her only as a woman of independent means and temper.

She passed the destroyers tied up in the Port d'Echouage, some singly and others in trots of three or four, and came to *Sparrow*. She tip-tapped precariously over the pavé on her high heels and called out from under the umbrella, "Good evening, young man!"

A voice answered from the head of the gangway in broad Scots. "Evening, ma'am!"

She knew *Sparrow* and her crew and thought they were a nice enough lot of boys. A little bit wild, maybe, but boys will be boys. Through a gap in the buildings that faced on to the quay she could see H.M. Barge *Arctic* in the basin beyond with the Coastal Motor Boats nestling alongside and she wondered if Jack Curtis's boat was in — was sure she saw it. She liked Jack Curtis and she missed her four boys, all of them at sea.

She walked on, crossed two locks and the fish-market and headed for the Rue de la Panne. Where it opened on to the quay was a small bar called Le Coq. Victoria was less than enthusiastic about the name but she had found the staff courteous and respectful and it was comfortable, though now the windows were shuttered and the door closed because of the black-out. She paused outside the door to shake the rain from her umbrella and to unpin her blue-ribbon badge of total abstinence from her coat lapel and put it carefully into her bag. A little of what you fancy did you good and what the ladies of Kent didn't see wouldn't hurt them. Besides, they didn't have to take a tug to sea. She peered back along the quay at a gangling RNVR figure striding long-legged towards her, recognised Jack Curtis and waved the umbrella at him, then entered Le Coq.

"Good evening, M'sieur Jacques. Two large cognacs, please. Mister Curtis will be here directly." And she settled behind her usual table opposite the door, sitting straight-backed as she had been taught with her hands in her lap, but surreptitiously easing the shoes from her feet.

She watched the door for Jack Curtis and thought absently that there'd been a lot of pinnaces and boats below the fish-market and then remembered that Commodore Trist would be giving his orders and the boats would have brought the officers. Trist. She sniffed. Bloody man? Bloody old woman! Then she boomed, "Ah! Jack!"

–

Trist's headquarters was in a big house in the Parc de la Marine. Trist's office was in a long, spacious room with tall windows that must once have been a ballroom or banqueting hall. There was a scattering of chairs around the walls but the highly polished floor was empty except for Trist's big desk and the high-backed chair behind it. He received his callers there, rising straight and tall, impressive. The wall behind his desk held a huge chart of the Channel and the North Sea. Smith thought uneasily that the whole setting was designed for effect. The long stretch of floor, the big, empty desk, the vast spread of the chart – why behind him, where he couldn't see the damn thing? Now it was evening, the curtains drawn across the tall windows, but there were only lights at the end of the room where Trist conducted his briefing like an actor on a stage before the little group of officers seated in a semi–circle around the chart. Smith wondered again if it was all arranged for effect – the thought came then: mere window–dressing like his flotilla.

Trist looked around at the assembled officers. He stood below the big chart holding a long pointer that he tapped in the palm of one hand and he looked very much the schoolmaster. His Flag-Lieutenant stood attentively by the chart, a thick file of instructions under one arm. Trist summed up: "So there you are, gentlemen. The main force under my command will fire on Zeebrugge while Commander Smith and his – flotilla, attends to Ostende. The tides are right and the weather forecast is – hopeful. There's nothing we haven't done before, but bombardment of these ports has driven the U-boats inland up the canals to Bruges and so hindered their operations." He smiled coldly at Smith. "Offensive action is nothing new to this command."

Smith did not respond.

Trist still watched him. "Questions, anyone?"

No one spoke.

"Comments?" And when still no one spoke: "Surely our new boy has some bright light from the world outside to shed on our little struggle here!" It was said jokingly but there was an acid edge to it. The Flag-Lieutenant smiled.

Smith's face twitched and Garrick sitting beside him stirred uneasily. Trist's eye was on them. Smith said reluctantly, "Bombardments help, sir, but they don't stop the U-boats, only make it harder for them. It's just more difficult and takes longer for them to make the passage to the sea. They still get out."

Trist snapped, "Where the patrols are waiting!" And when Smith was silent, "Well?"

The schoolmaster again – 'speak up, boy!' But Trist seemed an uneasy schoolmaster, uncertain – wanting to demonstrate his authority as if unsure of it? Smith answered, "A vessel on patrol finds it difficult to catch a U-boat. And so does a blockading vessel. In both cases the ship is looking for a U-boat that could be under the sea and hunting *her*." Trist was red in the face now but Smith pushed on. He might as well speak all of his mind and get it over with. "And blocking the entrance to a port is difficult if not impossible. A ship sunk in the entrance might stop a destroyer or cruiser getting out but a U-boat on the surface draws a lot less water and will get around the obstruction. No, sir. Since you asked my opinion, convoys I think are the—"

"Convoys!" Trist chuckled, seeming relieved. "We have a prophet of the convoy faith among us, gentlemen." He smiled tightly at Smith, confident now. "Convoys served in the days of sail but this is a modern war and the U-boat is a modern weapon. A convoy puts all your eggs into one basket. What a risk! Suppose a U-boat comes on a convoy of twenty ships, twenty fat targets? She'd wreak havoc!"

Smith thought the schoolmaster was trotting out phrases he had learnt from another, determined to play safe, take not a step beyond the rigid letter of his instructions. Smith said doggedly, "I don't believe that. It can be a well-escorted basket. If the same number of escorts patrol seaways they have thousands of square miles to try to protect and the U-boats pick off the merchantmen as they like."

And Garrick put in, "I agree, sir."

Trist looked at him, sniffed. "You would, of course, you're a disciple. I've explained to Commander Smith the arguments against convoy, that it is too great a risk. However, the decision to be taken is not ours. We simply do our duty as best we can. But I respect your loyalty although in this case it is misplaced! And talking of loyalty—" His eyes slid back to Smith. "I do not see Mr. Dunbar. Is there any good reason for his absence?"

Smith had no answer. "I don't know, sir."

"I see." Trist smacked the pointer into the palm of his hand. "Well. Dunbar is your affair." He said it with dislike. "See to it, please."

It was a rap across the knuckles for Smith before the other officers and he stared woodenly at the chart as Trist said, "Very well, gentlemen – until we sail."

Smith did not speak as he walked rapidly down to where *Marshall Marmont*'s pinnace lay. Garrick strode along gloomily at his elbow. He was not an over-sensitive or imaginative man but it was clear to him that Trist had his knife into Dunbar and Smith. And now he himself was classed as a 'disciple'. He said savagely, "Damn it to hell!"

Smith glanced across at him. Poor old Garrick. Promoted and given a command but all of it turned sour. He halted on the quay as a door opened to show a lighted bar and a table opposite the door where a man sprawled, head on his arms that were spread on the table. His naval cap rested by his head. The door closed and it was as if an eye had opened then shut. Smith was not sure, but was that Sanders, the young Sub-Lieutenant from *Sparrow*?

He hesitated, thinking about *Sparrow* – and Dunbar, then said to Garrick, "You go on. I want to walk around to *Sparrow*. You might take me off in about twenty minutes or so." He watched Garrick stride away and then turned again to the bar, crossed to its door and entered. As he walked the length of the room, threading between the tables, he put his cap under his arm. He had seen Sanders only once but a glance now told him this sprawled Sub-Lieutenant was not Sanders, who was regular Navy. This man looked to be taller and the thin gold ring on his cuff was the wavy one of the RNVR. Opposite him and facing out on to the room sat a stiff-backed, red-faced old lady. She watched Smith approach and her gaze was truculent.

Smith halted by the table. There were several empty glasses and two half-full, one before the officer and the other in the hand of the lady who sipped at it with little finger genteelly crooked. Smith asked, "Is this officer unwell?"

Victoria regarded naval officers with suspicion. She considered half of them too old for their posts and the other half too young, and none of them would order *her* about. An order she treated as a request that she criticised but complied with. A new officer was suspect until he proved himself and that to Victoria's satisfaction. This one was properly respectful but he had a cold eye and a stiff neck. She set her glass down and said tartly, "Don't see that it's any o' your business — but no, he's not *unwell*. An' he's not drunk either, if that's what you mean." Smith's gaze drifted to the empty glasses and she saw it. "The empties are mine. That's his first. Got halfway through it, the poor lamb, and then fell asleep. He was out on patrol for near thirty-six hours and he's wore out."

Victoria's voice was pitched in her conversational tone but it carried. The young Sub stirred and lifted his head to peer blearily around him. His eyes stopped on Smith, blinked, screwed shut then opened again and now they were aware and he climbed to his feet. It was a long climb. He was a very tall young man with a thatch of black curly hair that needed cutting and sleepy dark eyes. He said, "Curtis, sir. CMB 19."

Smith now recognised him as the commander of the boat that entered the Trystram lock and thought he also recognised the drawl. "Canadian?"

"No, sir. American."

Smith's eyebrows lifted. There were a number of Americans flying for the Allies before America had entered the war, and some in the Army – but in the Navy? "That's – unusual."

"Yes, sir. A little."

"You come from a Naval family?"

Curtis grinned. "Hell, no, sir. We're all farming stock. But I learned to handle a boat on the lake. Wisconsin, that is. Started in the creek near as soon as I could walk and moved out on the lake soon after." He paused, then: "A farmer turned sailor. Now that's unusual, sir."

"Not altogether." Smith was a country boy, brought up in a Norfolk village. But he did not elaborate. Instead he asked, "How long have you been in command?"

Victoria put in deeply, proud. "They promoted him into her. Should ha' had a medal but for that damn' red tape again."

Curtis shifted awkwardly, embarrassed at the interruption. "Now Mrs. Baines it wasn't like that at all. Fact is, sir, I was on vacation over here when the war started an' I just joined and got a temporary commission."

Smith thought it would not have been that easy, that Curtis under his country boy, innocent exterior must hide a shrewd brain and an ability to wangle. He said nothing.

Curtis went on: "We had a forty-footer and I was midshipman in her till along about the fall of '16 when we got shot up and the Sub-Lieutenant caught it so I sort of – inherited. Seems I ran her all right so they promoted me to command her permanent and later on they gave me 19. But anything I know about fighting a CMB I learned from Charlie... that was the Sub. He was a regular officer, a great guy."

Smith was interested by the tall, sleepy-eyed young man but he had a duty to carry out aboard *Sparrow*, an unpleasant duty but one that had to be done. Still, he asked one last question. "You like the boats?"

"Wouldn't change, sir." That was definite, but then Curtis added, "Except—" He stopped.

Smith prompted, "Except?"

Curtis's voice was still quiet but there was a hardness to it now. "Sometimes I think I'd like to catch up with that destroyer that shot us up, when I was in a ship with a real big gun. And I could shoot the hell out of 'em." He saw Smith staring and explained, "Just to even up for Charlie, sir."

Smith was silent, then: "I wouldn't harbour thoughts of revenge. You'll find there's little satisfaction in it. Good night." And to Victoria, "Good night, madam. My apologies for intruding."

Victoria answered dryly, "I'll see you tomorrow at sea – if you get that far."

Smith hung on his heel, taken aback. "You'll – at sea?"

Victoria said complacently, "My tug, *Lively Lady* is going with you."

"Of course I knew *Lively Lady* was to be with us, but – you'll be aboard?"

"She's my tug." That seemed sufficient answer for this old lady with her hat slightly askew despite the two pins. She touched it now, settled it askew on the other side.

Smith said, "I see." He did not, but later he would. "Good night."

He strode on, heading for where *Sparrow* was moored alongside the quay. Her commander had been absent from the Commodore's briefing. Now Smith wanted an explanation from Dunbar – and a very good one.

Smoke trailed from *Sparrow*'s three funnels and wisped across the quay on the wind; she was ready to slip at a minute's notice. The quay was dark, rain-swept, pools glinting from a tiny light at the head of the brow. He halted out in the darkness to look at her. *Sparrow* was armed with one twelve-pounder on her bridge, five six-pounders and two torpedo-tubes. She looked long but only because she was low and narrow. A man could have crossed her deck in half a dozen long steps except that it was so scattered with guns, boats, torpedo-tubes, ventilators and hatches that you couldn't take two long strides in any direction, let alone six. She was a little ship and fifty-eight men were crammed into her.

Now she and her men were Smith's.

He strode out of the dark and up the brow. A quartermaster stood on watch at the head of it and Smith demanded, "Where's your captain?"

"He's – I'll call the coxswain, sir." The man was rattled, caught off-guard by Smith's sudden appearance. Guilty? Of what? Had he been dozing? Pulling at a cigarette? Or was there something else? Smith sensed the man was hiding something, or trying to. He was Scots with a thick Glaswegian brogue.

Smith snapped, "Never mind the coxswain – and stand still!" The quartermaster had taken a quick step aft towards the wardroom hatch. "Mister Dunbar is below?"

"Er – yes, sir."

Smith stepped past him, stalked aft around the six-pounder and dropped down through the hatch that led to the wardroom below. At the foot of the ladder he almost stepped on Gow, the coxswain. He was a big man with long arms and a premature stoop that Smith supposed came from living aboard thirty-knotters. His hands seemed to hang by his knees. His head was bent under the deckhead now and he stood between Smith and the curtain that served as a door to the wardroom.

Gow whispered huskily, inevitably Scots, "Sir, if I could just say—"

"Later." Smith tried to step forward but it only brought him chest to chest with the coxswain, their faces only inches apart because Gow held his ground. Smith sniffed, smelt whisky on Gow's breath, and asked, "You've been drinking?"

"Just the one I couldn't help." Gow's long face was drawn longer with misery. "Sir—" Beyond him glass shattered in the wardroom and his face twitched.

Smith said, "What the *hell* is going on here, cox'n?"

"Ah'm trying to explain—"

But Smith had had enough. He jammed a shoulder into the coxswain, rocked him off balance and aside and took a stride. Gow's voice came behind him, still in that agonised whisper but higher. "He had some bad news about his wife and bairn. He was awfu' fond o' them, sir."

Smith was still a moment and heard a low voice pleading. It was the voice of Sanders the young Sub-Lieutenant. Then Dunbar's came, thick but clear enough. "Get out! Get the hell out and leave me alone!"

Smith said, "All right." He pushed through the curtain into the wardroom. Dunbar sat on one of the couches that ran down each side, elbows spread on the table. His cap lay beside him on the couch. He was a thick-set man with a weather-beaten, tough face but now the mouth was slack and the eyes vague. He held a bottle in one hand, a glass in the other and he was pouring the last of the bottle into the glass. Sanders stood by the table and turned now to blink worriedly at Smith, his boots crunching glass that was scattered on the deck.

Sanders said, "Sir? Good evening, sir."

Dunbar looked up, blearily startled, climbed to his feet and stood swaying. He shook the bottle and peered at it. "Empty. Join me in a drink, sir. 'Nother bottle, steward. *Brodie!*"

"Aye, aye, sir." The steward's face showed white in the doorway. He had a bottle in his hand but Smith's slow shake of the head sent him sliding away out of sight.

Smith said, "Thanks. But not just now." And: "All right, Sub. You'll be needed on deck."

Sanders edged around him and away. Dunbar swayed too far and sat down again, slopping whisky and dropping the bottle. He fumbled for it as it rolled across the couch but it escaped his clawing fingers and smashed on the deck. He said wearily, "Oh, Christ!"

Smith looked down at him and silently echoed the sentiment. He said, "I understand you've had bad news."

Dunbar took a swallow from the glass and shuddered, wiped his mouth with the back of his hand. "Letter. Navy always sends telegrams to them but I got a letter from her mother – the wife's mother. A letter! They've been dead these four days and in the grave now! But the auld witch never liked me. She wanted Jeanie to marry some feller in a bank. Influenza, she says it was. Influenza! That's something you cure wi' a hot dram an' a squeeze o' lemon, but this was some new kind o' germ. Her and the boy. It killed them."

Smith said, "I'll see you get leave. You can go—"

But Dunbar's head was already shaking a negative. "Not me. Not to stand at a graveside wi' that spiteful old woman sinking her knife into me. Here!" He shoved a hand in a pocket, pulled out a crumpled envelope and tossed it on the table. "Read that!"

Smith smoothed the creases from the sheet of notepaper. A letter written in a jagged copperplate. He read it, phrases stabbing out at him: 'shirking responsibilities... could have got a shore job... poor girl and her baby left to fend for themselves...' He folded the sheet carefully and handed the letter to Dunbar who crammed it in his pocket.

Dunbar said thickly, "Her and Trist are a bloody pair. Vicious old women." He took another swallow from the glass, shuddered and shook his head. "No, I'm not goin' home." He squinted up at Smith. "Don't you worry about me. I know fine we've sailing orders but don't you worry. The stuff's not touching me. I'm ready for sea. *You're* the one that needs to look out." He peered past Smith. "That steward out o' the way? Good. Yon Brodie's a good man but this is just between you and me." He muttered, "Wondered if I should – tricky, y'know, discussing a senior officer an' all that. But I've heard one or two things about you, and I had a chat wi' Garrick yesterday an' he told me a few more things though he's an awful close-mouthed feller. Thinks a lot o' you."

Smith thought that he ought to shut him up. But he didn't.

Dunbar mumbled, "Where was I? Oh, aye. D'ye know Trist, sir?" And when Smith shook his head, "I do. I've known him too long. I'll be honest – I don't like him. He doesn't like me. Not for what I've said and done but I think he knows I've rumbled him. He never does anything wrong because he never does anything he doesn't *have* to. He's got a gang around him that agree with everything he says. Now there's a lot of shouting for 'offensive action' against the U-boats and he's got to *do* something, or *somebody* has. What he's done looks all right, giving you this ship and *Wildfire* and maybe more to come but *we* know different. I think he realises he has to take a chance and this way he's only risking *us*. We'll be put up like targets to be shot at and if it goes wrong his hands will be clean. He'll have given you a command and a job and *you'll* have mucked it."

He was silent a moment, then: "Thought I might whisper a word in Garrick's ear and let him pass it on, but that's the way Trist works." He pulled a face. "Mister Cautious himself. That's all. Just a friendly warning to watch your step, sir."

He was staring past Smith now. "Bloody funny, really. I've been running back and forth across this neck o' water for near three years, fair weather and foul. Never got a scratch, spite o' U-boats, mines, and those bloody big destroyers o' Jerry's. While they sit comfortable at home—" He peered up again at Smith. He did not touch the whisky but he still swallowed and he said huskily, "It's not fair. Is it?"

"No." Smith watched his head droop slowly down on his folded arms, reached forward and removed the glass from the twitching fingers and stood holding it, watching Dunbar until the Lieutenant's breathing was regular, snoring. Then he stepped out of the wardroom and found Gow waiting. "Get the steward and see to Mr. Dunbar."

"Aye, aye, sir. *Brodie!*" The big man shouted for the steward then sidled around Smith, opened his mouth to speak but saw the young Commander's set face and thought better of it.

Smith was remembering that *Sparrow's* rendezvous with the bombarding force was at dawn. Dawn at the Cliffe d'Islande Bank, ten miles or so to the nor'-nor'-east of Dunkerque and at the southerly end of the mine-net barrage that ran down ten miles or so out from the Belgian coast, intended to stop the passage of U-boats from Oostende and Zeebrugge. The dawn rendezvous meant that Dunbar would have a few hours to sleep it off and be fit to take his ship to sea.

Sanders clattered down the ladder, held out a flimsy to Smith and said breathlessly, "Signal from the Commodore, sir."

Smith snatched it, read it and looked up as Gow appeared with Brodie. The white-coated steward was a small man, sandy-haired and dwarfed by the coxswain. Smith read aloud, "*Grimsby Lass* reports RE8 down in the sea off the Nieuport Bank. *Judy* is searching." He looked at Sanders and asked, "*Grimsby Lass? Judy?*"

Sanders said, "They're both drifters, sir. Some have wireless and I think *Grimsby Lass* is one of them."

Smith nodded. And the RE8, the Harry Tate, was a two-seater reconnaissance aircraft the work-horse of the Royal Flying Corps in France, but this one probably came from the Royal Naval Air Service field at St. Pol outside Dunkerque. He said, "*Sparrow* is ordered to search." He saw Sanders's stricken face as the young Sub realised what this mean that *Sparrow* had sailing orders and her captain was dead drunk. Smith said, "Thank you, Sub." And to Gow, "We're going to sea, cox'n."

"Aye, aye, sir." Gow said heavily and followed Sanders clattering up the ladder, Smith turned on Brodie and said quietly, "I want him sober in one hour. And keep your mouth shut."

"Ye've no need to fear about that, sir." answered Brodie. And: "Thank ye, sir."

Thank ye? What for? But Smith was climbing the ladder. He stood on the deck as the pipes shrilled and *Sparrow* came alive with the sound of running feet, shouted orders and here and there a curse. He found he gripped the crumpled flimsy in one hand and in the other was Dunbar's glass. He hurled it to smash against the quay.

Sanders stared at him, then said nervously, "Your boat is alongside, sir."

Smith turned from the quay, stepped around the after six-pounder and looked over the side into the monitor's pinnace. "Mister Garrick!"

"Sir?" Garrick's head was level with the deck and Smith's feet.

Smith said, "Go on to *Marshall Marmont*. *Sparrow* has orders to sail immediately, and I'm going along. There's a Harry Tate down in the sea. We'll rejoin in the morning at the rendezvous. Any questions?"

Garrick had a number but Smith was referring to the forthcoming operation and none of Garrick's questions related to that. He wondered what was going on, because Sanders's face was enough to tell him there *was* something going on. He knew enough of Smith by now to recognise that icy calm as a mask Smith put on at moments of stress. But after a moment's thought he only said, "No questions,

34

sir." Then: "Shall I send Buckley back in the pinnace, sir?" He added lamely, "In case *Sparrow* is short-handed."

Leading Seaman Buckley, who along with Garrick had served in the Pacific with Smith, would be an asset in any ship. But that was not why Garrick wanted him aboard *Sparrow*. Smith might need a familiar face on board, known and dependable. A man to look out for Smith if he did something reckless.

Smith guessed this but though his lips twitched as he hid the smile, he answered gravely, "Do that. But he must be quick. There are airmen in the sea out there and I won't wait."

He watched as the screw of the pinnace thrashed and she slid away into the night. He had been tempted to order Garrick to send one of his officers from *Marshall Marmont* to take command of *Sparrow* while he himself returned to the monitor. He should have done so. But then Garrick and the lieutenant taking command would have to be told the reason.

Smith swung on Sanders. The Sub-Lieutenant looked nervous and unhappy, trying to hide both and failing miserably. Smith remembered that Sanders was almost as much a stranger aboard this ship as he was himself. His promotion from midshipman had brought his appointment to *Bloody Mary* just two weeks ago. Smith sensed those weeks would not have been easy. When he had visited *Sparrow* that afternoon he had weighed up her commander and her crew and decided they were a tight-knit band of highly competent, hard-bitten veterans. The fresh young Sub would have a hard time fitting in, being accepted.

Now Trist had ordered a bombardment and given Ostende to Smith and his tiny flotilla. He hardly knew a man of them except Garrick. And thank God for him, burly, solid, stolid, hard-workingly efficient and loyal. A good man. And Smith knew that even now Garrick would be worrying about his unconventional, unpredictable Commander, with his black moods and prickly temper, left aboard this old thirty-knotter among strangers. Hence the offer of Buckley. Smith found he was grinning again at the thought, saw the bewildered look on Sanders's face and laughed outright. He saw Gow, the coxswain hauling his long frame up the ladder to the bridge, freeze at that laughter and peer aft, startled.

Smith said, "All right, Sub." He walked forward to the bridge. As the parties collected fore and aft and the little bridge filled up they glanced sideways at him, curious, new rumours flying now on the heels of others that had no doubt preceded him. Never mind. They would soon find the truth about each other.

He looked around the bridge, crowded now with Gow at the wheel, the signalman ready with his lamp, the bosun's mate at the engine-room telegraphs and the three man crew of the twelve-pounder. The bridge was hardly more than a platform for that gun. Smith knew about thirty-knotters, he had commanded one as a very young lieutenant and the memory was green. Like coming home? To a thirty-knotter? *Home?* That was funny and he was grinning again now. But this was his flotilla, his ships and his men, for better or for worse, and he was taking them to sea.

Sanders reported breathlessly, "Ready to proceed, sir."

It was time to start learning about this young man. Smith said, "Take her out, Sub."

Sparrow hove to outside in the Roads as *Marshall Marmont's* picket boat bucketted out of the darkness on a rising sea, bringing Leading Seaman Buckley to join the thirty-knotter. As she rocked to the sea and the wind that pushed her, Smith had doubts about Trist's confidence in the weather for the morrow. It was a pitch black night, overcast. The day might start clear enough for shooting, but later…

Gow glanced at Smith then quickly around the bridge. "Permission to speak freely, sir?"

Smith had not missed that careful glance. He stood at Gow's shoulder. Sanders had shifted out to the wing of the bridge where he watched as the pinnace came alongside. The bridge was still crowded but Gow was close and only Smith would hear him above the sound of the sea. He said, "Go on."

The coxswain said, "We've got a good ship's company, sir. She's a happy ship. I know the name she's got and there's no denying we've some hard cases that kick ower the traces and get intae trouble ashore, but at sea they're the best." He paused. When he did speak again it was as if he had changed his tack. "Yon Mr. Sanders, sir, is promising well. The skipper's a wee bit hard wi' the young officers but he likes them well enough. It's just that he wants a job done right and he's maybe a bit over strict and the young man takes it too much to heart. But I think he'll dae fine if Mr. Dunbar's left alone to bring him along." He paused again, then: "The skipper's a tough'un, sir, but fair. Well-liked. I reckon the Commodore has a down on him, sir. I think he doesn't like the skipper; he should ha' had promotion to a bigger ship long afore this. He's been in *Sparrow* since 1914 and—"

Smith cut him off. "*That's enough, Coxswain!*"

Gow's mouth shut like a trap and his eyes fixed on the compass. There came a yell from the waist and

Smith, looking aft, saw the pinnace hook on and Buckley swing himself up to the iron deck of the thirty-knotter. The pinnace sheered off, spun on her heel with smoke streaming from her stubby funnel then the midshipman at her wheel straightened her out and sent her plunging away into the night. Smith's eyes flicked over Gow as he turned back to the bridge, to Sanders coming back to con *Sparrow*. Smith swore under his breath, thinking that Gow had been rash to try to plead for his captain. He might have hardened Smith if the latter had been in doubt how to act over Dunbar. Smith had not been in doubt, had long ago made his decision, but − But? Gow did not seem a fool or a hasty man. So he had not been pleading but simply endorsing what he was certain was Smith's decision, expressing his gratitude. And Brodie, too, had said, 'Thank ye.'

Was it so obvious then that Smith intended to cover up for Dunbar? Was Smith's nature so plainly written in his face? He did not want his emotions read so easily. He growled bad-temperedly, "Let's get under way, Mr. Sanders."

"Aye, aye, sir! Half ahead both."

Brodie came on to the bridge, enamelled mugs hooked on the fingers of one hand, a jug of cocoa steaming in the other. Smith took the proffered mug and sipped at the cocoa that burned his tongue. He asked Brodie, "Well?"

"Aye, sir. Empty and sleeping." They were talking about Dunbar. Brodie had got the whisky out of him. He said, "It's a bluidy shame, sir." There was genuine concern in the steward's voice. Gow had said Dunbar was well-liked. Smith watched Brodie clamber down the ladder from the bridge and head aft. The little man had been given some training in first aid because thirty-knotters did not ship a doctor. So Brodie did the best he could for sick or wounded until they could be put ashore. It was a responsibility Smith would not have wanted.

As he turned to face forward he saw a burly figure at the back of the bridge. Buckley was a big man but he had slipped in there unobtrusively. Smith asked, "All right?"

"Aye, sir, thank ye." Buckley sounded cheerful and Smith reflected that life aboard a monitor swinging around her anchor in Dunkerque Roads would not suit Buckley and he was doubtless glad of this change.

Sanders conned *Sparrow* through the shipping anchored in the Roads and the shoals off Dunkerque. She slipped through the night past one shadowy, looming ship after another. Sanders's orders to Gow at the helm were crisp, but Smith could sense his nervousness that jerked the words out of him. The Sub was handling the ship for the first time under the eyes of this new Commander – and Smith knew his own reputation as a shiphandler. So he kept his voice quiet behind Sanders, steadying.

The Sub-Lieutenant was grateful for it. Another thirty-knotter came up at them out of the darkness, anchor party at work on her turtle-back fo'c'sle. *Sparrow* swept around her stern and Smith murmured, "That's *Gipsy*. She's escort to the other monitors."

The monitors and the drifters were assembling now at Hill's Pocket, the anchorage to the north-east of Dunkerque, and *Sparrow* was threading through them. He said, "*Marshall Marmont* fine on the port bow. You can just see that tall turret of hers."

Sanders could. That was distinctive enough. As *Sparrow* steamed past the monitor he saw that she, like *Gipsy*, was anchoring in the Pocket to wait for the dawn. But *Sparrow* steamed on. The port look-out called, "Ship on the port bow!"

Smith's head whipped around and he reached for the glasses that hung from their strap on his chest. He had borrowed them from Lorimer, the seventeen-year-old midshipman who was at the chart-table under its hood abaft the first funnel, keeping the ship's track. Smith started to lift the glasses, but paused. The ship was near enough and clear enough for him to see that she was no enemy destroyer but a drifter. "Ask her number."

The signal lamp clattered and seconds later light stuttered erratically from the drifter. The signalman read, "Seven... three... five." He looked at his list. "That's *Grimsby Lass*, sir."

Smith told Sanders, "Come about and run alongside her. I want to talk to her skipper." For *Sparrow* had been sent to look for two men and had precious little information on where to look. 'Off the Nieuport Bank' covered a large area of dark sea.

Sanders ordered, "Port ten." He sounded a little more confident now, not relaxing but not strung tight any more. Smith noted the tiny signs and grunted approvingly to himself.

"Port ten... Ten of port wheel on, sir." replied Gow.

Sparrow's head swung through a half-circle until Sanders said, "Ease to five... steady."

"Steady on two-oh-five, sir." intoned Gow.

Sparrow had turned into the drifter's wake, was now running down to overhaul her and Sanders waited, eyes on the narrowing gap, then ordered, "Slow ahead both." The bosun's mate worked the handles of the engine-room telegraphs and *Sparrow*'s speed fell away. The way on her took her alongside the drifter but there she stayed, keeping station.

Sanders ordered, "Hold her there, cox'n."

"Aye, aye, sir."

Sanders had timed it almost perfectly. Was it skill or luck? There had certainly been a little experienced anticipation on the part of Gow at the helm and Smith suspected Sanders was a shade relieved.

Smith grinned. "That was well done."

The drifter was one of scores sent to sea to lay nets or sweep mines, patrol the barrages or escort the fishing fleets. A fishing vessel herself, she was built of wood, around two hundred tons gross with a wheelhouse aft and a three-pounder that was no more than a pop-gun, right in the eyes of her before the foremast. *Grimsby Lass* was barely creeping, she looked to be wallowing along, lower in the sea than she should be and water jetted continuously in streams from her deck; she was pumping.

Smith used the bridge megaphone to hail her across the narrow strip of sea that boiled between her and *Sparrow*. "*Grimsby Lass!*"

He saw a figure drop down from the wheelhouse to the drifter's deck, caught the sheen of oilskins as the skipper lifted his hands to bawl between them, "Aye!"

"I'm off to search for that Harry Tate you reported down in the sea. What can you tell me?" Smith lowered the megaphone.

The drifter's skipper bawled. "We was out on the coast barrage but making for Dunkerque. She was in a fight north of us wi' three o' they German fighters. When they turned back for home she turned an' all and headed for Dunkerque but she was near down and her engine on fire when she passed over us. It was getting dark but near as we could see she came down to seaward of the Nieuport Bank. *Judy's* gone to look for her."

He paused and Smith said, "You're pumping. Are you holed?"

"Not holed. We were sweeping up some Jerry mines. Suppose some U-boat laid 'em. Anyhow, one went off a bit close and sprung the old girl's timbers. We're making water but we'll get home all right so long as we take it steady and keep pumping." He paused again, then added, "Wished I could ha' gone wi' Geordie Byers. He's skipper o' the *Judy* an' a good seaman but he's new to the Channel and a hare-brained bugger. You'll need to watch him. I says to him, 'You'll have your work cut out, Geordie, wi' the dark an all.' 'I can burn a flare,' he says! I told him not to be so bloody silly but I don't know if it did any good."

'Bloody silly' was a mild phrase. It would be madness to burn a flare when the Nieuport Bank was only three or four miles from the enemy-held Belgian coast and the guns there, and barely ten miles from Ostende where the Germans had destroyers and from whence came U-boats. Smith raised the megaphone. "I'll look out for him. Thank you."

The oilskinned figure lifted an arm in acknowledgment.

Smith ordered, "Port ten." And "I'll take her now, Sub."

Sanders said, "Lorimer reports course is six-seven degrees, sir, on this leg."

Smith had laid off that course himself before *Sparrow* got to sea. He told Gow, "Course six-seven degrees."

And to Sanders, "I want a good man in the chains." As they would be running through shoal waters.

"Aye, aye, sir." answered Sanders. He turned on the bosun's mate. "Get McGraw. Send him for'ard."

It was a long time since Smith had served in the Channel. He would have to remember a lot of things and very quickly. "Revolutions for ten knots." There were two men in the sea and it was *Sparrow*'s and Smith's job to try to save them, but it would do no good to run *Sparrow* aground or into collision and Geordie Byers' drifter *Judy* was somewhere in the darkness ahead.

They turned to starboard when short of the minefields that closed the gap at the southern end of the mine-net barrage, reduced to five knots and stole over the Smal Bank with McGraw in the chains and swinging the lead, chanting the soundings. *Sparrow* turned to port, increased to ten knots and headed up the West Deep. To starboard a searchlight stabbed at the night, swept briefly, went out. That was the monitor on guard at La Panne and a landmark for Smith. Nieuport was another, of sorts. There was a glow in the night off the starboard bow that faded then brightened, a pulsing glow from the guns' firing and the flares that went on through the night and every night. Men were dying there.

As the men in the RE8 might well be. If they were not already dead. Smith knew something of the effect of a flimsy aeroplane smashing into the solidity of the sea. It would break up. The engine would sink like a stone and drag some of the aircraft down with it. And maybe the men. There would be floating wreckage because the Harry Tate was mostly fabric and wood but spotting that wreckage on a night like this would not be easy. He knew what it must be like for the men in the sea and the darkness, the cold darkness. He shivered and one of the crew of the twelve-pounder looked at him curiously. This wasn't cold. Not really Channel-cold.

Chapter 2

They reached the Nieuport Bank. Smith ordered, "Revolutions for five knots."

Sanders spoke into the engine-room voice pipe and *Sparrow*'s speed fell from ten knots to a creeping five. Except for Gow at the wheel and intent on the compass, every man on the bridge and on deck was searching the dark sea for wreckage – or a man. Smith knew how easy it was to run down a man in the sea and so had reduced speed, but even so they would be on him almost as soon as they saw him.

Smith glanced around as someone climbed on to the bridge. It was Dunbar. Smith said, "Course is five – five degrees and that's Nieuport coming abeam. We're looking for a Harry Tate that crashed in the sea a couple of hours ago."

Dunbar was silent a moment then said huskily, "Poor devils. It'll be hell's own job finding them on a night like this." His head turned, eyes going over the ship.

Smith said dryly, "I haven't bent her nor lost the wireless shack overboard." *Sparrow* had not been designed for wireless so the equipment was housed in a shack erected between the first and second funnels.

Dunbar said stiffly, "Of course not, sir." Wooden. Formal.

It irritated Smith. Dunbar wasn't going to make excuses and he was being stiff-necked. Then Smith with his uncomfortable habit of self-criticism remembered somebody else who could take refuge in being stiff-necked and formal. He smiled wryly and said, "Sanders kept the log. All routine stuff, taking me aboard and so on. You'll need to make it up." The log seen by Trist would be completed by Dunbar and signed by him, showing him as being in command throughout.

"Aye, aye, sir." Dunbar was silent a moment as he took it in, then: "Thank you, sir."

Smith said nothing. That was the end of it so far as he was concerned but he knew it was not the end for Dunbar. The loss of his wife and child would haunt him for God only knew how long. Smith had not been hurt that way but he had been hurt. As a naval cadet he had been the odd man out, a solitary introspective small boy in a rough, extrovert society. He had been hurt physically and mentally but he had survived. Later there had been love affairs when he was a very young officer with only his pay, a ship and a career to fight his way through. No family, no home. Not a marriage prospect. Young women had hurt him then as the young always hurt each other. He was sorry for Dunbar but there was nothing that he could do.

There was silence on the crowded bridge, an edgy, taut-nerved silence. All of them peered into the night, searching for the airmen but with little hope. They were also looking for the enemy because *Sparrow* was in the Germans' backyard now. In one way the Royal Navy's command of the sea gave the Germans an advantage because they knew that any ship they met must be an enemy and so could shoot on sight while the Navy had to assume another ship was most likely friendly, and had to challenge. If *Sparrow* used her signal-lamp to challenge in these waters it was possible the only reply would be a shell screaming out of the night.

Smith said, "There's a drifter, *Judy*, out on the Bank somewhere."

He saw Dunbar nod and heard him answer, "I know her. That helps but there could be a score of us out here and still not find those airmen."

Smith thought of the men out there, if they *were* still alive out there, and wished to God that he could use a light.

It was as if his prayer was answered. For ahead of them came a spark of light that immediately blossomed and grew into a ball of fire that lit up the underside of the clouded sky, the dark sea and the tar-black shape of the drifter on which the flare burned. It burned from the foremast and in its light and with his glasses Smith could see her little gun and the men shifting about her deck. She was moving slowly across *Sparrow*'s course and a mile or so ahead.

Gow said, "God!"

Dunbar groaned, "Geordie Byers! Bloody fool!"

"Maybe he's seen something," ventured Sanders.

"And maybe somebody'll see him!"

"Quiet!" Smith rapped it and lifted his voice. "Keep a sharp look-out!" They might as well make use of the light now it was burning.

And there came a yell from the starboard look-out: "Twenty on the starboard bow! Right on the edge o' the light! There's summat in the water and I thought I saw it move!"

Smith used his glasses. There was something. Wreckage? And a man? He saw the movement that might have been one more shadow from the flare but it was an arm, he was certain, and there was a head. It was lost as it sank into the greater darkness of a trough then seen again as it lifted on a wave. A shape square-cut that would be wreckage, a pale splash above it that was the face.

Smith lowered the glasses. "It's a man. Skipper Byers must have seen him because the drifter's turned towards him."

The flare was burning low but it had served its purpose. Smith wished it was out, and swore softly. He could guess the cause of the skipper's rashness. Geordie Byers must have found some flotsam from the RE8 and known that a man might be close by. Smith saw Dunbar's head turning like his own, sharing his uneasiness. They were both aware that *Sparrow* made a prime target as she ran down on the drifter. The flare did not light *Sparrow* yet but to any craft or U-boat astern of her she would be silhouetted against its glare. A second was too long to be that kind of target. Geordie Byers and the other men aboard *Judy* had been lucky. But they would have to learn not to rely on luck if they were to survive in the Channel war.

Smith said, "We'll have a word with Skipper Byers."

Dunbar grunted acknowledgment, a hand to his head. Smith saw him wince.

The flare was dying, but still painfully bright...

The spurt of flame came fine on the port bow, beyond and to seaward of the drifter, a flash that burned itself on the eye and then was gone, but before that instant was past the shell burst on *Judy* and *that* flash was bigger, lighting her up again as they saw the wheelhouse blown away and breaking apart as it flew. Darkness closed in briefly and then flames flickered on the drifter.

Smith set the glasses to his eyes. "Full ahead, Mr. Dunbar! Load!"

"Full ahead both!" The bosun's mate yanked over the handles of the engine-room telegraphs and Dunbar ordered, "All guns load!"

Sanders repeated the order in a high yell, "*All guns load!*"

The killick, the leading-seaman gunner on the twelve-pounder echoed "—*load!*" The breech was thrown open, the shell rammed and the charge in its case inserted.

Dunbar swore. "Bluidy *wars!*" He shouted at Sanders, "Any word of Jerry having destroyers at sea?"

"No, sir!"

"It could still be a destroyer. If it's one o' those big boats…"

Dunbar did not finish but Smith knew what he was thinking. If that shell had come from one of the big, new German destroyers with four-inch guns then God help *Sparrow*. The enemy would not have seen *Sparrow* beyond the lake of light cast by the drifter's flare, the thirty-knotter being hidden in the outer darkness. So far. But *Sparrow* was racing down on that lake of light. A turn to starboard or port and she could run for her life. Nobody would ask her to take on one of those big, modern boats. It was ridiculous. But neither could she leave the drifter to her fate.

Another gun flash. A second between the flash and the flaming, thumping *crash!* as the shell exploded in *Judy*, and hurled blazing timbers into the sky in a shower of sparks and set new fires burning and rolling down smoke across the sea. Aboard *Sparrow* they heard the popping of the drifter's three-pounder. *Judy* was a wooden boat. She burned and in the light of her burning they could see the men working the gun.

Time of flight of the shell about one second, Smith thought, so range between one and two thousand yards and closing. About twenty seconds between rounds so only one gun firing. Why? It could be a destroyer bows-on to the drifter so that only the one gun on the foredeck would bear but he didn't believe it. Why didn't she turn to fire broadsides? But if it *was* a destroyer then *Sparrow* was roaring up to shove her head in the lion's mouth and it wouldn't come out again. Smith could lose half his flotilla right now. And he was commanding *Sparrow*, in the excitement he'd almost forgotten that. He gulped and somehow managed to drawl out. "Stand by to depth-charge."

Dunbar glanced at him but Sanders shouted into the voice pipe that led to the torpedo-gunner aft, "Stand by to depth-charge!"

Smith said to Dunbar, "I think it's a U-boat on the surface." It *had* to be. "If it is then he will see us before we see him."

Sparrow stood high out of the sea while the U-boat would be almost awash except for the conning-tower. And *Sparrow* was working up to fifteen knots now, throwing up a big white bow wave, and in seconds she would be running into the light from the burning drifter. Smith went on, "So try the searchlight. Dead ahead." To Sanders he said, "Range about one thousand I think."

He heard Sanders repeat it to the killick, and yell it to the six-pounders below the bridge as Dunbar shouted up at the rating on the searchlight platform at the back of and above the bridge. The carbons in the searchlight glowed and crackled as they struck arc and then the beam cut a path through the night ahead of *Sparrow*. It wavered, swept, then settled.

The U-boat lay in the beam, almost still, cruising but so slowly there was barely a ripple at her bow. No sign that she was preparing to submerge. There were men in the conning-tower and the four-inch gun forward was manned...

The twelve-pounder slammed and recoiled and its smoke whipped past Smith's face on the wind. Smith saw the shell burst in the sea and Sanders shouted, "Short!" He did not add a correction; *Sparrow* was closing the range at fifteen knots. The gun's crew jumped in on the twelve-pounder as the killick yelled and the breech-worker yanked at the handle. The breech opened and the fumes spilled out, the stink of cordite swirled across the bridge.

Dunbar shouted, "Must ha' been running on the surface to sneak past the barrage in the night. Bound for the Atlantic. Then came on *Judy*."

Smith nodded. U-boats from the German bases often went north-about around Scotland but those from the Flanders ports of Zeebrugge and Ostende could reach their Atlantic killing ground quicker by running on the surface at night and slipping over the mine-net barrage that was meant to bar their exit through the Channel.

He saw the wink of flame from the barrel of the gun on the U-boat and as he blinked the rip! became a *roar*! The blast threw him back into Buckley and both of them hard against the searchlight platform. Lights wheeled about Smith's head but then he was aware and clawing to his feet, Buckley thrusting him up. Gow still stood at the wheel. Sanders was pulling himself up by the screen and the crew of the twelve-pounder were on hands and knees but the killick was yelling at them, hauling them on to their feet. The searchlight still blazed, lighting them all. There was no sign of Dunbar.

Smith wavered forward and fetched up against the screen. He could see a tangle of twisted rails and a dent or a scar on the port side of the turtle-back below him. The shell must have exploded on impact, not penetrating. There were ragged holes in the splinter mattresses around the bridge. If there had been only a canvas screen those splinters would have scythed through the bridge staff and left a bloody shambles.

He looked up.

Sparrow was tearing through the circle of light shed by the fire that was *Judy* and now the drifter lay on the starboard beam. But right ahead lay the U-boat, the range was down to a bare five hundred yards and her gun was not manned. He fumbled at the glasses, set them to his eyes. There was no one in the conning-tower... He swung on Sanders. "She's diving! Tell the gunner!"

Sanders croaked down the voice pipe "Gunner! Yes, we're all OK up here except the skipper took a knock. *Listen*, Gunner! The sub's diving. We're going to depth-charge."

Smith called, "Where's Dunbar, Sub?"

Sanders turned to him a face painted yellow and black by light and shadow, excited. "On the deck at the foot of the ladder, sir. Blast must have blown him over. Brodie's down there with him though, and he gave me a 'thumb's up!'" Sanders stayed by the voice pipe.

Sparrow ran down on the U-boat that now was only a plunging conning-tower. Then that was gone and the searchlight's beam showed only the churned circle of water where the submarine had dived. Smith's eyes were fixed on that circle, watched it slip up to *Sparrow*'s stern, under it. He shouted, "Let go One!"

"Let go One!" repeated Sanders into the voice pipe.

The canister fat with three-hundred pounds of explosive rolled down the chute and plumped into the sea off *Sparrow*'s stern.

"Hard aport," ordered Smith. *Sparrow* swung into the turn and as Gow held it there came the *thump*! of the depth charge exploding and a tall column of water was hurled up from the boiling sea. The sweeping searchlight settled on it, the beam fidgeting like a blind man's searching fingers, looking for oil or the U-boat surfacing. *Sparrow* still turned. Smith said, "Ease to five! Steady! Steer that!"

Sparrow was heading back towards the blazing drifter but Smith did not see her, his eyes on the sea on the spot where he thought the U-boat might be if she had maintained her course. *Sparrow* plunged towards it. That was all Smith could do: try to anticipate the U-boat. New-fangled hydrophones were fitted in some ships but not in *Sparrow*. In any event they would only pick up the sound of a U-boat when the ship itself was stopped and there were no other engine noises about. They were useless for this kind of hunt.

Smith pointed a finger at Sanders. "Let go Two!"

"Let go Two!"

"Hard astarboard!" *Sparrow* turned, all of them on the bridge bracing themselves against the heel of her. And Smith wondered: What if the U-boat had not held that course, had immediately turned? Which way? The depth-charge exploded and he stared like all of them at another churned circle of water and saw – nothing.

"Ease to five!... Meet her! Steady!" Smith rubbed at his face.

Sparrow tore down past the drifter, passing her to port and a thousand yards away. She burned all along her length and Smith saw that she had a boat in the water now. *Sparrow* ran on, left the drifter astern. Smith ordered, "Douse that light!" The searchlight snapped off. It was serving no useful purpose for the moment and they were dangerously close to the shore batteries on the enemy-held coast and closing it with every second. The searchlight would make *Sparrow* an easy target.

"Port ten... Midships."

Sparrow turned to run north-east to the unseen coast. Sanders still stood crouched by the voice pipe but his eyes searched the sea. The towering flames on the burning drifter sent faint yellow light trembling over them on the bridge. The little wooden ship off the port bow was just a huge torch now. It lit the sea between—

"*Periscope!*" the lookout's voice was a shriek of excitement. Glasses held to his eyes with one hand, he pointed with the other.

"Hard aport!" Smith used his own glasses, seeking. Was it? So many reports of periscopes proved to be the result of excited imaginations. He saw it, held the glasses on it as *Sparrow's* head came around, banging on to the screen as the deck tilted.

It *was* a periscope. Between *Sparrow* and *Judy* and inshore of the drifter. Five hundred yards from *Sparrow's* stern – "Meet her! Steady! Steer that!"

He let the glasses fall and stared unblinking at the tiny stick-like thing poked up from the sea as *Sparrow* gobbled up the intervening distance. Almost on her. A hundred yards. The periscope dipped but too late this time. The

U-boat commander had turned when he submerged, slipped inshore of the drifter and then come up to look for *Sparrow* – hoping to launch a torpedo? That was more than likely. *Sparrow*'s stern knifed into the swirl that marked where the periscope had showed a second before and Smith shouted, "Let go One!"

"Let go One!" Sanders repeated.

Smith counted flying seconds, then: "Let go Two!" The second depth-charge rumbled down the chute as the first hurled water at the sky. "Hard aport!" Again that tight, hecling turn. Smith clung on and shouted, "Search-light!"

It crackled into life once more as the second depth-charge exploded, throwing green sea and foam higher than *Sparrow*'s masthead. The cone of light swept the foam-flecked, yeasty sea between and around the areas of the two explosions.

Sanders croaked excitedly, "She's coming up!" And then all of them were shouting it.

Smith bellowed above them, "All guns commence!" And then to Gow, "Midships!... Steady!"

The U-boat surfaced, at first just the conning-tower showing like a shark's fin but then she came up with a rush until all the shiny, slimy black back of her was clear of the water. The searchlight lit her up and Smith saw she was down by the stern. The twelve-pounder slammed and the shell burst on the bull just aft of the conning-tower. Then the six-pounders opened up. All the guns were firing at virtually point-blank range, well under a thousand yards and Smith could see them hitting. Figures showed in the conning-tower, spilled over on to the deck and into the sea. The twelve-pounder scored a hit on the conning-tower and an instant later there came an explosion from somewhere forward in the U-boat that drowned the guns' hammering and the bow lifted, dropped. As it did so the U-boat rolled over. She lay there bottom-up for only seconds then slipped down by the stern and out of sight, leaving a stain of oil. The guns ceased firing.

Some men had got out, but – survivors? Smith remembered the hail of fire that had burst on and around the U-boat and thought it was unlikely anyone had survived. All the same he ordered, "Slow ahead both. Port ten. Mr. Sanders! Nets over the side in case of survivors!"

"Aye, aye, sir!" Sanders was grinning. The crew of the twelve-pounder were cheering. As Sanders went to the ladder the killick slapped his back and Sanders laughed. Smith thought that was good. This one action had made Sanders accepted.

He rubbed at his face again but it seemed to have no feeling. He knew he was not grinning, that he was the only man aboard standing quite still, not elated, expressionless. As he had been throughout the action. He stayed apart and he could not help it.

Sparrow crept down on the circle of oil with the search-light's beam shifting over it and Smith thought that was a luxury they must soon dispense with. If there were men in the sea then Sanders and his party in the waist would see them now or not at all.

"Port bow, sir!" That was the look-out, pointing, but Smith had already seen him. Or them. At first he thought there was only one man but as his order to Gow edged *Sparrow* over he saw there was one swimmer supporting another.

"Stop both." The way came off *Sparrow* and she drifted down past the men in the sea. Smith made out two oil-smeared faces turned up to him, slipping past below him as he leaned out over the bridge screen. He saw Sanders's party in the waist with the nets hanging down the side and two men already down on the nets, their legs in the sea, held on by lines in the hands of the men on the deck above them. So they could cling to the nets with one hand while reaching out to grab at the swimmer and the man he supported.

Smith used the bridge megaphone to urge, "Quick as you can, Mr. Sanders!" He saw Sanders lift a hand in acknowledgment and turned to call up at the searchlight: "Douse!"

The light went out. Smith took a restless pace across the bridge so he could see the drifter. She was no longer a pillar of flame, had burned down to her water-line. Between her and *Sparrow* was a boat pulling towards the thirty-knotter. His gaze went beyond it, looking worriedly for the airman who had been there, it seemed so long ago though it had been only minutes. Had *Sparrow* run him down in her twisting pursuit of the U-boat? It was possible. They would have to search for him though they had been too long in these waters already. *Sparrow* was a sitting duck for the shore batteries lying stopped like this and lit up by the last of the burning *Judy*, with her only movement the slow roll and recover as a beam sea thrust at her. Under his breath he urged, "Come on, Sanders! Come *on*!" But he kept his mouth shut. The men were as aware as he of the danger and working as fast as they could.

With the engines stopped their voices came up to him, breathless as they laboured in the waist. In the light from the drifter he could see them and he glanced uneasily towards the unseen shore where the coastal batteries were mounted. He looked back to Sanders and his party and saw the survivors being manhandled up the nets, their faces pale and oil-stained – or was that blood? He could hear them coughing up the oil, rackingly. The men crowded the side and the cheering had stopped when the survivors drifted alongside. Now the hands were hauling them in, holding them up. "—'right, Jock. Easy now."... "'Old on to me. Come up, now."... "Fetch us some blankets. This puir bastar's frozen and shivering his teeth loose."

Smith thought he could hear the crackling of the drifter as she burned herself out. He could certainly smell her, tar- and wood-smoke over the reek of the cordite that still hung about the bridge.

He turned up his face to the sky, wincing, hearing now the whistle that was faint but became piercing, grew to a shriek that ripped overhead. The shell burst in the sea a cable's length to seaward of the drifter and the height of the water-spout it threw up showed it to be a biggish gun, six- or eight-inch. That would be from one of the batteries north of Nieuport.

Now Smith bellowed, "Get 'em in, Mr. Sanders!"

"All secure, sir!"

"Full astern port! Slow ahead starboard!" And as the engine-room telegraphs clanged he threw at Gow, "Port five!" *Sparrow*'s screws churned, she turned tightly and Smith watched her head come around. "Stop port... Slow ahead port... Starboard five!"

"Starboard five, sir!"

"Meet her... Steady!"

Sparrow headed for the *Judy*'s boat and Smith leaned out over the screen again to shout at Sanders in the waist, "Get ready to do your stuff, Sub! And this time really fast! Haul 'em in!"

"Aye, aye, sir!"

Smith snapped, "Stop both!" Again the way came off *Sparrow* as she ran down on the boat and again she lay and wallowed in the beam sea. Smith held his breath as another shell howled overhead and burst to seaward of the drifter. He swallowed. But the boat was hooked on to the netting and the crew of the drifter were scrambling up and tumbling inboard. One man was hauled up on a line; Smith saw them yank him up and in like a sack of potatoes, a dozen hands grabbing at him.

"All secure, sir!" Sanders yelled it. Then he added, "An' they picked up the airman, sir!"

That may have been the man on the line. Smith thought the airman was lucky to be alive – and aboard, because *Sparrow* could not search for anyone now she was under fire. "Full ahead both! Port ten!" The sooner he got them all out of these waters the better, but first he had to claw out to seaward of *Judy* so *Sparrow* would no longer be silhouetted against the glow of the drifter for the gunners ashore. "Ease to five... Midships!... Steady! Steer that!"

Sparrow ran past the drifter that could not last long, had lasted too long for Smith's liking, passed down her port side then left her astern. "Port five. Half ahead both... Midships. Steady. Two-four-oh."

Gow answered, "Course two-four-oh, sir!"

Sparrow headed back towards the West Deep and the Smal Bank. A minute or so later the drifter *Judy* sank. The glow of her was snuffed out like a candle as the sea claimed her. There were no more shells from the guns at Nieuport; they could not see a target.

Dunbar clambered up to the bridge, his head wrapped around with a white bandage, his cap stuck atop of it on the back of his head. Smith looked at him closely, saw his face pale as the bandage and asked him. "Are you all right?"

"Well enough, sir." Dunbar put a hand to the bandage, tenderly. "I had a hell of a headache to start with. Being thrown off the bridge hasn't helped it." He glanced at Smith. "Good thing you were here, sir. After three years we finally sank a U-boat and I was down in my bunk with Brodie tying my head up."

Smith shrugged. "You started the attack, anyway. After that your lads just did it by the book." He did not have to lift his voice for all of them on the bridge to hear him. "You've certainly worked them up well. They've probably called you all sorts of a slave-driving bastard in the last three years — but now all is forgiven." He saw the look-out grinning and heard the killick of the twelve-pounder snort with laughter.

"Glad we got her, anyway." But Dunbar did not sound as though he cared very much. He looked around. "I'm the better for being up here where I can breathe. And it's quieter. I looked in the wardroom and it's crammed full o' bodies. Brodie's got his hands full although he's got the cook to help him. I told Sanders to stay there."

Smith said, "They're coping?" It was more statement than question and Dunbar nodded. Smith thought that was how it was when you served in ships that were wrong for the job they were set, or built for the war of a generation ago. You had to act the doctor with a first-aid manual and a prayer. You coped. You had to.

Dunbar went on, "The drifter lost two men. When she caught alight her skipper went below to fetch up the engineer – she'd taken a hit in the engine-room. Neither of them came out. The airman seems all right, though I understand they had to bring him up on a line. He doesn't know what happened to his observer but he must have gone down with the Harry Tate. One of *Judy*'s crew has a broken leg. Sanders set a sentry over the two Germans, though I can't see them giving trouble. One of them is a seaman but the other is the boat's captain."

Smith said, "Is he, by God!" It was not often that a U-boat captain was taken prisoner.

"Aye." Dunbar nodded his head, winced and put a hand to it. "Brodie reckons the German skipper hasn't got long and I think he's right. He keeps coughing up blood and ranting and raving at the top of his voice. Sanders knows a bit of German and he says its gibberish. The man's delirious. I told Sanders to sit with him."

Smith nodded. "I'd better see that young airman. You're fit to stand a watch?"

"Aye. Better up here than laying down there, thinking—" Dunbar stopped, then went on shortly, "I'll take her, sir."

Better on the bridge than lying below, thinking of his wife and child. He had not mentioned them but he did not need to. Smith never heard Dunbar mention them again. Smith said, "Course is two-four-oh. You've another seven minutes on this leg – Lorimer's keeping the track. Nieuport on the port bow." He thought a moment then added, "You'd better get a signal off to the Commodore and Dunkerque, saying we're on our way to the rendezvous, we've got the pilot and sunk a U-boat.

Tell Dunkerque to repeat it to the R.N.A.S. at St. Pol. They'll want to know about the pilot."

"Aye, aye, sir. Well, they were shouting for anti-submarine action. You gave it to 'em quick enough."

Smith blinked. He had not thought of that. But he wanted to be away. He clambered down the ladder from the bridge to the iron deck and started aft, his legs loose and barely controlled. His hands had begun to tremble as they always did at this time, when the action was over. He thrust them in his pockets.

Behind him on the bridge Dunbar took a deep breath and blew it out. Gow cocked an eye at him. "Reckon we've got a live one, sir."

"I won't argue with you on that," Dunbar answered grimly. "Not after tonight."

And in the darkness at the back of the bridge, Buckley grinned.

Smith passed the starboard side six-pounder, its crew still excited, joking and laughing. One of them saw him stride by quickly with his hands driven deep in his pockets and his shoulders hunched, his face a pale smudge in the darkness, and unsmiling. The man stared but then Smith became aware of him and forced a smile. The seaman returned it and as he watched Smith's retreating back he wondered if he'd imagined that haunted look on the Commander's face.

Smith kept the grin on his face as he passed the after six-pounder, waved a hand at the torpedo-gunner and his party who were securing the depth-charges in the stern, and then dropped down the hatch, sliding down the ladder to the wardroom flat. He stood again at the foot of the ladder in the narrow empty space between the captain's cabin and the wardroom, slumped there for a minute with his folded arms on the ladder, eyes closed. But he could still see the gun flashes and the burning drifter, could still hear the crackling and smell the smoke of her that mixed with the cordite's tang. He could see again the twelve-pounder recoiling, the holes punched in the skin of the U-boat and how she had gone down with most of her crew trapped inside her. He could imagine that, the sea falling in and filling the compartments.

He stood with his eyes closed until he heard harsh shouting in the wardroom, the German captain's raving that Smith could not understand. He thrust away from the ladder and pushed through the curtain.

The wardroom was fifteen feet wide and twelve feet long. The couches down each side made beds for four. There were five of the drifter's crew, the airman, and the two Germans. Four of *Judy's* crew sat on the deck but the fifth, the one with the broken leg, and the two Germans and the airman, lay on beds. Brodie and the cook were at work on the man with the broken leg, Sanders crouched by the gasping, raving U-boat commander and a sentry armed with a Lee-Enfield rifle stood with his back to the bulkhead. The deadlights were tight-closed over the scuttles so what little light there was wouldn't escape. The depth-charges' kick or the guns' firing had put the circuits out of action and only a dim emergency lighting functioned. The atmosphere was thick with the smell of sweat and oil, smoke and salt, vomit and antiseptic. Smith gagged as he picked his way across the crowded deck to the airman who was wrapped in blankets and sitting up now with his legs stretched out. He was round-faced, pale. He, or someone, had rubbed at his wet-black hair with a towel so it stuck up in spikes. Smith thought he was probably twenty. He looked about fifteen.

"I am Commander Smith. How are you?" He sat on the edge of the couch.

The young man shoved himself up so he sat straighter. "Lieutenant Morris, sir. Royal Naval Air Service. An' I'm not too bad, sir, thank you. Starting to warm up a bit. Your Steward chappie gave me some cocoa. Said he'd put 'a dram o' the skipper's malt in it'."

Smith smiled faintly. The boy was a good mimic. That was Brodie to the life.

Morris said innocently, "Can't tell in this cocoa but I suppose that would be Scotch." He peered into the mug he clasped in both hands, and sniffed.

Smith said, "I think it would." In this ship it certainly would. He asked, "What happened?"

Morris glanced across the wardroom as the German officer bellowed with an edge of panic and clawed up in the bunk with Sanders holding on to him. He subsided into muttering, let Sanders push him gently down.

The man with the broken leg yelped and swore and Brodie said, "A' right! Ye'll dae fine! Easy now!"

Morris looked back at Smith. "Happened? Oh—" He hesitated, looking into the mug again, then asked, "No sign of Bill – my observer, sir?"

"No. I'm sorry."

Morris nodded. Briefly he looked a very old fifteen. He blinked up at Smith, his gaze empty. "Never saw him after we hit. I paddled around for a long time and shouted, but it was very dark. I never saw him."

Smith saw his mouth twitch. This wouldn't do. If the boy broke down before the others he would be ashamed of himself afterwards. Though he should not. Smith knew something of that. He asked quickly, "What were you doing?"

The boy blinked again but this time focusing on Smith, trying to think, remembering… "Fairly routine, run-of-the-mill stuff. Reconnaissance over Ostende and the coast north of it. Only thing is, we've been getting a bit of a pasting up there lately. Margaret was our fourth loss in ten days."

"Margaret?"

"My RE8, sir." A faint grin. "I called her after a girl I know."

Smith said, "I see. And you were the fourth?"

"Fourth aircraft lost. Nobody at all came back from the others. Henry – er, Squadron Commander Dennis, that is – he'll be glad I'm all right but he won't be too pleased about Margaret. Because of the other three he wasn't frightfully keen on my going but – orders is orders. Anyway. The other times they sent some cover, a flight of fighters, but that ended up in a dog-fight and more losses. So this time I thought: Why not try a bit of cunning? So we went without cover, flew off in the early evening, made a big circle out to sea and came in with the sun behind us."

He paused, sipped from the mug. Smith could smell the whisky, Brodie's dram had been a hefty one. Morris went on, "It turned out there wasn't much sun but the wheeze worked anyway, up to a point. We got in all right and I made a fast circle low over Ostende then ran inland and flew north. We ran right up to the north of De Haan, nearly up to Blankenberge and then we turned south along the coast." He looked at Smith and explained. "You see, sir, they've been keeping a fighting patrol flying over De Haan permanently. There's always one Albatros V-strutter in the air and they can whistle up a lot more in minutes."

Smith said, "Albatros what?"

Morris explained, "Albatros V-strutter. Their lower wing is shorter and narrower than the upper so the struts come down to a point like a V. They're hot stuff; two machine-guns. The Triplanes we've got at St. Pol can fight 'em because the 'Tripehound' is more manoeuvrable an' goes up like a rocket. But a Harry Tate hasn't got much hope."

Smith nodded and Morris went on, "So the idea was to come at them from the north. See? Not from the direction of France. Anyway, all the way up Bill had the camera going like mad but he kept shaking his head and making 'wash-out' signs with his hands meaning he couldn't see anything new. So then we turned south and ran back down the coast. Sneaking in like that we got away with it for a few minutes. The light was a bit dim by then; it had started to rain again. It's been raining a lot. Bill and me, we've got a cricket side together in the squadron but we haven't had a knock for days. Bloody weather…" Morris's voice trailed off and he was silent for a few seconds. When he went on his voice was a little louder, a little clearer, more deliberately casual. "I'd taken her down as low as I dared and Bill was hanging over the side of the cockpit and I had my head poked out so what there was to see, we saw. And there was nothing. Nothing new, that is. Except when we were just south of De Haan. There's a biggish wood runs inland from the coast and there were a lot of chaps on the beach there. They seemed to be bringing a boat up from the sea."

Smith broke in, "What kind of boat?"

"Well, we were over and past in a second." Morris screwed up his face, trying to remember, then shook his head. "Bill could have told you but I was trying to fly

66

as well. Might have been a fishing-boat. Seemed sort of wide-ish, blunt-ish. A bit like a shoe-box, it was so square. No armament, though, that's definite. I'd have noticed a gun. Bill was excited, seemed to think he could see something in the wood, had the camera going."

He took a swallow from the mug and Smith asked, "And that was all you saw?"

Morris nodded. "After that, for one reason and another I thought we might as well go home."

"What reasons?"

"The light was going bad on us, of course. On top of that we started to get a lot of Archie coming up from the wood."

Archie was anti-aircraft fire. Smith said quietly, "From the wood?"

Morris nodded. "*That* was new. We didn't know they had Archie hidden in the wood. It gave us a hell of a fright."

Smith could imagine it bursting around Morris and his observer, tossing their little aeroplane about the sky.

He sat very still as Morris went on, speaking more quickly, nearly finished and wanting to get it over. "I turned out to sea and got right down on it and that got us out of the Archie. But then that damned permanent patrol of theirs came down behind us and chased us out to sea. Albatros V-strutters, like I said. Three of them. They gave us a pasting until they turned back after a bit, but by then they knew they'd got us. The engine was dicky, smoking and burning. Just as it was getting dark I had to put her down in the sea. And that was that. I hung on to a lump of the fuselage and then your chaps pulled me out."

Smith imagined Morris in the sea, paddling about looking for Bill. Darkness all around him, hiding him, and the cold reaching out fingers to clutch at his heart. While all the time the observer lay dead far beneath him.

Smith said, "I think you did very well."

Morris shrugged, embarrassed, shuddered as he drained the mug. "Wish I could have saved the camera. I'm sure Bill got something at the end."

Smith felt a touch on his shoulder, looked around and saw Brodie. The steward said "Mr. Sanders would like a word sir. He says, would you go over, please."

Smith stood up and saw past Brodie's shoulder the face of Sanders, looking at him anxiously. He said to Morris, "I'm sorry about your observer. I should try to get some sleep if were you." He reached out and took the empty mug, passed it to Brodie and then asked Morris, "Anything you want?"

He shook his head. "No, sir. Thank you." The pilot huddled down into the blanket, pulled it over his head and rolled on to his side, turning his back on the wardroom, its sights, sounds and smells, turning his back on the world. Clearly he had taken all he could stand for that day.

Smith paused a moment, looking down at him. If the war went on long enough or Morris lived long enough then one day he would have taken all he could ever stand of war, and then they would send the wreckage home. They might call it shell shock or flying sickness D but it meant you were finished.

Smith swung away, sidled between two of *Judy*'s crew sprawled snoring on the deck and across to the couch where the U-boat commander lay. He looked to be a tall man. He lay on the couch with his head and shoulders propped up against the bulkhead. Brodie had set him up like that so he could still draw what breath was left to him. He was lean with a thin, hard-boned face that was pallid now and glistened oily with sweat in the dim yellow light. His eyes were closed but his mouth gaped as he fought for breath. He was naked under the blanket that was pulled up to his chest and that heaving chest was swathed in bandages. The rags of the uniform they had cut from him lay on the deck beside him. It was salt- and blood-stained and filthy with oil but the insignia was that of a Kapitänleutnant of the Imperial German Navy.

Sanders crouched right up against the bulkhead and Smith knelt beside him so their faces were close to each other and that of the Kapitänleutnant. Sanders's face was as pallid as the German's. He was not yet familiar with the sight of death. He whispered, "Brodie says his chest's stove in and he's all cut up about the body and legs. It must have happened when we shelled them, sir."

Smith nodded. The Kapitänleutnant had survived that and they had saved him from the sea. But only briefly. Brodie said the man had not got long and Smith agreed. He was a long way from being a doctor but he had seen men die before. Too many.

Sanders went on, but hesitantly, "I − think there is something you should hear, sir. He keeps repeating some odd phrases. Every now and again he starts shouting or talking and goes on till he collapses. Then after a bit he starts again, though he's getting weaker all the time. If you could wait, sir...?"

Smith nodded.

They waited.

Sanders said, "I talked to the other one. It seems she was a Flanders boat out of Ostende. I asked where she was bound but he just clammed up at that."

Smith asked, "Where did you learn German?"

"My father is a doctor. He had an old friend in practice in Berlin. I spent quite a few holidays there when I was a boy, and one or two leaves from the Navy, I don't speak German all that well but I can understand—" He broke off and lifted a warning hand.

The Kapitänleutnant's shallow breathing had quickened, the lips moved and the lids over the eyes twitched, lifted. He stared blankly. The flutter of breath between his lips was a whisper that grew into a mumble. The voice had some strength now, but still Smith could barely hear it though his head was bent close. He could feel the man's fluttering breath on his cheek but he could only pick out odd words from his slurred whispering: "Vater... Ilse..."

The mumbling went on, growing stronger. Sanders whispered, interpreting, "Talking about his father, his home... his girl, or his wife, I think... the boat. Now, maybe..."

The words were clearer now but still they meant nothing to Smith until Sanders whispered, "*Schwertträger* – hear that, sir?" And seconds of incomprehensible muttering later, "There, sir. Hear it?"

This time Smith did, his ear picking it out. "*Schwertträger.*"

Sanders said, "It means sword-bearer. It might be a ship, or a code-word, sir?"

The lights blinked, went out and the wardroom was plunged into pitch blackness. The Kapitänleutnant's voice went on, lifting and falling with Sanders's whispered interpretation like an echo: "*Hinterrücks anfallen* – that's stab in the back, sir – couldn't get any of that – *Springtau* – that's a skipping rope – he must be thinking of his children..." The voice in the darkness, disembodied, stopped.

A torch clicked on, held in the hand of the sentry, its beam directed at the German seaman who squinted at its glare. Enough of it spilled over to cast a glow on the face of the Kapitänleutnant just as his voice ceased. He was looking blankly into Smith's face then his eyes moved to Sanders and past him. The lights blinked, came on again. Somebody cheered, ironically. Smith was watching the Kapitänleutnant, saw his eyes going about the wardroom, then coming back to stare at Smith and Sanders. His face twisted with pain, he coughed, and he coughed up blood. Smith took his handkerchief and wiped the blood from the man's mouth.

The Kapitänleutnant's chest was heaving now, his back rigid with effort, head back. His whisper was almost a breathless shouting. Sweat shone on his face. "*Sie haben nicht gewonnen!*" He coughed, slumped but struggled to lift his head again, "*Bald kommt der entscheidender Schlag und wir werden diesen Krieg zu Ende führen!*" He slumped again, lapsing at once into unconsciousness.

Smith wiped the German's face as Sanders translated, "I think he said something like, 'You have not won. Soon the – the decisive blow will fall and we will – will end this war'."

Smith stood up slowly. The man had been aware, then. Just. A kind of drunken awareness. He knew where he was and who he was talking to, but he was not thinking clearly enough to guard his tongue. He should have kept his mouth shut but he was dying, slipping over the edge and the man knew that much and was shouting defiance. Guts made him speak. Valour was the better part of discretion. That had not been a threat so much as a promise. 'Soon the blow will fall… sword–bearer… stab in the back.' The words were a warning. But of what?

He asked, "Have you a notebook?"

"Yes, sir." answered Sanders.

"Stay with him. Note every word he says." They needed to know more.

Smith turned to leave and caught sight of the miserable face of the German seaman, his eyes fast on his dying officer. Smith patted the man's shoulder as he passed, a brief gesture of sympathy, and said to Brodie, "Can you get him a dram?"

"He's had one but I'll give him another. Aye, sir."

Smith left the stink of the wardroom and climbed to *Sparrow*'s deck and thence to her bridge. Dunbar turned his head with its turban of bandage but Smith looked blankly through him. '*Schwertträger... Hinterrücks anfallen.*' A threat, no doubt about that. But of what? A threat uttered by a U boat commander whose boat was headed for the Channel or the Atlantic beyond. So – a new submarine weapon, or a new submarine tactic that would send the figures of shipping losses soaring even higher?

That would do it. That would end the war.

Braddock had said so and he was neither pessimist nor scaremonger but a man who dealt in hard facts.

Smith brooded over it, standing at the back of the bridge with Buckley a yard behind him and looming like his shadow.

And then he thought about Morris and his report. Four aircraft destroyed on abortive reconnaissance missions to Ostende and the coast north of it. They had been getting a bit of a pasting lately! But that mystery had nothing to do with U-boats. De Haan was hardly more than a village. There was no harbour, not even a stream. The coast from Ostende to De Haan was shallow, shelving beach running up into dunes. A fishing boat could well be hauled up on, or launched from that beach, but that was all. There was nowhere on that coast between Ostende and Zeebrugge that could be used as a base by submarines or destroyers. The anti-aircraft batteries in the wood were new. Why? And why the continued patrol of Albatross V-strutters that reacted so quickly, that pursued the RE8 and sent it down in flames into the sea?

He thought of Morris, Bill and the young men like Bill in the other three aircraft who had not returned…

He swore and saw Dunbar glance at him quickly. There was another lonely man now, with thoughts, memories to bedevil him. Smith took a pace forward to stand by the Lieutenant and said, "I'm a new boy around here, newer even than Sanders. There are things I need to learn, need to know."

So he talked with Dunbar and set him talking as *Sparrow* picked her way through the shoals and the dying night. Among other things Dunbar told him about Victoria Baines, praising her until Smith was almost won over.

They talked until Dunbar said, "Should be getting light soon. We'll be up with the monitors and should be able to get that German to a doctor aboard one of them."

Smith only grunted and fell silent. He doubted that any doctor would help the Kapitänleutnant. And with the first grey light Sanders came to the bridge. He looked older now, the night in the wardroom had done that. He reported to Smith: "He's dead, sir." He held out a notebook.

Smith took it. "Did he say anything new?"

Sanders shook his head wearily. "No, sir. He babbled a lot but his speech got more and more slurred. There was very little I could make out and that was stuff we'd heard before. He was never really conscious again."

Smith put the notebook in his pocket and stood in silence looking out at the tendrils of mist that wisped across the cold sea in the pre-dawn light. Then he said, "I'm sorry." He was. The man was an enemy but the enemy had been a man. And Smith had killed him.

Part Two

To a Check…

Chapter 3

They came up with the rest of the bombarding force as that first grey light spread across the sea from the French coast. *Sparrow*, with the West Deep and the shoal water of the Smal Bank astern of her was about to turn on to a northerly course that would take her out to the Cliffe d'Islande Bank. Dunkerque was seven miles off the port bow, just seen from *Sparrow*'s bridge as a jumble of rooftops with the finger of the Belfroi tower pointing at the sky.

To starboard steamed the Dunkerque Squadron, already heading out to sea on a northerly course for the rendezvous before the bombardment. The drifters were leading the way and sweeping a channel free of mines for the rest of the Squadron. There were British minefields to starboard of the drifters and off *Sparrow*'s starboard quarter, and the drifters themselves ceaselessly swept for mines that might have been laid by U-boats in the night. The monitors followed directly behind them while motor launches patrolled on either flank. These were petrol-engined boats, acting now as light anti-submarine escorts, seventy-five feet long and each armed with a three-pounder gun in the bow. And then there were the destroyers, from the thirty-knotters to the fairly new and bigger Tribal class boats, still too slow and underarmed however to meet the new German boats on equal terms.

The ships were all worn and workmanlike. They had held the Straits for three years by a mixture of determination and bluff; the Germans saw the British daring to patrol off the Belgian coast, a bare thirty minutes' steaming from the destroyers based at Ostende and Zeebrugge, and believed the Dover Patrol and the Dunkerque Squadron to be far more powerful than in fact they were.

Smith watched them, grey ships under a grey sky, and felt a familiar justifiable pride. The depression of reaction had left him now and he was cheerful to match the elation of *Sparrow*'s crew. Hadn't they sunk a U-boat?

Erebus, Trist's flagship for the day, led the line of monitors and her searchlight blinked orders at *Sparrow*. In obedience to those orders Dunbar took *Sparrow* in a long, sweeping quartercircle to starboard to take station astern of the last monitor in the line: *Marshall Marmont*. Just ahead of her the tug *Lively Lady* plugged steadily on. There *Sparrow* stayed as the day grew and the sun climbed the sky. At the Cliffe d'Islande Bank the force turned northeast to steam along the outside of the mine-net barrage that Bacon, Vice-Admiral commanding the Dover Patrol, had laid along the Belgian coast. By mid-morning they were off Ostende, the main force steamed on and Smith and his two ships were left with six motor-launches.

At twelve miles distance the coast could not be seen from the bridge of a little ship like *Sparrow* but the gunnery officer in *Marshall Marmont* would see it from her fore-top high above the deck. Smith could only see the buildings of Ostende as a ragged edging to the horizon. North of Ostende, about where the village of De Haan lay beyond that horizon, an aircraft patrolled. He could just make it out with Lorimer's glasses and decided it had to be German or there would be anti-aircraft fire. He let the glasses hang on their strap. So that was the standing patrol that Morris, the airman, had spoken of.

There was a light breeze out of the north-west and that was what he wanted. So far the weather forecast was right. But the sky to seaward was clouding. The weather was turning bad as he'd guessed it would, and the wind would bring it down on them. But later. Meanwhile he had his orders.

To the signalman he said, "Make to *Marshall Marmont*: 'Anchor and prepare for action. Report when ready.' And tell the motor-launches: 'Anchor to leeward of *Marshall Marmont*.' And to *Lively Lady*: 'Patrol to seaward of *Marshall Marmont*.'"

The tug would be inside the line of *Sparrow*'s patrol but he did not want her to anchor. If a submarine appeared and slipped past *Sparrow* – God forbid! – then at least the tug would be moving. But it was a small point. A submarine would undoubtedly go for the monitor tethered like a helpless beast. She had to be. Bombardment of the port and its installations had to be highly accurate because the town was set close around it and its people must not suffer. Apart from common humanity there was the need not to antagonise them. So the monitor had to be anchored to provide a stationary, exact firing-platform for her two big guns.

Smith's gaze drifted over his little flotilla and he reflected that this was a first test for all of them. He was watching them and they were watching him – while Trist had hurried on to Zeebrugge where he would not have to watch at all. Smith had taken *Wildfire* and *Bloody Mary* off his hands.

That was one worry less for a very worried man. Smith shook his head, sorry for Trist. But then he remembered

78

Dunbar's warning, that Trist's caution could be dangerous to them.

The signal hoists broke out and were acknowledged by Garrick aboard the monitor, the leader of the motor launches and, belatedly, by the tug. As *Marshall Marmont* anchored so the launches anchored in a long-spread line between her and the shore and two or three cables from her. Smith watched them all as he conned *Sparrow* on her weaving patrol to seaward. The submerged mine-nets were their inshore defence against U-boats. On the southward leg of the patrol he saw the 'Ready' signal break out on the monitor. As *Sparrow* passed the tug she was steaming easily. Her master waved from the wheelhouse as the two ships passed and the dumpy figure in boilersuit and sea boots in the stern also lifted a hand. Smith thought absently that it was crazy for a woman to be at sea – and she had a line over the stern! Fishing! Dunbar had been frank about Victoria Baines's faults as he saw them. "She's got an edge to her tongue to take the skin off you and she can be pig-headed. But, by God! She's a seaman and she's doing a man's job and doing it bloody well."

Smith was prepared to give her the benefit of the doubt. But he reserved his verdict – a woman of sixty or more for God's sake, effectively commanding one of H.M. tugs in time of war?

The signalman said, "Monitor reports 'Ready' sir."

"Acknowledge." And: "Where's that aeroplane? It's due."

He was answered by a call from Buckley acting as look-out: "Four aircraft bearing green two-oh!" He saw the aircraft drifting below the cloud base and watched them through his glasses.

As the lower one approached Buckley called, "Harry Tate, sir!" That would be the RE8, that was to be the spotting aircraft for *Marshall Marmont*'s guns. Flying high above it were three Sopwith Triplanes, its escort. All of them were from the Royal Naval Air Service field at St. Pol outside Dunkerque. The escort would be needed.

Soon they were making a wide, slow circle overhead and the signalman reported, "From *Marshall Marmont*, sir: 'Aircraft in wireless contact.'"

"Reply: 'Open fire when ready.' Signal the launches to make smoke."

All straightforward so far, no hitches. This was a drill and they had done it before, knew what to expect. But they had not fired a round yet and this operation would follow a deadly dangerous, predictable course. A bombarding ship was always at risk, at a disadvantage against shore batteries if they were at all efficient and the batteries at Ostende were. Timing could mean the difference between life and death and it lay in his hands.

The RE8 buzzed away towards the coast with its escort climbing above it and the launches began making smoke with the smoke-making machines they carried. Dense clouds of it, mixed black and white poured out and rolled slowly downwind. It would hide them and the monitor from the shore batteries and was mixed black and white because when white smoke only had been used the black cordite of the monitor's guns had marked their position for the shore batteries. He thought that but for the smoke it might have been a deceptively peaceful scene, the monitor lying at anchor, the tug chugging up and down and *Sparrow* patrolling at an easy twelve knots. But the monitor's guns were trained on the shore, barrels at high elevation pointing skywards. Any moment now…

Marshall Marmont fired, a single gun thundering out, the flame jetting orange and smoke spurting black from the recoiling muzzle. The massive fifteen-inch shell, half a ton of it, went howling away into the clouds, soaring to nearly nine thousand feet high before starting on its downward path. It would fall in about forty-five seconds and some fifteen hundred yards short of Ostende. The spotting aircraft should be able to spot it there and order a correction.

Sparrow's patrolling course had taken her clear of the smokescreen and before she turned he saw the Harry Tate twisting and turning off Ostende and all around it the cotton-wool puffs in the sky that were the bursting of anti-aircraft shells. He saw something else and lifted his glasses. Was that a balloon rising over Ostende, the silver skin of it catching what leaden light there was? He was sure of it and knew what it meant. Just as the Harry Tate spotted for the monitor, so the observer in the basket swinging below the balloon served the shore batteries. Smith and his flotilla would be under fire soon. It was time for Garrick to cross his fingers. He found his own were crossed and shoved his hands in his pockets. Superstitious nonsense. But he kept them crossed.

Sanders said, "Balloon's gone up, sir."

Smith grunted. "That it has. Go round Sub, and tell 'em all to keep their eyes skinned for U-boats. I *know* they've been told. Tell 'em again."

"Aye, aye, sir."

A man could become bored staring at an empty sea and be distracted by the action elsewhere.

Smith was not bored. This was like walking out along a plank.

Marshall Marmont fired again.

81

So the observer in the Harry Tate had spotted the fall of the first shell and ordered a correction. Or he had not seen it and ordered a repeat. *Sparrow* patrolled her beat and each time she turned he had a view of the coast and the aircraft. Every two minutes or so *Marshall Marmont* fired a single, ranging round as the observer ordered corrections to bring the gun on for line and extended the range towards the target. Smith did not envy the observer his job, bucketing about in the cramped cockpit of the RE8 as it twisted and turned off Ostende. The German anti-aircraft gunners were banging away at him and he had to peer down over the side of the cockpit with the engine's clamour deafening him and the oil spraying back, watch for the shell's burst and then send his correction to the monitor.

The regular thumping *slam*! of the ranging gun marked the passage of time like the slow tick of a great clock. As *Sparrow* tacked up and down on her patrol and while he still concentrated on his command a part of Smith's mind worried at the mystery thrust upon him. "*Schwertträger…* *Hinterrücks anfallen.*" 'Sword-bearer' – a code name, obviously, but for what? And 'stab in the back'. That could mean the Atlantic shipping… There was another mystery. The patrol over De Haan that Morris had spoken of. Now he could see it.

He was jerked totally back to the present as the monitor fired a salvo, both guns. So she had ranged on to the target, the dockyard installations or a ship in the basin, or the lock gates. He saw the shock-wave send a shudder out across the sea.

The RE8 still circled and soared, though now the anti-aircraft guns had ceased firing. Instead there was a dog-fight going on involving half-a-dozen aircraft, the escorting Sopwiths and a flight of Albatros fighters swooping and climbing, diving, curling away. But he noticed one oddity. The single German aircraft to the north over De Haan had been joined by two others but they only patrolled, made no attempt to join the dog-fight. Strange, but—

"Port ten!" Dunbar ordered.

"Port ten, sir!" Gow answered.

Sparrow came steadily around.

"Meet her. Steer two-four-oh."

"Two-four-oh, sir!"

Sparrow steadied on the southward leg of her patrol. Buckley had stood a trick at the helm but now Gow, the coxswain, was again at the wheel. Or over it. His big body curled over it like a question mark, head bent above the compass card, long arms gripping the spokes. Gow was a good cox'n.

Sparrow rode well enough in this quiet sea but the sky was darkening. In bad weather she would be a pig. These ships, *this* ship, kept the sea right through the gales and foul weather of winter, though they were not really fit for the task. They demanded, therefore, a special breed of seaman. Smith stared out at *Marshall Marmont*, a ship seen through the haze of the smoke from her guns' firing and beyond her the rolling smoke of the screen. Flame, smoke and *slam!* as she fired. The barrels of the guns, the turret and her foredeck were stained black from the smoke of her firing.

His flotilla. One elderly, frail game chicken and one pot-bellied lame duck. They were his ships. But the men? Trist regarded both ships and their crews as problems. But Smith already had an affection for *Sparrow* and Garrick spoke well of *Marshall Marmont*'s crew. Garrick would always defend his crew but he was no fool and he was honest with Smith. So something could be, would be made of this flotilla...

He was still thinking about it when there was a whistling roar as a German salvo passed overhead and a second later burst in the sea in four massive spouts of upflung water. Well out to sea, well over, but that was a ranging salvo. The next would be shorter and these looked to be big shells, maybe eleven-inch, and they would be from the Tirpitz battery sited just south of Ostende. It was a well-hidden, well-protected battery. Over the last three years it had been shelled from the sea, from guns behind the lines at Nieuport, and the Royal Flying Corps had bombed it – but the Tirpitz battery was still intact and firing as well as ever.

The next salvo would be shorter – Smith called to the signalman, "Signal to Commodore: 'Under fire from Tirpitz battery. Continuing bombardment.'"

The signalman ripped the sheet from the pad and slapped it in the hand of the bridge messenger who slid down the ladder to the iron deck and ran aft to the wireless shack between the first and second funnels.

Smith took two restless paces across the bridge and returned. He wished the Sopwith Triplanes could have shot down that balloon but they had their hands full with the Albatros V-strutters and now Smith could see another flight of the German fighters climbing. A commander in this kind of operation had to consider the safety of his ships and the lives of his men. At the same time the operation had to be carried out, the attack pressed home. Hazarding ships and men could bring a charge of negligence, while failure to press home the attack might be regarded as cowardice; your senior officer might think you had cut and run too soon. It depended on his point of view and in this case it was Trist's point of view. Smith remembered Dunbar's outburst: 'We're going to be put up like targets to be shot at!' He shrugged uneasily. That was nonsense; this was just one more operation. But whatever Smith did, he had to be *right*. It was all a question of timing.

Brodie came up the ladder to the bridge with a biscuit-tin full of sandwiches, thick hunks of bread with cheese and pickles. The men were already eating at their posts and now Dunbar helped himself but Smith shook his head. He was not hungry.

Timing…

And here came the rain. A squall swept in from the sea, rain driven on the wind. From the look of the skyline, that, too, was only a ranging round and there was more to come. Dunbar called over his shoulder, "See if you can find me a spare oilskin. There should be one in my cabin."

He spoke from a full mouth, was talking to the bridge messenger. But it was Buckley who answered, "Aye, aye, sir," and dropped down the ladder to hurry aft as best he could on that cluttered deck.

Smith glanced absently across at Dunbar and noted that he already wore an oilskin, also that he was unshaven, pale under the blue-black stubble and his eyes were blood-shot. The bandage around his head was grimy now; you could not keep a bandage white on *Sparrow*'s bridge with the smoke and soot from her funnels rolling down over the bridge each time she turned. But appearances notwithstanding, Dunbar stood rock-steady and alert.

The next salvo from the Tirpitz battery came down nearer *Marshall Marmont*. So though the rain shrouded the ships it was obvious that the observer in the balloon, the *bloody* balloon, could see something. Enough. *Sparrow* was at the end of her southward patrol, clear of the smoke where the balloon and the darting aircraft showed still but the coast was hidden by rain clouds.

Dunbar ordered, "Port ten." *Sparrow* started the turn.

The signalman said, "Signal from *Marshall Marmont*, sir. 'Observer reports target obscured.'"

So the rain had reached Ostende. Smith could see nothing of it now because *Sparrow* was behind the smoke-screen again but he heard the salvo that howled in and plunged into the sea a bare cable to seaward, only two hundred yards from *Marshall Marmont*. He swallowed. That one must have lifted Garrick's cap. The pace was hotting-up, growing too hot altogether and the monitor could do no good now the aircraft could not see the target. He ordered, "Make to all ships: 'Discontinue the action. Weigh and take station as ordered.'"

He realised that Buckley was hovering behind him and holding up an oilskin – so Dunbar had sent for it for Smith. He pushed Buckley away impatiently. "Not *now*!" He wanted no distraction. He jammed hands in his pockets and hunched his shoulders against the rain that fell solidly now, and watched, outwardly calm but inwardly chafing as *Marshall Marmont* laboriously weighed anchor and got under way, started to turn. Had he given the order in time or was a salvo – "*What the hell is she doing?*" The monitor was turning not to seaward but towards the line of launches, their smoke dispersing, themselves getting under way. "Signalman! – No, wait!"

A hoist broke out from the signal yard of *Marshall Marmont*. He could see bustle on her bridge, through his glasses he saw Garrick's tall, bulky figure and his mouth opening and closing as he shouted his orders. The signalman read, "'Starboard engine out of action. Rudder jammed.'"

Dunbar gave a humourless bark of laughter. "Good old *Wildfire*! Up to her tricks again!"

Smith snapped, "Signal the launches to take evading action! And tell the tug to stand by." To Dunbar he said, "Close her a little. Not too close because we don't want her ramming us." But he wanted to be close enough to see through the fog of war, of smoke and spray and beating rain.

"Aye, aye, sir! Port ten, cox'n!"

"Port ten, sir."

"Steady! Steer that!"

Smith muttered, "If one of those shells hits *Marshall Marmont* it'll go clean through her deck and burst below."

Dunbar said, "If one of them hits *us* there'll be no deck or bottom or anything else!"

Sparrow closed the monitor and as she did so the salvo roared in and burst where *Marshall Marmont* had been anchored and dead ahead of *Sparrow*. Her bow lifted and dropped and they felt the tremor of it through the ship as if she had struck. She steamed on through hanging spray that stank of explosive and a sea that boiled. Smith wiped spray from his face. Well, he'd been right to shift the monitor. Now he had to get her out of this.

Dunbar said, "God A'mighty!" Peering through the rain that hissed into the sea, rattled on the bridge and the oilskins of the gun's crew, they all saw *Marshall Marmont* still turning in a tight circle, running down on the launches, one of which was having trouble with her own engines, barely moving as the others scattered. Smith held his breath then blew it out as the monitor lumbered by the launch, close enough for her bow-wave to heel the little craft on her side before passing on.

He looked around and saw the tug butting towards them. "Make to *Marshall Marmont*: 'Stand by for tow from tug.'"

The signalman's lamp started clacking, flashing its message through the murk and the monitor acknowledged.

Lively Lady was on a course to collide with *Sparrow* but Dunbar ordered, "Starboard ten!... Meet her!... Steady!" And *Sparrow* came around so she was broadside to the monitor and coming up on her starboard quarter with the tug forging up to pass between them.

Smith said, "Slow ahead both, Mr. Dunbar. I want to have a word with the tug." The engine-room telegraphs clanged and *Sparrow*'s speed dropped away as the tug chugged up along her port side.

Smith picked up the bridge megaphone and stepped to the rail but Victoria Baines showed at the door of the tug's wheelhouse, in yellow oilskins and a sou'wester dragged down over her ears. She bawled, "Don't you rub up against me, young man!"

Smith muttered, "God forbid!" He saw Sanders lift a hand to hide a grin. Another salvo from the Tirpitz battery roared in and burst, tearing through *Marshall Marmonts* signal yard and sending yard, blocks and rigging cascading to the deck. The signal was gone and what rigging was left hung tangled. Smith called across to the tug, "Quick as you can!"

And Victoria Baines bellowed irascibly. "Don't we know it! Business as bloody usual!"

"I'm glad to have you along, madam." Smith lifted a hand in polite salute.

The woman ignored the gesture. "Don't get in my way, damn your eyes!"

Smith winced and watched the tug pulling ahead of *Sparrow* as both of them came up with *Marshall Marmont*, her engines now stopped. He saw a crowd of men right in the bow, frenzied activity as they prepared the tow. And she'd lowered a boat that was pulling towards the bow. Garrick was going to use the boat to pass the tow, not wasting time with a heaving line. It could be done in this sea that was no sea at all. There was a lop, but no more than that. Garrick knew his business. For the rest, the rain poured down.

Smith allowed himself to be bundled belatedly into the oilskin by Buckley but broke away with the wind flapping it around him as another salvo came down inshore of *Marshall Marmont*. He peered anxiously through the rain then sighed with relief again as he saw the launches had not been touched. He lifted his gaze, looking for the shore, and though the smokescreen had dispersed he could make out nothing through the rain. The German observer would be equally blind but he would not waste ammunition. He must have seen the monitor's erratic manoeuvring and the tug hastening up before the weather closed in and made a shrewd deduction. They'd be laddering up and down on the last bearing, firing blind, but if they kept at it they could find the monitor or the tug or both where they lay still, passing the tow.

He said, "Steer north-east! Mr. Sanders! Make ready to drop one of the life-rafts over the side and get some waste and paraffin from the engine-room. I want the raft packed with waste and all well-soaked in paraffin."

"Aye, aye, sir." Sanders gave him a baffled look but dashed away.

Dunbar looked questioningly at Smith but got no explanation. Smith was shifting restlessly about the bridge, his gaze going from monitor to tug to the launches that were hauling out to seaward.

Sparrow came around and headed north-east, leaving the monitor and the tug astern as another salvo burst still farther inshore but still on that same bearing that lay across the monitor and now they would lift the range again, feeling towards her.

Sanders bawled up from the iron deck. "Raft's ready, sir!"

Smith snapped, "Stop her, Mr. Dunbar."

"Stop both!"

The way came off *Sparrow* and she rocked gently to the sea as the raft was lowered over the side, held briefly until Sanders, at Smith's shouted instructions, lit a handful of paraffin-soaked waste and dropped it on to the raft.

Sanders yelped, "Shove off!" The raft was thrust away, smouldered and smoked then burst into flame with a roar as *Sparrow* pulled away.

Smith wondered if it would work, thought it had a chance as he peered through his glasses at the monitor and the tug seen dimly through the murk and saw the salvoes come down, one short, then tense minutes later one just over, so close that the men on both ships must have been beaten by the spray, shaken by the blast.

Sparrow was heading back to them now, coming up with the monitor. He glanced astern and saw the flaming orange beacon that was the raft.

They waited for it. Then it came, the too-familiar, gut-tensing roar and shriek and they saw the salvo fall to seaward, a quarter-mile to seaward and astern; and it had been fired at the blazing raft.

Dunbar snorted, "Fooled 'em!" He grinned appreciatively.

Smith was just glad. And if the ruse had been successful it would not succeed for long. The raft would burn out and anyway the squall was passing and soon would no longer hide them. Set the launches to making smoke again? But the tug was easing away, making her own smoke as she slowly took up the slack of the tow. For an instant she checked with the tow barely curved. Smith held his breath. But Garrick would have that hawser made fast to a shackle of the monitor's anchor cable to give weight to the tow, more elasticity and thus more strength. *Lively Lady* nudged ahead and drew *Marshall Marmont* after her.

Smith thought it was none too soon, though Mrs. Baines had proved she knew her job, and more. He sent the launches off to find their own way home. *Sparrow* steamed around and around the monitor and tug, keeping again her watch for submarines and making smoke that was needed now to cover the creeping ships as the squall swept on and left the same grey sea and sky with a rare glimpse of a watery sun. The shore batteries shifted target from the burnt-out raft and fired steadily. They got close to the monitor and once, by mistake, dangerously close to *Sparrow*, the salvo bracketting her and setting her tossing, deafening all aboard, hurling spray that again stank of explosive across her decks. She steamed through it and as Smith's ears ceased ringing he heard one of the crew of the twelve-pounder singing dolefully, "Oh, I do like to be beside the sea-side! I do like to be beside the sea..."

Smith's little command limped away and gradually the range opened until the shore batteries ceased firing. For a few minutes there was peace as *Sparrow* swung around ahead of the tug and monitor and turned to pass down to seaward of them. Then came the look-out's yell, "Aircraft bearin' green two-oh!"

They were flying high, heading out from the Belgian coast, specks against the grey sky and now seen then lost as cloud hid them. But then they were coming down in a dive that was shallow at first as they turned towards the ships, then steepened. Smith watched them through his glasses until he could see the crosses on the wings and then lost those crosses as the machines swept down on the sea.

Smith said, "Take station astern of *Marshall Marmont*."

"Full ahead both!" Dunbar rapped it out then jammed the glasses to his eyes again. He said, "Rumplers."

Smith grunted, took his word for it. They were biplanes, buzzing like hornets as they came in low over the sea, barely a hundred feet above it. Heads showed like footballs above the open cockpits. There was a machine-gun mounted in the after cockpit and bombs in their racks under the wings. Their exhausts stuck straight up from the engines for a foot or more and seemingly right behind the propeller. They streamed oily smoke above the pilot's head.

Sparrow had run down past monitor and tug to seaward of them and swung around well astern of *Marshall Marmont* as Dunbar yelled, "All guns commence!"

Sparrow's guns opened fire, the six-pounders barking and the twelve-pounder slamming away on the bridge, the smoke whipping away on the wind of her passage, the ejected empty cartridge cases flying and clanging across the deck. *Marshall Marmont* was firing too. Not the huge fifteen-inch that would not bear aft anyway, but the two anti-aircraft guns she carried in the stern. And then as the

Rumplers tore in, their speed now suddenly apparent as they closed the ships, the Vickers machine-guns on the ships added their chatter to the din. There were bursts all around the aircraft but they grew in Smith's eyes until they lifted, snarled overhead and on, higher now, two hundred feet or more. One – two – three. A spread line, one behind the other, a couple of hundred yards apart, leaving *Sparrow* and heading for the fat target, the monitor dragged along at the end of the tow. They swept over her and Smith saw the bombs fall, the Rumplers shedding their entire load so the bombs seemed to rain down. They fell abeam and astern and ahead of her. The tug's stern lifted and fell and a tower of water half-bid her. Was the tug all right? The *Lively Lady* chugged on and *Marshall Marmont* followed her.

The guns ceased hammering and chattering in response to bellowed orders as the Rumplers shrank and became tiny with distance, climbing far ahead. But they were turning. They wheeled, seemingly slowly, and their formation broke up as they scattered to come back at Smith's flotilla, one on either side, one from ahead.

Sparrow was making twenty knots now and pouring out smoke from her funnels as she thrust up abreast of the monitor and tug and then passed them to take station ahead. Smith glanced astern and saw them receding, said quietly, "Good enough."

"Half-ahead both!" Dunbar ordered.

Now *Sparrow* was again where Smith wanted her, where she could meet the attack first but the Rumplers were split now – "Turn her broadside to 'em Mr. Dunbar!"

"Port ten!"

Sparrow turned, showing her side to the raiders so she could at any rate fire her puny broadside of the twelve-pounder and three of her six-pounders and they opened up as the Rumplers came in, starting to dive and weaving with their biplane wings rocking. They snarled in and passed low over the ships with the trails from their exhausts criss-crossing. The one that ripped over *Sparrow* seemed to flick past the masthead. Smith saw the scarf trailing back from the pilot's throat like a pennant, the machine-gunner standing up in the rear cockpit to fire down at the thirty-knotter right under him. Then the Rumplers were gone, forming up again beyond the ships and heading for the coast. The guns ceased firing.

Dunbar mused, "Unusual." And when Smith glanced at him, "They're usually content just to chase us off, stop us bombarding. They don't chivvy us like that."

Smith grunted. It was just another oddity. He had plenty to think about. He wondered about the aircraft endlessly patrolling over De Haan.

The rain came in squalls through the rest of that day and brought dusk early. As night was falling Garrick reported the monitor's rudder and engines repaired, just as the main force passed them, undamaged, returning from their bombardment of Zeebrugge at an easy ten knots. Trist signalled from his flahship-for-the-day, the monitor *Erebus*: 'Do you require assistance?'

Smith snapped, "Reply: 'Negative! This flotilla will cope!'" He saw the exchange of grins on the bridge.

They anchored for the night back in Dunkerque Roads, the spread line of monitors rocking together like a row of elephants, and as the whaler carried Smith from *Sparrow* to *Marshall Marmont* he reflected that now he knew what he had to deal with, to fight with. He was certain now that Trist had dumped his problem ships on him. He believed Dunbar; Trist was covering himself, and whatever went wrong in these 'offensive actions' would be laid at Smith's door. So he had to make certain nothing went wrong. Easier said than done.

Victoria Baines sat on her bunk, sank her feet tenderly into a basin of hot water and sighed with voluptuous pleasure. A minute before she had seen the whaler pass with the slight, thin-faced Commander sitting erect in the stern. Now she thought, Well, he managed that all right.

There was something about this one.

Chapter 4

Smith was up at dawn to write his reports; one for Trist and this time another for the Director of Naval Intelligence by way of Trist and this was a report on *Schwertträger*. When he had finished he read them through, flat statements of fact. A plain recounting of orders carried out and an equally plain record of the Kapitänleutnant's words and Sanders's translation. He added his commendations of Garrick and Dunbar and *Lively Lady*. He could not mention Victoria Baines because officially she had not been out with the flotilla.

He ate breakfast alone in his cabin then called for the pinnace and went on deck. Garrick had a party aloft, sending up a new yard and new rigging. Smith asked him, "Oiling and ammunition?"

"The ammunition comes alongside in an hour, sir. The oiler follows her."

Smith nodded. "I'll be back by then. Send the picket-boat in for me in an hour's time."

"Aye, aye, sir." And Garrick asked, "Shore leave, sir?"

"For one watch. Two hours when you're satisfied with the ship." That meant half of *Marshall Marmont*'s crew would get two precious hours ashore in Dunkerque. The rest of her crew would have to wait their turn, in a day or a week or longer.

Smith crossed in the pinnace to *Sparrow*. She was preparing to enter the port to coal and take on ammunition and also to put ashore her survivors. There was weak sunshine but a stiff breeze that had now veered around to the north-east, and a chop that set the pinnace pitching. Aboard *Sparrow* Smith said, "I see *Lord Clive* is leaving us." The twelve-inch gun monitor had already oiled and taken on ammunition and was now weighing anchor.

Smith nodded as Dunbar said, "Special operations." And added, "She's not the first. One by one they're going. Wonder what's up?"

So did Smith. Garrick's First Lieutenant had told him of four monitors that had sailed in recent weeks with those same vague orders: 'Special operations.' Not a word had come back concerning any of them. Whatever the secret was, it was well-kept. As it should be. Smith said, "None of our business."

Sparrow weighed and stood in to Dunkerque. They had a berth for her again in the Port d'Echouage opposite the shipyard. Dunbar said, "We'll get alongside for a few hours but it's a bit of luck if they have room for us tonight. Usually we lie out in the Roads like last night and in any sort of a sea there's damn-all sleep for anybody."

Smith grinned at him. One couldn't blame Trist for everything. Dunkerque was a busy and a crowded port. He said, "There won't be any sleep tonight, either." Because Trist's orders had already been issued and *Sparrow* was to sail at dusk to patrol the mine-net barrage across the straits.

Smith turned and saw Morris, the airman, standing in the waist and beckoned him. The Lieutenant came on to the bridge, fresh-faced and clear-eyed and Smith said,

"Your swim doesn't seem to have done any permanent damage."

Morris answered cheerfully, "No, sir. And your steward chappie looked after me very well, considering." Considering that Morris had shared the wardroom with all the other survivors. It had not been a pleasure trip. The rest of the survivors stood in the waist, with the German seaman under guard and dejected. Smith thought the man should cheer up because at least he was alive. The Kapitänleutnant lay a blanket-wrapped corpse on a stretcher. Brodie was already working on clearing up the wardroom so as to be fit for use by its usual occupants. Smith had heard his cursing as he came aboard.

Morris said hesitantly, "I'm very grateful, sir. When I woke up this morning I was thinking – it's a big sea to search for one man and that in the dark."

Smith smiled grimly. Morris was only alive because of the recklessness of Skipper Byers of the drifter *Judy*, who had paid for it with his own life. "A lot of us were lucky that night."

"It was quite a scrap, sir." Morris peered over the bridge screen at the scarred and dented turtleback fo'c'sle.

Smith agreed. "It was." Then he asked, "Have you remembered anything else to add to what you told me?"

Morris shook a tousled head. "No, sir. There was just this one boat, or raft hauled up on the beach that these chaps were working on. If it was a boat it was nearly square. And they'd used a team of horses to haul it up. That's all. Though I'm certain my observer saw something and got some photos."

But observer and camera lay in the sea somewhere off the Nieuport Bank.

Three CMBs slipped up the channel from the sea in line ahead, passing *Sparrow* on her way in also, throttled right back so they ran level and low in the water. They turned in succession towards the Trystram lock, weather-beaten, hard-worked little boats and Smith saw none of them carried torpedoes – now. The chutes in their sterns were empty.

He thought: A raft? Or a square boat? There was nothing sinister in that, it was almost comic: a square boat! Maybe some blunt-bowed, square-sterned fishing boat? But why the patrol over the wood, the anti-aircraft batteries...

Morris burst out, "There's Jack Curtis!" He yelled, "Jack! Hey, Jack!" And waved furiously. Dunbar scowled incredulously at this performance on his bridge but let it go. He stared as did Smith. A canoe was slipping out between the wide-open gates of the Trystram lock. Smith had seen pictures of canoes like that with painted braves in feathered head-dresses but Jack Curtis sat in the stern of this one and waved a paddle at Morris before sending the canoe spinning around and shooting back into the lock after the CMBs.

Morris said, "Jack commands one of those boats. American chap actually. He made that canoe himself out of ply and canvas. D'ye know him, sir?"

"We've met," answered Smith.

"He comes over to the mess at St. Pol sometimes. He promised to take me out in that canoe of his. I must take him up on it. Awfully nice chap."

Dunbar ordered, "Slow ahead both."

Sparrow was coming up to her berth at the quay and Smith pointed, saying, "That must be your transport, Mr. Morris."

Morris glanced across the quay at the big Rolls Royce that had come from St. Pol and returned the waves of the two wildly gesticulating young officers who stood beside it. *Sparrow* came alongside and tied up. Smith watched Morris walk down the brow and across the quay to have his back slapped by his friends. A cork popped and champagne frothed from a large bottle. Smith shook his head and grinned ruefully. Champagne in the forenoon! He said dryly to Dunbar, "Ah, youth! I'm going to the Commodore."

Dunbar glanced around but there was no one in earshot. He said, "I was near out o' my mind the night afore last and I'd taken drink beside. But I remember what I said and I meant it, sir."

Smith answered, "I'll remember it. But we'll not talk of it again." For it was dangerous talk.

Dunbar nodded. "No need, sir." He watched Smith stride off along the quay, a slight figure, a little shabby and walking quickly, with that sense of urgency there always was about him. Dunbar muttered, "Three years o' Trist but now at last—" He saw young Sanders in the waist and roared at him, "Sub! Hands to coal ship! And smile! Things are looking up!"

Smith found Trist in the long room, shuffling papers that littered his wide desk, gathering them together and stuffing them in a drawer. Smith wondered why Trist did not let his staff take the lot away to file or deal with. He suspected Trist was a man who wanted to deal with all of the paperwork, trusting nobody. The Commodore was immaculate but harassed, glancing at his watch. He seemed irritated at Smith's arrival, snatched the reports handed to him and stuffed them in the drawer.

Smith said, "I think that report to Intelligence is urgent, sir."

Trist stared at him. "You do, eh? What do you suggest, that I mark it, 'Commander Smith considers this urgent'?"

Smith swallowed his anger. "Sir, I—"

But Trist had stiffened, remembering. "What was the meaning of that insolent signal?"

Smith looked back at him blankly. "Insolent?"

"You know what I mean. 'This flotilla will cope.'"

"It wasn't intended to be insolent, sir. It was an answer and that's all. We could cope. And—" He hesitated, trying to put it into words. Trying to say that he wanted the flotilla to see itself as an entity with a life and spirit of its own and not just a pair of ships thrown together by words on paper—

Trist did not wait for him. "*I* consider it insolent and I will not brook a repetition. Is that understood?"

"Understood, sir." Smith bit off the words.

Trist glared at him. "Very well." He glanced at his watch again then down the length of the room to the double doors. The Lieutenant who always sat at a desk outside the doors, apparently on guard, had opened them to admit a party of marines carrying the planks and trestles of a table. Trist said impatiently, "I have representatives of the Army Staff, and possibly the General himself arriving for lunch. We are to discuss future operations. Needless to say, I have promised them maximum support."

Smith was being dismissed. He had wanted to talk to Trist about the future operations of his flotilla and tell him of *Schwertträger* – what there was to tell. Trist was in no mood to talk plans but Smith tried once more. "There's just one thing, sir, and it will only take a minute." He realised he was pleading for time and was angry again that he should have to. He controlled his voice and said patiently, "That second report, sir. I wish you would look at it and pass it on. And I'd be grateful for your opinion." That was true enough. He would be grateful to anyone who could possibly shed light on the mystery.

"Oh, all right!" Trist took out the report, scanned it and sniffed. "I suppose it might mean something to Intelligence, *if* it means anything; the babbling of a man in delirium. In any event it's their concern and not ours." He shouted to the Lieutenant and when he came hurrying, thrust the report at him. "For the Director, Naval Intelligence – Urgent." He looked at Smith. "Satisfied?"

Smith had got only part of what he wanted. He was not satisfied but he said, "Yes, sir." He left Trist looking at his watch again and chivvying the corporal of marines to "get a move on with that damn table."

Smith strode rapidly back along the quay, past the bars and cafés on his right hand, the French destroyers tied up at the quay on the other. He was certain now that Trist was a weak and insecure man under the show, anxious about his post, cultivating appearances – and acquaintances such as the General. He would be dangerous because of that, ready to let Smith or anyone else go hang to save his own career. Dunbar was right. Smith swore savagely. He had guessed almost from the beginning that this would be a difficult appointment but it looked worse with every passing day. But fast walking worked the frustration and anger out of him and his sense of humour came to his rescue.

Wildfire and *Bloody Mary*! He remembered his bellowed exchange with Victoria Baines. And Galt, that gunner on the twelve-pounder singing, 'I do like to be beside the seaside'. There were always compensations. He was grinning when he came to the Port d'Echouage and to *Sparrow*. But he could not waste a minute. This command was still new to him; he had a lot to learn and more to do and he hurried aboard.

Sparrow slipped and moved under the coal chutes. The railway wagons up on the staithes tipped their coal into the chutes and it roared down to crash into the bunkers in an explosion of choking, black dust. The little ship lay in a cloud of it. Smith moved about her deck in a boiler-suit he had borrowed from the Chief Engine-room Artificer, moved among the men toiling in that foul atmosphere. Mostly he watched in silence but now and again he exchanged a few words with one man or another and each time committed a name, a face and an impression of character to memory. He learned that Galt played the mouth organ.

Marshall Marmont's pinnace came for him but before he went down into her he told Dunbar, "You're on two hours notice for steam so you can grant shore leave to one of the watches." He stared up the basin to where it turned. Around that bend lay the Bassin du Commerce where the French destroyers lay – and the old seaman's quarter with its bars and cafés. The men would make a bee-line for it. He said, "Tell 'em to behave themselves."

"Aye, aye, sir." Dunbar knew exactly who he would speak to, familiar names recalled, familiar crimes. McGraw and Galt to start with...

Smith went down into the pinnace and so out to *Marshall Marmont* where she swung to her anchor in the Roads. The oiler was alongside her and oiling in progress with the fat hoses snaking and looping across the gap between the ships. He moved about the monitor as he had done in *Sparrow*. He spoke to a pair of young stokers. "This is better than coaling."

"Oh, aye, sir. You just connect up your hoses and away you go."

"I've just been aboard *Sparrow* while she coaled. There was a certain amount of bad language flying about but they seemed cheerful enough."

The two exchanged glances, grinned. One said, "Ah, well, sir. They're a mad lot in *Bloody Mary* – I mean *Sparrow*," he corrected hastily. "But after all, sir, you know what they say: 'If they can't take a joke they shouldn't ha' joined.'"

Smith returned the grin. "That's right."

He clambered around in the turret where the gunners worked in its dull-echoing steel cavern, cleaning and servicing the twin fifteen-inch guns. He poked his head in at the magazine where they were stowing ammunition. And when the liberty men were piped to go ashore for their two hours of leave he watched while they paraded in their best dress to be inspected and lectured by the officer of the watch.

He bathed and changed his clothes and ate in his cabin but this time had Garrick join him, listened to him talk of his ship and his crew and his plans. And finally Smith told Garrick something of his own plans. Garrick was startled but doubtfully agreed.

The tap came at the door and the messenger said, "Mr. Chivers's compliments, sir." Chivers had the watch. "Sorry to disturb you but there's a signal from the Provost Marshall. There's trouble ashore with the libertymen."

Garrick said, "Blast!"

"I'll come." Smith picked up his cap.

They went ashore in the pinnace, running up the channel past the lighthouse and up the length of the basin of the Port d'Echouage to the fish-market quay at the head of it. Smith climbed the steps with Garrick at his shoulder and found Dunbar already on the quay, pacing back and forth like a caged tiger and glowering at the party of seamen drawn up on the quay in four ranks. There were some thirty in all, a dejected, battered group. There were blood-stained jerseys and torn collars to be seen in plenty but few caps. Smith recognised men from *Sparrow* and *Marshall Marmont*, including the two young stokers from the monitor. The group was encircled by twenty or so military police and men of the Naval Shore Patrol under a petty officer.

Dunbar called them all to attention and Smith acknowledged his salute. "What happened?"

Dunbar nodded curtly at the petty officer, who barked in a monotone: "We was called along 'cause of a fight in that there bar, sir." He gave a sideways jerk of the head and Smith saw the glass-littered road and the shattered windows, the door hanging askew on its hinges. The petty officer went on reciting: "We found 'em smashing up each other an' the place in the bygoing. All well-known to me, sir. The same had hats from *Wildfire* and *Bloody Mary*—"

"That will do!" Smith's rasp cut the man short. He went on quietly, "Take your patrol away."

Garrick looked at him sharply when he heard that tone; he knew Smith a little now. The petty officer did not. He objected, "Sir! My orders was to see them embarked and—"

He stopped as Smith's eye turned from the bedraggled group to fall on him. Then he blinked and saluted, turned on his heel and bawled at his men, marched them away.

The corporal in the rear file said from the corner of his mouth, "What did he say, then?"

The petty officer muttered, "Nothing. Not a bloody word. But better them than me. He's got an eye as goes right through yer."

Smith looked at this sample of his flotilla. He knew he was no good at speeches and he would not make one now. He stood still, eyes going to each one in turn and holding theirs before passing on. A squall swept up the basin, hurling rain in the men's faces and they hunched their shoulders, bent their heads to it.

"Look up!" He did not shout but the order snapped them straight. "I have never been ashamed of any ship in which I have served and I will not start now. You're going to sea. All of you."

He turned to speak briefly to Dunbar and Garrick while the men cast uneasy glances at each other. If they were all going to sea then surely *Marshall Marmont's* orders must have been changed, they thought. But it was not so. Instead Garrick and Dunbar had to quickly compare notes and revise watch-bills. So that when *Sparrow* sailed an hour later a dozen of her complement who had not gone ashore were settling in bemusedly on board the anchored *Marshall Marmont*, while all the party from the quay were aboard *Sparrow*, as look-outs, ammunition numbers on the guns, or in the engine-room where two young stokers were being initiated into the painful and rigorous art of stoking a coal-burning ship. They were learning how to balance on the stoke-hold plating that in good weather rose and fell and tilted and in bad weather bucked like a horse. How to knock open the furnace door with the slice, the long-handled rake, probe with it at the white-hot embers and drag out the clinker and ash that pulsed with heat. How to shovel fresh coal into that roaring, red maw and spread it to burn evenly. Then move to the next furnace and do it all again. And again. Cursing their way steadily through the watch, the hours spent in sweltering heat, filth, steam, the deafening, churning thump of the engines and the roar of the draught that forced the furnaces to that white heat.

Sparrow's Chief grinned at them comfortably, "Well, if you can't take a joke you shouldn't ha' joined."

Sparrow ran down the channel in the last of the light with her crew manning the side. McGraw's head thumped with every turn of *Sparrow*'s screws but like the rest of the men on her deck he peered up at the bridge. Faintly on the wind came the sound of a mouth-organ. Smith was on the bridge and Galt was playing at his orders. 'Oh, I do like to be beside the sea-side!'

McGraw held his head. "Mad bastard!"

The next day Trist had a word with Smith. "That was a disgraceful business! I had a full report from the Provost Marshall. Disgraceful! The offenders have been dealt with?"

"Yes, sir. I took a very serious view of the affair." Smith slipped the question. He doubted whether Trist's view of suitable punishment coincided with his own.

Garrick had spoken to all of the offenders on the quay after Smith had gone, spoken in a voice tight with suppressed rage in a way that left them stiff-faced and silent. "You have commanding this flotilla the finest seaman and sea-fighter I've ever known. A man who will lead you and fight for you and never let you down. I won't let him down if I can help it and, by God, neither will you!"

So *Sparrow* entered again the grind of patrol work. But they were lucky. *Sparrow* had steamed her seventeen days and came up for boiler-clean, so they got a break early on. She was laid up for three days and her crew sent on leave.

Smith was explicit on that. He told Garrick and Dunbar, "The punishments I leave to you. Work them as much as you like but I want no man's leave stopped."

So the men got their leave.

–

Smith got a summons. Naval Intelligence wanted to talk to Sanders and himself about *Schwertträger*. Smith thought it would prove a waste of time but with Sanders he crossed to Dover and took a train to London. He was right. Intelligence appropriated Sanders's notebook with its record of the Kapitänleutnant's last words, and questioned the pair of them to see if there was any scrap of information that had been forgotten or overlooked and so omitted from Smith's report. There was none.

Sanders hurried off to his home in Wimbledon and a girl. Smith went to see Rear-Admiral Braddock – at Braddock's request. "Heard you were in the building and visiting Intelligence." He grinned at Smith. "I have an intelligence system of my own. A lot of people talk to me. Sometimes they even listen." He scowled at that. Then he said, eyeing Smith, "That reminds me. We're still pushing the convoy system and we're gaining ground. The counter-argument now is that we can't find enough ships for escorts. Rubbish! It's just a delaying tactic." He got up and took a turn around the room, stumping bad-temperedly.

Smith shifted restlessly in the chair.

Braddock said, "I hear you sank a U-boat."

"*Sparrow* did, sir."

"You didn't waste much time. Trist claims it proves that his idea of an anti-submarine flotilla works. Did you know that?"

Smith blinked "No, sir."

Braddock grumbled, "Lloyd George does. It got back to him, somehow. He wants my opinion. I want yours as the man commanding the anti-submarine flotilla, the man who sank the U-boat."

Smith hesitated, trying to pick his words because they might be repeated to the Prime Minister. The *Prime Minister*! But the careful, chosen words would not come and so he spoke his mind, harshly. "We found the U-boat by sheer luck; just ran across her. And she nearly got away, might as easily have sunk us. The flotilla is doing good work patrolling and bombarding – we have to hold the Straits and hit their bases – but it can't and won't stop the U-boats. Nor would a hundred anti-submarine flotillas. The ships would be better used escorting convoys, and convoys must come and soon."

Braddock stared at him for several seconds, as if letting the words soak in so as to repeat them later. Then he stirred, started prowling again. "And how is the flotilla?"

"I've no complaints, sir." Smith's face was blank now.

Braddock thought, so it's like that. He said slowly, "I know Trist. I knew the kind of flotilla it would be when I got you the appointment, but there were other suggestions designed to bury you alive in some shore job with a big title and no command. I thought you'd prefer the flotilla."

"Yes, sir." That was definite.

"Can you make something of them?"

"They can. There's good stuff there, sir."

"What? *Wildfire* and *Bloody Mary*?"

Smith blinked again. Braddock's intelligence system was impressive. "Yes. To start with there's Garrick and Dunbar..." He told Braddock about the ships and their men, at first stiffly, self-consciously, but soon his enthusiasm set him talking freely.

Braddock listened until Smith talked himself out and only then said dryly, as he opened the door to end the interview, "It's a good job Beatty can't hear you." Beatty now commanded the Grand Fleet. "If he believed you he'd want to swap for your paragons."

Smith went to his hotel. Sanders had diffidently invited Smith to spend the short leave at the house in Wimbledon but Smith knew about Sanders's girl and he wasn't going to get in the way there. Smith had no home to go to. The CPO and his wife who had brought up Smith had both died in his first year as a cadet in *Britannia*. But he had always managed happily enough in a hotel before. Now he stared out of the window and wasn't so sure. He had three days to get through. Get through? That was hardly the way to look at a short leave after a gruelling period of service in the Channel. He was used to being alone but now he felt lonely, a very different thing. He scowled moodily out at the rain that spotted the panes and thought about the ships.

–

She was fast and modern, slim and strong. Not a ship. Eleanor Hurst was twenty-four years old, with money of her own, and the man she wanted and could not get had been killed on the Somme. She sat at the table in the Savoy, between the subaltern and the young Lieutenant-Colonel with the red tabs of the Staff, and watched Smith. He was aware of her: pretty, blonde, the dress low-cut, the eyes watching him coolly. Not challenging, just watching. He wondered whether she was too cool; was there a tenseness about her?

The big room was brilliantly lit by the chandeliers, the orchestra played ragtime and the dance floor was filled with young officers and girls. The supper party was given by the subaltern's mother who was in a nervous state because he was returning to France and the Front the next day. The average life-span of a subaltern at the Front was three months. Smith sat between her and a Mrs. Pink – he couldn't remember her name but thought of her as Mrs. Pink. She was large and pink-faced and pink bosomed, expensively dressed and she kept laying her hand on his thigh under the table. Her shadowy, absent husband was making a lot of money, she was vocally patriotic and got on Smith's nerves.

Sanders sat opposite him with a pretty, dark-haired girl who laughed a great deal. Smith's invitation had come through Sanders because the subaltern and Sanders were old friends. Sanders had been apologetic. "I can put 'em off – make some excuse, you know – although they were very keen I should ask you." Smith had hesitated but accepted, telling himself it was a chance to relax and briefly forget the war, but now he was regretting it. He found he was something of a celebrity. A lot of people wanted to talk to him because the action in the Pacific had been widely reported. He did not like it. He told himself he should be pleased, he *was* pleased that some people thought well of him but the fact was that it embarrassed him and he did not wish to talk about the Pacific.

There was a lot he wanted to forget. He thought he might have enjoyed the luxury, war-time shabby though it was, the air of gaiety that sometimes bordered on wildness, if he could have been one of a party like those young Flying Corps officers. He envied them. They seemed to be Canadians and hell-bent on enjoying themselves. But then he told himself brutally that he was not one of them nor like them and if he was miserable it was his own bloody fault.

He found Eleanor Hurst's direct gaze disturbing. And Hacker, the remarkably young Lieutenant-Colonel on the Staff asked him some probing questions. There was a toughness about his dark good looks. The subaltern had muttered earlier, "Son of a friend of mother's. Wangled himself a cushy billet as a temporary Brasshat on movements or something in Dunkerque."

Hacker was attentive to Eleanor Hurst. They talked, sometimes in low tones, their heads close together. In the general conversation Smith learned that Hacker's commission was only for the duration of hostilities but he could hardly be called a 'temporary gentleman'. He was wealthy, an all-round athlete and a Doctor of Philosophy. Smith learned none of this from Hacker, who talked well but not of himself. Hacker made Smith feel shabby and awkward. This was very much Hacker's world.

Smith tried to stick it out but as Mrs. Pink badgered him with questions about the action in the Pacific his answers became monosyllabic. Until Mrs. Pink was leaning towards him, her voice shrill and affected, "You showed them, Commander! The only way! We've got to finish them off for good no matter what it costs!"

But Smith had taken all he could stand. He had a fleeting vision of the Kapitänleutnant dying before his eyes. 'No matter what it costs'? He knew the cost and had seen men paying it in blood and broken bodies. He shoved back his chair and made a little bow to his hostess. "If you will excuse me." To the subaltern: "Good luck." And then he was gone, walking quickly to the door and out of their sight.

In the Strand he turned towards the river, away from his hotel because it was too early to return there. This was summer but the night was chill and a fine rain falling. He walked quickly through the gloom of a wartime, blacked-out London, unaware of the rain. He knew that to most of them his behaviour had been offhand to the point of rudeness, but he could not help that. He was restless, on edge. He did not want to go back to sea nor to any more parties like that. He did not want to go back to the hotel. He did not know what he wanted.

The horse slowed from a trot to a walk and a cab rolled alongside him, keeping pace. He did not notice it until she called "Commander!"

He turned and saw the face of Eleanor Hurst at the pulled-down window of the cab and stared at that face, a pale smudge in the darkness of the cab with the eyes catching the faintest of light. The cab stopped and so did he. She said, "If that's the only uniform you have then you'd better keep it dry." She pushed the door open.

He still stared at her but after a moment he stumbled into the cab and sat in a corner and the cab jolted away. He did not say "Thank you". They sat in silence as the horse alternately trotted and walked eastward through the dimly-lit streets, it seemed for a long time. When the cab stopped for good it was in a street hard by the river, a cobbled street flanked by warehouses, but slotted between two of them was a little house. It looked to have been one of a terrace, the rest torn down on either side to make room for the warehouses. Its front door opened from the pavement without any garden or yard before it. A knocker and handle gleamed brassily and above the door was a fanlight.

Eleanor Hurst was down before he could precede her. The cabbie said, "One and tuppence, sir." Smith fumbled out his change and handed up three sixpences. "Thank ye, guv. G'night."

Eleanor had gone and the door stood open. He passed through and found himself in a sitting-room. There was a fire in the grate and before it a guard. In the firelight he saw her standing by the table in the middle of the small room, reaching up. She said, "Close the door." As he did so there was the snap of a match, then the brief hiss and *plop*! as the gas ignited and lit the room. He saw that at the back of it was a door that led to a kitchen. To his left a flight of stairs ran up out of the sitting-room to the floor above.

She still held the burning match in her fingers and looked at him over its flame until it burned down and she shook it out, dropped it in the fireplace.

"Would you like a drink, Commander?" She nodded to a glass-fronted cabinet that held a row of bottles, a syphon. Her voice was different now, husky. He shook his head, still standing by the door.

At the foot of the stairs she paused, her back to him. "Commander. What's your name? Your first name?"

"David."

She nodded and went up the stairs.

He should leave. This was a strange young woman; not bold, nor wild, but too cool. He knew nothing of her. He had got himself into trouble enough. The door was behind him. He was still wondering, hesitating, when she called him.

"David?" A question. Asked of herself? Doubting?

He went up to her.

In the night she woke and lifted on to one elbow to look down at him. She wondered if he thought she took home every man she met. At home in Dorset some had said that the Hurst girl would come to no good. She looked at him and thought they could be right but he had looked so – lost. Now he slept as if drugged but she was afraid and slid over on top of him, woke him, demanded him.

He stayed with her for the rest of his leave. On the first day he paid his bill at the hotel and brought back his valise and stood it against the wall close by the door. They took a train into the country and walked. Or they wandered down by the river. They did not go to the West End, to its shows or its restaurants. They went to bed when it suited them and lay late in the mornings. They did not talk much, but enough. He found she was cool and she was wild and she was bold. He thought he learned a great deal about her but in fact he did not.

On the second day of his leave they took a cab to the house of a distant cousin of Eleanor's. He was in France with the Royal Flying Corps and they borrowed his motor-car. In the cab Eleanor said, "It's a fourteen-horse Foy Steele two-seater with a double dickey-seat behind."

Smith said, "Oh." And: "There's a chauffeur?"

"A *chauffeur*? No!" She laughed. "Why?"

"Well, I can't steer one of the things. Never tried."

"That's all right. Driving is what I do. I drive a Staff car, carting Generals and what-not all over London. Just at the moment I'm on leave." She glanced at him, amused but with an edge to her voice now. "Or did you think I spent my time comforting lonely officers?"

"Good God, no!" said Smith, startled at the thought. "To tell you the truth I hadn't thought about you doing anything – although everybody seems to have a job now."

She drove him out of London in the Foy Steele and they explored the lanes of Surrey, lunched at a pub and walked in Oxshott woods. In the end she persuaded him to try to drive and it took little persuasion. He was eager. Only the certainty that he would make a fool of himself in front of a girl caused him to hesitate. Then he thought that it didn't matter if he *did* look a fool in front of this girl. She explained the workings of the clutch, gears and brakes and how to start and to adjust the mixture and he made a terrible hash of it. But finally he got something of the hang of it and took it careering for two or three miles until a near-collision with a farm cart decided Eleanor that it was enough for one day.

They drove back to London and left the car in its garage, ate dinner at a quiet restaurant and walked back to the little house.

That night she was afraid but did not tell him, clung to him.

They woke muzzily to the rumble and clank of the iron-wheeled milk cart with its churns and heard the boy come running to take their can, fill it and replace it on the front-door step. Between sleeping and waking he stared through half-open eyes at the ceiling and thought that today he had to go back to the flotilla. He thought about *Sparrow* and *Marshall Marmont*, and the U-boat commander, and young Morris, the airman… He hoped Naval Intelligence would make some sense of his report. He could not. But it haunted him. *Schwertträger…*

Hinterrücks anfallen… Springtau… He mumbled, "Damn silly. Skipping-rope!"

"What?" She turned and rolled into his arms.

"A word. German. *Springtau, springtie*, something like that. Sanders said it meant skipping-rope."

"*Springtij* isn't German. I'd have thought you knew that one, being a salty sailor." She snuggled into him.

"Not German?"

"No. It's Flemish."

He stared down at her. "How do you know?"

"Because my grandmother was Belgian and I've lived there a lot. I speak Flemish like I speak English. I said so that night at the Savoy but I don't suppose you heard me with that woman bawling in your ear. *Springtij* is the extra high tide you get once or twice a month."

"Twice." He was wide awake now. Flemish. *Springtij.* Spring tide. The exceptionally high twice-monthly tide. He rolled away from her and out of her bed, pulled on his bath-robe over his nakedness and made for the door.

She sat up in the bed. "Where are you going?"

"To make a cup of tea! Breakfast! I've thought of something I must tell the Admiralty!" His voice came up from the stairs.

"What have you thought of?"

"Can't tell you!" Flemish! Of course! The U-boat was out of a Flanders port and her commander had picked up the local term.

Eleanor Hurst said, "Oh!" He was leaving her today but she had known he would. She huddled down in the bed, shivering.

He told Intelligence about the spring tide because they had asked him to tell them anything he remembered but it did not help. A spring tide – but where? Flanders? Maybe.

But then what? They were no nearer solving the puzzle. He left the Admiralty and ran to catch a passing cab. He had to return to Dunkerque — but first he must go to Eleanor Hurst's house. He was ready to go back to sea but reluctant to say farewell to Eleanor Hurst. He worried at it as the cab rolled eastwards. How deep was her feeling towards him? He did not want to hurt her — and then he told himself coldly that he should have thought of that before. If he'd hurt her, then he was sorry. He had wanted her and taken her but — love? He was not sure, wary of the word.

"Wot ship, Cap'n?"

"Free cheers for the Nivy."

He was jerked out of his abstraction. The cab had slowed to round a corner and a group of urchins, ragged and dirty and mostly barefoot ran alongside. He grinned, lifted a hand in salute and they cheered. A tiny girl shrieked, "Touch your collar for luck!" But Smith was no bluejacket with a collar to touch and the cab was trotting on now, leaving them behind.

And his thoughts turned not to Eleanor Hurst but to *Marshall Marmont* and *Sparrow*. His mind was busy with them when the cab pulled up at the door of the little house and he jumped down and threw at the cabbie: "Wait!" He dug into his pocket for the key and opened the door. The house was still, the sitting-room and the kitchen beyond were empty. "Eleanor?" He called her name again as he ran up the stairs, tapped at the bedroom door and went in. She was where he had left her in the bed, curled small, her face turned towards the window.

He said tentatively, "Eleanor? Don't you feel well?"

"I'm not ill." The answer was flat and she did not look at him.

He went to sit on the edge of the bed and said awkwardly, "I'm sorry, but I have to go."

"All right." Her voice came muffled.

He was lost for words, knew vaguely what he wanted to say but not how to say it. He was sorry and grateful, fond of her. He picked up the leather case that held his razor, lather-brush and toothbrush and glanced around but there wasn't anything else. He looked at her and then down at the case and finally he said inadequately, "Thank you." He tried again: "I won't be far away and if I get leave I could come and—"

She said harshly, "No! You're off to the bloody war and you won't come back to me. Go away!"

There was a hammering at the door and the hoarse voice of the cabman called, "How long are you goin' to be, guv? 'Cos I'm booked for one o' my regulars an' I can't 'ang abaht!"

"Coming!" Smith shouted it. He turned back to the girl but she neither moved nor spoke. He stared at her helplessly. She had known what he was and that he would have to leave her. What had changed her? Only a few short hours ago... He burst out, "What the *hell's* the matter? What did you expect?"

She twisted in the bed and flung at him, "This! This is what I expected and I asked for it! Now get out!"

He shook his head, bewildered, and as the cabman banged again on the door said unhappily, "Well. Goodbye."

He walked down the stairs, jammed the leather case into his valise and opened the door to the cabman. "Take the bag out, will you?" The cabman heaved the valise into the cab. Smith put the key on the hall-stand, picked up his cap and closed the door behind him.

He said, "Victoria, please," and climbed into the cab. It lurched away as the horse broke into a weary trot. Smith ran his hand through his hair and jammed on his cap. He was sorry, and angry because he did not see what he had to be sorry for. It was a hell of a way to part. He glanced at his watch. There was a train he could just catch. If he went back to her now he would miss it. But for Eleanor, though, he would have spent the last two days wandering the city and making polite conversation with strangers because he would not impose on Sanders or the one or two like him. And there was more to it than that.

He shouted up at the driver, "Stop!"

The cabbie hauled on the reins, grumbling.

Smith looked out of the rear window and saw another cab leaving the house. A man stood at the door of the house, an Army officer, cap in hand. The door was opened and he stepped inside and out of sight.

Smith faced his front, staring blankly ahead. He could not believe it. She would not acquire another man, another lover so soon. It had to be coincidence… though she *had* known when Smith would leave because he had told her.

The cabbie complained, "Look 'ere, guv'nor—"

"All right! Get on!" The violence in the tone jerked the cabbie back in his seat. Smith glared ahead. That was that. Now there were only the ships, his command. But he would not forget her. Besides, he had recognised the officer, the tall young man in the red-tabbed uniform of a Lieutenant-Colonel on the Staff: Hacker…

It was only much later, staring out of the window of a train crowded with troops that he thought he was no nearer guessing the meaning of *Schwertträger*. And now a new dimension had been added: Spring tide. If the tide was significant then a time was set. But what time? And what was the threat? It was as if Eleanor Hurst's casual words had set a clock ticking. And there was nothing he could do about it.

She had run down the stairs with her robe clutched about her carelessly, thinking the knock at the door meant Smith had returned. Then she said, "You'd better come in."

Hacker stood by the table and said, "I have to go back to Dunkerque. What is your answer?"

She wondered if Smith had known she was afraid and did not believe so. He had taken what he wanted and what he needed and because she had not summoned up a brave smile to speed him on his way he had gone away miserably certain he had hurt her. She had learned a lot about him, knew that he wanted to be gentle. Well, she just wasn't feeling very brave, he had been leaving her alone and at the end her nerve cracked and she lashed out at him.

But she wouldn't crack again. She pulled the robe closer about her, looked up at the tall soldier and nodded. "Yes."

–

For Smith it was back to sea and the grind of patrols. *Marshall Marmont* he used as a floating base as she swung to her anchor in Dunkerque Roads. *Sparrow* always had a sprinkling of men from the monitor aboard her, giving some of *Sparrow*'s crew a comparative rest aboard *Marshall Marmont*. And that was just as well because *Sparrow* did more patrols than any other ship in Trist's command. And some of the monitor's men got first-hand experience of patrol work and even tasted the excitement of a U-boat stalk, though it was unsuccessful. But as McGraw told them philosophically as they stood down after the action, weary and deflated, "Still, the bastard didn't get us, either." The torpedo had missed *Sparrow* by scant feet.

Always now when she sailed she did so with Galt playing his mouth-organ. 'Oh, I do like to be beside the sea-side!' Again that was at Smith's order but Dunbar grinned at it. That was a rare sight. Dunbar was a more patient man these days but taciturn, unsmiling. He never mentioned his wife and child in all the long hours he shared the bridge with Smith. And Smith was aboard *Sparrow* on every patrol, with Buckley as a lookout or taking a trick at the wheel.

There was a bombardment when a dozen of *Sparrow*'s crew worked in *Marshall Marmont*'s turret and tasted the swallowing claustrophobia of entombment in an anchored ship under fire from big guns. The monitor made excellent shooting.

Finally *Sparrow* and *Marshall Marmont* formed part of the escort of a 'beef' convoy. Those convoys from neutral Holland to the Thames and the East coast carried beef but also butter, cheese and other foods. There was a theory it was purchased to stop the Germans buying it, an extension of the blockade, but Britain needed that food. The monitor was there only because the ships of the convoy were so old and slow that she was able to keep up. They joked that it was the slowest convoy of the war, or any other war, but when one ancient tramp was torpedoed it was *Marshall Marmont* who took the crippled ship in tow and *Sparrow* who shepherded them home.

McGraw bawled across from *Sparrow* when once during the tow she ran close alongside the monitor. "Ye cannae fool me! Yon tramp's pushin' ye!" And the men of

Marshall Marmont laughed. They knew McGraw now as he knew them.

When they returned to Dunkerque the monitor's engines broke down, she had to be towed to her anchorage in the Roads and her engineers said it was a job for the dockyard, but still they were a happy company. The ships were the same but the men were changed.

It was close to noon on what should have been a summer's day. It was the 9th of July, but a light rain fell steadily and a ground mist covered the land as Smith stood on the monitor's bridge and she was towed in. He was wearily content. He thought of Eleanor Hurst as he sometimes did and it still hurt. *Sparrow* had been laid up for another boiler-clean since Smith returned from London but he stayed aboard *Marshall Marmont* and sent Garrick on leave instead. He thought it was almost a month since he had seen her. It struck another chord of memory and he asked of the bridge at large, "When is the next spring tide on the Belgian coast?"

There was a stir on the bridge behind him, muttering. Smith grinned to himself. Did they think it was a trick question to keep them on their toes? Then Chivers, the gunnery officer, said, "Next spring tide is early on the 12th, sir, at 4.16 a.m., local time. That's just after first light, sir."

"Thank you." The Kapitänleutnant had said, 'Soon the blow will fall,' and it had not seemed an empty threat. He had spoken in the knowledge that his death was upon him… One spring tide had come and gone since he had died. Smith wondered uneasily if Naval Intelligence had solved the mystery or whether it would only be solved when the blow fell – and it was too late?

Soon.

But when? Where?

Brooding set him pacing out to the wing of the bridge but as he did so he caught Garrick watching him. Smith realised he was scowling at his own thoughts but Garrick must be wondering what he had to scowl about. He tried to throw off the mood because there was no point in worrying over a problem he could do nothing about. "I think the hands can keep to their own ships from now on."

Garrick nodded eagerly, emphatically, glad to see Smith smiling and to be able to agree. "It's worked, sir. The men didn't like being swapped about to start with and I was doubtful, but it worked. Dunbar is of the same mind." Garrick was happy with his ship now. But then he said, "There are rumours the Army are getting ready for another big push."

Smith grimaced. A 'big push' meant a big casualty list but that was the only thing certain about it. It might gain a few miles of ground or only a few yards.

Garrick said, "Wonder what the Commodore's got for us? But whatever it is," he added with satisfaction, "we're ready."

Smith thought that now, maybe, they were.

He knew he was sorry about Eleanor Hurst.

Part Three

From a Check...

Chapter 5

That evening Trist sent for Smith, the signal flickering out at *Sparrow* as she steamed up the channel and into the port of Dunkerque. Smith had transferred to her as *Marshall Marmont* anchored and now he watched the hands as Dunbar took her alongside. They were dog-tired but working cheerfully. He told Dunbar, "Coal and ammunition." They were the only reasons *Sparrow* had got into the port. "Tell 'em I'll give shore leave if I can but, of course, it will depend on what orders we're given." They all knew he thought they had done well; he had told them so.

If he had expected congratulations from his Commodore he would have been disappointed. He found Trist in a black mood, standing with his hands clasped behind his back and scowling at the big chart at the end of the long room, his Staff gathered around him. Or rather, scattered. They stood about in silence. As if they waited for Smith's arrival? He thought he saw glances exchanged that were relieved or uneasy. Relieved that the whipping-boy had come? Smith was angry that he thought of himself as such but the feeling persisted. And the uneasy ones, who did not meet his eyes?

Trist grumbled, "I'm getting reports that the men of *Marshall Marmont* and *Sparrow* are starting to regard themselves as an élite, almost as a separate Squadron."

Smith asked, "Reports from what source, sir?"

"That's my affair."

"The reports are incorrect. I believe the men have done well and I have told them so. That's all."

"I hope so," Trist shot a glance at Smith and it was nervous. "Those ships are part of the Dunkerque Squadron under my command and they should not forget it. *Nobody* should forget it."

Smith did not have an answer to that. He was bewildered. Did Trist seriously believe that Smith was trying to undermine his authority?

But Trist seemed to have finished with that topic. His eyes were on the chart again and he muttered, "They're badgering us again about offensive action against U-boats. They want to know why you haven't got more U-boats as you did that first one."

So Trist's boast about his idea of an anti-submarine flotilla working, had rebounded. Smith said, "We were lucky that night."

"You sank her just seaward of the Nieuport Bank. They may still be slipping through there."

Smith admitted, "It's possible, but—"

Trist pushed on, not listening, obviously following a preconceived train of thought, "It is your considered opinion that operations in those waters are practicable?"

Smith wondered at the point of the question. The Navy *did* operate in those waters, laying mines for one thing. But – "Yes, sir. I think—"

Trist said, "Very well. I'm prepared to authorise you to carry out a limited operation with the vessels at your disposal. You are to make a sweep along the coast by night to seek out and destroy U-boats entering or leaving their bases or trying to slip around the end of the mine-net barrage like the other one."

Smith said, "You mean – just *Sparrow*, sir?"

"Well, *Marshall Marmont* is hardly suitable." Trist's sarcasm brought a chuckle from one or two of his staff but the rest stayed silent.

Smith saw it. Trist was getting the best of both worlds. He was sending Smith and *Sparrow* on a sweep against U-boats that he could justify by the demands made on him for offensive action and by the precedent set by *Sparrow* when she sank a U-boat in those waters. Moreover, whatever went wrong he could lay at Smith's door because he had given his 'considered opinion' that operations in those waters were practicable. Smith wondered if that was why Trist had the Staff there, why some looked unhappy; were they there to bear witness? He knew he could hedge and put his objections in writing: that the chances of *Sparrow* sighting a U-boat, let alone sinking one, were remote; that the chances of her meeting a big destroyer that would blow her out of the water, were not.

He knew that if he did object Trist might seize on the chance to have him relieved; his little flotilla would cease to exist as such. And Trist might well order Dunbar to make the sweep instead, and when Dunbar objected as he undoubtedly would, then Trist would start using words like 'disloyalty' and 'collusion'.

Smith was getting to know Trist. There would be an unholy row and an inquiry that would uncover the truth about Dunbar being unfit to take his ship to sea because of drunkenness... 'Commander Smith! Did Lieutenant Dunbar, in your presence, make comments critical of your superior officer, Commodore Trist?' It would be bad for the flotilla, the Dunkerque Squadron, the entire Dover Patrol.

He thought the war had gone on too long for Trist, who was worried, cautious, trying to please his superiors and yet risk nothing. Or risk as little as possible: one small, old TBD with a captain Trist considered dumbly insolent and a Commander he regarded as a threat to his authority?

Smith swallowed the bitter pill because he had to. "I'll carry out the sweep, sir."

He was at the door when Trist called, "What do you think of Dunbar, now you've had him under your eye for a time?"

Smith stood there stiffly, resenting this discussion of another officer before the listening Staff. He answered, "A good officer, sir."

Trist pursed his lips. "Well, he's your responsibility." He had nailed that down in front of witnesses, too, but Smith did not care. He would answer for Dunbar and *Sparrow*, and Garrick and *Marshall Marmont* for that matter. Trist said, "I suggest you keep a close eye on him. You know my views on discipline. I will break any officer who falls short in that respect." And then he smiled, "Good luck."

Smith believed he meant it, really wished them luck, hoped *Sparrow* would come home with another sunken U-boat to report and so take the pressure off Trist, for a little while at least. "Thank you, sir." But as Smith strode from the big house into the air and breathed it deeply he thought, We'll need luck but not Trist's luck. That would not take them far. Trist had stated his intention, if obliquely: given the least excuse he would break Smith.

As he walked the last yards back towards *Sparrow* where she lay alongside the quay he looked beyond her and froze, seeing Hacker. The Lieutenant-Colonel on the Staff stood a hundred yards away by the Trystram lock, but despite the light rain and the ground mist that wisped in tendrils between, there was no mistaking that tall figure. Hacker was looking out over the channel with a hand raised, beckoning. Smith saw the canoe out there with the American, Curtis and Morris the airman aboard. Curtis paddled the canoe into the side of the quay at Hacker's urging and climbed up to talk with the soldier.

Morris climbed up also, but walked along the quay towards Smith, who tried to put Hacker − and Eleanor Hurst − out of his mind. Nevertheless, he wondered absently what a 'movements brass-hat' could want with the lanky commander of a Coastal Motor Boat. Then Morris said glumly, "Filthy weather, sir."

Smith smiled as he returned the salute. He liked Morris. "It keeps you on the ground. I'd have thought you liked that."

"Normally I would," Morris admitted frankly. "But I was hoping to have another go at flying over De Haan. The Squadron Commander won't have it, of course. He says we've had too many losses trying it and got nothing out of it except my report. And *that* wasn't much good."

"So?"

Morris grinned sheepishly, "Well, to tell the truth, sir, he's going into hospital in a couple of days − some shrapnel that got left in his knee they want to dig out − and as soon as he does go, *and* if the Army asks for a flight again, then I'll ask the second-in-command to send me. I think he will, provided the weather is fit for flying. But nobody's flown for the past two days." He saluted. "I'll be on my way, sir."

He turned, but Smith called after him, "You're quite determined. Why?"

Morris paused with rain dripping from the peak of his cap as he stared down at his boots. He had borrowed someone's trench-coat and it was too big for him. He said, "Because there must be something there. Bill, my observer, saw *something*. So − I suppose it's for him. If I don't do it then he was just − wasted." He looked up at Smith. "D'ye see, sir?"

Smith nodded. Morris said, "I thought you would."

Smith watched him trudge away across the pave then turned and boarded *Sparrow*.

−

Late that same evening, the 9th of July, *Sparrow* had taken on ammunition and coal; the signs of the latter were hosed away and the rain helped, falling steadily and bringing dusk early as *Sparrow* slipped, moved out into the channel and headed towards the sea and her U-boat sweep off the Nieuport Bank. Smith, huddled in oilskins on her bridge, listened to the jaunty notes of Galt's mouth-organ and watched the low, black shape of a CMB slide out from the Trystram lock ahead of them and turn seawards. The man at her wheel, also in oilskins, stood very tall in the cockpit and Smith thought it might be the American, Jack Curtis. But the light was going, the rain driving between, and the CMB hauled rapidly away and out of sight. When *Sparrow*'s stern lifted and dipped to the sea in the Roads there was still light to seaward, a greyness on the horizon and he could make out the low, fat bulk of the disabled *Marshall Marmont* where she lay at anchor with the other monitors. She was due to be towed into the dockyard for engine repairs. Garrick would see to it.

Sparrow picked her way through the shoals off Dunkerque and stole up the West Deep, a dark ship on a dark sea with the night and the rain folding her round. Smith said quietly, "Mr. Sanders."

"Sir?"

"Eyes skinned and ears pricked. Go around and rub it in." And Dunbar added, "Here are my keys. Unlock the small arms and issue 'em."

"Aye, aye, sir." Sanders disappeared from the bridge. Because *Sparrow* was sneaking into the enemy's backyard and ever since Evans's men in H.M. Destroyer *Broke* had fought hand-to-hand with the crew of a German destroyer in the Straits of Dover, small arms had been issued when action seemed likely.

Sanders's departure made a tiny bit more room on the bridge, crowded anyway with Smith and Dunbar, Gow hanging over the wheel, the signalman, the bosun's mate at the engine-room telegraphs, look-outs, the crew of the twelve-pounder. *Sparrow*'s crew was at action stations. Nieuport showed soon on the starboard bow and steadily drew abeam. Dirty night or no, they could see the town as a flickering glow against the low clouds and the sullen rumbling of the guns came to them across the sea. It fell behind as *Sparrow* fractionally altered course and headed farther out, running steadily, quietly through the night with only the low drum-beat of the engines.

Smith had told them where they were headed and why, that they were to hunt U-boats in the waters off Nieuport and north to Ostende and every one of them knew that 'hunt' was a double-edged word and *Sparrow* could become the prey. And they knew that there were German destroyers based at Ostende and Zeebrugge, big boats and faster than *Sparrow*. *Sparrow*'s only hope was to surprise a U-boat running on the surface because, with no reason to submerge, she could cruise faster and more economically on her diesels. But even a surfaced U-boat was hard to spot while *Sparrow* was a big, tall target and her smoke made her taller still.

Dunbar grumbled, "Black as the inside of your hat. More like winter than high summer." The rain had stopped but there was a chill dampness in the air, the clouds hanging low. There would be more rain. He grumbled but he knew very well that the last thing they wanted was a fine night.

Sanders was back on the bridge. He muttered uneasily, "Couldn't see a battleship in this, never mind a submarine."

So it was no surprise that they almost ran her down. They were so close to her that the look-out's yell of "Dead ahead! Boat—" formed part of a chorus.

Dunbar at the same instant rapped, "Port ten!"

And Smith: "CMB! Hold your fire!"

Sparrow's stern swung away even as it seemed to hang over the CMB and then the destroyer swept past her. She lay only feet away and they saw a blur of faces aboard her, a man crouched behind each of the Vickers machine-guns she carried, one forward, one aft. She rocked to *Sparrow*'s bow-wave and then to her wash as *Sparrow* drew past her.

Smith said, "She's stopped. Probably in trouble. Turn and close her."

Sparrow continued in her turn, came around as Dunbar ordered, "Slow ahead both." The engine-room telegraphs clanged and *Sparrow* slowed. They searched the darkness for the CMB, lost now, but – "Port beam, sir." The look-out pointed and there she was, still rocking. *Sparrow* crept down to her.

"Stop both," ordered Dunbar. *Sparrow* lay about ten feet away but drifting slowly down on the CMB. Smith saw that instead of torpedoes she carried a dinghy lashed on over the chutes. A party were already in *Sparrow*'s waist hanging fenders over the side to protect the CMB's fragile hull. As the gap closed, the men forward and aft aboard her threw lines that were caught and she was drawn in alongside. It was CMB 19.

Smith peered at her, lifted the megaphone and called, "Mr. Curtis?"

"Aye, aye, sir."

"Trouble?"

"Yes, sir. Can I come aboard?"

"Yes."

Smith slid down the ladder to the iron deck and walked aft to meet him. Curtis stank of petrol and oil and his face was smudged as if he'd drawn a dirty hand across it. He was naked except for his cotton drawers and his hair was plastered wetly to his skull. He was breathing heavily. "Sir! Am I glad to see you. We've fouled both our screws. Ran across a whole mess of wreckage, timber, with a trailing wire. The wire's wrapped around and around them. Me'n the engineer, we've been over the side working on it but it's nowhere near free."

Smith said, "All right. We'll tow you."

"Thank you, sir, but it's not that simple." He hesitated, glanced around at the surrounding seamen and said, "Can I talk with you privately, sir?"

Smith blinked. "If it's essential. But I don't want this ship lying stopped any longer than she's got to be. For obvious reasons."

"Yes, sir. Only take a minute and it *is* essential."

"Come on." Smith strode quickly aft until they were clear of the party in the waist. "This will have to do."

"Dandy, sir. Fact is, we're on detached duty and I understand it's Intelligence. That's all. Our orders are to pick up a party from the beach north of Ostende. There's a definite time and it's getting close. We can't make it, but I think somebody has to." He stared at Smith. "They'll be waiting."

"What time?"

"Twenty minutes after midnight."

Smith peered at his watch. It was 11.32. He snapped, "Show me on the chart," and hurried to the chart-table abaft the first funnel.

Midshipman Lorimer was stooped under the hood of the chart-table, recording their course. Smith dislodged him without ceremony and with Curtis at his side peered at the chart. Curtis picked up a pencil. Water dripped from his hair on to the chart and he swore softly and wiped at it with his hand. He used the ruler, measuring carefully and drew a neat cross on the chart.

"That's the spot, sir. I landed them there last night."

Smith saw it lay just south of the area of woodland at De Haan about forty miles from Dunkerque and fifteen from *Sparrow* now.

Curtis said, "It's a bit tricky but it worked out right last night. The idea was we should cruise about a mile off-shore. Two lights would be shown. I was told they were to be set up by a couple of people, farmers maybe, hanging lanterns in their barns so they'd be seen at sea and nowhere else. We were to get the lights in line and run in on that bearing real slow and quiet. When we were close inshore we were to wait for a signal. They tell me the Fritzes patrol the shore and we had to wait till somebody flashed an A and that meant the patrol had passed. We got the signal and landed them in the dinghy, then hauled out. The same schedule goes for tonight. The party we had to collect will flash an A when the coast is clear and then we were to take them off in the dinghy – the CMB's too noisy to run right in. But the timing is very important. The two lights to give the bearing will only be shown for fifteen minutes. They daren't risk any longer. So – whoever goes to make the pick-up has to be cruising on station at twenty after twelve. From then he'll just have fifteen minutes to pick up the lights and run in. And it's got to be done quietly. There are shore batteries at Ostende and light guns at De Haan and all down the coast and—"

Smith snapped irritably, "I know that, damn it!"

"Sure." Curtis pushed his hair back from his eyes. "Sorry, sir."

"How often have you done this?"

"This is the first time. I guess maybe it's the first time it *has* been done. I asked why and got told it was none of my damn business, but they did say the weather had been bad for flying people in and two of them meant two aeroplanes or two trips. And that there was someone able to get in and organise the reception committee so I didn't have to worry." He laughed shortly at that. "But that's all I know."

Someone able to get in? Maybe a neutral, a Dutchman whose business took him frequently into Belgium, who could arrange for the lights to be lit and the boat to be met, if it came, when the weather was right? It was a possible explanation but only that. And it was not Curtis's business, nor Smith's.

He stared at the chart, already seeing the problems, planning. "Anything else? A challenge? Passwords? And how many in the party?"

"Two, sir. And the challenge is 'Sword-bearer' and the answer 'Nineteen'. And one of the people is—"

"What?" Smith spun round from the chart. "*Sword-bearer!*"

Curtis glanced at him, startled. "That mean something to you, sir? Are you involved in this already?"

Smith took a breath. "I didn't think so." Sword-bearer. *Schwertträger.* It *couldn't* be coincidence. He pushed out from under the hood and said, "We'll try to do it."

Curtis looked relieved. He said, "I'm obliged, sir. I feel real bad about it, those people hanging on."

"Not your fault. Just bad luck." Smith eyed him. "I don't want to tow you now because I'll be in a hurry."

"Don't worry about us, sir." Curtis started to edge aft. "We'll clear those screws. You want us to follow on then?"

"No." The CMB would arrive too late to do any good and might get in the way if *Sparrow* had to fight or run and both were likely. "You can do no more. As soon as you get under way, head for home. Now get along."

"Aye, aye, sir."

Smith saw him start aft and himself turned back to the chart-table and laid off the course himself, checked it, showed it to Lorimer then ran forward. As he climbed on to the bridge he saw the CMB drifting away, Curtis already crouched in her stern by the dinghy there, waiting to go down into the sea again as soon as *Sparrow* pulled away and her wash had cleared them. Smith remembered Curtis had been about to tell him something. "One of the people is…" But whatever it was, it was not important enough to delay because every second counted. He ordered, "Course is six-five degrees! Revolutions for twenty knots!"

Dunbar ordered, "Starboard ten! Steer six-five."

Gow acknowledged, "Steer six-five degrees, sir!"

The engine-room telegraphs clanged and Dunbar spoke into the voice pipe. "Revolutions for twenty knots." *Sparrow*'s screws turned, slowly, then gradually the beat of the engines quickened. The CMB was left tossing astern of them.

Gow reported, "Course six-five degrees, sir."

Smith turned on Sanders and Dunbar. "We're going to take some people off the beach." Dunbar only grunted but Sanders's mouth opened in surprise. Smith told them Curtis's orders then went on: "I want the whaler ready to slip and I want two or three extra hands along." If they were discovered there might well be casualties and extra hands would be needed then. "Boat's compass and torches. Small arms for everybody. That means revolvers with an empty chamber under the hammer and safety catches on." He paused to take a breath and saw Sanders staring at him, swallowing with excitement. Smith went on, "I'll go in the whaler with Lorimer. Tell Buckley to come along as well. We'll need a buoy to rendezvous on. I want a boat anchor slung below a grating. On the top of the grating lash an empty oil drum with a crutch hanging inside on a length of twine. Understood?"

"Yes, sir." Sanders looked disappointed. Had he hoped to be going in the whaler? But Dunbar would have need of him.

"Get on with it, then."

"Aye, aye, sir."

Sparrow was running near twenty knots now, the wind plucking at them on the bridge and her engines pounding away, thick smoke rolling astern of them. They would make an easily-seen target but that was a risk that had to be taken. Curtis had said that time was important and it would be a close-run thing at twenty knots. Less would not do.

They raced on through the night and the report came up from where young Lorimer was hunched over the chart. "Ostende on the starboard beam."

No doubt it was but there was nothing to see, only the lowering black clouds that merged in the darkness with the oily sea, a sea split white by *Sparrow*'s bow wave that spread out on either side of her in phosphorescent silver to be swallowed by the wash from her whirling screws.

With Ostende astern *Sparrow* turned at Smith's order and closed the shore. "Half ahead both." *Sparrow* slowed and the vibrating of the frame eased. And later, "Slow ahead."

Sparrow was creeping on to her station but that station should have been taken by Curtis's CMB and she only drew three feet. *Sparrow* was drawing nine and Dunbar had a man in the chains just below the bridge with the lead going. His voice came up to them: "Quarter less three!" *Sparrow* had barely sixteen feet of water under her. She was not running aground but it was close enough.

Smith nodded at Dunbar and he ordered, "Port five." He stood by the compass as *Sparrow*'s head came round. "Steady... steer that."

Smith said, "Look out to starboard. For two lights." As if to frustrate them the darkness became impenetrable blackness as a squall swept over them, rain lashing down to drum on oilskins and wash over their faces as they strained their eyes into the night. Then the squall was gone but the darkness still hid the shore from them and nobody cursed that. *Sparrow* nudged steadily through the sea, a quiet ship now so they could have talked in normal tones but voices were hushed. The nearest of the German batteries at Ostende was barely three miles away to the south and the guns at De Haan no farther north. If *Sparrow* had ventured into the enemy's backyard before, now she was at his back door. Only the night protected them from that cross-fire.

Smith looked at his watch again. It was twenty-one minutes after midnight and *Sparrow* must turn soon, creep back along her course...

"Abeam!" Dunbar snapped it as Smith saw it – no, them. Two lights, almost in line and still closing...? Yes.

Smith said, "Stop her when they're in line! Stand by the whaler!" He saw the boat's crew milling aft, the whaler swung out on the davits. He told Dunbar: "Patrol along this line. You won't see that marker buoy we're putting over, nor hear it, but we'll find it. When we see you we'll flash a K and that's what you'll answer. Take care you don't run us down," he finished dryly.

Dunbar grinned tightly. "I'll watch it."

"It shouldn't take more than an hour. If we're not back in two then clear out and head for home. Is that understood?"

"Perfectly, sir." Not looking at Smith, both of them looking out to starboard at the twin pinpoints of light that were close together now – Dunbar ordered, "Stop both."

The way came off *Sparrow* as Smith slid down the ladder to the deck and hurried aft. Stroke and bow were already in the whaler, standing between the falls. He saw that stroke was McGraw, the tough. He was right for this job. He heard Lorimer order, "Lower away," and the boat was lowered into the sea and her crew dropped down into her. As Smith came up Lorimer held out a bundle and said breathlessly, "Pistol, sir. Checked as you said an' Mr.

Sanders checked all the others himself. Compass is aboard, and here's a torch."

"Very good."

Lorimer went over the side and into the whaler and Smith stripped off his oilskin, belted the big Webley pistol around his waist and jammed the torch in his pocket. He could see in the stern-sheets of the whaler the grating with the lashed-on drum. He looked up at the bridge for Dunbar but instead saw Sanders there. Then Dunbar stepped out of the shadows to say gruffly, "Look out for yourself, sir." Smith glanced at him, taken aback. Dunbar said, "You've done a hell of a lot for this gimcrack flotilla; you've made it work. You've done a lot for the men. And for me. I'm grateful."

Smith could not see Dunbar's face and hoped Dunbar could not see his. He muttered, "Rubbish!" And turned and climbed down into the whaler.

Dunbar shook his head and grinned to himself, said under his breath, "You hard-faced bastard." And lifted a hand.

As the whaler pulled away from *Sparrow*, Smith remembered he had told Trist that Dunbar was a good officer. He had meant it. He knew as the boat turned to point at the unseen shore that he could depend on Dunbar. That was reassuring, as was the crouched bulk of Buckley, set solidly right forward in the bow.

Once clear of *Sparrow* they stopped briefly to drop the grating over the side and saw that it rode to its anchor. From inside the drum came the metallic *clunk!* as the sea set the crutch, an iron row-lock dangling inside it on a length of twine, swinging to bang against the side. Smith saw *Sparrow* was under way and heard the beat of her engines. He turned away from her. Lorimer had the helm and was peering into the binnacle of the boat's compass. Smith asked, "Bearing?"

"Lights bear 132 degrees, sir."

Smith nodded. That checked with the bearing he had taken aboard *Sparrow*. He ordered, "Steer for the lights." And: "Tide's nearly full. Watch it doesn't set you to the south."

"Aye, aye, sir."

Smith stared ahead over the rhythmic bending and lifting of the men's heads as they pulled at the oars, and he watched the lights, looked for the shore.

The lights went out.

He looked at his watch. Thirty-five minutes after midnight. The men who set the lights had been as good as their word. He could imagine them crouched in their lofts with the lanterns, telling themselves the lights should only be seen at sea, but suppose a land patrol somehow caught a glimpse of them? Or a cruising German torpedo boat? Wondering if at any minute rifle butts would hammer on the door...

He shifted restlessly. Too much imagination.

Lorimer was steering by the compass now, the faint light from the binnacle on his face and showing it taut with concentration. Smith wondered if he was more afraid of the approaching enemy coast and its waiting guns – or of making a hash of the job with the Commander sitting by him. Smith remembered his own youth and thought it was an even bet and grinned, chuckled. He saw McGraw's startled face as he leaned forward on the oar and saw that grin, heard that chuckle. Smith straightened his face. The man would think him mad at a time like this.

He stared ahead and thought – at last he was sure he could see the shore. The phosphorescent line that marked the break of the surf on the beach was clear enough but now he could also see the lift of the dunes, a low black cliff against the sky. He called softly, "Oars."

The boat drifted.

There was the slap of small waves against the side of the whaler, the faint regular sigh of the surf on the beach. And still, though distantly and only a mutter now, the sound of the guns at Nieuport. How long must he wait? Was the party ashore lying hidden, waiting for some patrol to trudge past and away? Or had they been discovered? Were the enemy waiting in the dunes for the whaler and her crew?

Somebody coughed and Smith said softly, "Quiet!"

He was certain the tide was setting them to the south and he told Lorimer, "Pull slowly to the north-east." The oars came out and the men bent to the work again but pulling slowly now to hold them against the tide. Lorimer did not seem to be breathing, though his mouth was open. The other men's breathing came loud in that quiet as they bent and pulled, bent and pulled, a slow, quiet stroke. It would be slack water soon but they must move before then...

The light blinked, blinked again, was gone. It had flickered briefly, low on the shore, almost as if on the sea. A short and long flash: 'A'.

Smith said softly, "Steer for the light."

Lorimer obeyed and the whaler's head came round to point at the light. Smith saw the bulky figure of Buckley change shape in the bow as he turned to face the shore. Smith also saw the dull gleam of blued steel and knew that Buckley had his revolver ready, knew also that Buckley could be relied on not to blaze away wildly. He rose and crept forward along the boat between the men as they tugged at the oars until he crouched beside Buckley. And drew his own pistol. There was the shore now, the beach a paler shadow that started at the white line where the surf washed it and stretched back to the black shadow of the dunes that lifted steep as a wall for twenty or thirty feet.

Flick, flicker. The light again from the shadowing wall of the dunes: short, long. The whaler ran into the surf, the bow grounded and Buckley vaulted over the side to stand up to his knees in the sea, holding her there, head turned towards the shore.

All of them watched the shore.

The rain came again in a flurry on the wind, driving across their faces and they saw him as a shadow that broke from the great shadow of the dunes and moved jerkily, quickly down the beach towards them. He came down to them through the rain, boots slipping in the wet sand until they could see the white face of him and Smith called softly: "*Sword-bearer!*"

The man halted, panted, then: "*Nineteen!*" The answer came breathlessly and he wavered on until he almost fell against Buckley who caught him and held him. He stood with mouth gaping in his white face, the long moustache a bar across it. He gasped for breath. So far as Smith could see in the darkness he wore a shabby suit, underneath it a shirt, collarless, open at the neck.

Smith asked, "Where's the other one?" And peered past him towards the dunes.

The man shook his head. "Caught!"

"Get aboard."

He tried weakly to climb in and Buckley put a big hand under his rump and hoisted him inboard where he collapsed by Smith and said, "In a minute – all right. I ran a long way. But in a minute—" He nodded.

Buckley shoved off, leapt aboard and now it was crowded in the bow. Smith was going to move aft but first he asked: "What happened? Who are you?"

The man lifted his head, smiled shakily. "Now, I am Josef. I worked in a hotel in London before the war and I am Belgian and that is enough for now. You understand?" And when Smith nodded, "We got through the wire about an hour ago."

"What wire?" Smith interrupted.

Josef jerked a thumb to the north. "All around the wood. We were to find out what was in there. It seemed the only way was to break through the wire."

Smith stared at him. The wood at De Haan. Where the fighters patrolled.

But Josef was going on, "I think the wire had an alarm. Yes? A wire with electric to a bell somewhere, you know? I think so. A patrol came up. We had to run, broke apart, I got away." He was breathing easier now but his manner was abstracted, remembering, reliving the experience.

Smith asked, "Was your friend hurt?"

A shake of the head, but, "It was a waste of time. We learnt nothing."

So his friend had been taken prisoner. Smith thought it might have been as well if the patrol had shot him. A civilian caught trying to break into a prohibited zone? They would try him as a spy and shoot him anyway. The rain still fell but the night was still, only the faintest creak as the men tugged at the oars, the sound of their breathing. He and Josef had spoken normally. He was aware the men were listening eagerly, intently to every word and so was Lorimer. That was not surprising.

The Belgian's head came up. He said, "I fell in a ditch and crawled along it. I looked back for her but she had fallen. I saw them take her. I went on along the ditch and then ran again. I had to run a long way to get around them." His hands moved in a gesture sweeping a wide curve.

But Smith said, "*She?*" And saw the men's heads turning.

Josef nodded. "We posed as man and wife. A couple attracts less attention than a man alone. We had papers and a letter supposed to be from her sick mother in Clemskerke, asking us to visit her."

Smith remembered that Jack Curtis had tried to tell him something, "one of the people is—" A woman.

There was silence in the boat, then Buckley ventured, "They won't shoot a woman. Will they, sir?"

Smith thought they had before and they might again. And looked at with cold logic, as a spy a woman could wreak as much havoc as a man. He wondered how Buckley would feel if a woman betrayed his country, or his ship? If she was the cause of the destruction of *Sparrow* and all aboard her? But the crew of the whaler felt as Buckley did. A low mutter ran through them that was deep-throated like a growl.

Josef said bitterly, "They will shoot her."

That brought the growl again and then McGraw spoke up and gave it frustrated, baffled voice. "Somebody ought to do *somethin'!*"

Smith snapped, "Shut up!" He stared over their heads towards the shore that was lost to sight now. "Oars!" The men rested on their oars and the boat drifted. "Flask!" Lorimer passed it forward and it came from hand to hand up the boat to Smith who unscrewed the cap and handed the flask to the Belgian. He drank and sighed, rubbed his mouth with the back of a grimy hand. Smith had come prepared: the flask held navy rum and water, one to two.

Josef said, "They will take her to the guard-post and hold her there until transport comes from Ostende to fetch her. The Major will want to have first go at her, you see. He does not like the headquarters at Ostende so he will question her until he is sure he knows all there is to know. Then he will send her to Ostende. He will be able to—" He stopped, snapping his fingers for the phrase.

Smith supplied, "Crow over them."

Josef nodded. "Yes. He is that sort of man. Very efficient but old for a Major. He believes he should have been promoted."

"You know a lot about him."

"Soldiers talk among themselves and the people listen." Josef shrugged. "Also, this he did before when he caught a Belgian spying."

Smith looked at his watch. Ten minutes had passed since the whaler ran in towards the light. A rescue attempt was out of the question. Madness. He would not risk the lives of this handful of men on an unplanned adventure into enemy-held country on the chance of saving this woman. The Belgian might be right about the Major but he might also be wrong and the woman already on her way to Ostende.

And even if she was not, what chance was there of setting her free? None.

He asked, "Where is this guard-post?"

Josef said, "About a kilometre or more inland. In a village, if you can call it that. There is one big house that is the guard post now and some little houses around it."

"And the guard? What strength?"

"Company strength or more. A hundred to a hundred and fifty men. One third of them on patrol, you know? The rest in the house." He took another pull at the flask and then Smith took it from him. That would be enough. So was a hundred troops, more than enough to guard one woman, to prevent her escape... He paused and examined the thought. They would be careful she did not escape, their eyes turned inwards. But what of a rescue attempt from outside?

He would be a fool to try it.

He found them all watching him as he came out of his abstraction, and Buckley in particular with a knowing look that vanished into blankness as Smith's eyes found him. Smith snapped at him, at all of them. "What the hell are you all gawping at? Where do you think you are? Idling on the beach at Southend with a bag-full of winkles and a belly-full of beer? You're supposed to be keeping a sharp look-out! You're sitting right off a German shore!"

That set them looking about them.

And it had put off the decision.

Eleven minutes gone.

He glanced at Josef, feeling that he was being forced into this by a streak of soft sentimentality he had no right to possess, not as an officer in command, but he demanded, "You could take us there?" It was only just a question.

"To the guard-post?" The Belgian peered at him. "I could. But it would not be easy. There is barbed-wire strung all along the dunes and the Germans patrol the top. Every gap in the dunes is filled with wire strung like – like the web of a spider. There is a gun or a machine-gun every kilometre, sited to sweep the beach. Trenches are dug behind the dunes. When I made the signal to you I had to crawl into a gully so the men at the guns would not see the light. There are troops billeted or camped close to the trenches. If there was an attack alarm the trenches would be manned in minutes. A landing by troops would be very difficult, perhaps impossible. But one or two men, moving quietly and keeping away from the guns and patrols, that can be done. We did it last night. But when we get to the guard post? There is a company—"

Smith broke in, his mind made up, "I know. Will you take us?" And as the Belgian hesitated, "Then will you draw me a map?"

Josef's teeth showed in a wry grin. "A map would not get you through the dunes. But you're determined to try. So. I will take you there."

Smith asked, "You have a report to make?"

Josef made a rasping, derisive noise. "Whoever makes the report can tell Intelligence that Josef said: 'No luck. Keep trying.' It doesn't matter. They'll keep trying anyway."

Smith looked at Lorimer. "Did you hear that?"

"Yes, sir."

"Tell Mr. Dunbar. Now put us ashore."

"Aye, aye, sir." Lorimer's tone was apprehensive. The boat turned in its length at his order and ran back towards the shore, the crew pulling eagerly now so Smith had to growl at them, "Easy!"

He went on talking to Lorimer. "I'll take Buckley, McGraw, Galt and Finlay." McGraw and Galt the toughs. Finlay he knew as a taciturn, competent seaman. He was glad he had brought the extra men – Lorimer would have just enough hands for the whaler, as it was.

"As soon as we're ashore, run back on your course then lie by the buoy. When *Sparrow* comes she is to patrol as

circumstances dictate but we will look to see her in—"
He hesitated. A round trip of three kilometres but there
might be delays. *Delays!* He almost laughed at the word.
"Two hours. Say at two-forty. Lie at the buoy and from
two o'clock onwards you'll run in to the shore and out
again, watching for our signal. An 'A'. Understood?"

"Yes, sir."

But Smith still hesitated. The men's faces were turned
towards him, listening. He said, "You'll have your hands
full." And Lorimer was young, raw.

Smith stared at one face, older, weather-beaten, and
the man picked up his cue and said, "Maybe if I took the
helm, sir, so Mr. Lorimer can watch his heading?"

He was an old hand, Smith knew, come back to the
Navy from the fishing fleet, and he was privately telling
Smith that he would look out for Lorimer. And himself,
of course. Smith could read his mind: he didn't want to
pull around the North Sea all night while a green young
squirt tried his hand at small boat navigation.

Smith nodded. "Do that."

Buckley muttered, "Shore, sir."

Josef was peering. He whispered, "That way!" And
stuck out his left hand.

Smith hissed at Lorimer, "Ease to port!"

The helm went over and the whaler swung to port,
crept on and crabbed in towards the shore as the men
pulled slowly.

Josef whispered, "Here. The guns will not see us. We
must risk the patrols."

They swung to starboard, the men gave one last pull at
the oars and the whaler ran into the surf once more. Smith
strained his eyes against the darkness but saw only the pale
stretch of the beach and the black lift of the dunes. Was a

150

German patrol waiting for them up there? He could only hear the wash of the surf – then the whaler grounded. Smith and his little party tumbled out and Galt thrust at the bow of the whaler. It was backing off, turning, as they waded out of the sea and Smith led them at a trot up the beach, the big Webley revolver heavy in his hand. He ran crouching, expecting with every stride that the dunes would suddenly burst into the flash and rattle of rifle-fire. But then they were in the shadow of the wall of the dunes and he halted.

Josef looked about him, then pointed to his right. He led them now, along the wall of the dunes to where a gap like a gully cut in and upwards. He went on more slowly, a hand lifted cautioning, and Smith gestured the others into single file and followed on Josef's heels. They passed the gully and saw it criss-crossed with a cat's-cradle of barbed-wire. Just beyond the gully Josef began to climb the wall of the dunes using hands and toes. The wall was not so steep at that point. Smith followed him. As they came to the top the Belgian dropped on his knees, crawled to the summit then cautiously lifted his head. Smith could just see beyond him the posts marching away on either side with the barbed-wire strung between them. For a moment Josef knelt there, peering about him, then his hand lifted and he rose and led them on. They picked their way through the wire and beyond was a trench but it was no more than five feet wide and in turn they jumped it, crossed a track and followed the Belgian. Now they were winding through the dunes and after a minute or so he halted and turned to Smith.

"They patrol along the top of the dunes. You saw the track?" And as Smith nodded, "We were lucky. There will be other patrols but they keep to the road and the track. For most of the way we go—"

He stopped, searching again for a phrase and again Smith supplied it: "Across country."

Josef nodded. "We go, yes?" He looked at Smith.

Smith pondered. They were ashore in enemy-held country; they were committed. And the woods at De Haan must be less than a kilometre away to the north...

He said, "Go on."

Josef led on, the boots of all of them padding softly in the loose sand until they came out of the dunes. The ground beyond was open for a hundred yards but then a low shadow stretched across before them. Halfway across the open ground they came on a railway line, crossed its tracks and came to the shadow, that proved to be low scrub.

Smith whispered, "The railway. Where does it go?"

"Up to De Haan and on to Zeebrugge, or down through Ostende and right down the coast. The Germans use it, of course."

Smith nodded and followed him again as they skirted the scrub, keeping close to its shadow. He noted the abandoned ruin of a cottage or barn, stored it in his memory as he was trying to count the paces, keep an idea of his bearings. The rain came again falling steadily. They moved through the silent country for a quarter-mile or so, Josef halting to peer about him and cock his head, listening. Then they left the scrub and he led them angling to the right and they came to a hedge. He followed it down to a gap, stepped cautiously through, head turning, and then waved them on. They came out on to a dirt road slippery with mud under the rain and the Belgian whispered, "Now we must go carefully. The village is close."

On again with the squish and slither of their boots in the mud at the side of the road, the sound of their breathing and the tinkling trickle of a score of water courses. Josef in the lead, then Smith, McGraw, Galt, Finlay and Buckley at the tail. Until Josef stopped again and whispered, "The village."

Smith changed the Webley to his left hand and wiped the sweat from the right on his jacket.

There were lights, only three or four of them and giving little away, but lights all the same. The enemy could show them here; the village was a long way behind the line. Smith could make out buildings, the hard edges of roofs and walls where they stood among the softer lines of trees.

Josef whispered, "There is a patrol in the village. A non-com and two men."

Smith nodded.

Josef moved on until the village opened up. The road ran between houses into a square. They passed between the houses, hugging the wall on their left and came to the square, stopped at the corner of the last house. Smith stood at Josef's shoulder. The square was maybe three times the width of the road that ran through it, past a fountain that was not playing, and on out of the farther side of the square. The guard-post was obvious where it lay to the left, facing the square. It was a middle-sized house with a flagpole on its roof but no flag now. A short flight of steps led up to the front door and sentries stood on either side of the door in the shelter of the apron that projected out over the steps. Their rifles were slung on their shoulders. No one could enter the square without being seen.

Smith whispered, "What about the back?" There was a light behind the front door that showed in a thin crack at its foot and another in the room above the door. The window was curtained but a sliver of light showed at one side.

They turned, retraced their steps past the houses, climbed a low wall and trudged through a garden. Liquid mud sucked briefly and smellily at their boots as they passed a pig-sty and there was a rustling and grunting. They turned right round the back of the houses, came on a path, followed it.

Josef turned and waved frantically, ran crouching off the path and bellied down. They followed him and lay pressed against the wet earth, wet grass on their faces. Now they could hear the patrol pacing steadily, unhurriedly along the path. There was a mutter of voices that grew louder as the tramp of the boots grew louder. The voices were bored, soldiers trudging through a wet night, not for the first time, nor the last. They were passing...

They stopped.

Smith had his face pressed in his folded arms to hide it, the Webley under his chest. He peered up under his brows and saw the three soldiers close, winced as a match was scraped and the glare set him blinking, saw the man with the match hold it to the pipe, his cheeks sucking. The match went out, the pipe glowed then was cupped in one hand.

One of them spat out into the darkness and it landed before Smith's face.

Then they tramped on, out of sight and sound.

Josef got to his feet and Smith and the others followed him in file as he went along the path, moving more quickly now with the patrol behind them. So that they nearly ran into the sentry. They had come to a chest-high wall and Josef started to follow it then dropped down on all fours, pressed in tight against it. Smith, kneeling behind him, saw above the wall the head and shoulders, the rifle barrel, the flat round cap and caught a glimpse of the face below it, the round lenses of spectacles above a big moustache. Smith could see him against the glow of light in the building behind him but Smith and his party had moved against a background of trees, otherwise the sentry must have seen them. He passed them, his boots crunching on gravel on the far side of the wall, turned and passed them again, his back to them as he paced back along his beat. That beat was the length of the wall that was some fifty feet long with the break of a gate at its centre. He paced along the inside of the wall and they, crouching, tiptoed behind him outside.

The wall bounded the yard of the guard-house and that was about fifty feet square. At the head of it stood the house and there was an uncurtained window. Through it Smith could see a long room that ran the width of the ground floor. It was a dormitory with beds down each side and men sprawled on them fully-dressed. Rifles stood in racks in the aisle between the rows of beds. All this he saw by the light of the lamp that stood on the table in the middle of the room and half-a-dozen men sat there playing cards.

A sentry stood by the back door of the house, his back propped against the wall, clasped hands holding the muzzle of the rifle, its butt resting between his feet.

Smith went down again with the rest of them. The sentry was coming to the end of his beat. He turned and passed them, the crunch of his boots fading. Smith saw Josef's face turned pale towards him as he watched the sentry then he rose and moved on. He did not halt until they were well clear of the wall and then he looked at Smith. "Well?"

The back of the house was as hopeless as the front. They could do nothing. It had been a dangerous waste of time and they had a long way to go to get back to the ship. He looked at his watch and saw that forty-five minutes had passed since he sent Lorimer away and embarked on this folly. He had made a fool of himself and all of them would know it and Trist would smile. All for a woman just because she was a woman. Or was it because Buckley and the men expected him to perform some miracle and his vanity had led him to try?

They stood around him with their shoulders hunched against the rain, heads turning as they quartered the darkness but they shot quick glances at him. The carrot-headed Hec McGraw, and Galt, the mouth-organ playing tough. Dour Finlay and Buckley. He would have to tell them it was no good. He had risked their lives for nothing.

He asked, "Where does the path go?"

Josef shrugged. "I don't know but I suppose it runs into the road again on the far side, the inland side of the village."

"We'll keep on, then." Something nagged at him, something he should have thought of, that had eluded him so that he went over in his mind what he had seen, looking at it again as they walked on through the night, following the path as it bent slowly to the right. He recalled the road running between the houses and the sentries at the front of the house, at the rear. The wandering patrol. The single light on the upper floor suggested the woman might be there. Might? The square was empty so maybe the transport had not arrived and she was in there somewhere. It was too soon for the transport to have come and gone and surely they would have heard it, seen its lights – *That was it!*

He heard it then, and saw its lights as the factor that had eluded him snapped into place. The lights were moving, he could see them through the trees that ran in a line that marked the line of the road and he could hear the engine. The vehicle was about four hundred yards away and he was twenty yards from the road.

He started to run and shoved past Josef. "*Come* on!" He called it, not shouting but loud enough for all of them to hear and their boots pounded and splashed behind him. He made out two low gaps in the hedge and broke from the path that meandered on and ran straight through the long grass at one of the gaps and jumped it. He landed in the ditch beyond in a fountain of spray that stank and knee deep in water, fell forward, recovered and splashed out of the ditch and ran along the road towards the approaching lights. There were splashings and muttered curses in Scots accents and Buckley's hoarse chiding: "Shut that gab! Save your breath!"

They needed it. Smith was already panting but he kept on running as the lights came towards him. Two hundred yards away? He stopped and dragged his torch from his pocket, switched it on and shoved it at Josef. "Get in the road and stop him!" And crouched in the ditch, the water up to his middle, waved down the others as Josef stood on the crown of the road and waved his torch at the vehicle lumbering down on him.

Smith gasped, "Point the pistols but no shooting unless they try it. Understood? It's got to be *quiet!*" He saw them nod and his eyes swung back to the road.

It was a staff car. He saw that much behind the yellow orbs of its lights as it slowed, a mist of spray rising from its wheels, a leather or canvas top to it but no windows, open at the sides above the doors, two faces in the front…

It halted abreast of him, brakes squealing and only feet short of Josef. A head poked out at either side, one in a round cap, the other in a cap with a peak. A voice snapped a question, curt, impatient.

Smith could see faces in the back of the car now. Two? He shoved out of the ditch and straightened as he took the long stride that brought him up to the car to put his pistol to the face there. "Still!"

Buckley was around the other side, pistol pointing. So was Galt. McGraw was beside Smith and yanking open the rear door with his pistol pointed, threatening. "Keep still ye bastards or ah'll shoot ye where ye are!"

Smith doubted if the words meant anything to the two soldiers inside but the pistol did. Like the two in front they sat frozen. He snapped, "Get 'em out! Quick! And watch for any tricks!" He eased back half a pace, tugging the door open with his free hand then beckoning: "Out!" They all climbed down, hands lifted above their shoulders. The two in the back were infantrymen, their rifles left in the car. One from the front was the driver, the other, in the peaked cap, was a Major. Smith recognised that rank. He was young and hard-faced and the face was scarred. He was startled and wary but already recovering. He took in Smith's uniform and those of the men with him and broke into German.

"Shut up!" Smith told him.

For a moment he did. Then he started again. "You are English—"

Smith shoved him towards the ditch, snatched the cap from his head and snarled at him. "Shut your mouth or I'll shut it for good!"

He sounded as though he meant it. The Major believed him and was silent. But he was angry, not afraid.

Smith said, "Buckley, Galt, cover the other three. Finlay! You and McGraw make this officer fast and gag him. Use his belt, anything that'll do and sit him in the ditch."

He left them to it. He heard the start of an angry protest from the Major: "You cannot do—" It was suddenly cut short. Smith suspected the gag had been applied but he was inside the staff car, peering at the controls, trying to identify them from the memory of his one brief attempt at driving. He thought that the Major slipped easily into English and that he was probably another Sanders in reverse, spending long vacations in England before the war.

He heard Buckley say, "Same with the others, sir?" And nodded absently. The engine was still running and that was something. He didn't have to worry about starting, adjusting the mixture etc. He saw that the safety catch was applied on the Webley then tucked it in his belt and went over the procedure, muttering instructions to himself. He thought he had it – Buckley showed at the window. "All secure, sir."

He had to do it. "Finlay! McGraw!" As they came up he saw beyond them the heads of the Major and his men sticking out of the ditch at the edge of the road. He'd picked McGraw because he was a fighter and Finlay for his cool head. He would keep McGraw in check. He told all of them what he wanted and then looked at them. McGraw was enjoying himself, that was obvious, but Finlay was poker-faced. He sent those two off, carrying the soldiers' rifles and running for the path by which they had come.

"All right," he said, "the rest of you get in." Buckley sat in the front by Smith. Josef and Galt got in the back. He saw Josef holding the Major's Mauser pistol, checking the load, smacking the magazine home.

Smith took off his cap and crammed the Major's on his head so it rested on his ears. He jammed the car into gear and got it moving but jerkily so it shook them and he heard Galt swearing. Then it ran more smoothly and they were bumping over the pave, picking up speed as Smith clung to the wheel. Something moved at the edge of the light, came up at them as they closed the distance between and they saw the patrol they had seen earlier, still making their circuit of the village and about to cross the road. They waited for the car to pass, hunched under the rain and Smith told himself he had been right to order the prisoners to be gagged because a yell now would have given the game away. The patrol squinted against the lights but then the car was past them and running into the village. Smith only had time to be glad the patrol had not come five minutes sooner and then the little square showed ahead of him. He braked and they slowed a little but still swayed drunkenly as they took the tight turn into the square. The headlights swept around the faces of the houses and settled on the door with the two sentries. The car jolted down at them over the cobbles, swerving out and in as Smith swung it desperately around the fountain, straightening…

The car slid to a halt with its front wheels almost on the steps and the engine hiccupped and died. Smith stuck his head out of the side, mouth open to bark, "Komm!" But it was unnecessary: the sentries were already coming down the steps, blinking against the glare of the headlights. One of them saw the Major's cap and snapped to attention and the other followed suit. Smith said, "Out!" He thrust open the door and pointed his pistol at the nearest sentry. He saw Buckley menacing the other. Galt and Josef came slipping around to snatch the gaping sentries' rifles and Smith said, "Galt! You hold them!"

"Aye, aye, sir."

Smith ran at the door, twisted the handle and pushed it open. Beyond was a hall stretching towards the rear of the building. Empty. To the right a staircase led up and he took the stairs on the run, three at a time. On the landing he paused briefly. There were four doors on the landing but light showed under only one and that one of a room that faced the square. Buckley and Josef crowded behind him, breathing heavily. To Buckley he said softly, "Watch our backs." Then with Josef he moved to the door, paused to take a breath then seized the handle, twisted and shoved and burst in with the opening door.

It was an office. Opposite the door was the curtained window and on either side of the room stood a desk. An orderly sat at a typewriter behind the one on the left. Behind the other on the right sat an officer, bareheaded. His hands rested on the blotter before him. Another Major but this one's close-cropped head was grizzled and between his hands lay a Mauser automatic pistol like the one Josef held now. Between Smith and the Major sat a woman in a straight-backed chair, her back to Smith. A guard, rifle slung, stood stiffly at her shoulder. It was all taken in with one blink as he stood at the door and those in the room gaped at him, all except the woman who did not turn. For that blink of time all of them were frozen as if posed for a photograph.

Then Josef said, "That's her!"

The picture broke up, was smashed. The Major snatched at the pistol and fired at the same time as Smith and Josef. The reports were thunderous in the room. Something burred past Smith's head and the Major, half rising, went backwards over his chair to fall spread-eagled on the floor. The guard was unslinging his rifle but Josef was on him, hitting him wildly across the side of the head with the Mauser, a blow like a man chopping wood that jerked another shot out of the pistol to smash into the ceiling in a spurt of plaster and the guard fell against the desk and then to the floor. Josef grabbed at the woman's arm and she rose under that urging, turning. She wore a blouse and skirt, both cheap, and a shawl was wrapped around her shoulders. The dress of a peasant woman. Then she turned fully around and Smith saw the face, pale and tight-drawn. It was the face of Eleanor Hurst.

For a moment he could only stare, unable to take it in. Eleanor Hurst. *Eleanor!*

And though she in her turn gazed at him blankly, she recognised the face. But not the man. This man with his cold, savage stare was a stranger. But then Buckley yelled and a shot crashed out in the hall, a door slammed. Shooting broke out at the rear of the house, a fusillade, and there was the sound of shattering glass. Smith heard distant cheering and knew that was Finlay and McGraw but then there was firing closer, inside the house and he ran out on to the landing. Buckley stood crouching, wide-legged, pistol covering the landing. He turned his head fractionally. "A feller popped out of a door an' jumped back when he saw me. I fired a shot at him but he got away."

Smith answered breathlessly, "Let's see if we can do the same."

The orderly still sat frozen behind his desk. Smith ran for the stairs and down, Josef hustling the girl behind him, Buckley bringing up the rear. As they reached the hall a door at the back of the house burst open and a man came through it, pistol in hand, shouting. They all fired at him but all of them missed and he ran back through the door and they heard him shouting again.

Smith led them out of the house, down the steps and past the car. God knew if he could ever start it again – and where could it take them? He yelled at Galt but he was already coming. They crossed the square and at the corner of the houses where the road ran in, Smith halted and looked back. Men showed in the lighted doorway of the house but Smith and Galt fired at them and they disappeared. They ran after Josef and the girl, caught up with them and halted again at the last of the houses. Smith panted and rubbed at his face, peered into the darkness. The firing still crackled away at the rear of the house and flashes continually lit the sky. Then a klaxon brayed out its alarm over the countryside and he swore.

His orders to Finlay and McGraw had been: "When the shooting starts blaze off all your ammunition at the back of the house, rapid fire and no let-up; then run." Had one of them been wounded? Could they cope with a wounded man? He knew they could not but neither could he leave one behind.

Come on! Where the *hell* were...?

Finlay pelted out of the darkness and vaulted the low wall, McGraw tumbling over behind him. The latter grinned madly and shouted at Smith, "Yon patrol came chasin' back when the balloon went up an' Ah got the bloody lot!"

Smith shoved him down the road. "Good enough. Now run for it!"

Back along the road, through the hedge and into the open country, Josef and Galt with Eleanor Hurst, an arm apiece between them, Buckley and McGraw behind them. Smith came on the scrub, followed it, marked the ruined cottage coming up and knew the railway line should be...

There was a train on the line, the little engine puffing slowly, two coaches drawn along behind. He could see the glow on its footplate that silhouetted a man with a rifle. And still the klaxon blared behind them. He ran on because the train was stopping, he could see heads stuck out of windows, heard a voice bellowing. The train halted a hundred yards away in a hiss of steam as Smith jumped over the rails. He turned his head as he ran and saw the others were all close behind him and he saw the troops jumping down from the train. He thought briefly that it was probably a leave train or a draft for De Haan. But there was a whistle shrilling and the soldiers were starting to double after Smith and his little party.

The dunes. Breath rasping, a pain in his chest and legs like jelly, his boots floundering in the soft sand. A shipboard life did not make for distance running and a glance showed him the others in no better shape than he, barely trotting on unsteady legs.

The trench. Seeing it at the last instant and barely clearing it, staggering through the wire, falling and rolling on with a rip of cloth then on his knees and gasping out, "Down! Defensive fire! Hold 'em off!" He sprawled on the sand and tufted grass, fumbled the torch out of his pocket and flashed its beam at the sea. The beam wavered as he panted. Short. Long. – Short. Long. – Short...

Then a pistol cracked out behind him and Buckley yelled, "Patrol!"

Smith turned and saw them a hundred yards or so north, just vague, moving blobs of blacker shadow against the sky's darkness. They were on the track that ran along the top of the dunes, two – three of them as the group disintegrated at Buckley's shot, the men going down. Smith turned further, slithering right around on his stomach at the sound of more firing. The spurts of flame came from inland in the dunes and others close where Galt and Josef fired back at them. He looked again towards the sea and shouted hoarsely, "They're here!" It was no more than a shadow but he knew it was the whaler. He stared down the twenty foot drop at the beach below. With the ebbing of the tide there was now nearly a hundred yards of that smooth, open sand before the sea. A hundred yards under fire. The shore guns would be manned...

He wriggled back to Josef. "Give me that pistol!" He took it, then shouted, "Finlay! You and McGraw see these people to the boat! You can see it running in! We'll keep the patrol busy!"

He saw Eleanor Hurst's face pale in the darkness and her eyes watching him. Then Finlay and McGraw each grabbed one of her arms and the three of them went plunging, sliding down the wall of sand to the beach below and Josef went after them.

Smith shouted, "At the patrol! Rapid!" Because the patrol commanded the beach while the troops inland did not, though the muzzle flashes showed by their spreading that they were working around the flanks. Smith and Buckley and Galt fired away. The pistol-fire would hit no one, fired at that range and in the darkness but the patrol did not know that and Smith suspected they would be rear-echelon troops anyway. It worked. The patrol went to ground, their firing ceased and the figures running jerkily down across the sand to the surf passed unscathed.

But now? He could just make out the black shape of the whaler in the surf, and the jerking, running shadows blending with that shape. The beach stretched out in a long, long two hundred yards.

He said, "I'll hold them off! You two go now!" He tossed aside his empty pistol, exchanged it for the other.

Buckley said, "No bloody fear. We can go together an' make a running fight of it." Then he added, "sir."

Smith was speechless at this breach of discipline. And *Buckley*!

But then Galt gave his view without being asked: "Beggin' your pardon, sir, but ah don't fancy the idea o' leavin' you up here. If we all goes thegither then yin can help the other."

Before Smith could answer the decision was made for them. A machine-gun hammered from the surf and tracer slid through the night in a line pointed at the luckless patrol. Smith blessed Dunbar's foresight or caution in shipping the Vickers in the whaler. He shouted, "Right! Let's go!"

They jumped together. Smith had a brief, bizarre memory of playing like this as a child, falling through the air down the first steep drop then landing in a spurt of sand to slide down the last few feet of the wall to its foot. Then they were running for the whaler as the Vickers fired burst after racketing burst at the crest behind them until they drew close and the firing ceased. Smith could see the Vickers mounted in the bow, Finlay and McGraw nearly to their waists in the sea, and holding on to the whaler's stern. Smith splashed into the sea with the other two and waded out. The Vickers fired again right over their heads. *Tack! Tack! Tack!*…

Hands grabbed them from inside the boat and Finlay and McGraw shoved them up and out of the grasp of the sea, into the whaler. They stumbled between the men at the oars, Smith seeing Lorimer's face floating like a pale moon towards him, mouth opening and closing…"Shove off!"

Smith fell into the stern alongside Lorimer, sat down with a bang and gasped for breath, watching as the whaler backed off with the Vickers firing again, the line of tracers waving slowly back and forth like a warning finger, sweeping the crest of the dunes. Then the whaler spun on her heel and as Lorimer yelled "—together!" the oars dug in and she headed out to sea.

The Vickers was silent but a gun fired now from the crest of the dunes, it seemed right in their ears but it was about three hundred yards north. The shell screamed over the whaler and set them all ducking. Smith screwed his head around to peer at the shore receding behind him, the dunes fading into the darkness until only the line of surf marked the shore. The gun bellowed again, and again the shell was high. Rifle-fire came raggedly with flickering points of flame and the rattle of the reports coming flatly over the sea but the firing was blind and not a shot came near the whaler. He heard a whistle, faintly, and the firing stopped. Once more there was only the creak of the oars and the breathing of the men, the slap of the sea on the whaler's stern.

His chest ached, his legs were weak and the muscles trembled with reaction. He felt sick. "Well done." It was the least, the very least he could say to them but he could find no other words. He had taken appalling risks. It had been a mad, hare-brained operation… Or had it? They'd had surprise on their side, a huge factor, and he'd known that and felt there *was* a chance they could pull it off, known also that his conscience would plague him forever if he did not try it and simply left the woman to her fate.

The woman. Eleanor Hurst! He stared at her where she sat within arm's reach but her arms were folded on her knees and her bent head rested on them so he could not see her face. He had questions to ask her, but not now.

His eyes went to the men. Young Lorimer, intent on the compass, its glow dimly lighting his face. Buckley, his bulk unmistakable forward by the Vickers. McGraw, Finlay, Galt. And the others tugging at the oars as if they were just starting, rowing a clean stroke while he sat exhausted. They had backed him all the way. He was lucky, lucky in his men.

Chapter 6

Smith had the helm now. The boat crept on, moving in a darkly circumscribed little world of its own and all of them listening now until the sound came faintly but clearly across the sea: *Dunk!... Dunk-clunk!... Dunk!...* It was Smith's improvised buoy and he steered in the direction of the sound, at first tentatively because sound plays tricks in its passage over water; it is not easy always to mark the direction of its source. But it grew stronger.

Smith asked: "Did you have any trouble finding the buoy?"

"No, sir." answered Lorimer. That was true enough but he did not add that he had suffered an agonised minute before the buoy had made itself heard when he had sweated at the thought that he might miss it and lose the whaler in the North Sea. He had been glad of the stolid veteran seaman at his side, knew why Smith had set the man there and had suffered no injured pride. He had just been grateful and marvelled at Smith's insight.

Smith said, "There it is." The buoy was just a black lump swaying on the surface of the sea. As he eased the helm to bring the whaler's bow on to it he asked, "You heard our firing and came in?"

"We heard that klaxon and thought there must be something up, sir. That was some time after the gun-fire and we thought that might have been from De Haan but it sounded more as if it came from the sea, nor-east by north."

"Gun-fire?" Smith did not remember any gun-fire. "Heavy?"

"Just five or six reports, sir. That's all. And some time after that we heard the klaxon."

"Um." Smith thought about it. "Oars!"

The oars came in and Buckley in the bow reached with the boat-hook and hooked on to the buoy. The whaler lay rolling gently in the sea. The men rested and rubbed forearms over sweating faces and panted.

Galt said, "I never knew you could run that fast, Hec."

McGraw answered lugubriously, "Me neither! Must ha' lost a stone!"

Soft, wheezing, breathless chuckling. Reaction was setting in.

But they were not clear of trouble yet, not by a long shot – and with the proximity of the shore batteries that phrase was apposite. Smith said, "Quiet. Keep a sharp look-out."

Buckley was a hump in the bow where he squatted on his hunkers by the Vickers. Eleanor Hurst was slumped against Smith now, limp as if she slept but he could see her eyes wide.

He said softly, angrily, "What lunatic had this bright idea?"

She accepted now that the man was Smith. The man she had known. Still, she wondered at him, as she wondered at her own self-possession, surprised at how calm she was.

"What bright idea?"

"Putting you ashore to spy, of course."

She stirred and sat a little straighter but still close. "I can't tell you who he is but he isn't a lunatic. He said he'd come to me because I knew the country and spoke the language like a native. He told me what he wanted me to do and explained the risks. I volunteered. And for the most part it was simple enough."

"Simple!" Smith's voice lifted and he saw the men staring at him.

Eleanor Hurst shrugged. "I won't say I wasn't frightened because I was; even in London when we – were together. A motorboat landed us last night, a Belgian met us and we crept up from the beach and only once saw a patrol before we got to his house. During the day we wandered about peering at the woods from a distance. We were stopped by patrols a couple of times but the papers we had were all right. It wasn't till tonight that things became – complicated."

Smith stared out at the dark sea. The boat rocked slowly and the buoy gave its reverberating *dunk! dunk! dunk!* Where was *Sparrow*? He fingered the torch. She was long overdue and the light was growing; when Buckley turned his head Smith could make out his features now. He would have expected Dunbar to be early. He was uneasy.

He asked, "What were you looking for?"

"I shouldn't tell you, but we were just looking. We didn't know what was in those woods and we never got a chance to find out."

Smith said, "*Schwertträger.*"

Her head snapped around, eyes wide. She whispered, "How did you hear that?"

Josef was also staring.

Smith answered, "How did you?"

He saw her exchange glances with Josef, saw the Belgian nod. She said, "The man who came to me. He said they'd had reports by carrier pigeon – they drop them to the Belgians by parachute, you know?" Smith nodded. "Well. He said they had reports of something called *Schwertträger*. It was secret and connected with the woods south of De Haan and the Germans had sealed them off."

So somebody else knew about *Schwertträger*, or rather wanted to know about it. And someone had asked for reconnaissance flights over the woods.

The girl beside him shuddered – with the night's chill? She said stubbornly, "It was worth a try. I thought it worth trying."

But they had found nothing. What could it be? Some kind of tank? But why then would a U-boat commander be involved?

Josef said, "There was the train." Smith looked at him questioningly and the Belgian went on, "The – people we contacted, they told us that the train, the light railway, you know? It has been leaving Zeebrugge with Army engineers and marines and loaded with crates and timber in big sections. It arrives empty at Ostende."

Engineers – and marines?

He shifted restlessly. Where was *Sparrow*? He looked at his watch again. Dawn would come soon to expose them on this empty sea to anyone on the shore and that would be the end of it. He was certain they were on station but if Dunbar in *Sparrow* had made a mess of his navigation he might be patrolling a mile away. But he could not believe that. Dunbar was an old hand...

"Ship, sir." Buckley calling softly from the bow. "To star board."

Smith saw her bulk and used the torch to flash the long-short-long of a K as she came on, at first just a vague shape in the growing light under trailing smoke then the shape hardening as she trudged down on them...

"Oars!" He barked it at them and they jumped to it. She was not *Sparrow*, and she was going to run them down! "Give way!"

The oars dug in and heaved the boat forward as the men strained to drag it and themselves out of the path of the ship, and failed – just. Smith swung the boat away so the towering stern missed them but her bow-wave nearly turned them over and then her side hit them and stove in the boat with a smashing of oars.

They fell or jumped from it, yells cut short as they hit the water and went under. There was a minute of chaos as they thrashed around in the wake of the ship, paddling clumsily then all of them struck out for the wreckage of the boat that drifted among them. Smith blinked water from his eyes and saw the head of Eleanor Hurst, nearer the boat than he and swimming strongly for it. She grabbed hold and Smith laboured after her with the weight of his clothes dragging and hindering, reached it with one last desperate lunge and clung to it beside her, coughing.

They were all coughing, spitting out water. Smith started hoarsely calling the roll: "Buckley..."

They were all present.

Then he remembered. "Josef?"

No answer.

"Did anyone see the Belgian?"

No answer. They turned their heads to peer out over the waves. They called his name, shouting all together then stopping to listen. They never got an answer from

Josef. But a hail came out of the darkness and slowly the ship swept on them again from out of that darkness.

"*Wer da?*"

A light flashed out, wavered, then swept and found them.

Smith knew that much German. 'Who is there?' None of them answered. They could see the figures at the rail, that she was a small coaster of maybe eight hundred tons or less, her engines and funnel right aft. The figures stood in the bow staring down at the men in the water where they were lit by the pool of light from the torch. One of them leaned further over the rail, pointing, his hand with its prodding finger in the cone of light and he bawled, "*Engländer!*"

The ship had stopped and rolled gently in the beam sea. She'd made a lee for them and as she drifted down towards them the figures at the rail dropped ladders over the side. Smith could see the men clearly now, the bearded faces and blue jerseys, the soft caps with the peaks tugged down, the skipper with his head stuck out of the wheelhouse aft. He wore a homburg so he had to be the skipper. And then one came hurrying with two rifles so that as the first of Smith's crew dragged himself out of the sea and up the ladder the bolts of the rifles slid out then snicked home as the men worked them, feeding a round from magazine to breech.

Smith hung on to the ladder and pushed Eleanor Hurst on to it and thought they would be naval reservists because they handled the rifles with familiarity. Maybe too old for U-boats or the High Seas Fleet but not too old to run small cargoes down the coast under cover of darkness.

He saw all of his men aboard then followed them to join their dejected, dripping group. Someone had relieved the skipper at the wheel so he was able to stare at them in the light from a hurricane lamp he held over his head at arm's length. He was bearded, short but wide, made huge by a thick coat over a jersey. He conducted a brief interrogation.

"You. Englisch." He pointed at them. The men were all in working dress but they wore their badges of rank. Smith's jacket was unmistakable to these men.

Smith nodded. "Yes." There was the skipper and one other man with an apron knotted around his waist, doubtless the cook. Also the two men with rifles. All of them gaped at the little crowd of British sailors.

Then the light from the lantern fell on Eleanor Hurst, her hair unpinned and hanging limply to her breasts where the blouse clung to them. The skipper snatched off his hat, sought words and only found "Sprechen Sie Deutsch?"

Smith shook his head again and that ended the interrogation. The skipper burst into rapid German and the other three nodded. Smith caught the word "…Schiff!" The skipper's arm waved, pointing out into the darkness and he snapped a cover over the lantern. His conclusions were obvious: Smith and his men had come from a ship and it or another might be out somewhere in the night, seeking them, possibly close now.

Smith hoped so.

But the rifles waved, menacing, gesturing. Smith and his party obeyed the gestures and started to stumble aft along the deck. Dawn was close upon them but the shutting off of the light brought a temporary blindness so they stumbled over obstructions on the deck and the guards were not immune. There was a flash of flame that lit them all and the crack of the rifle set their ears ringing.

Smith heard someone yell, "God!"

His head turned. "Anyone hit? Anyone *hit*?"

The bullet could not have passed through the knot of them without striking someone. Smith thought the barrel of the rifle must have been pointed at the sky at the moment it fired because no one was hit.

The skipper had been ahead of the group, climbing into the wheelhouse. Now he yelled at the men with the rifles, furious. As well he might. The bullet could as easily have hit him. One of them muttered what might have been an apology but then the rifles gestured again.

They moved aft once more. McGraw muttered, "Somebody should tell you daft bastards to watch out! We're prisoners o' war and no' targets!"

Prisoners.

The word brought it home to Smith, to all of them. Heads turned as they exchanged glances.

Prisoners. Prisoners of war. Shut up in a camp for – how long? A year? Two? Longer? A year would be a lifetime.

They were herded down a companion and into a small, dark hole, crowded together, groping in the faint light that came down the companion. Then the hatch was closed and there was an instant of total darkness before a lantern was uncovered. One guard had been left with them. He hung the lantern on a hook and stood by the foot of the companion, rifle held ready across his chest. The engines started, thumping slowly then steadily.

They were in what would rank as the saloon in a ship of this size where all hands would mess together. There was a low deckhead that kept them stooping, bunks on either side, a table with benches flanking it on which some of them sat. The rest perched on bunks or squatted on the deck. Smith had been last down behind Eleanor Hurst and they were crowded into a corner near the guard. It was warm in the saloon, stuffy because the deadlights were tight-closed. They could not open one either for air or to try to signal *Sparrow*. The guard was there to stop that. Their clothes and bodies began to steam. Smith found there was a rifle-rack on the bulkhead behind him, empty now. So the two rifles he had seen comprised the ship's armament.

Prisoners of war. Then he remembered that was not true of all of them. He looked at Eleanor Hurst. She was a prisoner for the second time this night and she knew she was not a prisoner of war. There would be no camp for her. By comparison, the rest of them were lucky.

Escape? They had to escape, that was obvious. The method was not. But there must be some way...

Buckley said, one eye on the guard, "They've got the wind up about a ship. It's a fair chance *Sparrow* will run across us."

"Ah hope not." McGraw looked up from where he sat, elbows on the table, squeezed in among the others.

Smith glanced at him and McGraw said, "Did ye no' smell it as we came aboard, sir?" He looked around at them. "Petrol." Heads nodded. "There's drums of it stacked for'ard. Maybe they're moving it down tae Ostende for the seaplanes there. Anyhow, if Mr. Dunbar puts a round into this lot it'll go up like a bloody torch!"

And they were trapped below. There was an uneasy shifting among them that died away as the guard pushed away from the bulkhead, eyes flicking over them, hefting the rifle, reminding them. He eased back on to the bulkhead, balancing to the movement of the ship. He was a tough-looking, horny-handed seaman. He looked wary, as well he might, a Daniel in that crowded den of lions, but not worried. He had the rifle. His finger was laid along the trigger guard, not on the trigger, not after the near-calamity on deck.

Smith was prepared to bet the hatch was not locked. The guard would not be happy with it locked with the prospect of a shell smashing out of the night, and why should it be? He had them under his rifle and Smith was sure he would use it. He looked a solid, determined man. A respectable husband and father and kindly, but at this moment he was guarding his enemies... They had been excited on deck, startled, curious – but not triumphant. There had been no expressions of hatred... An attack on this man would fail but...

Feet thumped on the deck, the hatch opened to admit grey light and a hoarse voice, the skipper's, called down to the guard. Then the hatch slammed down but the guard relaxed slightly, settled himself more comfortably.

So it was light enough now for the skipper to see there was no British ship in sight. That would be the reason for the grin. What had happened to *Sparrow*? But this was the time, if ever.

It was worth a try. They *had* to try.

He said quietly, "Eleanor. Shiver."

She looked up at him, then shuddered. He started to tug off his jacket, talking to her, but he said, "Don't any of you look at me. I'm supposed to be talking to the lady." The glances shifted away. "Buckley. Get ready."

The guard was suspicious now. Smith was not looking at him but at the edge of his vision he saw him once again push away from the bulkhead. But a respectable, decent man... Smith said, "Take off the blouse." It was no longer sodden but it still clung to her. She was still a moment, seeing the men's eyes turn away. Then she started to unfasten the buttons, peeled the blouse away from her as Smith held out the jacket.

The guard averted his eyes. A decent man.

Smith had no time to be sorry. He slashed the jacket across the man's face and threw his weight into him, hurling him at Buckley. "Get the rifle!"

Buckley grabbed at the man, wrapped arms around him and grasped the rifle. It fired, once, the shot smashed into the deckhead then the others were piling on to the guard who went down under them kicking and fighting and bellowing in panic.

Smith was already on the companion, thrusting open the hatch and bursting out on to the deck. The light seemed bright in those first seconds and for one of them he hesitated. Then the skipper came hurrying aft around the wheelhouse and the man with the second rifle came running from the bow. He was shouting, lifting the rifle and Smith threw himself at the skipper. They wrestled clumsily, the skipper taken off guard and no more than trying to fend Smith off. Smith had to keep his feet and hold on to the skipper, hold him between the rifle and himself. The skipper's eyes squinted at him and his mouth gaped as he panted, breath smelling of tobacco in Smith's face. Beyond him, over the skipper's broad shoulder, Smith could see the man with the rifle. He was stopped short of them, the muzzle of the rifle a yard or so away, weaving as he tried to get in a shot. He edged to one side, shouting, but Smith heaved the skipper over, stopping his attempt to break free, stopping the rifle from firing. But the skipper was setting his feet now, seeing the object of Smith's wrestling and Smith could see the knowledge on his face. Where the *hell* were...

He saw Buckley suddenly straighten from the hatch and step up behind the man with the rifle.

Buckley also had a rifle.

The man was still. He twisted his head to look over his shoulder at the rifle Buckley had rammed into his back and stood so to let McGraw step up and twist away his weapon. Smith thrust the skipper towards Buckley then pointed a finger at McGraw. "Engines. Watch 'em. Make 'em see they do as they're told or else!" McGraw ran for the engine-room hatch. Smith threw at Buckley, "Get 'em all below and put a guard on them."

The cook was out of his galley, mechanically wiping fat hands on his apron as a pair of *Sparrow*'s men hustled him below to the saloon. The man from the wheelhouse followed him similarly escorted Smith finished, "And make sure they don't get out!"

"That they won't, sir." Buckley was grimly determined on that. He jerked the rifle at the skipper and his other prisoners.

"'Ere, you! Get below! Sharpish!"

Smith swung himself up into the wheelhouse and found Finlay at the wheel. Smith had watched him stand a trick at the wheel aboard *Sparrow*.

"Course, sir?" asked Finlay.

Course? Smith stared at the morning, grey, clouded, a fine drizzle falling, trying to catch his breath. He rubbed at the rain and sweat on his face as he took in the scene. They had seized the chance of escape only just in time — if in time. The sun was not up, but Ostende stood vague a bare mile away off the port bow. If this ship had not stopped and turned to pick up Smith and his men she would have reached Ostende at first light or before.

He ordered, "Starboard ten! Steer two-six-oh!" They were not going to Ostende. Not if he could help it. There were shore batteries that could sink them easily but this ship flew German colours. They might wonder at her change of course but they would know her because this was unlikely to be her first trip. They would not fire. There was a guard ship, what looked like one of the old torpedo-boats, patrolling slowly between the ship and Ostende. They were showing no interest. He stuck his head out of the wheelhouse and looked up at the yard at the hoist of flags there. Probably the skipper had run them up just before the escape and they were the identification. The coaster's bow had swung away from the port and now pointed out to sea. He bent to the voice pipe.

"McGraw!"

"Sir!"

"Full speed ahead!" He found Eleanor Hurst beside him, tucking in the blouse, pushing at a tendril of hair. She suggested, "*Schnell*."

He said, "Tell 'em *schnell*!"

"*Schnell!* Aye, aye, sir." Smith heard him bellow, "*Schnell!* D'ye hear? *Schnell! Schnell!*" There came the scrape and clang of a shovel.

Smith straightened. Lorimer stood at the wheelhouse door, red in the face and panting with excitement, brandishing a cook's carving-knife like a cutlass. "We've searched the ship, sir. Nobody aboard." Smith had seen them at it, scurrying like terriers.

Buckley appeared. "All secure under guard, sir. An' the cook had a pot o' coffee going and there's bread an' sausage. Foreign stuff o' course, but it smells good. Come to that, anything would." He was not looking at

Smith. Now he said, "That torpedo-boat sir. Reckon she's signalling to us?"

Smith grunted. He had no doubt of it. She lay astern of them now and she would be curious as they steamed away out to sea. "Run up a hoist." And as Buckley looked at him questioningly, "Any flags. Doesn't matter what it means, if anything. They'll think the skipper's got his signal-book upside down and try us again."

"Aye, aye, sir."

The engines were thumping away at a faster beat now and the coaster was slowly increasing speed. This was not *Sparrow*, though *she* was no ocean greyhound. This ship that had been toddling along at five or six knots might now slowly increase to eight. They were nowhere near running. But they were gaining time, gaining distance. The torpedo-boat still patrolled and was being left further and further astern.

"Sir!" Lorimer's voice was urgent. "Ship of some sort! Starboard bow!"

Smith swung around to stare out over the bow and saw her, about three miles away. A ship? It could be a ship, bows on but it was not *Sparrow*. There was no smoke and she was not big enough, smaller even than little *Sparrow*. His eyes searched the wheelhouse and then found the telescope in its clips above the wheel. He snatched it down and levelled it, searching again for the black object, the ship. It came up in the lens, the image blurred and dancing but he focused the telescope and steadied himself against the motion of the ship so the image came clear and full in the lens. He watched for several seconds then lowered the telescope. He said, "It's a U-boat. Heading for Ostende."

He stared at the U-boat, thinking, while the others watched him and looked at each other uneasily. He thought it was cruel luck. A little more time and they would have been beyond pursuit by the old torpedo-boat but the U-boat was on an opposite course to their own, running down on them. She was probably on the surface because she would make better speed. She might have sustained damage that prevented her submerging but that was a minimal possibility. The reason did not matter, anyway. The fact was she was running on the surface and making better speed than this old coaster ever could; she could make eleven or twelve knots if she had to. And she carried a four-inch gun forward, he could see, it and it was manned. That was enough to deal with the coaster and their two rifles. More than enough. One round from that gun landing in the deck cargo forward would make of the ship a furnace. If *Sparrow* was here or *Marshall Marmont* with her big guns, cranky engines or no – Cranky engines? His thoughts checked an instant then raced on.

Buckley said urgently, "Torpedo-boat's made his mind up, sir. He's turned an' he's coming after us an' cracking on speed."

Smith swung to stare out over the stern at the torpedo-boat, a white bone in her teeth now and showing a narrow silhouette as she surged after them. She had a gun forward too, a six-pounder it would be but she wouldn't fire, not with the U-boat coming down into range. He turned back to the U-boat. The combined speeds of coaster and U-boat had halved the distance between them. With the telescope he could see the men moving about the gun and the heads and shoulders of the little group in the conning-tower. There was a spark of light then. Someone in the conning-tower was using glasses. Inspecting the coaster. Seeing her colours but also noting her course and wondering. There was no chance of passing with a wave of the hand.

He jammed the telescope back in its clips and bellowed, "All hands!"

Buckley took up the yell and they came running, all but McGraw in the engine-room and the sentry below in the saloon. Smith told them what he wanted.

Lorimer looked around, then at Smith. "I'm the lightest, sir."

There was no doubt of that. Smith nodded and they scattered. To Eleanor Hurst he said, "I want you to wait aft of the wheelhouse, get down on the deck and under a tarpaulin or a blanket. Find a lifebelt and put it on or get hold of a lifebuoy."

"What are you going to do?"

He told her, not looking at her, head turning from the distant torpedo-boat to the nearer, now very near, U-boat. He finished, "So be ready to jump. I don't have to explain in detail?"

"No." She hesitated, then looked up at him. "It — it doesn't sound to have much of a chance."

He thought that was being optimistic. He said simply, "It's the only one we've got."

"You could surrender. You would surrender if it wasn't for me."

He tore his eyes away from the U-boat, looked seriously at her and shook his head. "No," he said. "No, I couldn't. If you weren't here I'd do the same." And he thought he probably would. Hoped he would. And was surprised at himself and the determination in his voice.

But Buckley was running aft with a coil of rope. Smith pushed her away. "Do as I said."

She watched him as he went to meet Buckley, watched him as she backed away, and only took her eyes from him to look briefly at the U-boat as she stepped behind the wheelhouse.

Smith swung himself up into the wheelhouse to stand by Finlay. A glance aft showed him that Buckley and his party were ready, Lorimer among them with the rope around him in a bowline on a bight. Smith faced forward, faced the U-boat drawing steadily down on them and ordered, "Hard aport!"

Finlay turned the wheel rapidly then gripped the spokes. "Helm's hard aport, sir."

The coaster's bow swung away from the U-boat and kept on swinging. Helm hard over she turned around through sixteen points and kept on turning through a full circle. As she swung broadside to the U-boat once more Smith glanced aft and saw little Lorimer had gone, knew he now dangled at the end of the rope, armed with a boat-hook and stabbing at some pretended obstruction of the rudder. The men in the U-boat would see the pantomime as Smith could see them in the conning-tower now, leaning out of the wheelhouse as the coaster churned again around the circle at juddering full speed.

Finlay said, "Just like the auld *Wildfire* the other day."

Smith said absently, "That's right."

He watched the U-boat as they swept around in the circle and was sure her speed was falling away. Her bow wave looked less; he reckoned she had reduced to less than eight knots as she kept her course towards the circling coaster. He looked back across the sea that separated them from the torpedo-boat. She was closer but still a fair distance off. He swung back again to stare at the U-boat. She was large in his vision now as they closed the third circle, the coaster still curving round to port, the U-boat still well off the port bow but the bow inching towards her.

Soon.

The bow was nearly – was pointing at the U-boat's stern and edging up her length as the coaster still turned but now the U-boat was turning. He fumbled for the telescope and through it saw the men on the conning-tower, faces filling the lens. He saw one of them was laughing, the others grinning, close as if he could hear that laughter. She was turning to run alongside the coaster as the latter went down around the circle again. In seconds the U-boat would be running alongside them and less than a cable's length away...

"Hard astarboard!"

The wheel spun again, stopped, and the coaster swung out of the circle, swung further.

"Meet her! – Steady!"

The coaster ran straight, the U-boat rushing up at them. They would pass astern of her. "Port five!" She was turning towards them, trying to edge aside. He could see their faces now without the telescope, see a mouth wide, bellowing. Her gun forward of the conning-tower flashed and slammed and the shell ripped over the wheelhouse.

Smith shouted aft, "Hold on!" He saw Lorimer dragged aboard by Buckley and shouted again, "*Hold on!*" He looked back to the U-boat and braced himself. That last correction of course had been enough. They were charging down on the U-boat. The gun's crew leapt desperately around the weapon, her commander shouted, she still turned but now there was nothing he could do, or Smith, or anyone to avert the inevitable collision. The coaster rammed her right aft. Smith thought he was braced for it but he was torn loose and hurled into Finlay who clung to the wheel. Smith hung on to him and saw through watery eyes the bow crashing into and on to the U-boat, riding down on her, rolling her over. He could see the conning-tower but whoever was in it must have rolled to the deck. A man lay on the steeply tilted deck behind the gun, clinging on. Others were already in the sea.

The engines had stopped and he shouted down the voice pipe, "Slow astern!"

No answer.

Then McGraw, swearing. Then: "Sir?"

"Slow astern!"

"Slow astern! Aye, aye, sir!" Then more distantly: "Slow astern you lot. Astern! *That* way for Christ's sake an' slow, sl-o-o-o-w!"

Smith could picture him gesturing, mouthing. But the engines started to turn, slowly, and slowly the coaster went astern, ground off and away from the U-boat that rolled sluggishly back to an even keel but now lay well down by the stern.

"Stop engines." And then: "Half ahead. Steer two-six-oh."

The coaster shivered then started to move ahead as the screws churned, slipping past the stern of the U-boat and heading for the open sea once more. A head showed in the U-boat's conning-tower.

Smith jumped down to the deck and shouted at the men aft, "Get forward and get down! Mr. Lorimer! Check that the prisoners are secure!" Smith could guess at the confusion and tension down in the saloon after the ramming because the prisoners and their guard had been given neither warning nor explanation. The prisoners were always at the back of his mind, a possible threat...

But Lorimer shrieked, "Secure, sir!" He came chasing after the party from the stern and he was still pulling the rope from around him. Smith wanted them out of the stern because while the U-boat's gun would not bear, she would have a machine-gun. He turned and saw Buckley already right forward in the bow, head craning over the side. Smith went to see for himself. He had smashed his knee against some obstruction in the ramming and it reduced him to a limping lope.

Buckley turned, wiping back-handed at a nose that dripped blood. He pointed, "She's all stove in, sir."

That she was, the sea washing in and out of the compartment below their feet. She was down by the head. But what did he expect? Much more important, she didn't *seem* to be sinking farther. He muttered, "The bulkhead forrard of the hold. If that's all right—"

"Shall I whip off one or two hatch-covers and 'ave a look, sir?"

Smith shook his head, looked back past the little crowd around them now, Lorimer at their head. Smith could not see the U-boat for the wheelhouse, she lay astern of them, so the machine-gunner would not see them. He told Lorimer, "See this lot over the side." He nodded at the drums that were lashed, stacked on the deck, then started aft. They would be better without the weight of the drums and their explosive threat. But they had no time to stop and attempt to plug that huge hole, even if it was possible. The torpedo-boat was driving on; he could see her over the port quarter and she was in range.

As he reached the wheelhouse the machine-gun opened up from the U-boat and bullets spanged and whirred off the coaster's stern and the galley abaft the wheelhouse. Smith crawled, wincing, along the sheltered side of the wheelhouse and past the galley. He smelt food; he was starved. He stopped at the corner of the galley. There was a break in the firing – the gunner changing the drum? He lifted on to one knee and now he could see the U-boat, down by the stern, men on her deck but she was not launching boats so she was not sinking. She was well astern now and the torpedo-boat beyond her but once the U-boat was no longer in the field of fire of the torpedo-boat's six-pounder... He ducked as the machine-gun opened up again, firing at long range now but still hitting. He crawled back past the galley and up the steps to the wheelhouse. Finlay was at the wheel, shoulders hunched as he listened to the machine-gun's hammering. And Eleanor Hurst stood at the back of the wheelhouse. He thought with shock that he had forgotten about her but pushed her down on to the deck and bawled down the voice pipe, "McGraw!"

"Sir!"

"That torpedo-boat's coming up. I want smoke. Do you know how?"

"Oh, aye. I've been in a stokehold."

No doubt he had, paying for his sins by labouring with a shovel.

Smith turned on Finlay. "Zig-zag. Five starboard, five port. Understood?"

"Aye, aye, sir."

Smith looked forward and saw Lorimer and his party had ripped away the lashings on the drums. As he watched the first of the drums was manhandled over the side. The machine-gun had stopped firing, out of range. He took a breath, then held it as the first shell from the torpedo-boat plunged into the sea abeam of the coaster. He sighed it out.

Now the torpedo-boat must have a clear field of fire. He jumped down from the wheelhouse and went forward, limping. He heard Buckley's yell, "Look at that!" And turned to see that McGraw had not failed him. Smoke was pouring from the coaster's funnel, huge billows of it rolling down and astern of them. Somebody cheered but Smith snapped, "All right! Let's get on with it!" Because he had caught a glimpse of the torpedo boat and she had hauled out to port. So the U-boat did not need her assistance. And the TB could charge on, seeking vengeance.

They worked furiously, panting, rolling the drums to the side and sending them over and all the time the stink of petrol around them, "Go steady! Strike one spark and it could touch this lot off!" So they laboured carefully, intent on the work but inwardly tensed for the next shell from the torpedo-boat. She was firing as fast as she could but she was hurling shells blindly into the smoke and Finlay had the coaster slowly weaving. Two fell close but the others were a long way off.

The last drum went over the side and Smith staggered and almost went with it. He rubbed at his face with a hand that stank of petrol, thought that the hole in the bow stopped them making a better speed, that the torpedo-boat would be overhauling them hand over fist, but that she would have done that anyway. He told Lorimer and Buckley, "Organise a damage-control party. See what equipment you can find and have it ready." Because they would need it. He walked unsteadily aft to pull himself into the wheelhouse with one more grateful look at the smoke they were making, and wondering what the *hell* he could do now.

Eleanor Hurst was squeezed in a corner, quiet, seeming calm enough. Smith spoke breathlessly into the voice pipe: "Engine-room."

"Engine-room! Chief McGraw here. Is the auld man still breaking his back?"

Smith straightened and cocked an eye at Finlay who watched his course with a frozen face. So he had been keeping McGraw up-to-date. Smith stooped again to the voice pipe. "He is not. He is asking you how things are below?"

He heard the startled grunt, then McGraw's voice came, re-signed. "All secure, sir."

"Very good." Smith paused, added drily, "You're doing a fine job, Chief."

"Thank ye, sir!" Relieved now. The skipper could take a joke, thank Christ. "He's not a bad auld lad, the engineer, sir. Been showing me photies of his wife and kids. He's got a daughter—"

"That's enough of that. You watch them. Under-stood?"

"Aye, aye, sir. It's just – ah feel a wee bit sorry for him, ye ken?"

"Feel sorry for him when you're out of this and that'll be a long time yet." Smith snapped the cover on the voice pipe, grinned faintly and shook his head. McGraw the tough, the hard man with a soft heart...

They were hit. The shock of it sent him reeling then he recovered and plunged out of the wheelhouse. The coaster had carried a boat right in the stern that now was a splintered wreck and there was a hole in her deck that wisped smoke. Smoke? Smith looked astern and saw McGraw's precious smoke being rolled away as a breath of wind tugged at it. He prayed that it was only a breath as he saw Buckley run up to the hole with two of the hands. They had found a canvas hose and dragged it along behind them. It spurted water into the hole and the wisping smoke died.

Smith hung over the hatch and shouted down the companion, "All secure below?"

A voice came up from the saloon. "Aye, aye, sir!"

"Don't take your eyes off 'em!" Smith warned. "If anyone of them tries to escape, shoot him! Understood?"

"Aye, aye, sir!"

Smith wiped at his face. He and his men had contrived to escape from that saloon. Their situation now was desperate enough without the prisoners breaking out. Another shell splashed into the sea twenty or thirty yards away. Smith found he was tensing himself for the next, tried to relax and failed, twitched and crouched too late as it howled over and hit them forward. He joined Buckley and his men at hauling on the hose until they were forward at the damage there. Flames flickered and ran about the deck where the petrol had been leaked and refused to be quenched by the water they poured over them. Smith wondered what was below them, whether it was more petrol, but then Lorimer and the rest of the hands came running with buckets of sand they had found ranged below the wheelhouse set there for just such an emergency. Sand was thrown on the fire, kicked over it, until it was doused.

He was conscious that the coaster was steering badly. Was Finlay day-dreaming? He walked wearily back to the wheelhouse, saw a shell fall short astern of them, a leap of water in amongst the smoke. Then another. He started to climb up into the wheelhouse then froze in the door. Finlay was on hands and knees, shaking his head and peering muzzily around him, dazed. Eleanor Hurst was at the wheel. Smith took a long stride and relieved her of the spokes. "What happened?"

She knelt by Finlay. "Something hit us and knocked us down but he must have hit his head. I went to help him and he said something about the wheel so I took it."

Smith had the coaster back on course. Finlay was climbing to his feet with the girl's hand under his arm. "I can take her now, sir."

"Sure you're all right?"

"Ah've a right bloody headache but ah can steer."

Smith turned the wheel over to him. To Eleanor Hurst he said, "Stay with him. If anything like that happens again, you yell." She nodded, did not say that she had screamed at them as they shifted vague in the fire's smoke and against the background of the running flames and they had been deaf to her. When they had come running for the sand at Lorimer's hoarse bellowing they still had not heard her.

They were hit forward again, a thumping crash and a spurt of smoke. As he jumped down from the wheelhouse he saw Buckley leaning over the side again. He ran to join him and Buckley said, "Just below the water-line, sir. See?"

Smith saw the gaping hole. They could, would *have* to contrive to rig some sort of patch over it. He straightened and lifted his head to peer around him. There was Ostende and the Belgian coast, on the horizon now. The German shore batteries could see them but they had not fired, might not fire. The coaster had made a lot of ground and they might have got clear away but for that torpedo-boat. She would haul up on them now and sink the coaster or board her, take him and his men prisoner. And Eleanor

Hurst? If she had looked to him then he had failed her. Christ! What a mess he'd made of it. And out there was the empty sea…

No, it *wasn't*. He stumbled back to the wheelhouse, shouting for Buckley, grabbed at the telescope and set it to his eye. There was the smoke, and under it –

He lowered the telescope and snapped at Buckley, "Hoist *Sparrow*'s number! She's there!" He pointed.

"*Sparrow*'s – Aye, aye, sir."

There was a locker below the telescope's clips. Smith opened it and found the signalling lamp, braced himself in the wheelhouse door and worked the lamp to wink his message at *Sparrow*. 'Stand by to take us off. Smith!'

He lifted the telescope again, watching for an acknowledgment. He had to wait, but it came. He worked the lamp again, 'Am under fire from TB.'

Again his signal was acknowledged. *Sparrow*'s silhouette foreshortened as she turned towards them. Now he saw the flick of light and puff of smoke as her twelve-pounder fired. He ran to see the fall of shot; two long, lunging strides across the wheelhouse, cannoning off Finlay. And saw nothing but their own smoke rolling astern of them. He turned to Finlay. "How is she handling?"

Finlay scowled worriedly. "She's getting very sluggish."

With water pouring into her she would be. And there would be gradually mounting pressure on the engine-room bulkhead.

He lifted the cover on the voice pipe. "McGraw!"

"Sir?"

"Keep an eye on the for'ard bulkhead. We're filling for'ard. And McGraw. *Sparrow*'s running down to us. We can expect to be taken off."

"*Sparrow*! Aye, aye, sir!"

Smith leaned on the door of the wheelhouse and thought it would need to be soon. They would nurse her but they had to keep going. The sooner they reached *Sparrow* and the less time she spent in these waters, the better. She should not be here anyway. With that he thought of Trist and swore under his breath. But then he forgot Trist. *Sparrow* was big now, dashing down on them. Her gun had ceased firing and there had been no firing from the torpedo-boat for some minutes but now one huge water-spout lifted astern and to port of *Sparrow*. It was a quarter-mile away but the shore batteries were seeking the range.

He ordered, "Starboard ten...Midships." And to McGraw: "Stop engines and chase them all on deck." To Lorimer: "Get the prisoners out."

He stood on the deck of the coaster as it filled with the prisoners and his men. He found Eleanor Hurst beside him holding a steadying hand under the arm of Finlay who seemed shaky on his legs. Smith thought she looked dead-tired but then his eyes left her and went to *Sparrow* and he saw now that her forward funnel was holed and leaking smoke, the wireless shack had gone and she had a hole in her hull just below the bridge. But she was sliding alongside, screws thrashing briefly astern, stopping. The hands were there slinging fenders over the side and the lines came snaking over. The two ships rubbed together for only seconds as the prisoners were urged to climb up on to *Sparrow*'s deck and the men followed, taking Finlay with them. Smith handed Eleanor over and then followed himself, the last to leave the sinking coaster.

A salvo burst in the sea inshore of the coaster and still a quarter-mile away but they would soon lift the range.

Sanders was leaning out from the bridge. "Is that the lot, sir?" Smith lifted a hand and Sanders bellowed, "Cast off!" He vanished and a moment later *Sparrow* throbbed to the beat of her engines and she pulled away from the coaster. As she did so a squall came in from the north-west, rolling *Sparrow*'s smoke down to coil around the listing coaster like a winding-sheet. With it came the rain, and the coast and Ostende were lost as its grey curtain came down. The shore-batteries fired no more.

Smith went to the bridge, pausing for only seconds to stare at what was left of the wireless shack; a buckled frame, splintered planks and the wireless a chunk of scrap. He moved on, found Sanders on the bridge and said, "We're very glad to see you. What happened?"

Sanders looked tired, drawn and pale. He spoke slowly, a sentence at a time as he remembered the incidents, getting his thoughts in order as he went. "We were patrolling, sir. Heading north. These two German boats came up on us from astern. We saw each other together, I think. The captain made a run for it and got away that time, but they hunted us, found us again when we tried to cut back. They fired at us and hit us, but we got away again. They still hunted us. Drove us right off station. When it was getting light and we could see they'd given up – probably thought we'd got round them somehow and gone home – the captain said we'd come back to look for you."

"He was taking a risk."

"Yes, sir. He said we had to. Couldn't leave you and scoot off home."

Smith thought they owed their freedom if not their lives to Dunbar. Nobody would have blamed him if he had refused to hazard his ship on the thin chance of finding

Smith's party. Sanders might prove a good officer in time but a decision like that...

He asked, "Where is the captain?"

Sanders looked at Gow where he hung over the wheel, long arms hanging to grip the spokes. Gow's face was expressionless. Sanders said, "When they hit us they killed the two Sparks and wounded the captain but he stayed on the bridge. Shortly before we sighted you he collapsed and we took him below. He died about ten minutes ago. Brodie says it was shock and loss of blood."

Smith looked at them, at the misery in Sanders's face and the mask clamped on Gow's. He said to them, "I'm very sorry. He — was a fine officer."

He could find nothing more to say. He had got away with it, but not Dunbar. The man had said he owed Smith a lot. He had paid in full; far too much. And the two wireless operators. He thought of Dunbar's private misery, never shown, never spoken of, but he knew it had been there. He did not believe this rubbish about dying of a broken heart. Men died for reasons like — loss of blood. Not a broken heart. Still...

He turned away from them to face forward. Eleanor Hurst was in the captain's cabin and Dunbar and the dead wireless operators in the wardroom. There was nowhere Smith could go. The bridge was crowded as always with its staff and the crew of the twelve-pounder. There was barely room for him to take a pace either way. He stood with legs braced against the motion of the ship and wrapped his hands around the mug of tea that came up from the galley and sipped at it and hunched wearily under the rain, the never-ending rain.

Dunbar. The appalling, bloody waste of a good man.

Chapter 7

Sparrow slipped into the harbour of Dunkerque in the forenoon. As she passed through the Roads, Smith saw *Marshall Marmont* was still at anchor. Her pinnace was in the water with steam up and an officer descending the ladder. *Sparrow* slid on past the lighthouse and the bastion where a French *poilu*, disconsolate in a dripping cape, stood guard with rifle and bayonet by the field gun that pointed at the sky. She tied up at her berth in the Port d'Echouage and on the quay a solitary figure awaited them, an Army officer in a trench-coat, cane tapping against his booted leg. The officer looked up at the bridge and saw Smith, lifted the cane in a wave. He was tall, handsome, but with a toughness about his good looks and Smith remembered him from the party at the Savoy a world away. And from three days later. He was the Lieutenant-Colonel on somebody's staff who had been a Doctor of Philosophy and now was something on movements in Dunkerque – Hacker. He called up at Smith, "Permission to come aboard, sir?"

Smith nodded slowly, putting two and two together. He turned his head and threw a reminder at Sanders: "Coal ship!" He started down from the bridge.

Sanders's "Aye, aye, sir!" followed him.

As he walked towards Hacker where he waited in the waist, Smith saw Brodie at the hatch that led down to the wardroom and the captain's cabin, holding down a hand. Another hand took his and he helped Eleanor Hurst up to the deck as Smith reached Hacker. The Colonel stared at the girl and let out a sigh of relief "Thank God for that!" He took off his cap and thrust his fingers through thick, black hair. He was freshly shaved but Smith suspected he had been up all night. He looked tired.

Smith was seeing some things very clearly now. He said, "You are a Lieutenant-Colonel in Intelligence and you sent that girl into Belgium."

Hacker did not hesitate, admitted it immediately, "Yes." He did not offer explanations, excuses or apologies.

Smith said, "I think we'd better talk."

Eleanor Hurst was close now. Garrick's voice spoke up behind Smith, "Welcome home, sir. We were starting to worry."

Hacker muttered, "Not as much as I was."

Smith turned to meet the grinning and obviously relieved Garrick and asked, "What news of the engines?"

"She's to be towed into the dockyard tonight or early tomorrow, sir."

Smith thought that was his 'ship of force': two big guns and no engines. And that his deck was getting crowded and the hands at work were having to climb around them. He said, "I think we'd better compare notes." He looked from Hacker to the girl. "Shall we go below? The men are making ready to coal ship and we're in the way."

They went down to the cabin and Smith crowded them in, Hacker and the girl sitting on the bunk, Garrick standing by the bulkhead. Brodie appeared before they were settled, carrying a tray with glasses, a bottle and a jug of water. "Thought you might fancy a drop o' something, sir."

"Did you?" Smith took the tray from him. "It's a bit early but the circumstances are unusual. Thank you."

Brodie left and Smith charged the glasses.

Hacker said, "*Sparrow*'s been knocked about a bit." When Smith nodded, Hacker went on, "Curtis told me when he got back here in the middle of the night that you'd gone to do the job. Then when you didn't show up at first light—" He shook his head, his cap now hooked on one knee, and smiled at Eleanor. "I was very worried, my dear. Oh, I know it was a job that had to be done and you had volunteered. But *I'd* let you go and – well, I'm damned glad to see you safe." He paused, then asked, "Josef?"

Smith answered, "We lost him." He explained briefly.

Hacker said nothing for a moment then he lifted his glass to Smith where he stood at the door. "Congratulations to you, anyway. And – 'absent friends'."

Smith lifted his. "Absent friends." This was Dunbar's cabin. There would be a stretcher party coming soon to take Dunbar and the wireless operators from the wardroom. He gulped at the whisky and felt it burn down into him. "There's no cause for congratulations. Josef and Miss Hurst found nothing. Just as the reconnaissance flights you asked for found nothing. Except that whatever is in those woods, the enemy are determined to keep it secret."

Hacker said, "You seem to know a great deal."

"I know about *Schwertträger*. I know you're trying everything you can to find out what's behind it." And Smith told him about the U-boat commander, and how it had been reported to Naval Intelligence and to Trist. He finished, "Now I find you're on the same trail. Does Trist know? Did *you* know what I'd told Trist?"

Hacker shook his head uncomfortably. "There's very little liaison of that kind. We're improving, but so far – no, there's no machinery for exchanging information." He added wryly, "I'm having difficulty in persuading my people that this thing could be important. They authorised reconnaissance flights, and this landing of Josef and Miss Hurst but only because of the reports from Belgium. And because I persuaded them there was something going on that we should know about."

Smith was silent for a moment, aware that Garrick was listening to all this with amazement. Smith looked at him, open-faced and honest and thought wearily, Thank God for Garrick in a mad world. He said quietly, "I believe that, because of the way they are guarded, the woods south of De Haan hold a secret that is a threat to us. Because of the connection with a U-boat commander and the mention of a spring tide that threat must be coming directly from the sea." He paused.

Hacker said, "That sounds sense."

Smith emptied his glass and looked from Hacker to the girl.

"I'm going to the Commodore to ask him to let me make a reconnaissance of that stretch of coast. Will you come with me?"

The two of them sitting on the bunk exchanged glances. Hacker said, "Well, I know Trist – but I think you're right. I'll come."

Eleanor Hurst stood up wearily. "Very well."

Garrick offered, "I'll come along if you like, sir." He said it unhappily, scenting trouble.

Smith turned him down. "But if you'd care to wait aboard I'll go with you in the picket-boat later."

He had no cap so he took Dunbar's. They walked up through the port, along the quays. As they crossed the fish-market where there was a new crater filled with rubble, the flag climbed up the staff on the Belfroi tower and the fog-horns sounded. The crews of the French destroyers lying alongside ran to their guns and the barrels lifted to point at the sky.

Eleanor Hurst asked, "What's going on?"

Smith answered shortly, "Air-raid," and kept up the fast pace he had set from the beginning.

At the house in the Parc de la Marine they found a line of Staff cars, the drivers in a lounging group that stiffened into cracking attention as a corporal among them bawled, "Heyes front!" And snapped up a salute. Smith returned it. The outer office was empty, the Lieutenant missing from his desk by the double-doors leading to Trist's room and those doors were half open. Smith and his little party could hear a murmur of voices, deep-toned laughter and he pushed the doors wide and walked in. He saw the Lieutenant who should have been guarding the doors hurrying down the room towards them, a startled look on his face. Beyond him there was a crowd of officers, Army and Royal Navy intermingled blue and khaki, gold braid and red tabs, glittering boots and buttons and silky-shining Sam Browne belts. They stood around the big map in little groups. Two stewards in dazzling white jackets were moving among them with trays of drinks and a long table was laid for lunch by the windows. Smith saw one tall figure in the uniform of a Brigadier-General in conversation with another tall, immaculate figure who smiled widely. Smith thought of Dunbar who had bled to death while he refused to leave his bridge, refused to abandon Smith and risked his little ship under the enemy guns. But Dunbar was at peace. Smith wanted something of Trist, had to have it. Then Trist saw Smith and his smile vanished.

The Lieutenant intercepted Smith. "Sir, if you would care to wait—"

"The door was open. I need to see the Commodore." Smith passed him and met Trist who was walking with rapid, long strides down the room.

Trist said softly, savagely, "What the devil do you want?"

"I'm sorry if I'm interrupting, sir, but there was no one around outside and the door was open. I have to see you."

Trist looked him up and down, at the salt-stained uniform, crumpled as it had dried on him, the hollow eyes in the unshaven face.

Smith guessed how he must look and was sorry, but: "It is urgent, sir—"

"This is a conference," Trist started, but Smith's eyes flicked past him to the group at the end of the room, the stewards and the drinks. Trist followed the direction of that gaze and saw curious glances turned towards himself and Smith. Gunfire sounded beyond the tall windows of the long room, some of it distant and some of it close. A shudder ran through the floor and the windows trembled making a soft rattling in the frames and then there came the far-off muffled *crump*! of the bomb. Hacker and Eleanor stood a yard inside the room, the Lieutenant hovering uncertainly. They watched the slight, bedraggled but straight figure of Smith standing under Trist's glare, refusing to be moved.

The Commodore smiled easily at the General across the room but muttered an obscenity under his breath. He said, "Very well. Outside."

And when they stood in the hallway, "What is it?"

"We've talked before about—" Smith hesitated. What to call it? "*Schwertträger*, whatever it may be."

Trist raised his eyes to heaven. "Not *again*!"

Smith said, "This gentleman is Lieutenant-Colonel Hacker of Army Intelligence. This lady is Miss Eleanor Hurst. If you would hear them, sir."

Hacker looked real, the soldier he was, but Eleanor Hurst still wore the blouse and skirt in which she had been captured and in which she had swum. She had dried them aboard *Sparrow* but they had not seen an iron. She looked a scarecrow figure and knew it, was aware of Trist's eyes running over her, amused and patronising.

Hacker told his tale, and Eleanor Hurst went stiff-faced and curtly through hers as Trist watched her with a cynical half-smile.

When they had finished he looked at Smith. "And I suppose you believe this lends weight to your arguments? That two wrongs make a right?" He glanced at the doors behind him and looked at his watch.

Smith said, "Before we only knew the Germans planned something called *Schwertträger*. We still don't know what it is or when it will be but we know *where* and that it is connected with the woods by De Haan."

"That may be," Trist admitted grudgingly. "But if Colonel Hacker had sent a more appropriate agent than an untried girl—"

"*I* was there only as – as part of a disguise!" Eleanor Hurst snapped it at him. "There was an expert with me, he tried all he knew and now he's dead. He did *not* die with his bottom stuck in a chair and a drink in his hand!"

Trist glared past her at Hacker. "Are you unable to discipline your assistants?"

The door opened behind Trist as the girl answered him. "He can't and neither can you! I'm a civilian! Thank God for that and that I don't have to take orders from a pompous windbag!"

The General and his aides stood in the door, and with them a Royal Navy Captain. Trist spun on his heel, saw them and snapped round again.

Hacker said, "Sir, I'm sorry. Miss Hurst has been under considerable strain and doesn't know what she's—"

"I know very well what I'm saying!" She was pale but she spoke very clearly.

Smith said savagely under his breath, "For God's sake, *shut up!*"

Her head jerked as if struck and she turned away.

Smith spoke to Trist, tried to retrieve the situation. "I think the Germans have something in those woods, sir. The aircraft patrolling over De Haan, the way they are very secretive about the area, how it is isolated, guarded and now this report that actually links *Schwertträger* with those woods — they all fit together now. I suggest that we try to reconnoitre that stretch of coast by making a landing, and the fact that Miss Hurst and myself have both landed there shows it can be done. I think we've got to make a reconnaissance backed by force and prepared to—"

"No!"

Smith thought he could not have made himself clear. He must try again. "If I could explain, sir—"

"*No!*" Trist almost shouted it. "You've already exceeded your authority in engaging in operations outside the orders I gave you. You're demanding a reconnaissance while one ship of your force is immobilised and now the other is damaged because of your actions!"

Dunbar. All the time came the sound and shudder of the bombs falling in the port and the constant racketing gunfire. Dunbar.

Smith heard himself saying, "With respect, my actions were dictated by circumstances and in the same circumstances I would act the same. The ship was knocked about and three good men killed, one of them a fine officer, because the orders from this headquarters sent her out alone into waters where she had no right to be and on a task she was unfit to undertake!" He shouted it at Trist.

The other man's mouth was open. The Army officers stood staring. Smith looked at them all and told himself his temper had wrecked everything.

Finally Trist said, "You – are – insubordinate!"

He was going to relieve Smith of his command. Smith knew it. It would be the first mistake Trist made because it would mean a court martial and though he had engineered matters so that he was covered, nevertheless some mud would stick.

But then the Captain stepped in and the four gold rings around his sleeve were interspersed with scarlet. He was the Fleet Surgeon. He said easily, "I really think, Commodore, that both this officer and the young lady are suffering from overstrain. I see a great deal of it and the signs are there if you know what to look for. I suggest release from all duties for a few days." He glanced meaningly at Trist. "I'll authorise that with your permission, sir." He was breaking it up, getting rid of the troublemakers.

Trist saw the opportunity to avoid a court martial and all it entailed. He hesitated, reluctant, then nodded. To Smith he whispered, *"Get out!"*

For a second or two Smith did not move. He was trying to find words to try again. And then he realised, slowly, that it was hopeless. Trist did not believe him, did not want to.

Dunbar was dead but Smith remembered his warning about Trist. "He never does anything he doesn't have to... Mister Cautious himself." Trist would not authorise any operation out of the ordinary. A bombardment, convoy escort, a sweep of the Belgian coast – all of them were arguably within the brief for Smith's flotilla. But not a reconnaissance in force off the coast by De Haan where no U-boat would or could have its base.

Trist would not authorise it.

Smith walked out.

They halted outside the house, for a moment a silent group. Smith was fighting down his anger with Trist, and with himself because he had let his temper run away with him again. He thought he had made a fool of himself, fouled it all up. If he had bided his time, got Trist alone, maybe buttered him up – No. He recoiled from that. But if he had to? No matter. He had handled it badly and now somehow he had to set it right.

There was a fire in the town, sparks flying up amidst the smoke. There was another across the basin that smelt like a paint-store burning. The smoke coiled across the water, acrid. The air-raid was over but as always there was the distant rumbling of the guns at Nieuport and this day they seemed louder, nearer.

Hacker said quietly, "I have some friends in London. I propose to go to them."

Smith nodded. Friends? He knew he had no influential friends. Except... "There's someone in London I might talk to as well," he said. There were rules and he was about to break one of them, or try to. He could see no other way.

Hacker asked, "When will you be ready to leave?"

Smith looked down at himself. His kit was in his cabin aboard *Marshall Marmont*. He had to get out to her.

Hacker said, "Curtis is in the basin and is still on detachment to me as requisite. He can take us across to Dover."

But Eleanor Hurst put in a word. "Look, I want a bath and my hair washed and clean clothes and I want to go home today, but before anything else I want to go somewhere and have a drink and sit quietly." She paused for breath. Her voice had a high pitch to it.

Hacker asked anxiously, "Are you all right? Do you feel ill? The doctor—" He gestured towards the house.

Eleanor said desperately, "I don't want the doctor and I'm not ill but I'm not all right, either. If you want to know how I feel then I feel as if I'd been captured as a spy and threatened with shooting. As if I'd been thrown out of a boat into the sea, hauled out of it again and then shot at. As if I'd been involved in a blazing row with a man I've never seen before and never want to see again."

Hacker put an arm around her shoulders and said gently, "Of course. I'm sorry."

She looked up at him. "Can't we just go somewhere where we can have a drink and sit quietly in a seat that doesn't go up and down and sideways? Just for a few minutes?" Her legs trembled under her and she was close to tears. Hacker was solicitous but awkward while Smith stood aloof and stared at her blank-faced.

But it was Smith who said, "Just down here." And took her arm.

He led her along the quay past the French destroyers where the hands were securing the guns and gathering up the spent brass cartridge-cases whose clanging sounded like a badly executed carillon. He led her to Le Coq, Hacker marching along stiffly on the other side of her. It was not yet noon and the bar was empty but for one customer. Mrs. Victoria Sevastopol Baines sat at her customary table at the back of the room with the customary glass before her. Smith thought that was one stroke of luck and delivered Eleanor Hurst over to her.

"Mrs. Baines, this is Eleanor Hurst. We had the good fortune to pick her up this morning when her ship went down." That was true enough and all he could say. He could sense Hacker's Secret Service eye on him, worrying. He explained to Eleanor, "Mrs. Baines owns a tug and she's helped me out of trouble on occasion."

Victoria fussed over Eleanor like a mother-hen and bawled at Jacques for cognac in a voice that shook the bar and made Eleanor flinch. But she found the old woman comforting.

Smith felt the cognac warm his stomach, felt his tense muscles relaxing and his thoughts begin to move again. He did not have to talk. Victoria Baines did the talking.

She asked only a couple of questions about the sinking and got brief, vague answers from Eleanor: a U-boat had attacked them and *Sparrow* had picked her up. It was enough for Victoria. She could fill in the details herself; she had seen enough ships sunk. Smith thought she probably assumed the sinking was somewhere in the Channel and that the ship had been British. Victoria chattered on, making plans. "There's a hotel in the town. I go up there to have a bath – there's nothing so grand as that in the *Lively Lady* though she's snug enough. You'll be able to have a bath and a sleep and I'm sure I can get you some nice clothes. I'll get Jacques to send out for a cab—"

Hacker stood up. "That won't be necessary. I have a car nearby. I'll go and whistle it up."

"That's very kind of you, Colonel, I'm sure. One of those Staff cars is it? Well, it'll be nice for it to be doing something useful for a change, won't it?"

Eleanor's lips twitched and Hacker said drily, "Yes, madame, it will."

He walked towards the door and Smith said, "I'll be waiting aboard *Marshall Marmont* within the hour."

"Right." Hacker passed out of the bar through the open door and as Smith watched his broad back receding down the quay, memory stirred.

He turned to Eleanor Hurst. "The day I left – I was going to come back but then I saw Hacker at your door—" He stopped.

There was a silence. Eleanor Hurst's face was blank for a moment as she stared at him but then her lips tightened and he thought, You bloody fool, you've done it again. He said lamely, "He'd come to see you about – this other business."

Now Victoria's face was blank, turning from one to the other but the bright eyes were watchful and she smelt a row brewing. "What about another drop o'—"

Eleanor said softly, "That's what you know *now*, but what did you think *then*?"

Smith could not answer her. He remembered her mood, her blazing anger in that bedroom and he waited for it to burst upon him now. He waited.

She laughed and that was worse than the outburst he had expected. She laughed and said, "Well, Commander, my life's my own and what I do with it is my business.

How I spend it and who I spend it with is my business. It has never been your concern and never will be. I'm grateful to you for saving my life but I think we're all square now."

Smith had deserved it, he knew that. But she had not deserved it. He said, "Eleanor, please—"

"Sir?"

He looked around at the interruption. It was Buckley, who said, "The captain sent me up to the Commodore's to find you but I spotted you in here, sir. I was to tell you we've shifted the picket boat; she's lying just at the end of the quay here."

Smith stared at him, trying to remember what he had been about to say to Eleanor. Buckley shifted under that taut, empty stare. "He thought you'd be in a hurry to get off, sir."

Hacker was to take him to Dover aboard Jack Curtis's CMB. Hacker had to see his friends and Smith had to talk to someone. The mystery of what was hidden in the woods by De Haan was still unsolved. *Schwertträger.* If he was right then the time was running out. Two days. Two days at the most...

He said, "Very good. I'll come now." He stood and picked up his cap as Buckley saluted and left.

Smith stooped over Eleanor. "I was wrong and it's not fair you should be hurt. I'm sorry."

She did not answer him or look at him, stared past him at the door. So he went to it and out, put on his cap and walked towards the end of the quay, the pinnace and London.

He and Hacker scrambled into a leave train as it pulled out of Dover and stood throughout the journey in the corridor. The train was packed with the men and their equipment, most of them still with boots and legs coated with Flanders mud. Hacker had telegraphed ahead and there was a car waiting for them at Victoria. A hospital train had preceded them and the station was crowded with ambulances, wounded on stretchers, wounded limping on crutches or with arms in slings, some with eyes bandaged and holding on to comrades. And there were the faces behind the barriers that waited and watched, anxious or hopeful. The one or two that lit up when they saw the man they waited for even though he might be a shattered wreck; he was alive and home and now that was enough. Smoke and steam hung in the station and their smells mingled with the smell of damp khaki serge, sweat, dirt, antiseptic and the exhaust fumes of the ambulances creeping through the crowd.

It happened every day. Often it happened all day and all night.

On the way from Dunkerque they had talked and learned a great deal about each other. Smith found that Hacker had been an artillery subaltern until Intelligence claimed him. "They seemed to think I'd be useful. Bit of luck, really. Most of the chaps I knew as a subaltern are dead. I had trouble getting things done at the start because I didn't know the strings to pull then. But once I learned that I got on all right. I mean, half-colonel isn't bad for a chap who's really a civilian. And it's an interesting job most of the time." He paused, then added, "Not too bloody funny sometimes, though." He appeared languid and easy-going. Smith found him to be hard-working and serious.

Now in the car Hacker said, "About Eleanor." He paused, for once embarrassed. "There was nothing between us except that I recruited her for the Belgian job.

She had a bad time and I'm sorry, though I had no choice. We *needed* her. But that was all there was to it. She's a fine girl."

Smith said, "I know." But he had already wrecked his chances with Eleanor Hurst.

He got out of the car at the Admiralty and stared up at the great building with the wireless aerials strung across its roof. Hacker handed him his bag and said, "When I have any news I'll come round to your hotel, but this will take time."

Smith answered, "I don't think we have much time."

"I'll do my best."

Smith shook his head. "We've *got* to make them believe!"

Hacker stared at his intensity as Smith went on, "We know the evidence is just words: soldiers in De Haan talking of *Schwertträger*. A U-boat Commander mumbling it when he was delirious, but he *wasn't* delirious when he told me: 'the blow will fall soon'. I *saw* him. And he talked about a spring tide. You get two of those a month when the tide is exceptionally high and the next one on the Belgian coast is early on the morning of the 12th. That's the day after tomorrow. That's *soon*! Whatever *Schwertträger* may mean it *is* a threat, it *is* connected with the woods south of De Haan and it could easily be timed to start on the morning of the 12th. *We've got to get them to see that!*"

Hacker was silent a moment, then said, "I believe you. And I know some strings to pull now. We'll make them believe."

The car pulled away. Smith watched it go and was glad he had Hacker on his side. He'd got to know the man and liked him; he could prove a friend. But now Smith had to test another and he turned towards the Admiralty.

—

Rear-Admiral Braddock growled, "What are you doing here?"

Smith came straight to the point. "I need help, sir."

"Sit down." Braddock looked thoughtfully across the desk at him. "The opinions you expressed on anti-submarine flotillas and convoys – I quoted them."

"Yes, sir?"

"They made an impression. Let's say that yours was one more vote that was counted. The convoy system is to be extended."

Smith said from the heart, "Thank God for that."

Braddock nodded. "I'm convinced it will be the saving of us. The reduction in shipping losses where convoys are used certainly indicates that. So you were right." He thought Smith could be a bad-tempered, moody, stiff-necked, hard-nosed, infuriating officer. But he was right when it mattered. He went on, "I hear you've been busy. How are you getting along with Trist?"

Smith said baldly, "I'm not."

The Admiral scowled, waited, and Smith told him the whole story, from his first hearing of *Schwertträger* to Trist's refusal to allow him to attempt a reconnaissance of the woods south of De Haan. And he said what he wanted to do.

Braddock still scowled. "I wouldn't say that you go looking for trouble as a rule, just that you seem to attract it. I promised you help, but coming to me for this, bypassing the chain of command! Trist will rightly say you're going behind his back."

"I know."

"It won't endear you to him, or to a lot of other people. I don't like it myself."

"I don't like it, sir, but I believe time is against us and there was no other way. I had to use the back door. A Lieutenant Colonel in Army Intelligence is trying the same method." He told Braddock about Hacker.

Braddock said, "Um. So the pair of you are trying to get orders for you, over Trist's head, to attempt this reconnaissance. Well, *I* can't give 'em."

"No, sir. But you're the only man I know who might be able to – or prepared to..." He stopped, uncertain how to put it.

The Admiral finished for him: "...persuade the right people." He was silent, thinking that while he knew something of this young man, he knew little about what he really wanted. Thinking also that he himself was nearing the end of a long and distinguished career – but for the war he would have been retired by now – and he did not want to tarnish it with some backstairs-engineered blunder. He shifted uncomfortably in his chair. Was that what was making him hesitate, the risk to his reputation? If he was worried about taking that sort of risk then he had stayed too long and he should get out. And what about Smith, sitting there expressionless as a Chinaman but ready to risk not only his career but his life? He thought of this young officer's seemingly wild escapades, the enormous risks he had taken, the women, the scandalous talk he had caused. Now he sat quiet. Not tall nor handsome. A little shabby and the fair hair needed cutting. No jutting jaw nor blazing eyes. The eyes looked tired now but were steady on Braddock.

Braddock said harshly, "You know what will happen to you if you're wrong, don't you?"

"Yes." Then Smith added, "But what may happen if I'm right and do nothing?"

"Nobody could blame *you*."

"No. The dead blame no one."

Braddock digested that and made his decision. "All right." He pushed out of his chair, looked at his watch then fumbled in his pocket, produced two slips of coloured paper and handed them to Smith. "I'll get in touch with your Colonel Hacker and I'll do what I can. You can do nothing, so go away and try to forget about it for a bit. There are a couple of tickets for *Maid of the Mountains*. They tell me it's a good show and I was going to take my wife but now it seems I'll be busy."

"I'm sorry, sir."

"No, you're not. And don't worry about my wife. She's used to this kind of last minute cancellation and I'll take her some other time. Now clear out and let me get on with it."

"Thank you, sir."

Smith used one of the tickets as he was told because he did not know what else to do. He left his bag at his hotel and went out to Daly's. There he sat through the first twenty minutes of *Maid of the Mountains*. It was a good show and the house was packed but he saw none of it. He saw a dark coast, the sea breaking gently on a shallow-shelving, long beach with a sharp lift of dunes beyond. And beyond them the loom of woodland, dark, silent. Secret.

He left the theatre and walked, lost in thoughts that revolved in his mind and threw up possible solutions to the mystery that he probed and worried at, but that remained just possibilities. There might be other possibilities that he could not dream of. It was a long time before the shrilling of the air-raid whistles brought him back to the present and he found he had been walking east. It seemed only minutes but his watch would have told him he had walked for an hour. He did not need to look at it because he knew where he was and that he was close to the little house belonging to Eleanor Hurst. But Eleanor was still in France. And besides, she wanted nothing more to do with him…

A fast-striding policeman, an elderly man, a 'special constable', peered at him and said, "Air-raid, sir. There's a shelter in the street you've just passed."

The warning was superfluous and the policeman looked at Smith curiously. There was gun-fire all around the eastern perimeter of the city, searchlights sweeping the sky and now the far-off but familiar whistle, glow and *crump*! Of an exploding bomb.

The 'special' said, "I suppose it's the Gothas again, sir." And then he shouted, "There y'are!" He pointed. In the sky to the east of the city the wavering beam of a searchlight had locked on to an aeroplane, a very high, tiny thing of silver in the light. But it was a Gotha. They were big biplanes, enormous compared to aircraft like the Harry Tate, with the range to reach London with a half-ton of bombs each. They had a ceiling of fifteen thousand feet but this one looked lower than that as it twisted and turned, but still the light held it and the gunfire burst around it.

"Go on! Blast the bleeder!" The 'special' ground it out.

But then the Gotha side-slipped out of the light. The searchlight beam swept the sky, searching, but did not find it again.

'The 'special' muttered savagely under his breath then glanced at Smith. "Be wise to take shelter, sir." He was disapproving. He obviously thought an officer should have more sense than to be walking the streets in an air-raid for no good reason.

Smith could not explain his presence but air-raids in the streets were the business of firemen and ambulancemen, and of the volunteer patrols formed in each street. He was none of these. If he could not help, then: "I'll go back to my hotel."

"You watch out then, sir."

Smith turned back. He had not covered fifty yards and was approaching a side street when he heard a far-off hiss climb quickly to a shriek and he threw himself down close by the wall. The pavement heaved under him and the blast sucked out the windows above his head to shower him with falling glass as the roar of the explosion battered his ear-drums. He saw the dust roll out in a cloud from the side street just ahead. The pavement heaved under him again and there was the *thump*! Of another bomb exploding but this one sounded further away. Dust still boiled out of the street ahead of him. He started to rise and was on hands and knees when the house groaned above him. He stared up and saw the whole wall of it toppling like a falling tree; he went down again with his hands over his head, pressed in tight against the wall. Then it burst about him and that was all he remembered.

–

There was light and there were voices. He heard the murmur of them as far away, deep but with a lighter tone among them, the voice of a woman. Eleanor Hurst? He heard them in the drowsy moments of slow awakening. Then there was a rustle as of a woman's skirts and the voice said softly, "Yes, I think he's waking."

He opened his eyes. She was young and pretty but she was not Eleanor Hurst. She was a nurse, a VAD and she stooped over him with a half-smile on her face but watching him intently. He thought she had a nice face, young, anxious. He turned his head on the pillow. There were screens around his bed and on a chair at one side sat Hacker, who now shot his cuff to glance at a gold wrist-watch and drawled, "About time." But he looked relieved.

Smith lay still for a moment thinking about it, drowsy but not tired, just waking slowly and drawing his world together again. He remembered the bomb, the toppling wall. He asked, "What is this place?"

Hacker answered, "A hospital for officers. One of those houses given up for the duration. Near Regents Park." He was shaved, neatly uniformed, buttons and Sam Browne belt gleaming but there were dark smudges under his eyes. "I went to your hotel this morning and found you hadn't got back last night and started searching. Had a hell of a job finding you. Wasn't till the forenoon—"

"Forenoon!" Smith jerked upright in the bed, fully awake now. He stared at Hacker and asked, "Well?"

Hacker nodded. "I've got your orders in my pocket. What you wanted."

And Smith thought that he had been sleeping the day away while time ran out – wasted!

The nurse returned. "I can't find Doctor Blair."

Smith asked quickly, "My clothes, please?"

"Well, the doctor will have to see you before—"

"But I'm all right! What was wrong with me?"

"You were unconscious and bruised. A few minor lacerations."

"That's nothing. I'm all *right*." He was. He was stiff and sore but he felt as though for once he had slept well; he was eager to be away.

The girl explained patiently, "A doctor must see you before you can be discharged."

"He has. Colonel Hacker is a doctor and he's just been looking at me. Right, Colonel?"

The girl looked at Hacker and he looked at Smith then said gruffly, "That's right."

The girl hesitated. "But the Colonel isn't Medical Corps—"

Smith said quickly, "Seconded for Staff duty."

Hacker nodded and smiled at the nurse.

The girl blushed and gave way. "Well, I suppose in that case—"

Smith jumped in. "Fine! Fetch my clothes, nurse, there's a dear girl."

She brought them and he saw someone had cleaned his uniform tolerably well and his boots had a shine to them. He dressed rapidly.

At the front door she admonished him, "But you must take care, sir. A wall fell on you. You looked an awful mess when they brought you in."

"I will." Smith could see Hacker's car waiting at the kerb with the driver at the wheel, the engine running and Hacker gesturing urgently from the rear seat. Smith added sincerely, "And thank you."

She looked over his shoulder. "Why, here's Doctor Blair now."

Smith saw him, a grey-haired man in a white coat walking across the road from a house opposite. "My compliments to him." Smith was across the pavement and into the car. He waved to her as it pulled away.

Hacker grumbled, "You really are the bloody limit, Smith."

"Well, you told me you were a doctor."

"Of *philosophy*, dammit! If they report this—"

Smith grinned. "You might get your name in the papers."

Hacker was not amused. "Along with the other dirty old men who impersonate doctors. Thank you. Oh, well, I'll go in and apologise when I get the chance."

"So will I. Where are my orders?" He ripped open the envelope Hacker gave him.

Hacker said, "We had to see a lot of people – that Admiral of yours is a demon! Had to do a lot of talking, a lot of persuading. But they came around. Mind you," he added cautiously, "they weren't enthusiastic. In fact they are just covering themselves."

Smith scanned the orders. He was required forthwith to reconnoitre with the force at his disposal the coast south of De Haan and take any requisite action. He was to be careful of hazarding his ships or his men.

It was sufficient, all he had hoped for because he knew his case was hard to argue; he had argued it enough to know. The Navy was fighting desperately against mounting losses of merchant shipping from U-boats and with one eye always on the German High Seas Fleet where it lurked, waiting, in its North Sea base in the Jade river. To the Admiralty the threat hidden in the woods south of De Haan was a problematical one and a sideshow at that.

He stuffed the orders in his pocket as Hacker said, "There's a train for Dover in half-an-hour. And I've sent a signal asking for another reconnaissance flight."

Smith said, "I don't think you'll get it. I talked to one of the pilots at St. Pol and he said it wasn't on. His Squadron Commander won't have it."

Hacker said, not looking at Smith, "It's worth a try." He thought there was only a slim chance that Smith might succeed. He did not say it but Smith could read the thought behind Hacker's face. He went on, "I intend to go myself as observer. I've done a bit of that." He settled back in the corner and tipped his cap forward over his eyes. "It was a long night, as the young lady said to the Colonel. Call me at Victoria."

Smith grinned but became serious as he stared forward, eyes vague and his thoughts racing ahead.

They were bound for Dunkerque and the war.

Chapter 8

They got a passage in a destroyer bound for Dunkerque and sailed from Dover under clear skies. As she approached Dunkerque Roads, Smith, standing on her bridge with her captain and Hacker, saw there were yet fewer monitors at anchor in the Roads – but *Marshall Marmont* was out there. He grinned at Hacker. "They've worked hard on her!" And as Hacker raised his eyebrows "The engineers told me it was a full day's work for the dockyard but she's out again already." Things were going right at last.

At his request the destroyer hoisted a signal and minutes later he saw *Marshall Marmont*'s pinnace following them into port. The destroyer was going on into the basin but she stopped and lowered a boat to set Smith and Hacker ashore on the quay where *Sparrow* was tied up in the Port d'Echouage. As he climbed the ladder to the quay he noted that some of *Sparrow*'s damage had been made good. There was a lot of raw, new paint and she had a whaler again but the wrecked wireless shack was still a wreck. As he strode along the quay towards her he saw Garrick climb up from *Marshall Marmont*'s pinnace that had hooked on near the Trystram lock and they met at the foot of *Sparrow*'s brow. Smith returned his salute and said, "Congratulations. You're ready for sea."

Garrick's face was set. He said bitterly, "No, sir. We're not. After you'd gone we received a signal from the

Commodore. The ship wasn't to be put into the dock-yard here. She's to go to Chatham instead. There's a tow arranged for tomorrow morning."

Smith stood on the quay taking it in, conscious of the orders in his pocket and a feeling of foreboding. As if to match his mood the clouds were breeding now and a shadow fell over them on the quay, the breeze turned chill. He could hear the gun-fire from the lines at Nieuport as always, but today it seemed louder and more continuous, a constant, distant thunder.

Hacker strode up and said, "The Naval Air Service people have sent a car. There's a Harry Tate waiting for me at St. Pol." He hesitated, then said, "Maybe we could get together for a drink. Afterwards."

Smith answered, "That's a good idea." Looking beyond Hacker he could see the familiar Rolls Royce. He shook the hand that Hacker stuck out and watched the soldier cross the quay and duck into the car. It pulled away.

He heard Garrick say, "Of course, I went to see Trist and told him you'd ordered me to see the repair carried out immediately. He only said that *he* was responsible for priorities. So I had a quiet word with the dockyard and they've got plenty of work but they would have taken us if Trist hadn't stopped them. Maybe you could put it to him better than I did, sir."

Smith said, "I doubt it." It would be too late, anyway. He needed the monitor to sail with *Sparrow* tonight. He wondered why Trist had done it. Surely not spite? No. Caution. Trist did not want to risk the ships, did not believe, or want to believe that the woods at De Haan were anything other than what they seemed. After all, he had not listened to the Kapitänleutnant gasping out his threat with the last of his life. Smith took a breath. "I'm going to see the Commodore anyway."

"Good luck, sir. I'll wait aboard *Sparrow* and have a jaw with young Sanders."

Smith nodded. "I'll see you there."

As Smith left him, Garrick called back, "Buckley asked to come along in case you wanted him, sir. He's in the pinnace."

Smith lifted a hand in acknowledgment. Buckley. Garrick. Loyalty. He walked on to meet Trist, crossing the locks and striding along past Le Coq and the other little bars up to the house at the Parc de la Marine. He thought that he had trodden this path too often but, one way or another, this would be the last time. After tonight he would not have this command, of that he was certain. He had stirred up a hornets' nest to get his way and Trist would see to it that he paid the price. Trist would get rid of him, somehow.

The Commodore received him in the long room. He sat in it alone, behind his desk at the head of it, an impressive figure as Smith walked the length of the room, heels clicking on the polished floor. Trist sat upright in the high-backed chair but he seemed relaxed.

He kept Smith standing.

Smith said, "I have orders from the Admiralty, sir."

He held out the paper and Trist took it, glanced at it casually then flipped it back. He smiled thinly. "Yes. I know all about it, of course. Their Lordships sent me a signal. As it should be, how things should be done. I may not have gone crawling to the seats of the mighty but I know more than you think."

Smith started, "Sir, with respect I did not—"

But Trist held up a hand. "Never mind. That's all behind us now. I had two signals. The second informed me that I am being, not promoted, but given another appointment. With a decoration, of course."

"I'm very glad, sir." Smith said it without expression.

He wondered if others had gone behind Trist's back. Had whispers reached the Admiralty from Trist's Staff? He remembered the unhappy faces of some of them when Trist had ordered *Sparrow* to make her 'offensive' patrol of the coast.

But Trist was saying, "My successor will find the affairs of my command in order. I have always contrived to keep up to date, with the help of a *loyal* Staff. It only remains for me to write my report and my reports on officers and make my recommendations."

Smith knew what that meant. Trist would report on him and it would be there in black and white, or knowing this devious, cautious man, dirty grey. Forever.

Trist said softly, "So. I have my orders and you have yours and your flotilla. Carry on with my blessing."

Smith stood in silence for a moment. Now he had to ask. Trist knew it and was waiting for him. He said slowly, "Sir. *Marshall Marmont's* engines—"

"Will be repaired at Chatham. I have issued the orders."

"Yes, sir. I know. But I need a monitor. My orders call for me to take appropriate action depending on what I find."

"Your orders call for you to act 'with the forces at your disposal'," Trist quoted. "Those forces you have."

"That's only Sparrow, sir! There are twelve-inch monitors lying in the Roads. If I might have one of those—"

"There are monitors in the Roads because I ordered them there. They are there for the defence of this port. This command has already been stretched thin by the appropriation of ships. You know of the monitors already detached. What you don't know is *why* they were detached. I will tell you, in strict secrecy. A landing is planned on the coast north of Nieuport. It is timed to link up with a big push on the Ypres front. That is why the General and his Staff were here yesterday. We were taking the planning a stage further. The intention is to capture the entire Belgian coast and deny the enemy the use of that coast and the ports of Ostende and Zeebrugge as bases for U-boats. These are matters of strategy which lie outside your sphere unless or until you are involved but I tell you for a reason."

Trist paused. Smith thought he was boasting, demonstrating his power, that he was privy to the innermost secrets of the conduct of the war. Why?

Trist went on: "I tell you because more ships are being demanded for the landing. The only ones I can spare are *Marshall Marmont* and the two other destroyers I promised you. Those two are at this moment sailing for convoy duty from Hook of Holland to the Thames; the convoy assembles off the Hook a couple of hours after first light tomorrow. When they return they and *Marshall Marmont* will be detached. I have made this commitment. My successor will have to honour it."

So he had destroyed Smith's flotilla. He was left with nothing but *Sparrow*. Trist had created it out of paper and now he had destroyed it with paper. Smith was silent. To attempt to carry out his orders with a single, old torpedo-boat destroyer would be madness. Trist knew it and was having his last laugh.

But the Commodore had not finished. "For the present – well, you can ask your friends to try to obtain further orders to augment your force but I don't think they'll find it easy. I told you I knew more than you thought. Quite simply, your mystery has been exploded. The enemy bombarded the lines at Nieuport for twenty-four hours, starting yesterday evening. You may know that. What you probably don't know, because you were scheming in London, is that they attacked today, and successfully. They've pushed forward to the Yser river. Not an attack inland but on this coast. There's your stab in the back! I expect the reserves they used were hidden in the woods by De Haan and brought up in the night." He smiled. "You have the satisfaction of knowing that you were at least partly right, there *was* a plan."

He was almost laughing. Smith thought Trist was relieved because a weight of responsibility was being lifted from him. And Smith, who had been a thorn in his side? Trist could stop him by just doing nothing. It was a perfect Trist solution. Smith rubbed at his face. Through the window he could see the leaden sky, rain spattered the panes. The room was a place of shadows.

Trist said, "The Admiralty knows this of course. I would not be surprised, therefore, if you were to receive further orders shortly. I suggest you return to *Marshall Marmont* and wait for them."

Trist was wrong. The attack on Nieuport was just another attack. Why should a U-boat commander be involved? Had the woods hidden nothing but the reserves for this one attack, and for weeks on end? No. The precautions, guards and Albatros fighters, were too elaborate. Trist was right in one respect: his information would raise doubts again in London and there would be orders coming for Smith to countermand those in his pocket. He could do nothing.

Sunset was three hours or more away but there was no sun. There was the lowering sky and the rain that drove in on the wind from the Roads, though the Roads were hidden in the rain's grey murk. He was striding blindly along, tramping through puddles that sprayed mud from under his boots when the shaft of yellow light blinked across the quay and was gone as the door closed. He came to a dead stop and stood under the rain with legs braced as if he was at sea and stared at the door. It was not the same door, not the same bar but – He stood irresolute for a moment, contemplating the risks, bearing the distant rumble of the guns at Nieuport but today there was also another, natural thunder and the light that flickered out to sea was not gun-me but lightning. The rain beat on him and he made his decision, then moved on, walking quickly again but now with a new purpose.

–

Victoria Baines parted the curtain that hung over the door of the bar and peered out through the chink at the quay. The rain was still falling but she thought she'd finish the glass and go back to the *Lively Lady* and tell them to stand down. She had told them to keep steam up and they'd wanted to argue about that because they weren't on call but she had refused to listen or explain. They could call it a woman's whim if they wanted but she commanded *Lively Lady* and if she wanted steam up she'd damn well have steam up. She did not know why. She was just – restless, uneasy in her mind. That Hurst girl with her calm face hiding her misery – but it was not only that. There was something brewing... she had felt like this the night before the captain was lost at sea and she prayed the boys were safe...

A band of yellow light from an opened door stretched pale across the quay in that early evening. Beyond it showed a solitary, slight figure seen like a wraith through the blurring rain. The light blinked out. For a moment she still stared out into the rain, then she closed the curtain.

Smith pushed in through the door of Le Coq, shut it behind him, shook water from his cap and looked to the back of the room. She sat at the same table, stiff-backed and red of face. She wore a black hat that was circled in flowers and sat slightly askew on the grey bun. She was sipping from a glass, daintily, and her little finger was fastidiously crooked. Again he hesitated, remembering the story he had been told of how she had bawled at an officer, "Put a poor old widder woman on the beach, would you? Take away her livelihood?" There could be more than a grain of truth in that and he did not want to be that officer but...

He went to her slowly and said, "Good evening, Mrs. Baines."

"Evening, Commander. Thought you'd gone to London."

"I did. May I?" He laid his hand on the back of the chair opposite her.

"Welcome, I'm sure." The china-blue eyes sharpened as he lowered himself into the chair. "You're looking peaky. Too thin and too tired. You youngsters are all the same, don't look after yourselves proper. I told Jack Curtis so the other day. Jack, I said—"

Smith broke in, "Where is he?"

"Gone over to St. Pol. That flying friend of his asked him over there. Some 'do' in the mess."

"What about his crew?"

"They'll be ashore. There's nowhere to sleep aboard those motor-boats so they've got billets just down the quay. I'm just drinking off. I can show you the house where Jack and his Snotty sleep but I'm not sure about the men." She paused, then asked, "Is that all you wanted? To find out about Jack?"

Smith said, "No. I want a great deal more than that."

She met his gaze and after a moment asked, "Are you in some sort o' trouble?"

"No. But I'm going to be."

She stared at him and he said, "Can we talk as we go?" And stood and offered her his arm.

He talked with Victoria Baines as she led him along the quay, walking cautiously on the pave in the high-heeled shoes. He had seen her squeeze her feet into them before they left Le Coq. She held up her umbrella against the rain and Smith had to look out for his eyes. She had paused once to stare at him incredulously. Then they walked the last yards in silence and she stopped before a house, neatly painted, the windows shuttered. "This is the place." And then, "I hope you know what you're doing…" She went on to warn him, but – "You're set on it, aren't you?" And when Smith nodded, she said, "All right, I'll do it."

She bobbled off along the quay, bag dangling from one lace-gloved hand, grey bun showing under the flowery hat. The picture of a respectable lady of advancing years and modest means. A nanny or a granny. Then the umbrella blew inside out and he heard the crisp oath, and smiled.

He rapped at the door and a minute later was talking to Midshipman Johnson who came down to him in the hall, sleepily and with a greatcoat over his pyjamas, the overlong legs of which concertina'd above his slippered feet. Smith looked at him and thought, They seem to be getting younger.

He said, "You're early to bed."

Johnson's hair stuck up in spikes. He said, "The old lady here was going to bring my supper up to me. She fusses over me a bit, sir." Smith could imagine it, looking at Johnson, who added defensively, "We've got all night in, sir."

"I'm afraid you haven't. Can you reach Mr. Curtis?"

"He's over at St. Pol, sir. Went over there for dinner but he left a note. There's a telephone there and—"

"Then telephone him. Ask him—" He stopped. That wasn't right. This was Smith's responsibility, he wanted that to be clear. He said, "Tell him he is to get straight over here. You know where *Sparrow* is lying?"

Johnson was wide-awake now. "Across from the ship-yard."

"That's right." Smith wrote rapidly in his notebook, tore out the page and handed it to Johnson. "Clear?"

Johnson read it carefully, blinked in surprise but said, "Yes, sir. I'll telephone Mr. Curtis and bring the boat alongside *Sparrow* and he can join her there."

"Get dressed and get on with it then."

Smith watched him run up the stairs, tripping over the bottoms of the pyjamas, sighed and shook his head and went out.

As he approached *Sparrow* he felt the wind on his face, coming off the sea and thought it was a fair wind. He saw them gathering on *Sparrow*'s cluttered little quarter-deck, Garrick's tall figure, Lorimer short and stocky and Sanders slim. The quartermaster on the side had obviously had orders to warn them of his coming.

As he stepped aboard he asked, "Ready to slip?"

"Yes, sir." answered Sanders.

"Lower the whaler." And then: "Now, gentlemen. First: Wireless silence until further orders. Understood?"

Sanders said, "We haven't got any wireless, sir."

Smith remembered that was so; there was just the gap between the first and second funnels where the shack had stood. He looked at Garrick, who nodded acknowledgment. So Smith went on to give them detailed orders. And – like Johnson and Mrs. Baines before them – they stared...

Marshall Marmont's pinnace slid past the lighthouse and headed along the channel towards the sea. She towed *Sparrow*'s whaler and had the crew of the whaler and Buckley aboard. Smith stood in the cockpit with Garrick as a light challenged them from the shore and the signalman clicked his lamp in reply. He knew Garrick was uneasy by the worried glances he shot at Smith, who ignored them because the only way he could lift that worry from Garrick's mind was to cancel the orders he had just given. He would not do that. It was not easy for Garrick, or Sanders. They were under his command but their orders were unusual, to say the least. He had offered to put them in writing, said he would accept their formal written objections if they wished. They had refused.

He wondered why they trusted him so.

They were challenged again in the Roads. There were a dozen ships anchored there and all of them wary of intruders. They passed ship after ship that loomed out of the rain, towered over them then slipped astern. Until *Marshall Marmont*'s squat profile showed blurred, hardened and the pinnace swung in alongside her and hooked on. Smith and Garrick boarded her and Smith walked forward past the bridge and the tall turret with the huge fifteen-inch guns. He heard Garrick rasping his orders and then the pipes shrilled and the ship came alive.

He stopped just forward of the turret and stood under the muzzles of the guns, watching as the men streamed past him into the bow. The rain was driving now. He looked at his watch, shifted impatiently and peered out into the murk. Nothing. He would have liked the night to cover him now but he could not wait. Time was against him and this rain-filled dusk would have to serve. He looked over his shoulder past the guns at *Marshall Marmont*'s single tall mast with its control top and the strung aerial of the wireless. If anyone called her she would hear but Smith had stilled her tongue; they would get no reply. They would acknowledge no orders that would countermand those he had in his pocket.

He turned forward, looked again at his watch and up – There she was! She came creeping in on them over the rain-swept sea, the tug *Lively Lady*, turning slowly on her heel then nuzzling her stern close in under the monitor's bow. He watched as the tow was passed and reported secure, winced as the capstan hammered and *Marshall Marmont*'s anchor was raised. The yell came: "*Anchor's aweigh!*"

The tug was moving ahead. There was a jerk as the loop of the tow became shallow and then *Marshall Marmont* was moving. The party still worked forward, securing the anchor for sea. He ssaw the motor-launch foam out of the night and swing alongside *Lively Lady* and he ran forward to stand in the bow.

The Lieutenant commanding the patrolling launch called through a megaphone, "I understood *Marshall Marmont* was to sail in the morning."

Smith held his breath. He saw Victoria Baines's dumpy figure on the deck of the tug and her bellow came back to him on the wind. "So did I! Till they got me outa me bed to tell me otherwise! Bloody Navy! You bluejackets are all the same! Work a poor old woman to death for the sake of a lot o' red tape an' paper work while you run around asking damn fool questions! Why don't you ask him back there?" She jerked a thumb at the monitor. "I reckon he'll give you an answer if I'm any judge of his temper!"

But the Lieutenant was not going to cross the hawse of a captain in a foul mood on a dirty night. He answered, "Goodnight, Mrs. Baines." The motor-launch sheered off and was lost in the premature dusk.

Smith blew out his pent breath. God bless Mrs. Baines! The Lieutenant would make a report, of course, but that would be too late.

He turned and strode aft, looking up at the open bridge, lifting an arm. He saw Garrick up there give an answering wave but then he was past. Aft, the whaler was hauled up short, her crew aboard her where she was towed along at the side of the monitor as she moved slowly ahead. They were holding her off from the side, bow and stern. The mast was shipped, the sail ready to hoist. Buckley sat in the stern sheets. Smith climbed down into her, sat by Buckley and the tow was slipped and the men at the oars tugged briefly to take the whaler out of the lee of the monitor then hoisted the sail. They had fallen astern of *Marshall Marmont* but they crept up past her with Smith at the helm and sailed up alongside the tug. Peering through the rain Smith could make out a figure at the wheelhouse door, the pale splash of a face. He called, "Thank you! Well done!"

"Good luck!" The call came back softly. Maybe Victoria was subdued now, impressed with the secrecy of their slipping away. And there was the tumbling water between, the thumping beat of the tug's engines and the churn of her screws.

He put over the helm and the whaler turned away from the tug and pointed her nodding stern at the port. The tug and the monitor had a long, weary haul ahead of them. Soon they were only vague shapes and then lost entirely. But he saw them once more as thunder growled and lightning stabbed down at them, saw them in the blink of an eye, the plodding tug and the unwieldy mass of *Marshall Marmont*, then the rain closed in. Victoria Baines had stared incredulously at him on the quay and muttered, "I hope you know what you're doing – or they'll hang the pair of us. You can't steal a warship from the Navy."

Couldn't he? Thunder rumbled again and he shivered again though he was not cold. He was soaked and the rain washed his face as the whaler soared and plunged, driving towards Dunkerque with that fair wind, but he was not cold. Buckley was whistling softly through his teeth and he and the crew of the whaler watched Smith covertly but he was unaware of it.

Jack Curtis waited for him aboard *Sparrow* in oilskins and seaboots, His CMB was tied up alongside the thirty-knotter. Smith glanced at it and saw that his orders had been carried out. As the sail came down and the whaler slid in against *Sparrow*, Smith saw that Curtis was talking with Sanders, the tall American and the shorter Scotsman side by side. They were of the same rank and age. Excited? He tried to remember how he had felt at that age and briefly felt a hundred years old but then he was climbing the ladder.

He called Curtis aside. "I want you and your boat to sail with me now."

"Yes, sir. That's what your note said." Curtis was understandably guarded. Smith was a superior officer giving him an order. On the other hand the CMB was not seconded or attached to Smith's command.

Smith asked, "No one will question your sailing?"

"No, sir. We're still on this detached duty. Colonel Hacker, sir."

Smith said, "Colonel Hacker will have no objection." He smiled wryly. "But you must have some questions."

Curtis grinned sheepishly. "Well, yes, sir. I sure do." He paused and shifted his weight from one leg to the other, wondering where to start. "Well. What are we going to do?"

"That calls for a fairly long answer and I'll give you details later. But briefly, I intend to find out what is hidden in the woods south of De Haan. And then – what was that phrase of yours? – shoot the hell out of it."

Curtis stared at him, swallowed, then said, "Well, that seems to answer one question, sir."

Smith said quietly, "Then I'll ask one. I'm giving you an order. Suppose I made it a request? Would you go?"

Jack Curtis was silent a moment, looking at this Commander who seemed scarcely older than himself, that he knew little except by reputation and that reputation was of a stormy petrel; Smith and bloody action went together. He was a lonely, aloof figure, yet men followed him and Sanders and Buckley came close to hero-worship. Curtis wondered why and then heard himself say, "Sounds like a good idea, sir. I'm in."

Smith said, "I'm sorry about your party at St. Pol."

Curtis was silent a moment then answered, "It was cancelled anyway, sir. Seems there was a call for a reconnaissance flight that their Commander had said he wouldn't let anybody fly but himself. But he's away in hospital and my friend Morris pushed for it and they let him go. He was shot down by Archie over Ostende. I talked to one of the guys in the Triplanes that flew as escort. He said the Harry Tate went into the ground like a bomb, exploded and burned as it struck. There was Morris and an observer – some Army officer. Both gone."

Hacker had tried to hedge his bets, tried to uncover the secret of the woods at De Haan by flying a reconnaissance because there were very long odds against Smith succeeding. The odds had proved no better for Hacker. Smith thought Curtis was not the only one to lose a friend this day.

Sparrow went to sea with Jack Curtis's CMB in tow, to save the motor-boat's fuel.

Part Four

To a View

Chapter 9

Sparrow was sliding furtively through the night now, a night that was oppressive, the air thick around them so she seemed to push through it over a sea like black glass, calm as if flattened by that pressure. The mine-net barrage lay far out in the darkness to port. It might have been a good idea to creep close to it. The enemy knew very well that it was there and so could be expected to steer clear of it. On the other hand there was always a fair chance that a destroyer and a mine-sweeper might be out to try to do it damage. The enemy might be anywhere. This course was closer to the coast but it saved time and time was short on these summer nights. De Haan was still more than forty nautical miles from Dunkerque and some of it shoal. One more risk to be calculated and accepted. *Sparrow*'s crew was at action stations and the look-outs strained their eyes into the darkness.

The signalman muttered, "Bleedin' rain!" and hunched his shoulders at it. It was soft summer rain, almost warm, but it worked inside Smith's clothes and left them clammy against his skin. He was glad of it. A fine summer night would have left *Sparrow* naked. He had that restlessness, that itch that almost always preceded action. And this time they weren't searching blindly for they knew not what. They knew where they were going, if not what they would find.

It was hard to be restless in that tiny space that was more gun-platform than bridge, crowded with the crew of the twelve-pounder and the bridge staff. Buckley stood right at the back below the searchlight platform. Smith took a couple of strides then forced himself to stand still on the gently heaving bridge and stare aft. He could just make out the CMB because her bow wave blended with *Sparrow's* wash where the thirty-knotter towed her. Curtis's little craft looked top-heavy now with the hump of tarpaulin forward of her cockpit. He was glad Curtis commanded her. He had faith in that young man, trusted him. What was more important was that Curtis trusted him. Smith had told Curtis what he intended to do and the American had volunteered. Not rashly: he was a long way from being a fool and was well aware of the risks. So he must trust Smith.

Smith wondered why?

He turned forward and saw Sanders as restless as himself, the Sub's fingers curling and twitching on the glasses that hung against his chest. It was no wonder that Sanders was nervous. He had done well when Dunbar was killed but he would have his hands full tonight. He was young...

The voice of Lorimer called through the pipe from the chart-table where he was plotting their course, "Six minutes on this leg, sir. An'— and that's it."

"Thank you." Smith answered absently, thinking that if Sanders was a boy, then what about the seventeen-year-old Lorimer? An infant. He felt again very old and muttered, "Don't be a bloody fool."

Sanders turned. "Sir?"

"Nothing. You know what you have to do?"

"Yes, sir. I patrol, passing your start–point every fifteen minutes."

"For two hours. And then?"

"I go to wait at the rendezvous for *Marshall Marmont* and inform her captain that the force is to return to Dunkerque."

Two hours was enough. "And if the enemy sights you?"

"I run like hell, sir." Sanders sounded doleful.

"Correct." Smith was quietly emphatic. It was not an order in the tradition of Nelson, but Sanders was not a Nelson and it was odds–on that any enemy boat would be twice *Sparrow*'s size. Smith flinched at the thought of Sanders becoming involved in any such night action.

He looked at his watch just as Lorimer called, "Time, sir."

"Stop both!"

The engines slowed, stopped, but an instant later the engine of the CMB roared into life then throttled back to a throaty mutter. She cast off her tow and sidled alongside *Sparrow*. A grimy stoker passed a bucket down to the CMB. Smith climbed down the ladder into the cockpit beside Curtis who stood at the wheel. "Carry on."

"Aye, aye, sir."

The CMB swung away from *Sparrow* and the mutter of the engines became a growl as she worked up speed. Smith, looking back caught a last glimpse of *Sparrow* and thought he saw her already moving ahead. Sanders was on his own now.

Curtis took the CMB up to only twelve knots and held her there, hardly cruising, but keeping the speed down kept down her bow-wave also and the wash that would otherwise mark her in the night. She slipped on through the sea, lifting and falling, bow smacking from wave to wave, so even at that speed and in that calm the spray came inboard.

To the south-east a flare hung in the sky, faded, died. A searchlight's beam wandered, was still, went out. There were gun flashes. Those were the lines of the trenches at Nieuport. The British would be licking their wounds and re-grouping, the Germans consolidating the ground won and preparing themselves against the inevitable counter-attack. The same old stalemate, the armies wrestling back and forth across the lines of trenches, gaining a few yards here, losing them there. Losing men all the time. Smith was certain the attack on the lines at Nieuport, successful though it had been, was not *Schwertträger*. It was nothing new, just another attack.

But they were closing the shore now, though it was still unseen. He thought they could damn near run aground before they saw the dunes on a night like this. Then the engines slowed to a mutter and Curtis said huskily, "Lights, dead ahead." Smith stared over the bow as it sank into the sea with the way coming off the boat. He saw the lights that blinked and were lost in the rain, come again so that they seemed to twinkle like distant stars or to move like fireflies but they were neither. They were lights on the shore or in the woods by De Haan.

He swallowed his excitement and kept his voice steady as he asked, "Are we on station?"

Curtis answered, "Almost, sir. I reckon we're less than a mile from the beach."

"Carry on."

The CMB puttered on softly; all of them, Curtis in the cockpit and Smith and Midshipman Johnson alongside it, the two men manning the Vickers guns forward and aft, all watched the lights.

Until the seaman forward at the Vickers called hoarsely, urgently, "Ship fine on the starboard bow!"

Curtis spun the CMB to port. They saw the black lift of the ship but only because she stood against the lights on the shore. She was making only a thread of smoke and was anchored, showing no lights at all. As they swung away the rain hid her completely but she had seemed so close that Smith's order was almost whispered. "Good enough. Stop her."

The way fell off the CMB and she lay hardly moving on that dead calm sea under the beat and hiss of the rain with the engines grumbling below. Had the lookouts on the enemy ship seen them? The CMB had seemed right on top of her but then Smith thought how the rain was falling and the CMB had made hardly any bow-wave or wash and had been throttled right back. No challenge came. No gun blazed at them out of the night and he said softly, "Let's get on with it."

Curtis turned over the wheel to Johnson. "You've got her, Mid." His two seamen set to work forward, casting off the lashings that held the tarpaulined hump on the fore-deck. It was Curtis's Red Indian canoe that he had made out of canvas and ply and paddled around Dunkerque harbour.

Smith and Curtis threw aside their oilskins and dragged off their boots. One of the seamen handling the canoe slipped and staggered as the CMB rolled gently under their shifting weight. Curtis called softly, pained, "Christ! Be careful! That's not a whaler you're banging about there!"

Smith dipped his hands into the bucket by his feet. It was a present from *Sparrow*'s stoke-hold and it held grease and soot. He smeared the blackness over his face and hands and Curtis did the same. It was a rough expedient but it served. All of them kept one eye and both ears cocked towards the unseen ship that yet was so close. Smith told Johnson, "When we've gone, haul clear of that ship, anchor and wait for us with the engines running, ready to slip if you have to make a bolt for it. Got that?"

The midshipman nodded, swallowed.

The canoe dropped into the sea and one seaman held it alongside while Curtis lowered himself gingerly into the stern and Smith cautiously followed in stockinged feet and sat down ahead of him. To Smith, used to dinghy and whaler, the canoe sat lightly on top of the water, seemed ready to dance on the surface of the sea. He took the compass and the paddle a seaman passed him but Curtis said, "Better if you just hang on to that paddle in case, sir, and let me do the work. There's a knack to this."

Smith nodded. Curtis said, "Shove off."

The seaman pushed the canoe out from the CMB and it bobbed there alarmingly until Curtis dug in his paddle and it slid forward. The CMB was lost in the darkness and they were alone on the dark sea though it was a minute or so before the mutter of the engines finally faded behind them. The canoe was a new experience for Smith, so light and so low in the water that it was as if he were swimming. She rode the quiet sea well enough but inevitably water slopped in. Curtis used the paddle with an experienced economy of movement, steadily and without a deal of splashing that would have made a white blaze in the dark, pointing the bow of the canoe at the pin-pricks of lights on the shore. He was heading to the north of them so as not to lose ground to the tide that was streaming south-west now. They were not alone for long. The enemy ship was first a shadow that blotted out some of the lights and then a silhouette, taking shape against them. She was still seen only fuzzily through the rain but she was so close! Smith gestured with his left hand and Curtis wheeled the canoe to port to take them past the stern of the ship. Smith could make out a gun forward, two funnels, another gun amidships and a third right aft. She was a big boat, even allowing for the tricks played by darkness and his position right down on the sea. He thought she might be one of the S class boats and those guns would be four-inch. As the canoe slipped on she came abeam. She was anchored fore and aft to hold her against the tide.

"Sir!" Curtis's hiss snapped Smith's head around and he saw a second ship to port. Her stern lifted tall out of the sea where she too was anchored and that stern was little more than a cable's length from the first destroyer in line ahead. The canoe was slipping between them but was only a shadow on a sea filled with shadows. He could see the barrel of the gun on the destroyer's foredeck, behind it the lift of the bridge and the tracery of mast and rigging.

Two of them. At anchor. If they had been at sea and met *Sparrow*! Were there others ahead or astern of them? Why were they anchored here?

The canoe slipped on as Curtis thrust steadily with the paddle. There was water slapping around Smith's thighs now and he used his cupped hands to bail but only for a few moments. The destroyers were barely lost behind them when Curtis swung the bow of the canoe to port again. Another ship grew out of the night ahead of them, lower in the water this one and smaller, with one tall funnel amidships and a box of a wheelhouse before it. A tug. They swung around her stern and she, too, was anchored fore and aft and as they swept almost under her counter, light spilled across her deck and the sea as a hatch was opened. They heard the wheeze of a concertina and a man singing slowly, sadly, then the hatch closed and chopped off the light and the voice. For long seconds their night vision was destroyed, then slowly the lights grew out of the darkness again as Curtis drove the canoe on towards the shore. Smith watched the lights come up, thinking. Two big destroyers anchored close inshore, so close inshore as to have precious little water under them at low tide though the tide was flowing now. Were there more? A tug anchored a cable's length inshore of the destroyers. Was she alone or was there another?

But now he could see more than just the lights, unaware that he was leaning far forward, bent almost double in his eagerness. He could see among them and beyond them and he heard the startled intake of breath behind him as Curtis also stared ahead at the beach and the scene took on shape and life as the canoe closed the shore, as if a curtain were lifted on a stage.

The stage was set. Smith thought: *Schwertträger!*

The lights were like fireflies, not like stars now because they darted and hovered and he could see the hurrying figures of the men who carried them. But he did not look at the men or the lights but at what they showed. He could see them in the dancing light of the electric torches, and count them. He counted twenty but thought there were more further along the beach that he could not make out, the rain blurring them. The twenty he had counted lay at the water's edge, stern to the sea and so close to each other they were almost touching. They were square-ended lighters and looked to be around thirty to forty feet long and over ten feet wide. Morris, the airman, had said, 'Like a shoebox.

There were others still coming down to the sea. A team of horses, six of them harnessed two by two, laboured down the beach under a cracking whip, hauling a wide-wheeled bogey on which rested another of the lighters. Behind it was another team and another lighter. Morris had said they were hauling the boat in. No doubt they had been. But before that they had hauled it *out* to the water's edge, the engineers rehearsing their parts for this, the performance. They were hauling the lighters down through a gap in the wall of the dunes from the woods where they had been collected and hidden. Smith turned to look at Curtis and saw his face glistening oily black under the rain with the whites of the eyes showing and a flash of teeth. He was not paddling but breathing softly through his mouth as if even the sound of his breathing might give them away. Smith called softly, "Closer."

Curtis glanced at him, then at the beach that already seemed too close for comfort, then back at Smith. But Smith was certain the rain and the darkness would hide them from the engineers who swarmed on the beach, who were working like demons against the clock because they had to beat the tide. And the tugs and destroyers were too far out to spot the tiny black shadow on the sea that was the canoe.

Curtis thought, Much closer an' you can step over the side and wade in for a real good look. But he wielded the paddle so that the canoe pointed its stern towards the shore again and crept in on the lighters. They crept in until what was a murmur of sound became clear orders, bawled across and up the beach. Voices became linked with individuals, figures; Smith could almost hear the words as they carried over the soft wash of the surf. Now the lighters and the men were close and Smith could judge the size of the lighters against the quick-moving figures of the men and it only confirmed his original estimate of their size.

He saw the team of horses turning then backing down the last shallow slope of the beach with men at their heads as other men heaved at the wheels of the bogey, running it into the surf. The team stopped and engineers moved in on the shoreward end of the bogey. He saw them working and that the bow of the lighter was rising. The front of the bogey was being jacked up; the lighter slid slowly back off as the whip cracked and the horses plunged then settled to the collar and drew the bogey away. The lighter rested on the shore with its stern in the surf. A torch moved for a second over the stern of the lighter and Smith saw the propeller, the rudder, and thought each boat probably had a small petrol engine. He could smell petrol.

Forty of them, and more. As the canoe pushed through the darkness against the set of the tide and parallel to the shore he could see the line of lighters still stretching on into the night. Each would hold – what? A platoon – more likely half a company? The men were coming down the beach now as the last of the lighters were brought down, moving in black phalanxes tipped by a rippling fringe of muzzles of slung rifles. The marines who had boarded the train at Zeebrugge but never arrived at Ostende. A phalanx headed for each lighter and they looked to be half a company or close to it. One-two-three thousand men? A ghost army, their boots stepping rigidly in time but silent on the sand against the cracking of the whips and the bawled orders.

And guns. They were being hauled down by teams of horses and there was a crane on a bogey to hoist each gun into a lighter. The guns rolled on wheels inordinately wide, wheels wide as barrels so they rode easier and those wide wheels would have even more point when the guns had to be disembarked because there would be no horses on the waiting beach...

Curtis paddled delicately, slowly, seeing those troops close, the engineers at work, thinking, How much farther? How much longer? For God's sake! Does he want to count their buttons?

Smith still stared at the shore. A flat calm. A dark, rainy night. A spring tide that would be high at 4.10 a.m., just before dawn, in that first twilight before the sun rose. The tugs to tow the lighters to Nieuport and the destroyers as escort for all of them. They would be less than three hours at sea and the tugs would slip the lighters and Morris's shoe-boxes would start their little engines that would yet be big enough to drive the lighters inshore on a flowing tide, through the last of the shallows that the tugs could not pass and into the surf to ground on the beach...

Time.

That first grey light was barely four hours away. The German engineers had run a race against the clock. They'd had to start bringing down the lighters as the tide still fell so that they would be lined along the beach ready to float when the tide started to flow and with four hours or more to spare before high water. The lighters would have to be worked out until the tugs could pick them up and pass the tow. Then three hours at sea at four or five knots. They'd had no more than two hours between the ebbing of the tide below the water-line now and this moment when the sea returned – but they had done it. So the lighters would be loaded with their men and their guns easily while their flat bottoms rested solidly on the shore. No soldier would need to wade out to a lighter to climb aboard.

The crane was whirring and engineers were climbing over the gun, ducking under the barrel, fixing the strops. The whirring note of the crane rose and so did the gun and it was swung into one of the lighters. As the strops were thrown off so lashings were put on, securing it against the sea passage.

The engineers had won their race.

Smith had his still to run. He turned and saw Curtis's eyes, white against the black goo on his face, flicking towards the beach. His mouth was wide but whether to breathe or just gaping Smith could not tell. Smith said softly, "Home!"

Curtis's eyes flicked back to him and he nodded. A stroke of the paddle spun the prow of the canoe away from the shore and it headed out to sea. Smith bailed but with his head turned on his shoulder and watching the beach. The surf was nudging at the sterns of the lighters, reaching halfway up towards their blunt bows. They would float on the tide in less than an hour.

He looked down at the compass and checked their heading, looked up and saw the tug but knew it was not the one they had seen on the way in. This one seemed bigger, standing higher out of the water but her mast was shorter. So there were two at least. At least. There were more than forty lighters to be towed.

They shot past her stern and on into the night. Curtis still drove steadily, unhurriedly, with the paddle. A third destroyer loomed and Curtis tried to haul off from her but with only partial success as the tide was setting them down on her. They passed her close, too close for Curtis who swore softly. The canoe was low in the sea, far below the destroyer's deck but the lights from the shore were behind them, might show them up. He worked the paddle with his shoulders hunched for the shouted challenge, the shot, but it did not come.

How many destroyers might there be, anchored in that long line offshore? Smith calculated, guessed: five, six? He thought five, at least. He bent over the compass, watched their heading and stuck out right hand or left as a helm order to Curtis.

And he thought it was so simple and how could it have eluded him? The lighters were no more than timber boxes, probably brought down to the woods by De Haan in sections and then put together. He had seen timber lighters like this used for landing troops in the Dardanelles. A spring tide at Nieuport. Yesterday's attack there had taken the enemy to the north bank of the Yser. There they were halted but the crossing would come tomorrow. With that first grey dawning the lighters would run aground behind the British lines at Nieuport and the troops would charge ashore. They might have a hatch to let out the guns but more likely they would just smash out a section of the box-like bow and run the guns ashore and up the beach on their fat wheels. In the first half-light the British at Nieuport would be attacked in the rear by two or three thousand crack troops, picked men with their own field-guns, as the other attack came in across the Yser. Once across the Yser they could sweep down the coast to Dunkerque, turning the flank of the British Army, cutting the lines of its communications and supplies, thrusting on to Calais...

The U-boat commander had been involved and Smith could guess how; they would have sent him and his boat to creep off Nieuport one night and confirm the depths along the line of the shore. And when he did not return they'd then sent another.

A spring tide because, though it only came twice a month, it rose higher than the normal tides by two to three feet. So on that shallow beach the grounding lighters would discharge their racing troops much nearer their objective.

Schwertträger... sword–bearer... stab in the back.

It was so obvious now. For three years the Generals had schemed and planned to try to break the deadlock on the Western Front. What was more obvious than an attack in rear? Trist had even given him the answer, thrust it under his nose only hours before when he said the British planned a landing on this coast to take the Germans in the rear. Even then Smith had not seen it.

Schwertträger had one subtlety. The obvious places on this coast to assemble lighters were the ports of Ostende and Zeebrugge. They could be brought down the canals. But the Navy bombarded both ports and there were thousands of Belgian eyes to note the massing of the lighters and pass word of the concentration by means of pigeons or secret agents like Josef. So. Don't use a port at all. Use a stretch of coast suitable for nothing but fishing boats, where there were few people and woods right down to the dunes to hide the lighters. And seal it off.

If only he'd had the courage of his convictions, if he had not bungled, if he had somehow seen to it that this reconnaissance was made twenty–four hours earlier. But he had not and the force was on the point of sailing. *For Christ's sake where was Curtis's CMB?*

Then he heard the mutter of its idling engines and the muttering grew into a low throbbing and it was suddenly there, the low, black hull, nearly as invisible as the canoe, lifting out of the darkness.

Curtis steered towards it. A seaman crouched just aft of the cockpit called softly and raised an arm. They slid in alongside the CMB with a final thrust of Curtis's paddle. Smith grabbed at the side and as the seaman reached out to hold on to the canoe, Smith shoved the compass at him and hurled himself aboard the CMB. "Slip! Full speed ahead for *Sparrow!*" He saw Curtis following, wide-mouthed and panting, face running with sweat as he shoved into the cockpit and took the wheel from Johnson.

The seaman was tugging at the canoe and Smith snapped, "Shove it off! Leave it!"

"Slipped!" The shout came from forward where a seaman crouched in the bow. The engines' note rose and the bow of the boat with it as she accelerated, starting to work up to her full speed of close on forty knots.

Smith sat down and pulled on his boots, dragging them on over wet socks. He was stiff and aching, soaked from backside to feet and stood up easing the clothes from his skin. He went to stand beside Curtis and stare ahead. After a moment he said, "You did very well. I'm sorry about your canoe but we're short of time."

Curtis shrugged and grinned. "To tell you the truth, sir, I was a sight more concerned about getting *me* back aboard this boat in one piece. I've never seen so many Germans and guns that close before." He did not add how he had watched Smith peering curiously, coldly, at the lighters, the troops, noting every detail on the beach. As if he was merely a spectator and they were not within hailing distance of a German beach and thousands of the enemy, and inshore of two or more destroyers. He glanced at Smith who stood with his arms crossed on the cockpit screen staring ahead as the spray wet his face and the wind blew at the fair hair. The fingers of one hand tapped restlessly, were still, and tapped again.

Smith thought that *Marshall Marmont* should be up with them at first light but first light would be too late; by then the lighters would be aground at Nieuport. He could run at full speed for Dunkerque and give the alarm but still the lighters would sail and once at sea they would be part of an armada. The destroyers from Zeebrugge would also be out in force and this time they would not 'shoot and scoot' to maintain a threat in being, because they could not abandon the lighters. They would fight. They could not win a battle like that but they would fight it to its bloody end. Both sides would lose and Britain the more because she could not afford such losses, she had to keep the sea.

There was no decision to make; his duty was obvious.

Spray soaked him now. The wind of the swift cruising of the CMB set the clothes dank against his skin and he shuddered all the time as he stared into the dark.

Curtis eyed him covertly and wondered what he would do. What could he do? Curtis was not a fool and had drawn his own conclusions and they were close to those of Smith.

Rain drove in on top of the spray, rain that was warm but stung their faces. Smith narrowed his eyes against it and saw the dark blur of her under the plume of her smoke as Curtis said, "*Sparrow* on the port bow."

The midshipman worked the lamp, a brief stab of light that was instantly acknowledged by a flicker from *Sparrow* taking shape before them, slipping slow and slower across their bow as the engines of the CMB dropped in tone from a rumble to a mutter. Curtis swung her around and slid her in towards the larger boat.

Sparrow was hardly moving now, and looked very small, even from the CMB – small and narrow and low in the water. She was not a ship to fight in a big action against odds but one to patrol, to observe and report. This was not a man-of-war, but an errand boy. But sometimes you had to call on a boy to do a man's work and more. Smith saw the figure of Sanders on her bridge, dwarfed by the towering bulk of the coxswain. He had confidence in Sanders now.

Lines came flying down from the deck of *Sparrow* and the CMB was drawn in alongside. Smith climbed aboard, ducked under the hood of the chart-table and bent over the chart, seeing the pencilled line of their track, their present position. Then with Curtis he went to the bridge where Sanders waited, relieved to see them, but on edge. Lorimer came on the run and Smith gathered them together and gave his orders. He had only to tell them what they were to do and that did not take long. He asked, "Any questions?"

They stood silently a moment then shook their heads. "No, sir." The rain felt warm on their faces, the air was thick, sultry, as *Sparrow* lay barely moving.

Smith wiped at his face and peered at them. "Remember the prime objective. The lighters must be destroyed. I don't need to tell you that the attack must be pressed home at all costs."

He did not and they knew what such an attack would mean.

Curtis went down into his CMB and she cast off and edged away with him standing tall at the wheel. Johnson sat at the torpedo firing controls. Her slim shape had the deadliness of a sword blade but she was as fragile as a match-box. She was to attack the centre of the line of destroyers while *Sparrow* struck at the head.

Smith ordered, "Full ahead both. Starboard ten."

Gow answered, "Starboard ten, sir."

Sparrow began to move forward through the sea and the darkness and her bow swung towards the unseen coast as Smith stood at the compass. "Meet her... Steady. Steer that."

"Course one-five-oh, sir."

The beat of the engines increased, built up slowly, steadily. Ten knots... fifteen... until the frame of the old ship began to tremble. The rain was still with them but slashing now as they drove into it, the air fresh on their faces. Thunder rumbled suddenly close as if the guns at Nieuport had crept up on them in the night. The rain was good. They needed it more than ever now.

Twenty knots and the darkness still shrouded them but now there was a glow at the tops of *Sparrow*'s funnels and a flick of flame against the cloud-hung sky. The engines' racing set the whole fabric of the ship to shaking and rattled every loose object aboard.

Soon now. The coxswain stood rock-steady, swaying to the motion. Spray from the tearing stern was bursting back over the turtle-back foredeck and over the bridge screen. Sanders stood with one steadying hand on the screen and its splinter mattress and the vibration that shook the ship seemed to be transmitted through him. His face was taut, nerves strung tight.

Smith stooped over the voice pipe. "Gunner!"

"Sir!" The torpedo-gunner's voice came from his position aft on the torpedo platform.

"We'll engage to port."

"Port! Aye, aye, sir!"

257

The look-outs on the German destroyers would have their eyes screwed against the rain and maybe, just maybe, shirking the job. But still they must see the whiff of flame from each of *Sparrow*'s three funnels. Smith stared briefly out to port and astern. Curtis and his CMB should be out there somewhere keeping station on *Sparrow* and he thought he saw the white flash of a bow-wave but could not be sure. Looking ahead he could see the lights on the shore now and *Sparrow*'s bow pointed at the southern end of them. He knew there were two destroyers anchored there and he believed a line of them stretched north, parallel with the lights and with a cable's length between ships it could be a line a thousand yards long.

And then the lightning struck down at the sea. It stood a jagged, blue-white blaze for a second and it showed them in that camera-shutter glimpse the destroyers ahead, anchored in a long line across *Sparrow*'s course and stretching away – five, *six* of them! Then the lightning was gone and the night came down as the thunder cracked again and close now.

Six. But he had guessed right: a line of a thousand yards.

Sparrow charged down on them out of the night, making better than twenty knots and in the stokehold they were still furiously stoking the fires. The flames now licked long tongues from the tops of her funnels. A winking light pricked the darkness and that was a German challenge. For once, right on their own coast and under their own batteries they were uncertain whether another ship was friend or foe. Smith shouted up at the rating on the searchlight platform, "Now!" And at Sanders: "All guns commence!"

"All guns commence!" Sanders's piercing yell came as the searchlight stabbed its beam across the night to dart about the surface of the sea then settle, glaring, on the second destroyer in the line. Smith could see the one ahead of her and the other astern as shadows outside the searchlight's beam. The twelve-pounder right alongside Smith on the bridge kicked, spat flame and roared. The smoke whipped past him and the killick's yell came, "Load!" as the empty case bounced across the deck. The two six-pounders below the bridge, one on either side, opened up together, snapping quickly away, a sharper note to the slower slamming of the twelve-pounder. Sanders crouched over the torpedo-sight by the voice pipe running aft to the torpedo-gunner and he would be aiming at the third or fourth in the line. As they tore down on the line so the silhouettes of the ships foreshortened in the torpedo-sight but so would the gaps between them. A miss would be nearly impossible.

Sparrow was on a course to ram the leading destroyer that was racing up at them out of the night, but Smith held on until Sanders shouted, "Fire!" He saw the torpedo leap out from *Sparrow*'s side and plunge into the sea.

Then he ordered, shouting at Gow's ear, "Port ten!" And: "Slow ahead!" He saw the wheel going over in Gow's long fingers and the engine-room telegraphs worked but did not hear their clanging. Every gun in the ship except the six-pounder right aft was firing now and *Sparrow* was scoring hits on both the leading destroyer and the second in line that was still in the searchlight's beam. The enemy destroyers were firing back, a ripple of flashes running down that long line of shadowy ships but they hadn't had time to get the range and *Sparrow* was a flying figure half-hidden in the dark. Smith did not see a shell fall near them but that would not last. The destroyers would get their chance. He bawled at the rating above him: "Douse that light!" The beam was cut off, the carbons in the lamp glowed briefly and died. The searchlight was a finger that pointed both ways, would point out *Sparrow* to the enemy destroyers.

Sparrow's head was coming around and he ordered, "Meet her! Steady! Steer that!"

Sparrow raced into the gap between the first and second destroyers though the way was coming off her rapidly now with the screws turning slow ahead. That was what Smith wanted. Speed, what *Sparrow* had of it, had served its turn. Now it was manoeuvrability and steadiness that was needed and as the thirty-knotter shot between the two big boats he ordered, "Port ten!" *Sparrow*'s head came around again. As she swung to point her stern to run down inshore of the destroyers' line her way took her on, sliding sideways. The first of the tugs was suddenly close and from *Sparrow*'s bridge they were looking down on her deck and seeing the faces in her wheelhouse as the lightning struck down again. "Meet her! Steady on that!" *Sparrow* thrust away from the tug and left her astern. The turtle-back bow was riding steady now and the stern sent no spray flying. *Sparrow* was down below ten knots and her speed still falling.

Sanders stared miserably at Smith. "Torpedo must have missed, sir. Sorry."

Smith shrugged. "You'll get another chance." Maybe. But it was cruel luck to miss that almost unbroken line of ships. Maybe the torpedo veered away or dived too deep or just didn't damn well work. It happened.

And where was Curtis?

Curtis had been ordered to attack the centre of the line as *Sparrow* broke through at the head of it. He had held the CMB to port of *Sparrow* and astern of her until the searchlight's beam stabbed out from her bridge. Then he thrust the throttle wide open and turned to shout at Johnson, "Attacking!" He saw young Midshipman Johnson nod where he crouched over the torpedoes then Curtis turned forward. The CMB had been cruising at twenty knots but now she had her stern tucked down and her bow was lifting. He saw *Sparrow* fire her torpedo and start to turn. Then the CMB slid up level with the old thirty-knotter seen as a shadow at the thin end of a searchlight beam, a shadow sprouting flame from her funnels – and from her guns. She trailed smoke from both. The CMB was abreast of her an instant then racing on. Rain battered against the screen and Curtis squinted against it, head half-turned as the CMB tore in at thirty knots and still accelerating.

He first saw them as shadows like clouds but a split second later they took shape as ships that lifted huge and clear out of the darkness, ships that were firing every gun they had and one or two of them at the CMB because Curtis saw the spouts of water as shells landed in the sea. He wanted one ship. He picked the one and eased the wheel over so that the stern, out of the sea and bouncing now as the CMB ripped across that calm sea, pointed at the bridge of the destroyer fourth in the line.

Steady.

Tracer like bright beads sliding at him out of the night, going over his head...

Steady... Now!

"*Fire!*"

He was ready to turn the wheel as soon as the torpedo took the water, to swing the CMB out of the torpedo's track. He was ready for the kick of the hydraulic ram and to feel the plunge and lift as the torpedo was fired stern-first out of the chute.

Johnson bawled, "Firing gear jammed!"

"Secure!" Curtis turned the wheel and the CMB swung away from the destroyer in a tight, wheeling curve and raced into the night. He eased the throttle back so the boat cruised again at around twenty knots and looked around to see Johnson and the torpedoman crouched over the firing gear. Curtis shouted, "What about it?" And: "You've got ten seconds!"

The torpedoman gave a wash-out sign with his hands. "No go, sir!"

"We'll try the other tube!" Curtis turned his head, turned the boat and opened the throttle. Smith had been relying on him for a diversion. Jammed firing gear. *Bloody* luck!

Sparrow hauled away from the tug and Smith used the megaphone to bawl down the deck on the starboard, shoreward side: "Lighters first! Pass the word!" He saw McGraw, layer of the six-pounder in the waist, lift a hand in acknowledgment then turn his head to bawl aft. There was no need to give any orders to the guns on the port side. The destroyers loomed close, a bare hundred yards away and asking to be hit.

As *Sparrow* hauled away from that first tug the shore opened up and Smith shouted up at the searchlight plat-form: "Expose!" He pointed. The searchlight crackled into life as the carbons struck arc and the beam leapt out to sweep the shore. A second later it was joined by the searchlight aft and the two white fingers lit up the box-like lighters in the surf, showing the gun barrels protruding, the heads of the men already aboard, the troops still filing down the beach. The range was about eight hundred yards. *Sparrow* was only moving at seven or eight knots and she rode rock-steady now in that flat calm. She pushed down between the two lines, of anchored destroyers to seaward and anchored tugs inshore with the lighters eight hundred yards beyond the tugs. The lines were a couple of hundred yards apart and she ran down between them firing every gun including the Vickers machine guns. And the destroyers, because their own tugs were so close, held their fire.

McGraw shouted, "It's like shooting clay-pipes in a bluidy fairground!"

The six-pounder was firing as fast as his loader could ram the projectile and close the breech. *Sparrow* fired at point-blank range into the helpless destroyers with the flash of discharge and then of burst seeming to come as one. The storm was right over them now. Over the hammering of the guns was the continual *crack!* and rumble of thunder, lightning stabbed again and again at the sea that hissed under the rain. Smith could see wreckage leaping skywards, holes suddenly punched in hulls, smoke swirling on the wind and flame that spurted, subsided, but grew again to breed more smoke. *Sparrow* scored hits on the destroyers but she utterly destroyed the lighters as she steamed down between the lines. The destroyers were built to fight, to take punishment, but the lighters were timber and built for one short sea passage in quiet waters. Even the little shells from the six-pounders smashed holes in them, tore through from bow to stern and set the timber smouldering. In seconds one of the petrol engines ignited and that lighter burned and they lay within arms-reach of one another. As *Sparrow* moved down the line, raking the lighters, Smith saw the troops in those ahead scrambling over the side and running up the beach. An officer with drawn sword stood on the beach trying to hold them but they ran clear of the line of fire that was reducing the fleet of lighters to matchwood. And like matchwood it was burning.

McGraw said, "Jesus! Did ye iver see the like o' that?"

He laid the gun, blinked as a tug showed between *Sparrow* and the shore. The loader shouted, "Skipper said the boats!"

McGraw muttered, "Take her *and* the boats," jerked the lanyard and bawled, "Load!" The shell tore through the tug's funnel.

"Ready!"

McGraw's eye went to the sight as the shore and the lighters showed again under the sweeping beams of the searchlights. The six-pounder jerked and recoiled.

Sparrow steamed down to the end of the line and as she reached it they saw the last tug trying to weigh anchor with the capstan hammering. The twelve-pounder fired into her on the water-line and below the funnel and she blew off steam. "Port ten! Douse the lights!" The searchlights' beams snapped off. Smith's voice was hoarse. "Mr. Sanders! I'm going back down the line! You'll get a chance with the other tube! Engage to starboard!"

"Starboard! Aye, aye, sir." Sanders bent to the voice pipe to tell the torpedo-gunner. "We'll engage to starboard!"

Smith ordered, "Midships!... Starboard ten!" *Sparrow* had swung around past the stern of the last destroyer in the line and he saw that she had slipped and was moving, going astern to get clear of the line but her head swinging seawards. He shouted at Sanders and pointed and Sanders waved. The starboard helm brought *Sparrow*'s head turning towards the shore again so she was describing a tight circle. Sanders crouched over the torpedo sight. The destroyer that had way on her was over *Sparrow*'s starboard quarter... now coming abeam as *Sparrow* came around...

Sanders croaked, "Fire!" He sounded as hoarse as Smith felt.

The torpedo, *Sparrow*'s second and last plunged over the side into the sea and its track ran away into the night. The German boat was boxing the compass as she tried to turn on her heel and haul out of the line. Smith saw her steady then and ease forward, heading seaward and he thought: We'll miss her! And: She won't miss us. The destroyer was firing and there was a crash aft and they felt the jar of it through the deck and the blast that pushed at them. Splinters clanged off the funnel and whirred across the bridge.

Sanders reported, "Think it was the tubes, sir." And a moment later: "Gunner doesn't answer." Another crash aft and Smith winced. That destroyer was firing her four-inch guns and *Sparrow* could not stand much of that. He saw Buckley still at the back of the bridge below the searchlight platform and beckoned him. As *Sparrow*'s stern pointed again at the gap between the lines of anchored destroyers and tugs he ordered, "Meet her..."

To Buckley: "Report the damage aft!"

"Aye, aye, sir!"

Smith told Gow, "Steer that!" But Gow knew already, was holding *Sparrow* on the line to take her back between tugs and destroyers, a line as if ruled in chalk on a board.

Sanders was squinting at his watch and now looked at Smith. "Missed again, sir."

"Not surprised, the way she was shifting about to haul out of the line."

The voice pipe from the torpedo-platform whistled and Smith bent to it. "Bridge!"

Buckley's voice came up the pipe. "Gunner's hurt bad, sir. They're taking him below, an' the crew of the six-pounder right aft, but the gun's all right. I've got a feller here to load for me an' I'll work it with your permission, sir."

"Carry on!"

"Aye, aye, sir!"

Smith straightened then ducked instinctively as another four-inch shell from the destroyer ripped over the mast-head. He could see her, just, and she was turning her head from the sea so as to fire broadside at her target. The gap between the lines of destroyers and tugs offered some sort of brief sanctuary again but *Sparrow* had yet to reach it. Lightning played far down the line and showed others of the destroyers moving, one of the tugs swinging inshore from her bow anchor.

Still no sign of Curtis. He wondered if the CMB had taken an unlucky hit right at the start. One of those four-inch shells would blow the fragile little craft apart.

The CMB was up on the step and tearing in again towards the coast and the ships. Curtis prayed that the second torpedo would not jam. For a second he had *Sparrow*'s searchlights as a mark then they went out but now he could see the destroyers against the light of the fires that burned along the shore and he knew what the fires were. He saw he was heading for the tail of the line but held his course. There was a ship, a destroyer there, last of the line and she was hauling out of it, her silhouette foreshortening as her bow pointed towards him. All this seen over the bucking bow of the CMB through the spray that came back in two long, white wings as if she was nearly flying.

Curtis shouted again, "Attacking!"

The destroyer was still turning, presenting her side to him and as he looked past her bow, to port that is, he could make out another ship beyond her. *Sparrow?* Both of them flickered with muzzle-flashes, both of them firing hard. *Sparrow* seemed to be only creeping – was she disabled? He swore softly. But the German boat was leaping up at them and broadside now. He saw no water-spouts but heard the rip of the shells overhead and knew they were firing over, the speed of the CMB cheating the layers. Then the lightning came again and a clap of thunder like the last trump that even drowned the roar of the engines. In that split-second, blue-white blaze he saw the destroyer and she was big ahead of him.

Close!

Nearly...

Now! "*Fire!*" And this time he felt the kick at the stern and his heart leapt with it. He turned to port to swing out of the torpedo's track and away from the destroyer and the CMB hurtled out into the dark with the guns still vainly following her, shells falling now in her wake.

Smith saw the CMB in that frozen instant of light that showed the big destroyer and the now ragged line of the rest of them, the tugs, the burning lighters with the flames momentarily made pale, the tiny scurrying figures on the shore. He saw the CMB without Sanders's high-pitched yell and out-thrust, pointing finger. She was racing in with her stern high and the rest of her almost hidden by the curtain of spray that glittered in the light. Then the night clamped down around them once more and their night vision was lost, though the burning lighters were still clear. Firing briefly ceased as the layers rubbed at their eyes and blinked away the wheeling stars.

The flame seemed hardly more than a muzzle-flash but it showed the climbing spout of water on the far side of the destroyer at the tail of the line and showed her lurch, then the thump of the explosion came shuddering across the sea and Lorimer shouted, "Got him! Oh, bloody good, Curtis!"

The explosion was followed an instant later by another. This time the flame could not be taken for a muzzle-flash. It soared out of the waist of the ship as if it would never cease climbing and with it went whirling debris and after it poured the smoke. This time Lorimer did not shout but gaped silently as the flame dwindled, the smoke spread and the destroyer rolled over on her side and showed her bottom.

A flash from the torpedo's explosion igniting a magazine? Smith thought so. But the certainty was that she would sink in seconds.

He turned away. "Full ahead both!"

The rain became a deluge. They were back between the lines, running through that narrow neck of water and now some of the destroyers' guns, tormented beyond bearing by this wisp of a ship that had fired on them with impunity, fired in return. They took the chance of hitting a tug, of firing on their own ships, and some of them did. But some of them hit *Sparrow*. This time Buckley pumped shell after shell at what remained of the lighters and into the tugs. McGraw found he had a different kettle of fish. His targets, the destroyers, loomed big as houses but these were firing back. He still fired the little six-pounder as fast as his sweating, swearing loader could feed it.

For long, mad minutes they were between the lines but then they came up on the last destroyer and she had slipped and was moving ahead. Smith shouted, "Starboard ten!" *Sparrow* swung to slide past the big boat's stern and the open sea lay before her. Out of the night burst the CMB with both of her Vickers machine-guns manned and hammering away at the destroyers' decks and bridges as she tore past them. She spun away from the line, the machine-guns fell silent and that tight turn brought her sweeping close to *Sparrow* before racing out into the darkness again.

Smith ordered the signalman, "Make the 'recall' to the CMB." The light flickered and out in the darkness another replied.

Sparrow was working up speed again now and making fifteen knots. The crew of the twelve-pounder stood around panting, with heaving chests. They were stripped to the waist, soot-smeared, running with sweat and the rain that coursed down over their heads and bodies. Their gun would no longer bear on the ships lying astern. The six-pounders aft and in the waist still banged away and *Sparrow* was still under fire. Rain hid the ships now but their gun flashes marked them and Smith knew that was all Buckley and McGraw had to aim at, and that was the case with their opposite numbers in the enemy destroyers.

He told Sanders, "Cease firing!"

In the ringing silence that followed he ordered, "Revolutions for fifteen knots." If there was pursuit they would elude it by stealth and not speed, not by hammering away with flames from the funnels to give them away. He found he was moving slowly and it was an effort to think. The men stood around dumbly, numbly under the rain. Maybe they weren't sure that they were still alive? He wasn't sure himself. He had no right to be. He had known it was an awful risk from the beginning but surprise had carried them through the first of it. Then when he had steered to enter that narrow lane again he had known it was a death trap, that the destroyer firing at him at the tail of the line would run along the outside of it and catch him as he came out. It was a box that he and *Sparrow* would never get out of. But then Curtis had attacked. He could close his eyes and see the CMB roaring in...

He said, "Mr. Lorimer! Get back to your chart and keep our track. I want to be outside the nets before daylight. Mr. Sanders! Check every gun and report to me. We stay at action stations till I order otherwise." There was no bridge messenger. "I want a messenger on the bridge. Whoever you send, tell him first to get hold of the cooks and they're to produce a hot drink and any grub for the men that they can knock up."

The ship came to slow life again as the hands turned to, repairing damage where they could, clearing the rolling, empty cartridge cases from the deck, throwing wreckage over the side. Brodie reported three dead, one of them the gunner, and eleven wounded. Smith heard him tell McGraw and heard his reply: "The rest of us are bloody lucky to be alive. I cannae believe it."

Smith stood on the bridge and when his hands started to shake he jammed them in his pockets.

Lucky to be alive. But it was over now.

There was no more lightning and the thunder rumbled away in the distance. The rain eased, stopped. When *Sparrow* stole cautiously through the gap in the mine-nets the cloud-cover was breaking up and stars showed. It was now just a warm, still summer's night.

Chapter 10

He stood on *Sparrow*'s bridge and he was very tired but he told himself it was over now, that he only had to wait awhile until it was day to see the end of it. *Sparrow* slipped softly over that still, dark sea at an easy ten knots, steadily patrolling up and down outside the mine-net barrage and waiting for dawn. Smith wanted to see the results of the night's action, and proposed to run in through the gap in the mine-nets and close the shore until he could see. He was certain there would be nothing but the wreckage of the lighters but he wanted to present a visual report of that. And if, incredibly, the big destroyers still lay there? Well, *Marshall Marmont* should be up soon with her two big guns to give him cover. He did not believe they would be needed. After the night attack the enemy would suspect that a large force was at sea and *Sparrow* only a small part of it. They would have gone home.

He would go when he had finished the job.

Sanders stepped up on to the bridge with a mug of tea steaming in either hand and offered one to Smith. Sanders, like all of them, like the ship herself, was the worse for wear. His jacket was scorched and had great holes burnt in it. What light there was showed him hollow-eyed. Smith thought the boy would sleep for a week when they reached port and that he had earned it, as *Sparrow* had earned the rest she would get in dockyard hands. Both torpedo-tubes were mangled, one of her six-pounders was twisted and useless and another had been blown over the side. At the moment it did not matter about the tubes because she had no torpedoes left to fire anyway. But there was a hole in the deck aft, a lump chewed out of her stern and another hole in the turtle-back fo'c'sle. A shell had burst between the first and second funnels and blasted away more of the wreckage of the wireless shack. It was a bitterly ironic thought that if the wireless operators had survived *Sparrow's* previous actions they would still have died in this one. Yet miraculously she still functioned as a fighting-ship. She had the twelve-pounder and three of her six-pounders and they had been cleared of what wreckage could be cut away. She had not been holed below or near the water-line and her engines were intact.

Like the rest of them, she had survived.

Not all. There were the three dead and eleven wounded men below in the wardroom.

The crew were still at action stations but though the look-outs were awake, the men at the guns slept where they were, curled on the deck or propped against the mountings. Smith could see them heaped around the twelve-pounder. They sprawled as if struck down and slept like the dead. He envied them.

He turned and looked astern to where the CMB kept station on them but all he could see was the white splash of her bow-wave. Earlier she had run alongside and Smith had seen that she, too, was scarred but Curtis had reported the torpedo firing-gear repaired. And said longingly, "What a night for a man to go fishing."

Smith grinned tiredly. Victoria Baines had taught that boy some bad habits. Fishing from one of His Majesty's ships! Or had he taught her, as he had fished when a farmer's son in the creek by his home? And that was not so long ago.

His smile faded as he faced forward. It was quiet. So quiet that but for the hum of the fans and the engines' soft beat they would be able to hear the guns at Nieuport that never stopped. He thought that in the German lines the troops would be standing to for the dawn and maybe a British counter-attack. But not to attack themselves. Not now. It would start to get light soon. Already he thought the visibility was gradually...

"Ship fine on the starboard bow!" The look-out called hoarsely, pointed. "Think it's the tug, sir!" It was the tug *Lively Lady* trudging down on them and as the gap between them closed Smith made out, astern of her at the end of the tow, the flat-iron shape of *Marshall Marmont*.

Sanders said, "She's right on time, sir." And when Smith grunted, sipping at the tea, "Pity we didn't leave her anything to do."

"I'm glad to see them." For he had sent them on a risky passage, at night and without an escort. Because it was another proof of the loyalty of Garrick, of all of them. They deserved to, and would, share in the success and that was what it was. *Marshall Marmont* would follow *Sparrow* home and nobody would laugh. He said, "Make to both of them: 'Well done. Good to see you.'"

The lamp clattered and a light winked in reply from the bridge of the monitor. "Glad to be here."

Marshall Marmont, his 'ship of force'. God, he was tired! When they got back there would be a blazing row over the way he had stolen her but he didn't care. The landing had been stopped, and he had been proved right.

He ordered, "Starboard ten." *Sparrow* had passed the monitor and now turned to swing around her stern and come up on her seaward side.

The landing. It had been a bold scheme and if it had gone through... He wondered absently how he would have done it, his weary mind trying to put himself in the enemy's place. Nieuport. There were shore batteries and a monitor was anchored at La Panne to defend against a landing but not such a one as this. Those little lighters would be close inshore before any alarm was given, would be on the beach before they came under fire and the destroyers would back them up. But how would the German attacking force defend itself from attack from the sea? He would want to create a diversion. That answer was obvious and so was the nature of the diversion: a threat to Dunkerque or the cross-Channel traffic of heavily-laden troop transports, so that the little ships of the Dover Patrol and the Dunkerque Squadron were torn two ways, a monstrous threat that they could not handle and for that he would want...

"Signal from *Marshall Marmont*, sir!"

Smith saw the light blinking urgently from her bridge as *Sparrow* came up level with her.

The signalman read, "Wireless from *Gipsy*: 'Enemy battlecruiser in sight. Course north-east. My position 51° 15' N 2° 15° E.'"

Gipsy was another old thirty-knotter. He thought she must have been very close to the battlecruiser to have seen her, lucky to have survived to send her message, but the night would help her.

He tried to take it in with all its implications, saw the signalman waiting, excited. He said thickly, "Acknowledge."

His interrupted train of thought lurched on – a monstrous threat to the cross-Channel traffic and Dunkerque. For that the enemy would want a ship of force, big, fast and heavily armed. A real ship of force slipping swiftly down the Dutch coast in the night to be on station in the Straits as the lighters ran in to the shore, ready to use her big guns to blast any ship in the Straits and to support the landing…

Boots hammered on the iron deck and Sanders hurled himself panting on to the bridge. "*Gipsy*'s just to the west of the Bergues Bank, sir." He had run to check the position on the chart.

Smith nodded. But the planned landing was now still-born. The battlecruiser knew and she had turned back – due north-east, because that was her course for home. He turned to stare into the night astern, to where she was somewhere over the rim of the world. He did not need to look at the compass to know he faced south-west. She was heading straight for him and his little flotilla.

There was a greyness to the night now. The day was coming.

Sparrow was nearly up with *Lively Lady* as the tug butted steadily onwards. Smith saw the signalman shaking the crew of the twelve-pounder into life, heard the killick's startled: "*battlecruiser!* Suffering Je—" Garrick would be looking across at him from the monitor's bridge, looking to him for orders while Garrick's ship was an inert mass dragged along by a tug under the command of an old woman and the battlecruiser was running down on them. Orders?

He said, "Make to both: Turn sixteen points to port. Course Two-three-oh!" And to Gow at the wheel: "Port ten."

"Port ten, sir."

Sparrow started to turn.

The battlecruiser would be racing; running for home she would work up to close on thirty knots. *Sparrow* could not make that but it would be forty-five minutes or so before the battlecruiser was in sight and that was time enough for Smith and *Sparrow* to scurry out to sea and out of the way. It was not time enough for the tug and Garrick and *Marshall Marmont*. The battlecruiser would hammer them to pieces. And then? North lay the crossing between the Hook of Holland and England and on that crossing was the 'beef' convoy. Trist had told him that the two thirty-knotters that should have been Smith's had been sent to help escort it. The convoy was assembling a couple of hours after first light and would sail at the speed of the slowest ship, eight knots if they were lucky but it might be less. Smith had bitter experience of that. The convoy would be strung out over twenty miles of sea and the escort would be a few thirty-knotters and armed yachts, one or two newer destroyers and, barely possibly, a light cruiser. They, too, would be spread over twenty miles of sea. The battlecruiser would come on them when they were an hour or so out and they couldn't scuttle back into Dutch waters. She would steam down the line of the convoy and through it and leave a trail of shattered and sunken ships.

Pakenham with the British battlecruiser force was in the Firth of Forth. But even if, by coincidence and a huge stroke of luck they received *Gipsy*'s signal and were ready to slip immediately they would never arrive in time. The Harwich force was closer but still not close enough. Both had the North Sea to cross. If Smith had forced a reconnaissance, got into the woods and discovered the lighters twenty-four hours earlier *and* thought the plan through, the Navy would have had a battleship force steaming this way...

If? That kind of speculation was useless, a waste of time. Again he tried to put himself in the enemy's place. Did the enemy know that his attack on the lighters had been a spur-of-the-moment decision forced on him? No. They would be thinking more reasonably that he *knew* they were there and his attack was planned, and *Sparrow* was only one part of a larger force...

Sparrow was on course now and so was the tug and *Marshall Marmont* but they had fallen astern as they had taken the wider turn and more slowly. He said rapidly, trying to keep pace with his racing thoughts, "Slow ahead both. Make to *Marshall Marmont* and *Lively Lady*: Cast off tow. *Marshall Marmont* will anchor and prepare for action." And to Gow: "Starboard five. Lay us alongside the tug."

As her speed fell away *Sparrow* sidled in alongside the oncoming tug until she ran along a dozen feet away. The tug was also slowing, tow drooping, two men working in the stern of her where the tow was secured. Smith stepped to the port wing of the bridge and made a funnel of his hands. "*Lively Lady!*" In that first grey light he could only see that the wheelhouse held a blur of faces but then its door opened, out came Victoria Baines and... He still held his hands cupped before his face and stared over them at Eleanor Hurst. On that warm morning she wore only a white blouse and a long skirt that the breeze of the tug's passage pressed against her legs. She held a hand to her hair. He stared until Victoria Baines called deeply, "What's the matter?"

He did not look at her but spoke to Eleanor Hurst, voicing his disbelief. "What are you doing aboard this tug?"

Victoria Baines snapped tartly, "Don't get on your high horse with me, young man! There's nothing wrong with this tug. I took the gel to a hotel so she got a bath. But then she was so wore-out she couldn't travel home so I found her a berth and just as well I did. She'd took a chill and spent most o' yesterday in her bunk. A sight better and safer than in a hotel full o' Frenchmen. And last night I told her where we were going but she wouldn't go ashore. Can't say as I blame her, either."

Eleanor said, "I spoke to you last night when you came alongside in the sailing boat." She sounded amused.

Smith accepted the situation because he had to. The girl looked pale and tired in that grey light but she was still smiling, watching him.

He looked away to Victoria Baines. "Cast off the tow and steer north-east. There's an enemy battlecruiser coming up and you'll be as well out of the way. Run into the Schelde if necessary." In the estuary of that Dutch, neutral river the tug would be safe from attack.

"What are you going to do?"

"Just keep an eye on things."

Victoria warned him, "Mind *you* don't get in the way of that battlecruiser. It looks as if you've been in enough trouble already."

"I'm not taking unnecessary risks. I don't believe in them." But anything that might save the convoy was necessary.

Victoria said severely, "Well, you be careful. How's that Curtis boy?"

Smith said dryly, "He's well – and wanting to go fishing."

She was laughing as she waddled aft to the tow, Tweedledum in her boiler-suit. "Fred! *Fred!* Where *is* that bloody man?"

Sparrow was pulling away from the tug, the gap widening between him and Eleanor Hurst. There was a lot he wanted to say but he only stared at her where she stood with hands at her sides and looked up at him. Until he ordered, "Starboard ten." *Sparrow* swung around the bow of the stopped tug, and the girl was hidden from him.

He said, "Mr. Sanders! Tell Mr. Curtis I want to see him aboard. And get the—" He could not say the dead. "Clear the wardroom. I'm transferring them all to *Marshall Marmont*. Make a signal to her that we're going alongside to do that." The monitor's surgeon would need that short notice to prepare for the wounded.

Sparrow turned a slow circle and nudged in alongside the monitor, was made fast. Smith went across to her where Garrick awaited him on the monitor's deck. Smith could see he had been up all night and was tense and anxious now but he grinned when he saw Smith. "Grand to see you, sir."

"And you!" Smith glanced around the deck. The anchor parties were hard at work fore and aft and they looked excited but cheerful enough. The wounded – and the dead – were coming across from *Sparrow* to be gently carried below.

Smith said, "I want a dozen men off your four-inch guns. Now. They come as they are."

Garrick shouted the order, then asked, "What do you plan to do, sir?"

Smith told him in a few sentences, held out his hand and Garrick shook it. There was no more to say and no time to waste. *Sparrow*, battered and filthy and ancient, sagged against the monitor as if weary to death – but she was ready to go. *Marshall Marmont* wasn't going anywhere.

He returned to *Sparrow* and found the draft of a dozen men from the monitor being given a rude but warm welcome, the CMB alongside and Curtis waiting for him in the waist. He gave the Sub-Lieutenant his orders and asked, "The boat's all right? And the firing-gear?"

"Raring to go, sir."

Smith looked at the tall young man a moment. He hoped Curtis would come through. He said, "Remember to wait your time and then – stop at nothing! Understood?" He saw Curtis over the side into the CMB and heard the engines started with a roar then throttled down to a burble as the slender, low little craft pulled away with Curtis in the cockpit at the wheel.

"*Stop at nothing!*" Curtis understood all right. Smith watched him go, bitterly sorry and angry, and swore. He snapped, "Cast off…"

As *Sparrow* eased away from *Marshall Marmont* he saw Garrick climbing up to his open bridge. Yelled comments were tossed across the widening gap between the ships. The monitor looked fat and ugly where she now lay anchored fore and aft with her stern towards the invisible shore, her guns pointing seaward. *Sparrow* turned away from her as Smith ordered, "Starboard ten!… Meet her. Steer nor-west by west."

"Nor-west by west, sir."

"Revolutions for twenty knots."

She turned away from *Marshall Marmont* and from the tug *Lively Lady* that was puffing north-eastwards towards neutral Dutch waters. The old thirty-knotter headed out to sea with the revolutions of her engines gradually increasing. The brownish vapour at the tops of her three funnels thickened into plumes of smoke she trailed behind her as her stern sank lower in the sea and the turtle-back curve of her bow lifted.

Smith said to Sanders, "Pass the word: I expect we'll be in action within the hour." That would only be confirmation. The rumour must have flown long ago.

"Aye, aye, sir."

The clock that Eleanor Hurst had set ticking when she translated 'spring tide' had not yet stopped. But soon it would.

For a time the CMB kept company abeam; for her twenty knots was just cruising. Then after ten or fifteen minutes she eased and slowed, stopped. The day was close on them now, the light growing. Smith watched her and lifted a hand as she fell astern of *Sparrow* and saw a hand lifted above her cockpit, waving. He turned away. When he looked again she was well astern and he had to search to find her. Without her bow-wave and wash to mark her she was a slender splinter on the surface of the sea.

Sparrow ran on. Sanders had returned to the bridge and like Smith was using glasses to search the horizon to the south-west but that horizon was still a false one and close, limited by the light. The true horizon lay far beyond.

But still they searched as *Sparrow* ran out to sea and slowly the day came and the visibility lengthened until it was close to sunrise. Now the horizon was real enough but the heat and the storm had left a mist as the world steamed so a haze lay along that horizon. Then the tip of the sun showed and the first rays set the quiet sea to sparkling. And Sanders said, "Smoke on the beam, sir!"

"Seen," Smith answered. He could just make out the stain of it above the haze and lowered the glasses to rest his eyes, rubbed at them. They were sore. He wished he had ordered Brodie to brew more tea; his mouth was dry. He said, "Port five." *Sparrow* turned until her bow pointed at the distant smoke. "Meet her... steer that."

Gow reported, "Steady – two–one–five, sir."

Smith said quietly, "Just keep her head on that smoke."

"Aye, aye, sir."

No one was sleeping now. The men stood to the guns. They were quiet, waiting, blinking tired eyes.

The clock was running down now and these last minutes passed with awful slowness. The smoke spread on the horizon. More than one ship. Of course. He swept the glasses around a quarter circle to seek *Marshall Marmont* but did not find her. Over half-an-hour's steaming seaward had taken *Sparrow* twelve miles to the north-westward of her and she was hull-down over the horizon. Her control-top would be showing above that horizon but he could not see it because of the haze and the distance, it was just too small. The sun hurt his eyes.

They formed the three points of a triangle: the monitor inshore, *Sparrow* twelve miles to seaward and the battle-cruiser steaming up to pass between them. She would be about ten or twelve miles from *Sparrow* and further from *Marshall Marmont* but still in range...

Sanders yelled, "*Marshall Marmont's* just fired, sir!"

Smith answered again, "Seen." He had also caught the wink of flame, the barest wisp of smoke. They would never hear the report above *Sparrow's* engines nor see the burst over the horizon. He lowered the glasses. But whether those hells hit or fell short or over they would come as a nasty shock to the battlecruiser. She was under fire from the big guns of a ship she could not see; *Marshall Marmont* was making no smoke except from her guns and Smith and Sanders had seen that only because they were looking for it. And *Marshall Marmont* was still out of range of the battlecruiser's twelve-inch guns.

Aboard the monitor Garrick would be sending the signal, "Am engaging enemy battlecruiser." Giving her position, course and speed. Pakenham's battlecruisers would be leaving the Firth of Forth, the Harwich force putting to sea and the destroyers of the Dover Patrol and the Dunkerque Squadron in hot pursuit of the battle-cruiser. They would all be too late.

He ordered, "Full ahead both." And: "Signalman! Get on the searchlight and start signalling westward as soon as I give the word. Anything you like as long as that battlecruiser can see it when she comes up."

"Aye, aye, sir!" The signalman swung himself up on to the searchlight platform at the back of the bridge and trained the searchlight around to starboard.

Smith called up to him. "But keep a sharp look-out as well! If you see any ship I want to know!" There was always the chance of a miracle, that a British force was already at sea and closing them.

He told Gow, "Keep her head on that smoke now."

Gow answered patiently, "Aye, aye, sir."

Smith shut his mouth. That had been an unnecessary order.

From twenty knots *Sparrow* was steadily working up to her full speed of twenty-six. She trembled and racketed along with the pounding thrust of her engines. The bridge vibrated under their feet and the kettle that had held the tea for the twelve-pounder's crew danced across the gun-platform until the killick grabbed it, swearing, and jammed it in a corner of the screen. Smith looked back at the smoke pouring from the three funnels, then up at the ensigns that streamed spread flat on the wind with now and again a *crack!* like a pistol shot. There were two of them because early in the war the white ensign had been mistaken for the German so ships were ordered to hoist two to avoid a mistake but there could be no mistake today. *Sparrow* flew two because they were all she had. Smith would have flown a dozen if *Sparrow* had them.

He faced forward. Now they were counting the time in flying seconds. The sun was sucking up the haze and the ships came on out of it, for an instant only vague phantoms, but then clear and hard. There were two destroyers a mile apart leading the force then one by one the others came up, still hull-down over the horizon but their upperworks clear enough. Two more destroyers. And two more still just smoke and masts. And in the centre of the group of six destroyers that was her escort, the tripod mast of a battlecruiser...

In his mind he flicked through the pages of the silhouette book, comparing the remembered shapes with the dancing image in the lenses of the glasses until he found a match.

Sanders ventured, "I think, sir, she might be *Siegfried*."

She might be any one of four German battlecruisers, seen at that distance and coming out of the haze, but – "That's right." Smith was certain. Eight twelve-inch guns and twelve 5.9-inch. Twenty-seven or -eight knots and twenty-seven thousand tons with a belt of armour a foot thick and more than a thousand men aboard.

Sanders said with reluctant admiration, "Got to admit it, sir, she's a beauty."

She was. Steaming at full speed, big, swift and powerful, yet graceful. Smith let the glasses hang on his chest and peered about him at the battered *Sparrow*. Less than four hundred tons, one twelve-pounder gun and fifty-odd dog-tired men. He lifted the glasses again and so saw the water-spouts rise out of the sea and to seaward of the battlecruiser.

Sanders yelled, "*Marshall Marmont's* ranging on her!"

The shells had fallen four or five hundred yards over but that would be little consolation to *Siegfried's* commander. Her guns were trained around to meet the distant threat but they did not fire. She was out of range. He would know the firing came from inshore because the salvo had roared over his head and maybe some eagle-eyed look-out in the control-top had picked up the tell-tale spurt of smoke and flame of the monitor's firing, but he would be hard put to it, straining his eyes against that low sun. And *Marshall Marmont* was trailing no banner of smoke to lead the eye on.

But now Smith lowered the glasses fractionally, seeking and finding the leading destroyers. They were scouting a good mile or more ahead of *Siegfried*, the one to port turning towards the shore, a signal flying, obviously being sent to investigate the ship that was firing. He saw the one to starboard turning until she was head-on and pointing at *Sparrow*. He could guess her orders. He saw the smoke and flame from the four-inch on her foredeck and ordered, "Port five!"

"Port five, sir."

"Midships!"

He shouted up at the signalman on the searchlight platform: "Now!" The light on its mounting was only feet from his head but he could barely hear the clacking of its shutter above the engines' din and the roaring fans. He saw it blinking rapidly, longs and shorts and wondered briefly what obscenities or prayers the signalman was flashing at an unresponsive horizon.

He faced forward to see the shell fall to starboard and ordered, "Starboard five!... Midships!"

He saw the intercepting destroyer charging out at them and beyond her, *Siegfried*. Who must be able to see *Sparrow* signalling frantically to the west, wondering whether she was bluffing or was there really a supporting fleet out there that *Sparrow* could see but was beyond *Siegfried*'s horizon? And the little destroyer was attacking. Would she attack without a supporting fleet?

The bluff seemed to be working. *Siegfried* and the rest of her escort maintained their course, preferring the devil they knew to the devil they did not, and not trying to haul out to seaward to get away from the big gun threat. That threat was emphasised as another salvo from *Marshall Marmont* plunged into the sea, short of *Siegfried* by three or four hundred yards. Still she did not fire, but soon she would be in range and *Marshall Marmont* and Garrick would feel the weight of those twelve-inch guns. They knew what they had to do. They would carry out his orders and he would answer for it. If he answered for anything.

All of it thought in a second.

That was *Marshall Marmont*'s fight.

This was *Sparrow*'s.

He took one final glance around from the twelve-pounder and its clustering crew, along the dented iron deck where Lorimer was shrieking orders at the crews of the six-pounders, right aft to the six-pounder on the juddering stern that bounced on a cushion of foam spreading into the boiling wake astern. He saw Buckley by that six-pounder, standing easily, patient. And McGraw on the other six-pounder aft on the starboard side. Then he turned to face the first of his enemies.

The German destroyer was a big boat and closing them at a combined speed of sixty knots because she was capable of thirty-five and making it with a big white bow-wave. She carried four-inch guns with a range of ten thousand yards or more but head-on like this she could only use the one in her bow that jetted flame now.

"Port five!"

"Port five, sir!"

"Meet her... steady!"

Sparrow swerved, deck heeling, all of them holding on, then steadied on the new course with the enemy boat fine on the starboard bow.

"All guns commence!"

The twelve-pounder slammed, shaking the already shuddering bridge and the starboard six-pounder barked right under the bridge. Smoke swirled and the cartridge case bounced on the deck as the breech was opened. A shell came down off the starboard bow and Smith turned *Sparrow* to starboard towards it. So *Sparrow* weaved erratically along the main course that still pointed her at the battlecruiser and the closing destroyer, that fired and fired again as the range closed and she came up bigger and bigger. Her firing was regular and rapid and accurate, only *Sparrow*'s jinking taking her clear as shell after shell plunged into the sea, sometimes close and sometimes near-misses and once a near-miss that burst right by the bridge and swept them with spray on top of the spray that *Sparrow* made as she charged down on the Squadron.

Sparrow scored a hit on the destroyer's bow and took one aft on an already mangled torpedo-tube.

The hit shook her. Smith heard yelling aft and one voice, high pitched, that was Lorimer's and knew that the boy was leading a fire-fighting and damage control party. Lorimer sent a man running to report, "Knocked the tube about a bit more, but that's all, sir."

"Very good."

But one bit was too many. "Starboard ten!... Midships!"

Sparrow swung away from her head-on charge at the German boat and turned broadside to her. Now the six-pounders cracked away and the German boat eased to starboard in her turn and all her guns fired at virtually point-blank range. Through the din Smith yelled, "Look out for torpedoes!" Because they would come. And they did. He saw them, two of them, leap from the side of the big destroyer and plunge into the sea. Seconds later he saw their tracks as Sanders shouted and pointed, as the guns slammed and recoiled and *Sparrow* was hit and hit again, hammer blows punching into her, punishment she could not take.

"Port ten!... Meet her!"

Gow had been waiting for it. *Sparrow* swerved and heeled again to turn inside of those twin tracks, to tear down past the torpedoes that raced away down her starboard side, and tore on, firing and being hit – and passing astern of the German boat.

A slamming, clanging explosion aft and Smith whirled to see the aftermost of the three funnels cut in half, the top half blasted away and going over the side, dragging *Sparrow* over, so for a second she steamed with the sea reaching up for her deck. Then she recovered. He stared forward, ordered, "Starboard five! Midships! Steer that!" Shouting it almost in Gow's ear against the bedlam of pounding engines, bellowed orders and the *crack!* and *slam!* of the guns. Gow's long face was twisted tight with concentration and his eyes were slitted as he glared ahead at *Siegfried, Sparrow* now steaming on a course to intercept her.

Smith shot a swift glance astern and glimpsed through *Sparrow*'s rolling smoke Buckley loading the six-pounder himself, his loader sprawled on the deck. And beyond was the enemy destroyer, heeled over in a tight turn, turning to chase *Sparrow*. All that smoke was not from the funnels, there was a fire aft, he saw Lorimer and two men dragging a hose. He faced forward. That destroyer had been intended to beat off *Sparrow* or destroy her and the little ship had been mauled but not stopped. *Siegfried* was only three or four miles away, signals flying from her yard and a light winking rapidly. But the other two destroyers to port of the battlecruiser had closed up, overhauled her and were now obeying those desperate signals, their shapes foreshortening till they were bows-on and pointing at *Sparrow*.

They were firing and he staggered as *Sparrow* was hit again and the air around him was alive with droning, snarling splinters, something plucked at his arm and he saw the sleeve was ripped. Gow was on his knees, clawing back to his feet and standing on one leg, the foot of the other just balancing him. *Sparrow* wavered, then steadied as the cox'n's big hands clamped on the wheel. His cap had gone and the grizzled hair had a monk's bald patch that was streaked with blood. There were four men sprawled on the bridge, the signalman was one of them and the engine-room telegraphs were unmanned but the twelve-pounder still fired at the two destroyers as they came on.

They roared down on *Sparrow* with deadly purpose. She could not be allowed within torpedo range of *Siegfried* so they came on with big white bow-waves and their forward four-inch guns firing rapidly and they were going to sink *Sparrow*. They were not going to fight her, engage her with guns or torpedoes though they were using the one and the other would come. They had no time for fighting because *Sparrow* was too close to the battlecruiser. The little ship that had seemed to pose no threat was now a real danger, could be mounting a torpedo attack on the giant the destroyers were there to protect. They had been ordered to get rid of her and they would run her down.

Smith knew it and that he could not stop it.

He looked just once more at the battlecruiser as she steamed on, saw that her secondary armament was firing and realised the big 5.9's were firing at *Sparrow*. The water-spouts alongside were huge now, but he also saw that *Siegfried* had been hit and had fires, so *Marshall Marmont* had hurt her. He turned to look at the course *Siegfried* was taking, at the quiet sea that lay ahead of her, sparkling with sunlight. *Sparrow* had to keep on a little longer. Just a little longer. And God help them all...

He put a hand on Gow's shoulder. "Starboard five... meet her... Steady. Keep her head on that destroyer."

"Aye, sir!"

Sparrow's stern pointed at one of the oncoming destroyers. The other was fine on Sparrow's starboard bow and about two cables astern of the first. Both of them were firing hard and Smith could feel them hitting. The crack and blast of the bursts were enough but he could feel the shock of each hit shudder through the ship and she was slowing like a fighter who had not been hit in a vital spot but had simply soaked up too much punishment, an accumulation of blows. Sanders clawed his way up a twisted ladder on to the bridge to bawl at Smith. "Holed four places – two on the water-line – the carpenter's trying to plug 'em but we're making water!"

Smith nodded but he was intent on the destroyers that filled his vision and claimed him totally. He heard Sanders say hoarsely, "God!" He had just seen the enemy within a thousand yards, bows high and sterns tucked right down and the smoke and flame of their guns flickering and blossoming. They were growing with every second, filling the eye and the mind so that the great mass of *Siegfried* faded into a moving backdrop as she slid along with a distant, silent grace. Only the destroyers existed.

But *Siegfried* had to be the target. She was not firing now because the destroyers were too close to *Sparrow*. Smith ordered "Port five... steer that." So *Sparrow*'s bow edged away from the destroyers and she was on a course to meet *Siegfried* and the destroyers were on her starboard bow. And they turned so they were on a course to meet her before she could reach *Siegfried* or get within torpedo range of her. And they were still firing. Broadside to them like this, *Sparrow* should have been firing three or four guns but only the twelve-pounder banged away.

Smith shouted, "All other guns out of action?"

"Yes, sir." Sanders added, eyes on the destroyers, "Brodie's got his hands full." The little steward would be trying again to cope with the wounded but there would be too many. Smith could see the deck astern seemed impassable because of twisted steel and the ripped plates of the iron deck. The funnels, what was left of them, were shot full of holes that spurted flame and *Sparrow* dragged their smoke and the smoke from her fires that Lorimer was fighting and she dragged it in a thick black trail. It was an empty deck; he could see just one man, Lorimer, peering up at the bridge as he staggered aft. This was not a battleship nor a cruiser. There was no big crew so you could move men from one part of the ship to another to meet an emergency. This was a little, old TBD and her crew was small. Some of them were below manning her engines or stoking. Some of them were dead or near it so he looked at a bridge and a deck near-deserted. He did not want to think about the wounded and dying crammed into the wardroom now. He had no time.

Brodie was trying to hold the man down to put a tourniquet on his leg but he was insane with pain and writhing on the wardroom table. Brodie was sprayed with blood. The wardroom stank of antiseptic, blood, vomit and smoke that coiled. There were holes in the side and the deckhead that Brodie had tried to plug with blankets and the wounded lay on the couches or the deck where the water swilled inches deep and sometimes washed over their faces as the ship heeled. Brodie dressed or stitched their wounds and then they were left to fend for themselves. He could do no more.

Lorimer saw the ready-use charges burning by the wrecked six-pounder under the bridge and kicked them over the side. As he started aft, seeing flames there, he tripped and fell. A bursting shell had minutes ago hurled him across the deck and now something ground in his arm; every movement was agony. He sobbed with pain and frustration but got up. He was the sole survivor of the damage-control party. He could see Smith on the bridge, saw his head turn and met the cool stare, saw Smith grin at him. Lorimer started aft again. He would carry on.

He had heard the other shells, but this one he did not.

Buckley slapped open the breech of the six-pounder, turned to seek the next round. It felt as if he was kicked. When he came round he was sprawled on the deck with his head near the side and the seas bursting over him. As he dragged himself inboard and on to his feet he saw the six-pounder was dismounted. His head ached. He staggered forward and almost fell over a body, unrecognisable but the uniform, what was left of it, was of a midshipman. So it had to be Lorimer. Buckley shook his aching head, sick, and went to help McGraw.

Sanders shouted, "I think — they're going to ram!"

Smith nodded. They were rushing down on *Sparrow*, big as houses and growing bigger and making all their thirty-odd knots. Bare seconds away now and *Sparrow* was slowing. "Hard astarboard... meet her... Steady!" *Sparrow* swung sluggishly but her falling speed made her turn the shorter and just in time so she turned from broadside to the big boats, bow swinging until it pointed at the gap between them, but the one to port would be the closer, very close. She was hurtling down on *Sparrow* like a train but she would miss now. Her captain was trying to turn but his speed was against him and he would be too late. She was firing every gun that would bear, *Sparrow* was hit every second and machine-guns were rattling now. The other boat was not too late, had room and time to turn and would ram *Sparrow*. Smith whispered, "Come on, old lady." He shouted, "*Hard aport!*" And into the voice pipes, "*Stand by to ram!*"

Sparrow turned in on the big German boat and Gow collapsed over the wheel. Smith grabbed at him and the wheel together and held *Sparrow* steady, feeling the blood on his hands and the spokes as *Sparrow* crossed the narrow strip of sea in brief seconds but even then the destroyer raced ahead, slipping across *Sparrow*'s bow that pointed at her bridge and then was ticking off the funnels as the high length of her went streaking past, but not all of her. *Sparrow*'s stern struck her ten feet from her stern.

Smith held on and had his arms nearly jerked from their sockets as *Sparrow* changed from a warship charging along at fifteen knots to a steel wreck. Her bow had cut into the destroyer's stern but Smith could see *Sparrow*'s turtle-back bow was crumpled and twisted upwards. The German boat was not stopped, though her engines had stopped. The way still on her dragged *Sparrow* along until the old thirty-knotter tore loose, as the big boat shook her off.

The crew of the twelve-pounder was standing in on the gun but there were only two of them now. Sanders was shouting, "Shift target! Destroyer on the port beam!" And jumping to heave the gun around. Smith saw that the captain of the other destroyer had seen *Sparrow* stopped and crippled and changed his mind about ramming. He had reduced speed, slipped past *Sparrow*'s stern and was now turning to close on his crippled consort and to deal with *Sparrow* on the way.

A messenger appeared below the bridge. The ladder had gone altogether now and he bawled up, "Forrard bulkhead's stove in and the sea's coming in!" It was McGraw, naked to the waist and the sweat running down his body. He shook his head. "There's nae stoppin' it, sir!"

The twelve-pounder slammed and at the same instant *Sparrow* was hit forward on that crumpled turtle-back. Smith's eyes caught the flash as the blast-wave hit him and threw him off the bridge.

He lay on the iron deck and stared across the sunlit sea at the destroyer, cruising slowly now, guns flaming, pounding the life out of the already dying *Sparrow*. He lay and seemed remote from it all. He tried to get to his feet but his legs would not work properly. Then he saw Sanders climbing down from the bridge and felt a hand grip his arm and lift him so he stood wide-legged and wavering. It was Buckley.

Smith said thickly, "Thought you were on the after six-pounder."

"Was, sir. Got knocked out, it an' me together. Come around wi' the sea washing in on me. Got a bang but me skull's too thick, I suppose."

Sparrow was listing and down by the head. He remembered McGraw's message. And here came the Chief, black with oil and soot and the hair scorched from one side of his head. "Engine-room's filling up, sir. I've pulled the lads out."

Smith turned on Sanders. "Get the wounded up. Get them all out, Sub. Abandon ship." And to Buckley: "Let go of me and lend a hand with the wounded."

"Sure you'll be all right, sir?" They both peered at him, concerned, where he stood holding on to a buckled stanchion.

He snapped irritably, "Yes, damn it! Get on!"

They left him, and he almost fell.

The destroyer had ceased firing. She was passing a tow to the other that was down by the stern but she could have kept up that terrible pounding just the same. Her captain must have seen that *Sparrow* was finished and ordered the ceasefire. That was an act of humanity.

Beyond the destroyers, beyond the drifting smoke and the smell of burning the battlecruiser *Siegfried* moved in another world. Smith stared at her. She had been hit, was on fire and the damage inflicted by *Marshall*

Marmont might make her leave the convoy alone – but only 'might' because the damage had not slowed her. Her twelve-inch turrets were trained around towards the invisible shore, long barrels at high elevation. They fired. So now she could reach *Marshall Marmont*, was firing at her. Sleek, smooth and swift, she was running on, her course unchanged, running for home and towards the convoy.

Smith watched her and waited. *Sparrow* had done all she could and so had *Marshall Marmont* and he thought they had done enough. He could only watch and wait as they dragged up the wounded from the wardroom through the hatch aft one at a time and laid them on the deck in a rapidly lengthening line. A fire burned in the waist because there were no hoses, no pumps, no pressure on the water, and nobody to fight it. The smoke hung around *Sparrow* where she lay heeling, sinking under him. He seemed to watch it all from a distance as if he floated above the deck. His vision would blur and then clear and he clung to the stanchion and peered out through the smoke to the bright, blue sunlit sea beyond.

–

Marshall Marmont was Garrick's first command in action. He did not bemoan the fact that she was a ship only in that she floated. *Marshall Marmont* was his and Smith had given him the chance and he was grateful. He was an unimaginative man but he saw very clearly that it was an opportunity he might regret and he might be lucky even to live to regret it. That was irrelevant. He had a command and an action to fight. He stood on his bridge and through his glasses he watched *Sparrow*'s smoke that showed where she steamed hull-down over the horizon and saw from that smoke that she had turned. Towards the enemy, of course. He turned, sea and sky blurring in the glasses, then stopped, steadied them. He could see a lot of smoke but there would be more than one ship because the battlecruiser would have an escort.

"'Guns' reports enemy in sight, sir! Twenty thousand yards!"

Garrick grunted, acknowledging the report, not lowering the glasses, and ordered, "Open fire!"

That was how Smith would have done it. The imitation was unconscious.

The Gunnery Officer high in the control top would see more than Garrick below him. Garrick thought that the battlecruiser would have vision equally as good as 'Guns' but not the indications he had, the smoke to lead him on to the tiny speck of the ship beneath. And the men in the battlecruiser were staring straight into the morning sun. It would be a miracle, or rather the devil's own luck, if they saw *Marshall Marmont* where she lay low in the water.

The twin fifteen-inch fired and the long barrels recoiled, licking out long tongues of flame and pouring smoke. Garrick stood as immobile as the ship, as quiet as the sea on which she lay as the salvoes roared out again and again.

"Leading destroyer altered course towards us, sir!"

"Seen." Garrick thought, sent to look for us. And take us on? Through the glasses he saw her head-on, high-sterned with a big white bone in her teeth as she came on at full speed.

"Battlecruiser's signalling, sir!"

He lifted the glasses fractionally and the battlecruiser swam in the lenses and then was still. He just caught the final blinking of the searchlight and then it stopped.

"Destroyer's turning, sir."

He grunted again. She was turning away towards the battlecruiser. So the big ship was calling back her escort, as if, now that the destroyer had reported the solitary monitor, the enemy commander was guarding against another threat, leaving the monitor to his big guns. Another threat? *Sparrow?* Ridiculous! Then maybe the battlecruiser, eight miles or so to westward could see something he could not?

Or had Smith contrived something?

He grinned with the rest of them when 'Guns' reported a hit and then another, and ducked inside himself though he never visibly flinched as the first salvo from the battlecruiser howled overhead and into the sea four hundred yards inshore. Then into one voice pipe he said, "Good shooting, 'Guns'. Keep it up!" And into another, "Baker. Got your damage-control party alert?"

"Aye, aye, sir."

"Keep 'em on their toes. You'll be busy soon."

When Garrick had served under Smith not long ago in the Pacific the ship had been almost totally destroyed beneath them. He would never forget that. He knew the horrors to come. But he watched the battlecruiser through his glasses as she came on, steaming hard inside her destroyer screen and he saw she had been hurt. *Marshall Marmont* could not kill her but she bore the marks of this action in the smoke she trailed that was not funnel smoke and the yellow flick of flame that marked a fire.

In the control-top 'Guns', Lieutenant Chivers, short and stocky and crouched like a gnome over the director sight, saw the damage he had done. This was justification, reward, for all the training, practice shoots, and the coastal bombardments of targets unseen over the horizon; this sight of a big ship being hit by his guns. He had never been in a big ship action, and never expected to be, not in *Marshall Marmont*. He did not know what was to come but he knew the German gunnery was good and they were seeking him out, that they were firing eight-gun salvoes and the range was closing, that *Marshall Marmont* was a stationary target to be shot at. He knew these things and he could have drawn some unpleasant conclusions if he had let his imagination run away with him but he refused to allow that, huddled lower over the sight and grew hoarser as he called his orders. His thumb punched the salvo button again and in the turret the bells rang and the twin fifteen-inch fired. He thought they would hit, the sight and deflection right, the battlecruiser a clean-cut target. He thought she might be *Siegfried*.

That was his last thought.

Garrick's stolid, appreciating glance took in that the battlecruiser was hit but maintaining course and speed, that ahead of her and to seaward destroyers were fighting an action, tiny ships flickering with gunfire as they seemed to creep towards each other. He never heard the salvo that hit them and blasted the control-top into wreckage that went over the side. He found he was on his face on the deck and his nose was bleeding. He climbed to his feet to receive reports and coughing in the smoke he ordered the guns: "Independent firing!" Before they could fire, another salvo hit *Marshall Marmont* and he sprawled again, rose again, holding on to keep his balance in a reeling world and saw through the smoke and flames surrounding the bridge that the turret leaned drunkenly on its mounting. He found he was the only man on his feet on the bridge and set himself to gathering reports, staggering to the voice pipes, stubbornly determined to fight his ship to the last, to save her.

Then the last salvo plunged down.

Jack Curtis had climbed the single mast of the CMB and clung there with one leg over the yard, watching, waiting. From there he could see *Marshall Marmont* firing and he saw *Sparrow* start her charge. He saw *Siegfried* heave up over the horizon and swallowed at the sight of her. He watched and waited as *Sparrow* charged in and slipped one destroyer then was lost in the smoke that rolled across the sea and hid her and the others. He watched and waited till then, seeing the fires start on *Siegfried* and then others start on *Marshall Marmont* as she was hit again and again and became a ship aflame. He felt sick and angry, frightened and cold and eager. But this was the moment that Smith had ordered and *Siegfried* was only two miles away and his CMB lay dead ahead of her.

He slid down the mast, burning the inside of his thighs, said, "Start—" But his throat was choked up and he had to cough to clear it. This time his voice croaked harshly, "Start up!" The engines burst into life with a roar and CMB 19 moved ahead. Curtis stood in the cockpit behind the wheel and stared through the already lifting spray at the knife-edge bow of the battlecruiser, the big turrets and the superstructure that climbed up to the control top and stood like a castle out of the sea. The CMB was alive now, smacking across the wave crests and now she would not be invisible. Bow-wave and wash would mark her like banners, plainer than the big ensign she flew and that cracked above Curtis. He glanced up at it then back at the midshipman. He shouted, "Ready?" And when Johnson lifted a hand and gave him a tight grin: "You'd better be! Only get one chance!"

He turned away and gulped. In those few seconds the battle-cruiser had seemed to leap towards him. The CMB was up on the step now, making her thirty-odd knots and still accelerating. She was closing the battlecruiser at their combined speeds of nearly seventy miles an hour and she was too quick and too sudden for *Siegfried* and the destroyers. They picked her out but not until she began to move, making that bow-wave and wash. Till then she lay unseen, a splinter on the surface of the sea while a tethered monitor fired big gun salvoes from inshore and an old torpedo-boat-destroyer manned by lunatics charged in from the sea. Now they saw her and it was too late. She had raced in under their noses and the seaward destroyer screen was involved with *Sparrow*. The others tried to intercept her and fired on her but she was too close and too fast for them to hit.

Curtis steered the boat and thought with a part of his mind that he and his little crew might be the only men still alive in Smith's flotilla and he must not waste the chance that the rest, that Smith, had thrust upon him. He hunched over the wheel and stuck his jaw out as he peered over the screen and through the spray at the battlecruiser. The midshipman watched him and thought, You can see by the look of him he's goin' to set his teeth into this one. Christ! He's whistling!

Curtis's lips were pursed and he was whistling as he might have whistled when baiting a line. The same frown of concentration was there. It was a toneless whistle and his lips were dry. The CMB fled over the sea with her fore half lifted clear of the water and her stern dug in and the battlecruiser grew to a giant and then a monster. Curtis eased on the wheel as the thought registered 'seven hundred yards', and the CMB spun away to starboard out of the path of *Siegfried*. The sea lifted in tall towers of upflung water ahead of him and alongside and he could see from the corner of his eye the destroyer to port and plunging across towards him. But he eased the wheel back and the CMB spun again and this time turned in towards *Siegfried*.

Aboard her they saw the motorboat off the port bow and looking to be standing on end in the sea as she snarled in at them. Curtis peered over the lifted stern and watched the bow of *Siegfried*, gauging her speed and how she lay to the boat, the distance between. He lifted one hand. The midshipman had been waiting for it, for seconds had been begging for it. Come on. Come on! Any closer and you'll run *aboard* her? *Come* on! Curtis held on because *Siegfried* was no destroyer under which a torpedo might run if he fired too near her. She was a deep-draughted ship so he would get in close.

Nearly there.

Nearly...

Now!

He cut down the hand, felt the jar, then the leap of the stern as Johnson yanked the release handle and fired the torpedo stern first into the sea. Curtis turned the wheel and the CMB spun to starboard, laid right over in a skidding turn. He held the wheel but sat half-turned in the seat shooting glances astern. The midshipman was yelling, red-faced with excitement, both hands lifted in a 'thumbs-up' sign and beyond him Curtis saw the track of the torpedo. He had held on to the last split-second to be certain and now he could watch the track and knew it could not miss. *Siegfried* was trying to turn away but he had run too close and she had no time. She was firing every gun that would bear, hurling ton after ton of steel and high explosive at the slender, flitting, bouncing black speck in its shifting curtain of spray that jinked and swerved and ran for dear life.

Aboard *Sparrow* Sanders came up to Smith and reported, "The wounded are on deck. All clear below." And warned: "She's making water fast, sir."

Smith could feel it in the way she listed under him, see it in the way the sea was reaching up on her. "No boats, Sub?"

"No, sir."

"Rafts, then. Wounded first."

There were few rafts intact on that shattered deck and it was hell's own job to clear them, but they got enough over the side to take the wounded and passed them down. The ship was still, lying lifeless in the sea. The big destroyers were moving now, slowly edging away, the one that *Sparrow* had rammed being towed by the other. Smith could still hear firing and saw that *Siegfried* had steamed on and left the two destroyers to their own devices. It was the battlecruiser firing and the remainder of her destroyer screen were increasing speed as if to concentrate ahead of her.

He helped the last of the wounded down to a raft and Sanders at his elbow said, "Here, sir." And thrust a lifebelt at him. "She's going, sir."

Smith held the lifebelt but turned away and started to scramble painfully up to the wrecked bridge again. Sanders shouted after him. "Sir! She'll go any *minute*, sir!" But Smith ignored him. He reached the bridge and climbed up on to the searchlight platform at the back of it. The light was shattered and the mounting twisted so he could not get on to the platform. He climbed carefully up on to the lamp itself and slowly straightened, balanced there. The glasses still swung on his chest from their strap and he set them to his eyes. *Siegfried* was easy to find, plunging along with guns blazing. He brought the lenses creeping down, searching the sea – and caught the flying CMB as it hurtled in on the battlecruiser, closer and closer until it spun away and raced past *Siegfried*'s stern. Smith held his breath.

Curtis steered with one hand and one eye past the battlecruiser's stern, starting to tear away to safety but still half-turned in the cockpit watching for the torpedo. And because she was steaming at nearly thirty knots and starting to turn, *Siegfried* almost drew clear of the torpedo and left it astern.

Almost.

But Curtis had gone in to ram it down their throats.

He saw the sea heave at *Siegfried*'s stern and saw the stern, twenty-eight thousand tons or so, lifted out of the sea by the burst of the torpedo. Johnson was capering like a monkey in the torpedo bay, yelling and waving his arms. The destroyer astern of *Siegfried* was firing, the shells falling close as the CMB swerved and ran away but no one aboard her noticed. Curtis's leading hand was hammering him on the back and bawling something about "bloody marvellous." Curtis was numb. The CMB flew over the sea to the south-west and soon the guns ceased firing.

Smith saw the sea spout at *Siegfried*'s stern and seconds later the *thump!* came dully across the sea. He saw her speed fall away, she slewed off course and the screening destroyers turned to her. That was all he saw but it was enough.

He turned and found Buckley on the bridge below him and realised Buckley was bellowing at him, had been bellowing for some time, "For Gawd's sake, sir! She's near awash!"

He looked and saw that Buckley was right and *Sparrow* was settling under them. He started down, slipped and fell but Buckley caught him. The burly seaman was muttering under his breath and scowling, for once out of patience with his wayward officer. But he got Smith down to the deck and into his life jacket. With Sanders, they jumped.

The rafts were crowded but they found hand-holds on the lines of one of them and hung there watching as *Sparrow* sank, slowly at first but then at the last with a rush as if to get it over with.

McGraw said, "Puir auld cow."

Siegfried and her escorts had made off to the northeast, were small with distance when Curtis came seeking *Sparrow*'s survivors, the CMB riding high and fast 'on the step' and sweeping in wide, lazy arcs until someone aboard her spotted the rafts in the sea. Then she straightened out to point at them and the bow dropped, her speed fell away as the engines' snarl faded to a low grumbling and she slipped slowly down on them, gently probing her way through the litter of flotsam that was all that was left of *Sparrow*. Curtis took all of the survivors aboard, cramming them in the torpedo bay, taking them on the deck, anywhere they could hold on. There were thirty-four survivors and of that number fifteen were wounded, one of them, a stoker, severely. Him they settled in the cockpit by Curtis's legs.

The CMB sat low in the water under its heaped human load, but Curtis said. "Won't be for long, sir. I made a signal to *Marshall Marmont* to tell 'em I was going to look for you an' I asked if there was anything I could do for them. They said, 'This ship will cope.'"

Smith saw one or two grins on the faces of *Sparrow*'s survivors. They remembered that signal.

Curtis went on, "So I suppose she's floating and I can transfer your crew when we come up with her."

Smith nodded. He sat on top of the cockpit so Curtis was speaking in his ear. Buckley crouched on the deck by his shoulder. As the CMB got cautiously under way and her bow swung around he looked ahead and saw the smoke that marked *Marshall Marmont*. He watched all through the long minutes as the CMB cruised steadily towards her.

There was no billowing cloud of smoke now though a blue haze still hung around her. Smith could see no flames. It was impossible to tell whether she lay lower in the water; she was always low. Her silhouette was changed because the tall mast and control top had gone and the bridge was a heap of wreckage. The turret was there but twisted at a crazy angle, the long barrels of the guns pointing at the sky. He said huskily, "Ask her condition."

Johnson found himself room to stand on the deck and worked the hand signal lamp. They waited.

Smith's eyes drifted around the horizon, seeing the smoke far off and the tiny specks of ships beneath that were the limping battlecruiser and her escort. Closer, much closer and inshore was the tug *Lively Lady*, bustling up and making plenty of smoke about it.

Eleanor Hurst...

A light winked rapidly from the monitor's deck and Johnson spelled it out: "Fires out. Stopped making water. Ready for tow as usual. Ingram in command."

Smith sat in silence a moment. 'Ready for tow as usual.' 'As usual!' Ingram had a sense of humour. But he was in command? Whatever had happened to Garrick, there were two other officers senior to Ingram who should have taken command. What had happened to them? And

Garrick? Smith had to know. He said, "Ask condition of captain."

And waited for an eternity until the light winked again from *Marshall Marmont* that was closer now so he could see a great hole torn in her, right forward of the bow, and the men working on her deck in that blue haze.

Johnson reported, "Multiple wounds. Condition fair."

That explained the delay. Ingram had sent a messenger scurrying down to the surgeon for a report on Garrick. He felt not relief, but hope. Garrick was alive at any rate.

They were closing *Marshall Marmont*. He had lost his glasses but he reached for those of Curtis that he saw hanging in the cockpit, stood up and carefully swept a full circle of the sea around them. The battlecruiser was hull-down. She would get home but she would never attack the convoy, crippled as she was. There was smoke to the south-east and that meant that help was racing towards them from Dunkerque and Dover. He lowered the glasses wearily, the sun hot on his shoulders, and saw the clothes of the men crowded on the CMB were steaming. He was aware of cheering and that the motorboat was sliding gently, slowly in alongside *Marshall Marmont*.

He stepped over the gap to grab at the dangling ladder and climbed slowly to the deck to stand and stare at the destruction he found there. Everything on the monitor's deck was smashed down so she looked more like a battered pontoon than a ship. But the men on her deck were cheering. So were those in the CMB and those climbing aboard from it. He saw Buckley at their head. He saw Curtis with his cap in his up-stretched hand leading the cheering and yelling himself hoarse.

The tug *Lively Lady* was passing close alongside with Victoria Baines on her deck but Victoria was stooped now and suddenly a very old woman. He saw Eleanor Hurst…

They were bringing the wounded aboard. There was a man they had sat in the cockpit by Curtis's knees. He was naked to the waist and his chest was swathed in bandages. His face was deathly white, his eyes closed, his lips moved as he mumbled in delirium and his chest heaved as he fought for each breath. He was dying as another man had died aboard *Sparrow* a hundred years ago.

Eleanor Hurst stared into Smith's face, into his eyes. She knew that she could never hold him, that he would leave her as he left her before but she accepted that. He needed her now and she wanted him back if only for now.

He stood lonely on the torn deck as the cheering beat about him, with the sun, he was sure it was the sun, setting his eyes to blinking.